IN THE TRADITION OF
JOAN VINGE AND VONDA McINTYRE

"A big, old-fashioned sense-of-wonder interplanetary exploration/biological puzzle novel with feminist overtones."
—*Orlando Sentinel*

"Combines the themes of *The Handmaid's Tale* with a well-researched, frighteningly original approach to genetics . . . science fiction at its best. Highly recommended."
—*Starlog*

"A well-thought-out, powerful, and often devastating feminist polemic."
—*Kirkus* (starred review)

"Displays immense promise . . . a rewarding and interesting novel that I do expect to see on award ballots."
—*Analog*

"A really interesting book."
—*Locus*

"A truly expertly constructed picture of what really might occur in the distant future."
—Andre Norton

"The sexual politics central to the plot is explored with subtlety and imagination as well as plain, in-your-face horror . . . Ms. Collins provides plenty of lively surprises and discoveries to keep the reader engaged."
—Suzy McKee Charnas

"An extravagant trip through fairy-tale on the wings of some of the most intriguing anthropological sf I've read in a long time."
—Ellen Kushner

MUTAGENESIS

HELEN COLLINS

A TOM DOHERTY ASSOCIATES BOOK
NEW YORK

MUTAGENESIS

Cover art by Nick Jainschigg

A Tor Book
Published by Tom Doherty Associates, Inc.
175 Firth Avenue
New York, N.Y. 10010

Edited by David G. Hartwell

Tor ® is a registered trademark of Tom Doherty Associates, Inc.

ISBN: 0-812-52163-3
Library of Congress Catalog Card Number: 92-21573

First edition: February 1993
First mass market printing: January 1994

Printed in the United States of America

0 9 8 7 6 5 4 3 2 1

To Lynn

Contents

"I have examined myself lately with more care than formerly, and find that to deaden is not to calm the mind. Aiming at tranquility, I have almost destroyed all the energy of my soul—almost rooted out what renders it estimable. . . ."

—Mary Wollstonecraft

Prologue

2635

The ship's bio-lab was so small that they could smell each other in spite of the hamsters, rabbits, rats, and thousand chemicals. Dr. Mattie Manan floated in a sitting posture before the open hamster cage.

Barney raced in place, the wheel spinning invisibly under his tiny paws. The female lay still, as if dead, in the cage corner.

"What's the matter with it?" Parn asked.

"Heavy."

"Heavy? But we're still in freefall."

"Guilt."

"What?"

"Heavy with guilt. Incest."

"Incest . . . ? Oh, Mattie!" Parn said. "For a second I believed—"

"True. He's her father. Grandfather actually. Cousin on her mother's side, grandfather on her father's. But definitely a father figure."

Dr. Parn Ramsey, holding himself by his fingertips from the rim of the cage, studied the female with a solemn Freudian frown. "Indeed I see symptoms of hysteria, female hysteria."

"This is serious," Mattie said. "I've tried hormones. Changed their diet. It must be something to do with freefall."

Mattie reached into the cage with her left hand, syringe in her right. The hamster tried to shrink and back away at the same time. Mattie pulled it out and inserted the needle between the softly furred skin and the stomach wall. As she pressed the plunger with her right thumb, she absently stroked the top of the tiny head with her left. She put the animal back into the cage, directly in front of the male, Barney, presenting it to him, an offering. Nothing.

Parn watched, kicking his feet gently, treading water, as if trying to keep place, like a kid hanging onto the raft in summer camp.

"The difference," he said, "between plant and animal biology is the illusion of personality."

"You know I was joking," Mattie said, giving her left leg a vague shove but achieving no advantage, no stronghold. "I'm not anthropomorphic."

"Not descriptively. But in a part of your perception. You named him. Didn't you name him Barney or something?"

"You know I named him Barney. So what?"

"I don't name my plants."

"You are saying that I am so personal that I have to personify, that I can't . . . I," she laughed, "I who have been accused of inhuman objectivity." A hard woman?

"That too," he said.

She kicked at him then but freefall was a poor medium for an efficient gesture. They were not underwater. A rough motion was too rough. The cage started to come with them, not down but up and over, on and by. They grabbed at it, twisting.

The hamster, Barney, flew like a squirrel. But the female seemed glued.

"The male is frenetic; the female comatose," Mattie said as she relatched the cage to the bench. "Barney, I'm going to use one of your brothers instead of you if you don't 'make love' fast! . . . Anthropomorphism indeed!"

Parn pushed off to his section of their lab, shaking his head backward at her, long lock of dark hair bobbing over his light tan forehead. "Maybe some kind of marriage counseling," he said. "Kyly is supposed to be a psychologist. Why not—?"

"Kyly is a turd!" Rol Addle shouted, pushing himself into

the cabin. In spite of freefall, in spite of his obvious youth and strength, he was struggling, panting.

"Kyly is many things," Parn said. "We thought he might solve Mattie's hamster problem. Celibacy."

"Kyly is lying. We'll be landing in the wrong place, not the one with the best crops. Not a many. Not the right kinds. Or maybe none at all."

"Why? Why would Kyly want us to miss the stuff? He's not involved in crops or foods."

"That's just it. Kyly doesn't care about grasses at all. Who knows how many more monocultured species have died out while we've been gone. People are starving, but Kyly, Professor Kyly, wants artifacts."

"So you think he's skewing the information?" Parn's soft drawl flowed around and under Rol's louder, urgent tones.

"The whole expedition, everything we are here for—"

"Aren't you just guessing, Rol?" Mattie asked. "Nat drew the plans with Kyly."

"That . . . that social scientist! We're going to land in the wrong place. I've been looking at their charts, all the data in the vid. Do you hear me? He's destroying the whole mission."

"It's a little late for him to do that, isn't it?" Parn asked. "We're in orbit. We land tomorrow."

"That's it! Where are we landing? We're landing in the wrong place. Kyly's been screwing it up from the beginning. I'm going to talk to Nat and the OC before Marker starts his meeting."

"Are you sure you want to do this, Rol? Nat's the navigator," Parn said. "He wouldn't land us in—"

"But Nat's plans are all based on Kyly's old records and maps. Kyly's."

Between four hundred and five hundred years ago, after the first development of interstellar travel, people from Earth colonized several habitable planets, including Anu. Within a hundred years, when the Wars destroyed most scientific knowledge and all hard tech-

nology, the settlements were cut off before they had
time to develop independent means of survival.

We know very little about Anu or its Earth immigrants, the records having been destroyed with all
other electronic data during the Wars.

Since the reconstruction period, the reestablishment
of interstellar travel, and the centralization of Earthstates, all planets have been visited except Anu, which
was last settled and farthest out. Earthstates Council
has deemed that such an expedition is not cost effec-
tive.

K. Kyly, Ph.D., Aa.Dp.
Volume 3 of *The Journal of PreEs History*—Es2628

The narrow rear end of Kyly, anthropologist, archeologist,
historian, linguist, and psychologist, hovered a scant centi-
meter above the floor, almost but never quite touching; his
back was bent into the hull's curve, and his chin rested on
his chest. It seemed to Mattie that he had been sitting in the
same place in the same way since they left Earth. She had
spent two precious years of her adult life looking at the
wisps of thin hair on the top of his narrow head.

Mattie moved down to the business end of the lounge
where the OC and Nat Smythy sat by the OC's platform,
screens, and the holovid. In it was a hologram, a large
sphere—globe model of the planet Anu. It looked, not like
a world, Mattie thought, but a mended antique bowl. There
were no oceans. The waterways, while wider than Earth's
rivers, were still so narrow and so many that the land
masses seemed pieced together.

"Come to the control room next shift and I'll show you
the real thing, Mattie," Nat said. "We should have perfect
planet view without solar interference."

Nat Smythy was wonderful to view himself. He was the
only one who had discarded the regulation navy shirt. He
wore a white lab jacket opened low to expose a strong,
sleek, dark brown throat and hairless muscled chest hand-
somely set off by a single, thick gold chain. His hair was

bleached so that it graduated from black at the roots to bronze and then to almost white on the very tips. It rose straight up from his forehead for several inches to where the lightest part just started to curl over forward, to almost topple like ocean waves caught forever just before they break. Mattie and Nat were each at the extreme ends of the human color continuum.

"I'd love to see it," Mattie said, "but it will be better to be on it, moving away from each other."

"Had enough of us all, have you?" the OC asked.

"Not you, of course," Mattie said, "but yes. Everyone seems a grotesque of what he was when we left Earth. Every hobby and interest has become an obsession. Kyly. Rol Addle. Even—"

Rol Addle had come in and launched himself across the cabin at the OC and Nat. Parn followed in a slow leap and dropped into his usual slouch, legs stretched out into common space.

"The object of this mission," Rol said, looking back over his shoulder at Kyly, "is the recovery of food grasses. We have to find the old varieties, the strains that were allowed to die out on Earth—"

"We know all this, Rol," Nat said.

"But, damn it, Nat, I think Kyly may have been changing the data—"

"Professor Kyly," the OC called. "Will you come over here please."

Kyly's narrow, pale face appeared above his knees.

The OC waited until he straightened, stood, and moved across the cabin. "It seems that we have a new question here, Professor. It concerns your evaluation of our landing sites."

Kyly's browless, colorless eyes closed slightly as his lips began to move. There was a half-second delay, as if he practiced speech soundlessly before voicing his words.

"Any one of the three possible landing places may or may not satisfy all our purposes. I recommended our target—" He stopped and blinked.

"He can't know all this. His own articles say we know nothing about preWar history. All records were lost," Rol said.

"Written records, hard copy, were not all lost," Nat said. "Here is where we believe they settled." Three points of light appeared on one patch, a "continent" on the model of Anu, and a few inches away another single point. "We will land here." One of the three grew brighter.

"But how do you know it is optimal? Our whole objective is the food, the old varieties of Earth species the settlers brought," Rol said. "Nothing else—"

"*My* objective is greater, Dr. Addle," Kyly said. "You confuse technology with civilization. What we want are the shards, jars, perhaps written records, the ruins of the structures and the ships, artifacts of an ancient, extinct branch of the human race. Anu is the archeologist's fantasy. Through these things we may learn the customs and taboos not only of an unimportant 'primitive' society but of our own ancestors who sent them. The folkways—"

"We are interested in food grasses," Rol said. "Plants, Kyly. Not 'folkways.' "

Kyly's mouth worked silently for a few seconds and his voice when it came was still barely more than a whisper. "Dr. Addle, you have talked about food to the point of tedium. Your narrow understanding, undeveloped sensibilities, limited education, and general ignorance blind you to all higher values of tradition and culture. You medical doctors and hard scientists are all mere technicians."

He turned and went out of the lounge, passing the rest of the crew just coming in for Delt Marker's meeting.

Sem the Doc, oldest member of the mission, paused to stare after him for a second before crossing the cabin to sit with Parn and Mattie. Mr. Ricco, officer second in command to the OC, strode in, body at attention; no part of him ever fell free, with or without gravity. Rachel Mallove, the only woman besides Mattie, dietician and horticulturalist, took no notice either of Kyly or the silence he had left behind. She sat herself on her heels before one of the small personal vid-screens.

Last by an exact three minutes, Delt Marker came in and crossed to the OC's bench.

"Staff, doctors," he said in several directions, "you are all aware that our long journey now nears its end. Through vast distances we bring the spirit and courage of Earthstates. Our endeavors—"

"Delt, why did you call this meeting?" Sem the Doc asked.

"Protocol requires that the transition period be . . . Some of you do not seem to be aware of my position on planet . . . This present discussion concerns matters of government priorities, of responsibilities unrelated to ship patterns or, one might say, hierarchical authority."

"What's he talking about?" Rol asked.

"That he's going to be the boss when we land," Parn said.

Marker resumed his address as though they had not spoken.

Mattie looked at the others, so familiar, too familiar. On her soft breast, just below her slightly open collar, Rachel wore a little ribbon, bright against the common navy of her ship suit. To brighten the day, she said. To make a small statement against uniformity. She had a different color for each day of the week. Seven colors. All the weeks they had been on the ship. Over and over. Today was pink; today was Tuesday.

Rachel's wide brown eyes were fixed on some point just above Delt's head. No doubt she was mentally playing or replaying some private story—more exciting than the wornout plots in the ship's vid. But Mattie did not know Rachel's fantasies.

And were the men's fantasies different in kind?

Rol seemed to be looking at Rachel; once in a while his sex drive interfered with his concentration on his work. While Mattie had not been so kind as to relieve him of this distraction, she thought perhaps Rachel had. But his dream was not romance or sex but the heroic quest. He would find and restore to the people of Earth every strain of every species of Earth crops that had been lost, all the rices, wheats, perhaps coffee. He saw himself as the hero who defeats the old evils, monoculturing, irresponsible genetic engineering, greed.

Nat Smythy was not so easy to read. After only one more shift they would land according to Nat's own astrophysical calculations and ancient, perhaps unreliable, maps. If there were a mistake, if he brought them down on the wrong side of the planet, everything would be lost. Was that his nightmare?

And Delt? Mattie looked up at him, the solemn expression on a face the perfect median shade of gold. He illustrated each remark with careful, rehearsed gestures. He was the only official member of the government on the mission, but hardly an ambassador. Ambassador to what or whom? More likely Es Council wanted someone to keep a watch on all the mad scientists and on military personnel—the OC and Mr. Ricco. So, Mattie guessed, they had picked an expendable minor official who had not excelled in his own field—diplomacy. And Delt did not know it.

"And now my third point—" he said.

"Delt, please," Sem the Doc said. "I'm old and growing older. I haven't the time."

"And I have much to do," Nat Smythy said, checking the portentous rise of his hair with a light caress of fingertips as he moved toward the door.

Dr. Mattine Manan and her assistant are inside a cell. The plasma, with its accidents of green gas, has engulfed and dyed them. They stand, ridiculous smoke-green human silhouettes, between the membrane that is the cell wall and the huge sloppy, hovering nucleus.

Smaller than the nucleus but larger than their heads, the mitochondria also seem to float, moving about beside and behind them vaguely, silently, and apparently randomly.

The monster cell with its human invaders fills only the center of the stage of a round surgical theater, its green glow dimly lighting the faces of those in the first row, but leaving the rest of the audience, encircling the stage in thirty tiers, in complete darkness.

It is not a vid cube; it is more than a hologram, more than a three-dimensional analog, more than an illusion. Tangible, tactile, palpable. An embodied spectral manifestation, an idea made flesh. It is actually an organic image of a brown-bear gamete cell enlarged two million times.

Dr. Manan says: "The laser technique and organic image analog is even more revealing when we fuse cells. In this case, we have only rearranged the genetic information, and perhaps the developmental sequence, within one cell rather than deleting or adding to it from outside; in other words I have recombined the grouping of the same genes in the individual so that the genome will be altered without our altering, deleting or splicing in new genes."

"Abomination! You are a devil," a Fanatick calls from a high tier in the dark outermost circle. "You play God."

Dr. Manan says: "I am a biologist, a metaphysicist but not a metaphysician."

Vid tape—Studio of Biological
Experimentation—Es2632

The corridors had been dimmed for the last night-shift, but most of the crew were not asleep. They prowled the ship, passing and repassing each other in the corridors and common rooms, like a reprise of the last two years.

Mattie found Sem the Doc alone in the galley. His skin was like some ancient parchment, yellow and finely cracked, and when he smiled up at her, the cracks tripled and his brows rose high up into his forehead. Whenever and wherever she came upon him, he looked astonished and delighted, as if their meeting were an unlikely but welcome accident.

"By the way, what happened with the hamsters?" he asked.

"The same," she said.

"Something you did to their genes?"

"No."

"Ah. Well, perhaps when we land," he said. "Gravity."

"I'll have no time, then," Mattie said. "You and I will be collecting Anunna! We will have no interest in Earthlings like Barney and his daughters."

When Sem the Doc laughed aloud, his eyes disappeared, becoming just another crease among many. "Anunna! Salamanders, batrachia, if we're lucky. More likely amoebas, single-celled but a single cell is all we need."

As a biogeneticist, Sem the Doc was Mattie's assistant; as exozoologist he was his own man.

The OC came over to their table, sat, and tilted his head back—the better to see Mattie from under his bushy eyebrows. His skin tones were deeper than Sem the Doc's, bronze next to the white of his hair and mustache.

"I still don't know why I was selected," Mattie said.

"Volunteered?" the OC asked.

"Not me. I didn't volunteer."

"Well, they had to have you because you're the best in your field, right, Sem the Doc?"

"She is that," Sem the Doc said.

"Thank you," Mattie said, "but I'm a biologist. Mainly mammalian. There are no mammals on Anu. The sun is too young."

"You never asked them why you?" the OC asked.

"Of course. Very often. They said it was the micro part. Microbiology—like Parn. Cellular. Molecules—and genes. I'm supposed to watch all our genes. In transit and on a planet with an alien ecosystem. And Barney's genes. And the genes of a whole lot of Earth bacteria."

"I saw you in a cell once," Sem the Doc said. "It was

three years ago. You demonstrated a laser technique. Geneticists in several fields were—"

"You were there, Sem the Doc?" Mattie asked.

"I was there. I sat near the Fanaticks that day," Sem the Doc said. "Dangerous ignorance. They were—"

"But I never saw you!"

"How would you have? I was in one of the darkest, highest, most rearward tiers, as befitting my status and achievements in our field."

Anu is a massive-2e, dry planet made up of steppes, plains that are actually plateaus. Its waters are a latticework of deep gorges, fiords, narrow cuts; "sea" level is a mile below the plains, which make up almost the entire surface of the planet. In two Earth years, au2, Anu circles an F5 sun which has twice the luminosity of Sol and 1.25 the mass. There is little heavy metal so in spite of its mass Anu's gravity is .9. Because of a 10% axial tilt, seasonal change is negligible. Anu is perfect for grass farming. Since its sun is so young, less than 6 billion years, the planet has no highly evolved native life-forms.

Nathan Smythy—Bureau of AstroReasearch—Es2631

It was dark in the small alcove Nat Smythy called a bridge. He had the shields up, all internal lighting off. Behind them, in the larger control room, lights flickered silently on screens and scopes.

"Wait," Nat said, and then, "Now!"

White light.

Mattie thought for a second that Nat had made a mistake and she was looking at a sun.

But the arc of pure white bisecting the window was the planet itself, Anu, reflecting the light of its star, a star with "twice the luminosity of Earth's Sol." The tiny cabin had become a cathedral with one luminous leaded window, translucent rather than reflective. Nat, Mattie, and the OC coming in behind them breathed together in silence, reverent.

There was no sign of the patchwork surface the globe model showed. No demarcation, no vein, no line marred the white radiance.

The OC touched her arm, and Mattie followed, leaving Nat in the dark behind, keeping watch at the window. They passed through the unattended control room, flickering votary candles, sibilant hissing like whispered prayers, and into the corridor where the sudden artificial light was plain and bare and metal-gray walls seemed almost green. The ship seemed as unfamiliar and close to Mattie again as it had been before, in those first early weeks out from Earth.

"What about Rol's questions about the landing site?" Mattie asked when they reached her cabin.

The OC shrugged. "Nat says no evidence. Addle's obsessed himself. No matter which one we picked he'd think another was better. Besides, everything was set."

He shaped himself into a chair, apparently contemplative. And tired.

"And now it's time to wait," he said.

For a moment he looked like her father although his skin was brown. His white hair was straight, silky, not grizzled, and only slightly thin in front. Thick white brows and mustache balanced the broad cheekbones and wide jawline. And the lips were surprisingly thin and soft under the mustache.

When he turned toward her, she looked away.

"Do you want to play strip in the exercise room?"

"What?"

"Strip. Will you play?"

"No, sir."

There was silence. He looked away again but his expression was benign. Perhaps amused.

"Why not?"

"I don't play well enough. I'd lose."

"I'd give a handicap of three garments."

Why now, after two years, within a shift of landing?

What a strange way to play. It must belong to some other generation—not hers.

"I'm only wearing three ... garments," she said finally. "You have many." She did not know why she was discussing the absurd as though it were rational.

"No, I don't. And if I forfeit three, we'll be fairly even."

"I can't ... play with you. We can't. You're the OC. It's against the rules. It wouldn't be fair to ..."

"Then you're saying no?"

She said no.

He sat awhile, smiling faintly, looking into the medium distance. Then he rose slowly, as though with difficulty. He managed to lumber with solid authority even though he floated. He had given up. He was going.

When suddenly he turned to her and bent over, arms at his side, she thought he was going to kiss the top of her head—like a father. He put his lips on hers, lightly, so lightly that it was surely still a good-bye kiss. Then he touched her lower lip with the tip of his tongue.

Her body reacted.

He straigtened up and turned to leave and she stood too and stared after him. He came back.

His touch was so gentle, so light that even when he put his arms around her she felt no pressure. He held her as though she were fragile. Respect or frailty? But whose frailty?

Then why was he doing it?

But the moving lips and tongue—not jamming fatly into her throat—fluttering.

He touched open the z-cling of her shirt, held her breast with his hand, bent his head to taste her nipple. The tongue played over it, dancing, gentle.

Too gentle. She pulled forward with her right arm high around his neck—he seemed taller than she had thought—and stretched and arched her body up to him. With her left hand she held his buttock and pulled him hard against her.

She froze, stunned. Was it possible that she was grabbing the OC's ass?

She wasn't going to do this. She let go, turned without looking back, and left him alone in her cabin.

Only much later did she grow angry and then, lying in her bunk, angrier. Damn the old man. She had trusted him.

Although in spite of its mass Anu's gravity is only 90% that of Earth, for us it will seem greater. We have been two years with only 10 to 40% of our weight. Of course, time of readjustment will depend on age, fitness (the diligence with which you have used the exercise room), and genes. I come in last in all three.

Sem Lac Omang—Lecture to crew—Es2635

At first the weight was not her own. It had fallen on her, and then it just lay on her, flattened her, pressed her into her bunk. For a moment it seemed to flatten her lungs, too, and collapse her laugh into a gurgle.

So she laughed again and tried to push it up away from her like the Poe character pushing the lid of his coffin.

Only when she consciously repossessed the weight, reclaimed it as her own, was she easier. With lead fingers she unstrapped her harness and pulled herself to her feet. Her legs wobbled and there were irregular tremors in her muscles. It was like standing and waking up onto the sand after a long swim in the ocean. Her left knee gave up and she allowed the rest of her body to sink down to the floor, her head falling back against the curved hull. This body wouldn't rush or leap ever again. Had she actually weighed more on Earth?

Finally she stood again and made her way slowly from her cabin down—down—to the hatch area. The familiar corridor was now an odd, vertical shaft; the bars for handholds in freefall were a ladder. She moved carefully, like someone recovering from a long sickness, yet she wasn't the last to join the small gathering in front of the OC and Delt Marker as the hatch opened.

"My God! There are people down there."

Elizabeth

In the late white light of early morning losos are dressing daughters in the city familydaughterrooms. There are shouts and cries outside. Elizabeth has never heard fathers behave so childishly except once just before the tornado destroyed their silos many harvests ago. She is afraid a tornado is going to destroy the city and kill them. (Elizabeth knows what the word "death" means.)

She pulls her hat from loso's hands. Fathers can still be heard shouting.

"It is coming down from the sky," one is saying. It must be a tornado, Elizabeth thinks. They must hide in the root cellars!

The daughters run into the main hall of the citybuilding and follow the fathers and brothers who are hurrying outside, also not knowing.

Everyone is pointing upward to the sky above the "landing place museum" outside the city. Elizabeth sees something shine white and then flash. She thinks the object has exploded but it has only reflected a ray of the fierce sunlight. As it comes nearer, it no longer flashes but shines the white light back at them as steadily and brightly as the sun itself. They cannot look at it as it lands.

All together, fathers, brothers, and daughters, they have been walking slowly in the direction of the landing field. Now the fathers are again behaving with dignity. They look around and call their own families together. They caution and warn but they do not explain. Maybe they have no explanation, Elizabeth thinks. Except for her pater, Father Jeremiah, of course. He wisely thinks it best to wait and see.

Bravely—because they are all afraid—they walk up to the

metal silo. Elizabeth has never before seen more than one or two small pieces of metal.

Above them metal stairs slide themselves to the ground and an oval door, also metal, slides itself sideways. People come out, strangely dressed fathers, and walk down the stairs slowly.

The daughters are serene but some smallbrothers speak and question the fathers.

The skypeople seem weak. Their bodies shake. Maybe they are afraid too.

Halfway down, the skyleader starts to speak and Elizabeth cannot understand him. It is always hard to understand fathertalk, and Elizabeth doesn't mind, but then she sees that no one, even Pater, is understanding. Yet they all listen until he stops.

The strange fathers all have hair cut so short that it cannot hide them from the sun and yet they are without hats. Their faces are faded, but their clothing looks new, freshly dyed, a deep and undignified dark blue like new ribbons, and fitted around the middle. They all look the same.

Pater has moved up ahead to stand before the stairs with two other leading familyfathers. He says greetings very slowly and carefully, and Elizabeth understands when he tells them to come to the pavilion to get their naked heads out of the sun. He points back to pavilion to be sure they understand.

The open field is not a good place to be for so long. It is hot for daughters. Losos are not with them. It hurts to look at the metal. It is too hot for Elizabeth to think what the new fathers are, but she is the only daughter who reads. Then she remembers that they are earthfathers.

They turn around to walk to the pavilion, which stands in an open field between the landing place and the city, Dagda's great city, rising large and long, like palaces.

After harvest familyfathers come to the city to visit the market where Eastcountrymen trade new things and answer questions about old things.

The fathers bring some of their daughters to the Eastcountry hospital for health. Elizabeth's eyes and skin are still good. She understood when the Eastcountrydoctors said to the fathers that all her parts were healthy.

Elizabeth wishes to be home. Her fingers move, wanting to work on the pater-and-smallbrother-Thomas portrait, which waits for her without patience, hidden in her attic "studio." Without her painting and books, wickedwitch things, her life is as flat as the world.

In the pavilion Elizabeth sits by Erin. (Only Erin and Lucilla like talking more than singing.) There is loso and shade. It is better. Elizabeth turns to watch the earthfathers.

And she sees that they are not all alike after all. Some of their faces are brown, burnt sienna and umber, some yellow, ochre and gold and tan, and some white. And one of them is Ariella! How can he be Ariella?

The fathers preach and tell.

Erin's familyoldfather stands tall, his hair still Fergus-red mixed with white, skin many colors and many old lumps, eyes almost gone; he says a holysong.

Then the earthfathers preach—strangely. Their bodies twitch and jump. The speak rudely, quickly and slowly, with no meter, just as they walked over the fields to the pavilion, not steadily, not smoothly. They breathe too loudly and wipe their foreheads. The do no respect their oldfathers.

The Ariella/earthfather sits very near and looks everywhere. Elizabeth watches him. He seems to be Ariella.

"Ariella?" Elizabeth asks before she knows she will.

The earthfather says something right to Elizabeth. He speaks to her.

He is not Ariella, of course. His eyes are dark, purple or black like Ariella's, but his face is pure white. Elizabeth has never seen such paleness. He seems to be a youngbrother, his skin is so smooth and his voice so high, but he acts like an oldfather—with dignity.

"—am Mattie M—," he says to Elizabeth. "What is—?" Elizabeth thinks that he asks her name! Erin, did he?

Fathers talk.

Did he ask Elizabeth's name? Erin doesn't know but she thinks so.

"Father?" Elizabeth says.

The father hears and Elizabeth says, "I am Elizabeth," but then Ioso is there, and she cannot see the earthfather. Why is it tending a father?

Her earthfather—Matty?—suddenly stands and raises his arm to the leaders and starts to speak to all the people. He stands tall and his form is clear.

He is a daughter.

"Abomination," the fathers say.

"Earthmen. Devils sent to destroy us."

The fathers rise and move forward like a great and silent wall. Elizabeth stumbles before them to the edge of the pavilion. Her head turns by itself, and she is looking back over the empty tables into the eyes of the earth . . . daughter.

Mattie

They couldn't have survived. Mattie knew they couldn't be there.

But there they were—people—standing below the ship.

Everyone was silent. Sem the Doc's hard breathing was the only sound.

So the data was wrong. Or this was the wrong planet. Earth. They were back on Earth somehow.

Delt Marker moved first. He raised his hand in a weak salute. No one below responded.

There were perhaps seventy-five of them, loosely gathered, almost motionless, looking up without joy, surprise—or fear.

The crew merged slowly and awkwardly into single file to descend the stairs.

"Explain it, Mattie," Parn whispered. Sem the Doc looked at her over his shoulder and shook his head.

"You said these people died when the Wars . . . four hundred years ago," Rachel said.

The upturned faces were too sharply defined, deeply shaded in blue, glaringly highlighted, overexposed, drained of color, haloed and blurred in the white sun. Rather than descendants of the original Anunnan settlers, they might be their ghosts.

Mattie stumbled and had to watch her feet. She held the rail tightly, tried to steady knees trembling under unfamiliar weight. Only when she was halfway down was she able to look out again. The Anunna were now just a few feet below.

There were large hats everywhere. Straw hats, woven hats, grass hats, and wide-brimmed cotton bonnets with huge visors on the little girls.

The men's faces were serious, wrinkled; they held their thin bodies straight with a courtly dignity. At first their box-like suits seemed vaguely familiar from historical "photographs" and antique vid images, but there was something odd about the color and material. Deep brown in the creases, but broadly mottled with irregular, large, faded areas everywhere else. And the fabric, in spite of rectangular tailoring, seemed to float lightly, loosely, like that of togas or tunics.

The girls looked like dried strawflowers, petaled rather than clothed in colorless layers of material left unfaded only in the folds. Ribbons were tied everywhere, around their waists, wrists, and hung from under the hats in unlikely cascades. The dresses were voluminous, the skirts billowing, just ankle-length. Impractical and overwhelmingly hot in this climate. But then the air was so dry that perhaps all this material and haberdashery protected them from the ultraviolet of the young sun. Without humidity . . .

As Mattie stepped onto the ground just after Sem the Doc, she spotted a small boy standing between two old men, a very small boy. She looked from him to the little girls and saw that they weren't little at all. They were women, grotesque women. Elephantine little-bo-peeps. Great big Alices at the Mad Hatter's tea party.

"Welcome to Dagda," said an old man.

Less than a hundred altogether, natives and Earth people, they were a small uneven motion against the vast, flat, still landscape, as they walked north from the ship to a low wooden pavilion whose interior was an inky shadow a few hundred yards in the distance.

They walked informally, the visitors among the natives but not with them, behind but not quite following the leaders.

It was too hot immediately. The sun, though still low, burned their heads and faces, and their solid navy clothes absorbed and held its radiation. The scientists' open-necked shirts tucked into loose pants were not much better than the tighter, tailored uniforms of the OC and crew.

There was none of the talk, murmuring, one would expect of such a large crowd of people who must know each other well. Next to the Anunna, the Earth people seemed hyperkinetic, restless, chattering. Their voices overlapped, empty, thin, without echo in the open. Mattie heard Rol Addle remark to Parn about the grass under their feet; Rachel was speaking to everyone about the shocking distance of the horizon; Mr. Ricco said something technical to the OC about the landing. No one said that these people could not be alive.

The land was stunningly and totally flat. Except for the pavilion just ahead and the insignificant interruption of a small cluster of low wooden structures some indeterminate distance beyond it, all around them was an immensity of featureless plain without relief or change, white-gold.

A hot, white, and heavy land. The Earth people began to drag, officers and scientists. There were straggling, as disorderly as children following the stiff, tall, narrow backs of the elderly men.

They tried. The OC himself "threw his shoulders back" to deny the pull of gravity on his girth, and Mr. Ricco's stiffness was a qualified if meaningless victory. Delt Marker cleared his throat too loudly, quickened his stride to match that of the man who had first greeted them, opened his mouth, said nothing. That leader, an old man with tufted brows, slowed slightly, accommodating, said nothing.

The Earth people, not the Anunna, seemed to be the lost children at last recovered. And, Mattie thought, there was solemnity and politeness, but no joy, in the fathers' reaction to the return of the prodigal sons.

Finally just outside the pavilion, only two or three short steps away from its exquisite shade, Parn reached down to pick some wisp of weed growing next to the first wooden step; he pinched it, crushed it, smelled it, wrinkled his nose and frowned.

Suddenly standing next to Mattie—looming over her—was a seven-foot, dark brown, heavily furred animal.

"My God! Parn!"

Parn saw it. He stood gaping, weed in hand. Behind them the OC shouted and pushed forward.

And there were more of the things—going in and out of the pavilion, moving among the women.

The natives took no notice of the animals or of the agitation of the Earth people. The old men gestured and bowed them up into the pavilion.

"Harmless," Delt Marker said and followed the natives.

"What kind of animal is it?" the OC asked Mattie.

Mattie shook her head and tried to examine the nearest of the creatures. It had incredible hands, prehensile and primate, narrow, with long, supple, hairless fingers.

These Anunna could not be capable of such a result. They seemed to be simple dirt farmers, maybe a primitive religious sect. And there was no sign of technology.

She tried to study the face but the thing would not bend down to her. Its features were small, eyes hidden in fur, snout not apelike.

Where was Sem the Doc? He was the only other person besides Mattie who might see the beasts for what they were.

"Dr. Manan." Marker was signaling insistently that she and the others come into the pavilion. She wrenched herself away from the animal. Later she would have all the time on this world to measure and probe.

Inside, Mattie's eyes ached with a green burn of afterimage. It was difficult at first to see the outlines of the long wooden tables and benches, and the wood itself took on a fuzzy blue haze. Because the horizon was so distant, they could not see the sky from inside. Through the open sides of the pavilion the horizontal plain created the illusion of vertical walls, glaring, brilliant walls enwrapping the pavilion full circle.

Mattie let herself drop onto a bench next to Parn.

"Mattie, are these things intelligent?" he pointed to the

animals, moving about among the tables, apparently doing things for—or to—the native women.

"I don't know," she said. But she did know that they were impossible.

Delt Marker was already talking. Weaving and swaying visibly with unaccustomed weight, he remained standing while he delivered a long, diplomatic address to the natives. They were all quiet.

Mattie looked around among them for signs of inbreeding. Surely after more than four hundred years such a small gene pool would have produced serious abnormalities, deformities. There were none.

The skin of most of the older people was scarred, seared, and tumorous, but that would be a normal effect of the radiant F5 sun. Some of the young, in fact, were remarkably untouched by it. A red-haired female at the next table had skin impossibly pure, without blemish. Skin that could never have seen the Anunne sun. Perhaps a mutation. Adaptation . . .

"We too are glad that you exist." An Anunnan was speaking at last, the old man who had greeted them so briefly.

The attention of all the Earth people was instantly concentrated. They strained to understand. Rol Addle, who had been walking around the edges of the pavilion to stare yearningly at distant grasses, turned to hear.

The Anunna spoke an English almost exactly as it had been spoken in many places on Earth five hundred years earlier. All linguistic evolution had taken place in the Earthstates; almost no change could have occurred in this isolated pocket with such a limited number of speakers. Some phrases were unintelligible, but generally the curious accent was comprehensible.

"There were rumors of war," the old man said, "and then there was nothing. No one ever came to Dagda again. Our fathers said that there must have been total destruction. Our fathers said that Earth and the most wicked of its children had finally suffered the wrath of God." The man had begun to chant or intone. "Our fathers saw Dagda as an Ark. Our fathers thanked god for sparing them and promised to serve Him and shun wickedness and guide their daughters in the ways of righteousness. It is our duty now to continue their work, to preserve the animals and the land in our care."

This speech, which had started out with the tones and inflections of spontaneous utterance, had changed into a monotonous song, a flat cant, rehearsed, ritualized. And when he stopped, the thing seemed unfinished. The visitors sat in awkward silence.

"Well, yes," Marker said finally, "but we ... uh ... we weren't annihilated, were we? I mean our ancestors.

"And we are glad to recover you! Wonderful and brave people to have survived unimaginable hardships, cut off when so young a colony from the nurture of Mother Earth ... as it were."

There was a flicker of unease, the first native reaction to any of their words.

Another man stood then, older than the first. He had red strands mixed with his sparse, white hair, and his skin was tortured from the sun's radiation. He said: "God our father preserved and provided for us and we have done His will to the best of our ability. Our daughters live in holy silence; our ..." The intoning became an incomprehensible litany.

Mattie glanced at the "daughters," soundless bundles of material. Shapeless lumps. As serene, as expressionless, as mute as the animals moving among them.

They were like stuffed dolls, overdressed by some child's aunt in skirt upon skirt upon underskirt, blank homemade faces sewn not quite right, looking not quite at anything.

And the same amateur seamstress had forgotten to do the animals' faces, too. One noticed a mouth, a canine nose, imagined button eyes under the fur. Otherwise there was nothing there. The maker was not skilled enough to create definition in form or face in either toy.

Could the women be deaf? A congenital defect—a result of inbreeding affecting, somehow, only the X chromosome. Or perhaps an adaptation for some benefit yet to be ascertained.

That would explain it all. What a horror. No wonder the men talked of caring for their daughters. The quiet. The blankness. The mutual isolation.

"Ah . . . ree . . . ahlah?"

They weren't deaf. One of them had spoken. Her face was narrow, freckled, thin-lipped. Plain.

A long neck, the head turning now, like some goose above the fat goose skirts. The light brown hair was streaked with blond. A golden goose girl.

Had she asked Mattie a question? Was is some archaic phrase?

"I do not understand you," Mattie said clearly, slowly, and loudly enough that Marker glanced her way.

The woman—she was not a child—did not answer. She turned to the one next to her, the porcelain doll with red hair.

They said nothing.

Parn said that the red-haired one was beautiful, but that the rest were the most uninteresting females he had ever seen. Mattie brushed his words away.

"I am Mattie Manan, Doctor Manan," she said to the women. "What are your names?"

They stared at her.

"Your grasses," Rol Addle asked the leaders loudly, almost shouting, hurrying his words, "are they native or from original Earth material? . . . How have they adapted to the planet's ecosystem? Has there been natural mutation?" He hesitated. There was silence; the elders were looking at him politely.

"What is that crop that we see in the distance?"

"We reap the harvest that we sow," an elderly leader said to Rol.

"What I meant, sir, was . . . well, we can offer you help. We have the techniques now to alter the range and type of genetic variability of—"

Another native male rose to his feet and said, "We gathered corn as the sand of the sea, very much, and stored it in our silos against the years of famine that God promised Pharaoh."

"The one talking is only about thirty," Parn whispered. "They're not all elderly. They seem to be pretending to be old men."

All the men—even the boys—bore themselves with the dignity of the very old trying to remain upright against the gravity of years. They moved and spoke with deliberation, a slow and grave caution, which gave importance and authority to every gesture and expression.

But two or three of those who had done most of the speaking were indeed elderly; and they behaved like leaders—over or under what kind of governmental organization, the Earth people had as yet no idea.

"Father?" Mattie jumped. It was the plain woman apparently addressing her again. The other one blushed.

"Me?" Mattie pointed to herself.

The woman smiled and her gray eyes narrowed and warmed and her lips formed a lopsided curve, higher on the right. She had a single narrow dimple. Not plain.

"Elizabeth," she said. "I am Elizabeth."

One of the animals came between Mattie and Elizabeth and wiped at Mattie's face with some kind of cloth. Mattie grabbed at its arm to keep it, but it walked away.

"What the hell!" Parn said. "God, they're huge . . . I thought this planet had no highly developed life-forms."

"It doesn't," Mattie said.

She jumped to her feet, forgetting her weight. She had to hold the table edge for a second, staggering, to keep from sitting back down hard.

"Your animals," she shouted toward the leaders. "One can see that they are the result of an advanced state of genetic engineering. How . . . ?" She saw the OC frown and Marker shake his head slightly. She calmed herself, drew a long breath, and stood straighter.

"I am Mattine Manan and my field is genetics, mammalian microbiology. Gene—"

"A daughter." The whisper was clear throughout the pavilion.

The men rose as one on all sides. In almost total silence they moved toward the women, who stood and walked before them to the north side of the pavilion.

"God was right to destroy them."

The pavilion was emptied with solemnity and dignity. The last Mattie saw of the Anunna were the eyes of the Golden Goose Girl looking back at her over the shoulder of the gray-haired leader.

Bitter Waters

According to the fragmentary Earth records that remained from before the Wars, Anu had been settled by at least four different, independent groups: "The Celtic Guild," a political association rather than ethnic in spite of its name; farmers, "Plainsmen," from the western hemisphere, less lettered, less verbal, communal but not communist; a small scientific community of which there is almost no information; and another group of farmers or perhaps villagers from somewhere in the center of old Europe. All the groups were, of course, preconstruction, racial as well as civil. The lack of racial mixing may mean that the strains were genetically weak.

K. Kyly Es2631—*Lost Earth Society Journal*

"Damn, it's dark in here!" Parn said. He was lying on the floor, shoulders against the bulkhead.

"Dark is good," Nat said. "I was blind in the sun out there. And the heat!"

The ship shut out the heat and light but not the gravity. The men had just dragged themselves back from a second meeting with the Dagdan "fathers." They were collapsed on the benches, sprawled over the tables, and flattened across the floor like hay after a windstorm.

The OC, heaviest of all, sat leaning over the bench, head propped on elbows. Next to him Sem the Doc lay over the table, the thousand lines of his face hidden now on his folded arms.

None of them looked at Mattie or at Rachel, who sat in

a low hammock, one toe touching the floor to rock herself in a nervous, repetitive, swing motion.

"What did they say?" Mattie asked.

No one answered.

"Parn?" She could see only the dark curls on the top of his head.

"Much of it was impossible to follow." It was the OC who finally spoke. "That droning—"

"Mattie, they're crazy," Parn said.

"We're not sure what's growing in the cultivated fields," Rol said. "We couldn't get near them."

"Quiet, Addle," the OC said.

"They chanted just the way they did the first time, when you were there. It was hard to understand," Sem the Doc said. "At one point I think they said their fathers 'were led out of the land of Earth and through the vast deeps to the wilderness of Dagda. / And when they came to Plain, they could not drink of the waters of Plain, for they were bitter.'"

"And then Marker chanted: 'We will sweeten your waters!' " Parn said.

All the men laughed, including Marker. "Well, at least I tried to speak in a way they would understand," he said.

"They interpolate the Bible with their own history," Sem the Doc said. "Dagda sounds like the name for the whole planet, for Anu, and Plain a local place."

"You certainly remember every word, Sem the Doc," Rachel said.

"I was raised on the Bible."

"Just like them," Mr. Ricco said.

"Hardly. All I have in common with them is advanced age."

"But most of them just look old."

"I can't understand this," Parn said. "According to Kyly, some of the people who founded these colonies were supposed to have been botanists and plant breeders, however rudimentary. But these people look like some kind of religious fundamentalists. They'd think 'germ plasm' was dirty language."

"Yeah, but look at the fields, flat beautiful fields," said Rol Addle. "We can't tell what is growing out there from this distance, but they must know what they're doing."

"But they seem so—so primitive. They went on about innocence and serenity and protecting the females from evil," Parn said. "Mattie, they said that their 'daughters' do not move to care for themselves. Their every need is satisfied."

"Lilies of the field," Sem the Doc said, "true children of God."

"Well, what did you say to them?" Mattie asked.

"We said our women were godless, daughters of the devil," Parn said.

"I told them that in Earthstates women are doctors and teachers," the OC said, ignoring Parn.

"Ah, but they answered you," Sem the Doc said. " 'But I suffer not a woman to teach, nor to usurp authority over the man, but to be in silence. / For Adam was first formed, then Eve.' "

"I heard the silence," Mattie said.

"Ignorance is blessed. Sin and knowledge seem confused."

"That is not a confusion, Dr. Ramsay," Kyly whispered from his place on the floor. "It is a common theme in human history. They are protecting the women, saving their souls. And it is true the females do no work."

"How do you know what's true?" Delt Marker asked.

"I talked alone with one of the younger men. Remember, I can speak their dialect quite convincingly." Kyly coughed his wispy cough.

"They're just protecting their own power," Mattie said.

Kyly smiled—pained but patience. "It certainly is not the first time in history that people were kept in the dark for their own good. In the early Christian centuries only priest were taught to read. It wasn't only the peasants—and—and women, of course—who were illiterate, but the nobility . . ."

"That was how the Church kept its power over the secular authorities. It's always power, control," Mattie said.

"There were once 'belles,' wives and daughters of rich

men, whose idleness was prized as much as their chastity. They enjoyed . . ." Kyly hesitated. "No, that's not the best example. Nuns. Throughout the earlier history of Western civilization the females in religious orders were illiterate and celibate. In the contemplative orders they did little or no work. Those of the aristocracy, that is. Nuns deriving from the lower economic classes labored to sustain—"

"And speaking of celibacy, what about sex, Kyly?" Parn asked.

"Is that part of their ignorance?" Mattie asked.

"As I said, their mores and customs, folkways if you will, have developed over centuries. Belief systems and values, which may be incomprehensible or even distasteful to the layman, may, in fact, contain deep truths and wisdom we have not yet acquired ourselves—or have lost. We must not let the ignorant among us tamper with the values and customs of these people."

"Did you ask him about the crops?" Ron Addle shouted. "What is growing here? Is it Earth species? Is it . . ."

"Shut up, Rol, will you! This is more important," Mattie said.

"Nothing is more important! I'm not going to have the mission ruined by a stupid . . ."

"Enough, Rol," The OC said. "Let's get back to the point, dealing with these people."

"When I talk to them myself . . ." Mattie said.

The men were suddenly quiet again. The only motion in the cabin was the swing of Rachel's hammock.

"They refuse to accept any of us if we insist upon including you or Racey," the OC said.

"What?"

"You have to stay on the ship."

"You didn't agree to such a—"

"We had no choice."

"But there must be some sane people on this planet."

The O.C. shook his head.

"This is not possible! No one else is qualified to study the animal life on this planet."

"The botanists have the important function on this expedition," Marker said. "Yours was not—"

"But that has all changed! These people are a biological treasure. Hundreds of years of breeding within the confines of a definitive gene pool. Also the animals! Didn't you notice them?" Mattie asked. "Sem the Doc, you saw? Without me half the scientific benefit of the mission will be lost."

"If we let you off the ship, it will all be lost," Kyly said.

Rol Addle nodded, agreeing with Kyly for the first time.

"Why can't we go somewhere else?" asked Rachel.

"We can't take the ship," Nat said. "There is no programming for a takeoff into an atmosphere, no shuttle facilities. We would have to wait for the right time, go into deep space, return into orbit, and then land as if on arrival. There is no way we can travel overland. This planet is twice e-mass."

"Delt," Mattie said, "can't you make a deal with them? Refuse to give them all the tech, all the help, unless they accept our terms?"

"That's the strange thing, Mattie," Parn answered instead. "They don't seem to care about our tech."

"Or simply do not understand the subject," Nat said.

"Doctor Manan was . . . is Earth's leading microbiologist," Sem the Doc said, his wrinkles dropping into a clownlike etching of sadness. "It is wrong, a grievous waste to confine her. I suggest we vote."

Except for Sem the Doc and Mattie, everyone—including Rachel—voted that the two women remain on the ship.

"No," Mattie said.

"Mattie, we'll bring you specimens, everything," said Parn. "You'd be working in the ship's lab anyway."

"Specimens! I could have stayed on Earth and you would have brought me specimens. You have no right to make such a decision. No authority. I . . . we were selected by the Earthstates Council of . . ."

Mattie turned to the OC, who said, "Sorry, Dr. Manan."

* * *

The ship had been the means but now it was the end. Before they had left Earth Mattie had seen the mission as a narrow, long tunnel—ship-width, two years long, fifteen lightyears deep—a tunnel through time and space. But open-ended. She had imagined they were tunneling their way up and out onto the surface of an immense, wide-open, bright land.

And it was true. Outside there were no walls, no verticals, just vast openness—but the distance itself was the prison. Mattie was in a prison within a prison, her cabin a cell. The keepers were old, narrow men; and the turnkeys, her own shipmates.

Paint

Families walk together from the train halt, moving solemnly eastward on the hard paths through the newly harvested fields. Motes of grain and larger bits of dry grass are visible in the light of the slowly setting sun.

The oldfathers lead. Losos carry goods from the city aloft like tabernacles while others bear the few daughters on their backs. Smallbrothers and tallbrothers carry the family bags and packs and food.

The procession winds its way around one great field that remains ungleaned. Its hay is so high now that the people are half in blue shade, half in white light, as if they wade to the waist in the deep blue water of some other planet.

Before them the horizon disappears in a deep purple. Some of the fathers begin to chant a holystory. The others walk behind them in silence and dignity although they are all tired from the day's train ride.

It is early dark night when they get to Lords. Fagot torches burn for them on the porches and in barn doorways.

Brothers and youngfathers coming from the city tell brothers and fathers who stayed home about the earthpeople. Some younger ones shout out through the dark as they pack away goods and close the sheds. The oldfathers hush them with their own silences.

As she is going to the daughterrooms to sleep, Elizabeth passes smallbrother Thomas. His mouth is wrong. Age has tightened it since she painted him. Painting from pictures in the mind is long and hard.

* * *

"The flood story is in this book. I can't see it very well; the letters are so small and thin and faded." Elizabeth holds the open Bible up to the pearl-white window light.

" 'And it came to pass, when men began to multiply on the face of the earth, and daughters were born unto them, / That the sons of God saw the daughters of men that they were fair; and they took them wives of all which they chose.' "

When Elizabeth finishes the story of Noah and the Ark, it is dark in the attic room.

Erin and Ariella sit staring in silence. They can sing angel-stories but they cannot read.

"The earthfathers . . . male and female, came out of the ship . . . at the landing field. Out of Noah's Ark . . . they came 'forth,' 'male and female,' 'the male and the female,' " Erin says. She is asking Elizabeth a question.

Elizabeth says: "Remember it said, 'the sons of God came in unto the daughters of men, and they bare children to them'? And in another place it said, 'Adam knew Eve his wife; and she conceived, and bare Cain . . .' Babies come from daughters, from their bodies. Fathers put seeds into them and they grow in them until . . ."

"Abomination!" The word came as a hiss from the darkness in front of the doorway. "Corrupter" is a whisper, spit.

Elizabeth stares blindly at the dark place. The only sounds are a cry from Erin and a sharp breath from Ariella.

A match scrapes and a candle lights youngfather Lucius's fat face, flesh hanging loose in emptiness.

Elizabeth's throat aches. Her mouth is open, stretched and paralyzed.

Lucius moves to the center of the room. He stares down at Elizabeth and the Bible. Red candle wax drips onto its pale page and Elizabeth's fingers. Hot.

She can almost see his smile, his joy.

He leans over her; she can smell his mouth, his body. She knows he wants to burn her, the witch, with his fire.

A form is standing tall beside her, facing Lucius. It is Ariella.

His eye-flesh tightens as he stumbles a small step backward, away from her.

To disguise the weakness he turns about, holds the candle high, studies the room. The pater portrait.

He is on top of it, the candle a sword, penetrating, ripping and burning. He thrusts again and again. Then he knocks it to the floor with his left hand.

Ariella jumps too late. Erin runs forward.

He is afraid of them. He does not look at their faces. At the door he mutters, "Pater."

Get Off

Mattie stepped through the hatch in the middle of the third Dagdan night. She took only water, rations, a blanket, a few instruments—as nonexpendable as a cook's knives—and the fingercube remote.

No one saw her go. It had not occurred to the OC that anyone in his command would disobey an order. Besides, where would she go?

The sky was huge, horrifyingly huge, and empty. The ship was the highest point and yet so tiny it was swallowed in the empty immensity. A needle engulfed in the blankness.

Blank not black. But Dagda had no moon. Mattie began to see a few faint stars overhead, but they were insignificant. Yet the night was not dark.

Gingerly, still heavily, she descended the steps. On the ground she discovered, low in the southern sky behind her, no longer hidden by the ship, two very bright objects, one a brilliant point of light just touching the horizon. Planets. Planets closer to Anu's sun than Anu . . . Dagda. She couldn't remember what Nat had called them. Larger planets than those of Earth's solar system, reflecting a larger and brighter sun. It was these two alone that lit the night sky and reflected ghosty pallor onto the land. It must be black indeed when they were set.

She made her way across the empty landing field without beaming her fingercube. The distance between the ship and the pavilion seemed greater than she remembered. Her weight tied her to the ground; she was pulled back and down by an undertow.

She stopped to rest in the pavilion. The "city" beyond

seemed abandoned, a "ghost town," illuminated only by the light of the sky.

Suddenly a small animal ran over her outstretched ankle. She leaped, beamed her fingercube, and ran after it.

And caught it. She was staring closely into the buggy eyes of a tiny lizard thing.

A real native. An Anunnan.

Mattie held it still in the light of the fingercube and checked its parts, classified, calculated. Like a lizard but not a lizard. Far lower on the evolutionary scale. Definitely not of earth by direct or indirect route. Natural or "changed"? Natural. Even without laboratory evidence she was certain.

She named it Parn, stuck it in her pocket, and walked on.

Mattie came to a low gate made of some kind of light wood, very dry, almost dusty to the touch. She studied it with half her mind as she swung it open.

With the fingers of her left hand she had been absently examining the folds in Parn's epidermis. Now she shifted the weight of her pack onto her left shoulder and rubbed her eyes. Dust. Particles of grain and flakes of leaves had also begun to irritate the skin of her neck and upper back. She stood still, looking around, scratching.

She was already there. It was not a city or even a town or village. Perhaps a marketplace. The structures were more like old, country hostels than the private houses Mattie had allowed herself to imagine.

The third building on the second side street had a porch, a "verandah." This single human touch led Mattie to it. She climbed the steps and knocked on the door. One of the large furry beasts opened it and let her in.

Folly

Just a little water to keep the flower alive. Not more than half a scoop. No waste. It is waste water anyway from the wash.

The wooden handle is strong and strangely light. The scoop feels good, springy and whiplike, in Elizabeth's hand. It is some kind of newood from Eastcountry which is supposed someday to replace all driwood.

Elizabeth touches the flower's petal, bright red and soft. How can such a thing—a deep, wet thing—exist in this place of hay and pale strawflowers? The oldfathers say daughters are flowers like these. Dear to sustain. Earthseed. *Promulgated* in Eastcountry. Wrong word. Elizabeth turns away from the windowsill to reach for the little dictionary but forgets her purpose and walks instead to the easel where form and color are becoming Ariella's face.

Which Ariella will it be? Elizabeth cannot yet make out the expression. She must work at it more before she can see who it is.

Her hand reaches for a brush and it, too, stops. Why go on? It will never be finished. Or it will end like the pater painting. She glances toward the cabinet shelf where she and Erin lay its pathetic shreds before loso cleaned it away. Erin said it could be pasted together and copied. Elizabeth knows better. The painting will never be again. It is no longer true. A different Elizabeth painted it.

Instead she came back up to her studio and started Ariella from the picture in her mind. In almost total darkness, all the Dagdan night, and then in the long dawning hours of wonderful white light, ignoring loso's distress, she worked, worked without thought.

There are household sounds and shuffling loso feet below in the daughterrooms. Everything as usual before morning food. No. Nothing as usual ever again.

Elizabeth takes up the brush after all, clucks at the dust, the *ubiquitous* dust, which has already settled on the painting, and opens one of the tiny hardwood-and-clay jars of paint.

Maybe a red, deep and wet, vermilion—with crimson?—shadowed, something below the face, very little, a ribbon here.

It is right. Exactly what is needed. In fact, it shows all Ariellas—daughters and doctors—at once, as one somehow. Elizabeth laughs and says good-bye to it.

She packs her paints and dictionary into a straw basket, listens for loso, goes down two wooden flights, and out the daughtersidedoor. She crosses the house gardens and circles the gazebo without attracting the attention of loso or man.

At first, Elizabeth sees before her not a flat, featureless plain but places that were and places to be. In growing season the paths and shallow hollows are daughtersecret tunnels and rooms; with each harvest they are violated, open to the sky, and erased. Now most fields are freshly harvested, some still stubble and others already planted, long rows of tiny sprouts, a shocking fresh green against dusty pale brown and gold.

She pictures the red wax on the floor beneath the easel. Is killing cruelty? The fathers are never cruel. Except Lucius. But Elizabeth has not been able, even before last night, to see Lucius as a father. He is only a harvest older than she. It is hard, even for good daughters, when younger and younger brothers turn into fathers.

The early morning air is already parched. She passes the "totem pole," a lone, broken fence post on which she once painted strange and mysterious images with magical meaning from angelstory lore. Traces of the color can still be seen on the far side.

Elizabeth is not a good daughter—or a bad daughter. Not a daughter at all. Never again a daughter. "Daughters of men." "The sons of God saw the daughters of men that they were fair."

She jumps over the castle moat, a rut at the end of the hayfield that is sometimes damp. (One sowingseason— when she and Erin were twenty-two harvests—it had a trickle of water.)

Lucilla and Rebekah chanted and played here with them. Lucilla accepted any role, dragon, youngfather hero, leadingoldfather, but always seemed amused. The only adult daughter.

Elizabeth squints and her eyes water when she tries to look ahead. Her wide hat-brim is no protection from the white glare that is the horizon sky or from the painful light reflecting up from the earth itself. How do fathers—*men*— and losos work in the fields?

She will be missed now.

It is growing hotter.

Of course she has not thought to bring water. Loso's job.

Maybe she will die, die dead out here in the open field like a dried up losobit. What difference can it make now?

Cynically? Elizabeth touches the dictionary in her basket. I am *cynical,* she thinks.

She should have brought water. Should have eaten. Should have run away before harvest.

Elizabeth resigns herself to fate, whatever it might be. The uselessness of resistance becomes sadly, sharply clear as the endless burning fields stretch on and on before her. Hopeless. Helpless. She will burn her dictionary. Let the fathers slave in the fields.

She comes to Ariella's house, Brens, by herself.

"You are a hero, Elizabeth," Ariella sings. "You have escaped a terrible fate. You have dared the dangers of . . ."

"This is no escape, Ariella. This is what there is, all that there is. Fields and fathers and daughters."

Grounded

The animal ate Parn—lizard Parn. It had brushed the dirt from Mattie's pants, slipped its long narrow hand lightly into her pocket and pulled out the prize. Fast, before she could react, it had dropped him into its mouth and swallowed. It was already going about the business of wiping dust off her shoes.

"Leave me alone." It didn't heed if it heard.

This thing, a bear with primate hands, seemed to be the only one home. But the hands were not just primate, not ape. Nor were they human, though there were human elements in them, frightening even to Mattie's cold molecular eye. Those fingers were supple, flexible, light and quick, but, as she was discovering, very strong.

"Let me go!"

There was a sound, footsteps above. Human maybe. Certainly not the brush-drag of this thing's feet, if feet they were. Mattie looked down at them. Paws. Big blocks, chunky and wide. Maybe if she stepped on one—hard.

If it felt the pain, she could not recognize the signal. It made no sound. It displayed none of the characteristic primate gestures or facial movement.

But it did pick her up off her feet and off its feet. It tried to sit her on a chair, but she stood instead on the seat in order to study its head. Was it mainly a bear? The ears were cupped, erect, almost canine. She poked one open and tried to look down into the canal, but the light coming from candles on a low table and the top of a cabinet shone at the wrong angle.

There was a woman standing in a doorway watching Mattie.

"You are . . . a witch . . . I saw you." The antique dialect was flat.

"Don't be afraid of me. I . . ."

The woman said: "Is . . . it a magic potion . . . in loso's ear?" She chanted or intoned the words "magic potion."

"Is this animal called Loso? Is it male or female?" Mattie said, trying to see its genitals, which were hidden by thick brown fur and a fat belly.

No answer. In spite of the shapeless dress, and all the ribbons tying back the hair, the hair itself was gray-streaked and the face fortyish. Yet the manner belonged to a child.

"Where . . . are . . . your fathers?" she asked.

"My fathers are on the ship. . . . I don't have any fathers. . . . What kind of an animal is Loso?"

The woman said nothing.

"But what is its name?"

"Sylvia."

"Sylvia? You're Sylvia? Where do your people get these animals?"

"You . . . are not . . . serene," Sylvia said.

The animal was touching the fastenings of Mattie's shirt. It couldn't work the Z-cling and tried to pull the garment over her head.

"What is it doing?"

Sylvia said nothing.

"Are there other women here?" Mattie asked. Perhaps this Sylvia was exceptional.

Sylvia turned and walked out of the room. That was the last Mattie saw of her. She expected alarms and delegations of the family males to come after her but there was nothing.

In an adjacent room she discovered "daughter" clothing, and in spite of the help of the loso, she changed into a miserable long garment.

There was no mirror. Mattie cursed and tried to smooth down the layers of light, faded blue material. And the infernal ribbons, of course. Dark blue. Around the collar and the waist and the sleeves. She had no hair to tie back but let one ribbon dangle from under the most concealing straw hat she could find.

The loso had taken hold of her old suit as soon as she removed it. Mattie snatched it back, stuffed it in her instrument sack, and headed for the door. The animal came along with her.

Outside, the long dawn had begun whitely. Mattie and the loso walked through the city on roads paved in luminous, ghostly gray dust.

It was too early to try another house. She would wait until she heard stirring.

As they rounded a corner, Mattie heard voices. And it was already too late to retreat. A group of losos and human beings were standing and sitting on benches along the length of a low platform, a simple staging. The loso went ahead of her up the single step; several of the men watched, some casually, others with open curiosity. The females gaped with blank, broad faces.

One among the nearest group of males spoke to her.

"Are you not a Brendaughter?" His voice was low, slow, old, a bit creaky, and his face under the wide hat-brim was browner than his faded, light-cotton cloak. But in spite of the deep squint-lines around his eyes and the stoop of his shoulders, Mattie saw that he was not more than thirty-five.

She nodded.

He and the others up and down the platform continued to stare at her silently. She didn't know whether to allow her discomfort to show. A daughter by herself in public was perhaps expected to be uncomfortable.

"Brens brought no daughters to the city this harvest," he said.

She said nothing.

"Brens went back already," said another man, a genuinely old person. "Why is she here?" He was asking the other men, not Mattie.

"Odd," said another. "Do you suppose something's wrong among them?"

Mattie almost answered and realized that it was not expected. They just looked sometime longer.

"Well, she'll catch the train, then," the first man said finally.

The train?

Train. The platform was indeed a station. On the ground before it, inconspicuous in the dust, passed the rails, a single pair of wooden runners so narrow that they became a line and then invisible almost before the "track" had cleared the last city building to the north. The vast, flat, characterless fields beyond extended blankly to the impossibly distant horizon. The railroad apparently originated among the wooden structures to the right beyond which the light in the eastern sky was already intolerably bright.

From that direction came a line of three flatcars and one boxcar, on wheels, winched together and pulled by a small locomotive, made of wood, wood on the outside at least. The flatcars looked like a string of canopied beds, each having four corner-posts over which stretched a tightly woven awning. The first was piled with goods, crates, wicker and straw baskets, farm implements, small plows, twine and ropes, and earthenware containers, crocks, great clay jars and canisters with, of course, wooden lids.

The next two cars had raised platforms in the center upon which some people were seating themselves while others stood, balancing against them. Younger men, boys, and losos sat on the floor, legs crossed or dangling from the sides.

As Mattie moved to step up, loso hands reached out and lifted her as if she were a bundle. Only when she was fully seated on the rear end of the raised platform did she see that "her" loso had stayed back. It was already turning the corner, going back the way they had come. For a mad moment she regretted its loss.

Before she could examine the females grouped near her, the train began to move. It started and stopped, and started again with abrupt jerks. These were mild compared to the grinding and jolting of the rail bed; there were, of course,

no springs. Grooved wagon wheels churning wooden tracks.
Was there such a thing as oil? she wondered—absently because her attention was suddenly focused on two figures
standing slightly apart at the front of the first passenger car.

Something more than space separated these men from the
other men. They seemed narrower and straighter, somehow
younger at a distance. She could see only one man's profile
and that told her little. The clothing seemed at first similar
but with a closer inspection stronger, less vaguely colored,
less wispy. But most important was their attitude: they carried themselves without the fathers' aged dignity and sense
of patriarchal wisdom, yet seemed to convey more of another kind of authority or knowledge. Like their clothing,
they projected a more solid identity. Perhaps she was imagining the distinctions, but if there was any way to move
closer, to listen to their conversation—without revealing her
identity—she would try it.

"You . . . are not . . . Ariella Bren," said the girl next to
her.

The car lurched with a screech. Mattie recovered her balance.

Three of the women were looking into her face, no ex-
pressions on their own. Blank-faced like the endless, empty
land the tiny train of cars had begun to cross. Bland, ageless
children. How much of a threat were they?

"Yes," Mattie said, and assumed as blank and simple a
look as she could. Were these woman capable of recogniz-
ing her offworld accent for what it was?

"She . . . is . . . Ariella," announced another. She leaned
forward to peer at Mattie. The move was not precarious
since she was held in position by volumes of stiff material.
They were all wrapped bundles of cotton stuffed together on
a shelf. No one could get loose to fall.

"I . . . know . . . Ariella," the first said without animosity
or tone of any kind.

Mattie waited for her to call out to one of the men, but
the girl continued her solemn study.

"She looks like . . . like . . ." She simply stopped talking and stared to the side at nothing.

"Ariella is younger . . . serene."

"Ariella Bren is the . . . most serene daughter in Plain . . . and Fian." The third speaker was much older than the first two although her dress was, if anything, more doll-like. The outer layer of the skirt pointed skyward at belly-level; her feet hung out of sight somewhere below. Her broad face was red, her beribboned hair grayer than poor Sylvia's. Her tone was righteous; Mattie expected the worst.

"Are you one of the Brendaughters from Fian?" the woman asked. ". . . You do not live in Plain."

"I do now. I have just been sent there from F-Feen to-day." Mattie took the chance. She spoke as slowly as she could and tried to mimic the flat tones of the daughters

Mattie decided to explain nothing more. Their concentration spans seemed as short as their logic. They were distracted by nothing at all and all three now sat staring outward.

Mattie, too, although she knew better, found herself looking at the immensity of the terrain and searching the horizon for a change in contour, for the hills or mountains that should mark the end of the flatlands, for the trees that would act as watershed or announce the presence of a river. But, of course, there was nothing.

The horizon was half again the distance of Earth's. The continent they had landed on—like the rest of the planet—was almost totally flat. Steppes. It was actually a plateau, one massive featureless plateau.

The only change finally was not visible ahead of time: the land, which just north of the city lay as fallow prairie, became patched here and there with a few small fields, squares of newly turned, light-brown soil. Nothing growing to report to Rol Addle.

With the "daughters" silent, Mattie strained to overhear the conversations of the men, but the squeaking of the wheels on the dusty rails was always louder than their mumbling voices.

The sun was still low in the sky but hot. The air seemed to be drier if that was possible. Mattie tried to sit as still as the others in spite of the scratching and weight of her dress.

How was she going to pass herself off as a relative at the Bren house? And what good would it do? So far she had seen only one female face lit by any sense at all, the one who had spoken to her at the pavilion. And then what? They would send her back to the ship. This endless trek over nothing toward nothing would be for nothing.

She felt eyes and turned toward the front of the car. One of the two odd men out was studying her. Why? She checked her posture. A lack of repose? Did she look abnormally alert?

She decided to identify herself. Why not? Maybe he at least had some brains and . . . no. It was something about his face. Something she didn't like and Mattie was never fanciful.

"Who are those . . . those fathers in front?" she asked the nearest girl.

"Fathers?" the older woman responded instead.

"At the front of this car."

"No fathers. . . . Eastcountrymen."

To ask more would be to reveal ignorance beyond even a "Feen" daughter.

What could she safely ask? Not where "Feen" is. Where is Eastcountry? Would they have been to these places?

"Do you have any children?" she asked the older woman.

"We . . . have more . . . than . . . than they do," said the one sitting next to Mattie.

"Five smallbrothers."

"Six. . . . Brother Jacob is still a smallbrother . . . until next harvest." Again, as if after great exertion, they lapsed into silence. Mattie sighed and slumped, wishing for a backrest. She glanced at her fingercube.

"How far is it to Plain?" she asked a few minutes later. She could tell that this question made no sense to them at all.

Mattie tried not to fidget but the physical conditions were

bad and worsening as the sun rose. She remembered rue-
fully the interminable ship meetings. In a controlled—
cool—environment! In freefall! In a loose, light, soft lab
suit!

Men began to drink from small wooden glasses; the animals were handing packets of food around. Mattie remembered she had eaten little and not slept in almost two days.

Long arms ... definitely more primate than ursine, she
noted ... lifted her down onto the car floor, back against the
side of the platform. It put one of the young women next to
her and gave them tepid tea and bowls of barley.

The horizon disappeared in brightness. Mattie's eyes
burned. The two Eastcountrymen seemed to be out of focus,
vibrating. And she was heavy. Heavy and hot and dried out
to nothing.

Mattie dreamt she was surgically removing a patch of
hairy dermis from someone. It had come from a bad gene
combination. If she could just find the right gene sequence
for humidity control, the operation would be a success.

When she awoke, the western sky was still white but the
two planets were already bright in the south, and the ground
everywhere was blue like a motionless ocean, a painted
ocean.

The little train had stopped at a long shedlike structure
standing in the middle of an endless field. There were fewer
people than there had been and all of them, except the two
Eastcountrymen, were getting off. Mattie wondered how
many stations she had missed. Only the oldest of the three
women remained and she was helped off the car ahead of
Mattie. She walked away among a few of the men and animals, never looking back or saying good-bye.

"Come on, then," said a young male voice just behind
Mattie, "we and loso are to go along with you to Brens."
The speaker was a teenage boy. He and another boy, only
slightly older, passed Mattie and followed a path that she
would never have noticed in the dusky blue earth. A loso
was next to her and started forward. As she took the first
step away from the car, her knee trembled and let go. She

slipped to the ground, still clutching her bundle of instruments and unsuitable suit.

"Fallen, daughter?" The words tumbled down softly, insolently from above, the seductive mockery falling on her, coldly and heavily, like lead.

She turned and strained to look up at the figure standing above on the edge of the flatcar. He was a tall, narrow, deep violet silhouette against the radiant white sky. His face, too, was long and narrow, but the features were lost in the dark. Only the eyes glistened, reflecting light from the southern sky.

Mattie would not speak; if she did, he would know who she was or at least who she was not.

She hid herself in blankness and stared up blindly.

As the loso animal picked her up and carried her away into deeper darkness, she heard the Eastcountryman laughing.

Brens

Mattie understood that one boy was called a "tallbrother" and the other a "veryyoungfather," but the voices she listened to as they walked just ahead of her in the dark belonged to elderly men, humorless and reserved. No foolish talk, no display of youthful energy even though they were out of the watch of authority, observed only by a mindless daughter and a mute animal.

These two talked first of wood, new wood. It was very good. It could be rounded or turned into a something. Their accent and diction were still not redundant for her and they mumbled. Droned, really. New wood was better than dry wood because it was lighter, stronger, could be shaped. This would interest Parn. More, they said, was expected soon from Eastcountry. Eastcountry? Eastcountrymen?

Was this loso creature also from Eastcountry? Mattie was glad to rest on its shoulders as it carried her, shuffling smoothly along behind the elderly boys. Her fingers moved along its throat, felt the cords of its neck, examined by touch those curious ears. Her scalpel was in her bag. If she had the light, the equipment . . .

"Eastcountrymen would like the Earth metal. Forget the newood."

"I know. Did you ever see so much metal? With all that you might trade for . . ."

"Our grandfathers had more than that when they came."

"They did not. Their ships were smaller."

"No."

"Yes."

"You're cot. How could they fit everyone?"

"You've seen the pictures at the landing museum."

"You can't tell by that."

Mattie thought they almost sounded normal.

Then there were dark buildings ahead on the right blocking out very small chunks of sky. Lifeless black. Barns, no doubt.

"There is some trouble between the Brens in Fian and Eastcountrydoctors."

"I know."

"There were wicked ways there."

"I know."

They spoke clearly right in front of Mattie—even though they believed her to be a member of the family they discussed.

There was a flare ahead. The path had widened into a road and beyond were houses.

They approached another boy, somewhat younger than Mattie's guides.

"I haven't been told of it," the Bren boy said, "but let her go over to the daughterhouse, I suppose. It's Ariella. Just let her go then."

As he looked closer, he frowned slightly, seemed puzzled. To hide her face Mattie ducked her head in the little bow she had seen the women make.

"Fathers met yesterday at Lords," he added to the others.

"Any Eastcountrydoctors come?"

"No."

"The two on train today said not a word to anyone about the Earth ship."

The boy gestured and the loso put Mattie on her feet. She stood uncertain. Now which way to go?

The young men went on talking.

"You see the Earth men?" the Brens boy asked.

"Just the first time," the tallbrother said.

"I was at both gatherings," the youngfather said.

"What did . . . what did the daughter look like?"

"Horror," the brother said.

"The witch was . . ."

Mattie could not stay to hear what she was. She walked

"serenely" toward the smaller of two houses and through an open door.

It smelled like a granary rather than a human dwelling.

Two squat candles burned on a long, simple wooden table, a torch flamed in a sconce on the rear wall, and just to the right of the door an oil lamp burned. Yet the room was dim.

A female voice chanted in the flat, repetitive phrasing of bead-telling. It was the recitation of material so rote, so familiar that all expression had been dropped and replaced with a rhythm, a rise and fall of pitch, and a pattern of stress unrelated to meaning. In fact the accenting so defeated sense that Mattie thought at first she was hearing prayers in some archaic religious language not understood by the speakers themselves.

It was quite different from the solemn chanting of the men in that it was not a litany and not a song.

The speaker was one of three women or girls—Mattie could not tell their ages—at the far end of the low-ceilinged room. She thought at first they might be members of some religious order except for their lack of regimentation. One was eating and another seemed to be asleep.

Then she recognized words: "spin the hay into gold," "castle," and "a great moat," in the English these people spoke. They were telling themselves stories, apparently fairytales, old Earth fairytales.

Losos were walking around the room, carrying things in and out. Food. Mattie recognized the smell even though it blended almost indistinguishably with all the other dried vegetation odors. She swayed, stepped toward the near end of the table, and realized with a jolt that four women were sitting directly in front of her, just inside the door. Not even their breathing had been audible. Mattie thought again of huge stuffed dolls.

Surely they saw her. She waited, frozen, for an alarm.

Finally she stepped to the table and sat next to them. Only then did the bulky figures seem to move, to turn toward her, but she kept her face carefully averted and reached for what looked like bread.

It was bread. And there were bowls of grain dishes, both moist and dry. Mattie took a clunky wooden spoon and a shallow wooden bowl and helped herself. She didn't care at all that everything was bland.

She was desperately thirsty but there was nothing to drink. Instantly a loso was next to her with an earthenware mug. It was filled with lukewarm water with a faint chamomile flavor. Mattie drank all of it.

She risked a glance at the tall woman sitting opposite and saw a broad-boned face, and hair that seemed brown in the dim, uneven light. Large sad eyes looked back.

The one on Mattie's right stirred, a motion of such relative energy that it was startling. Mattie turned to look into an astonishing face; it was animated, beautiful, and painfully familiar. It pulled on her memory. She knew the face. It was her mother when Mattie was a child.

She looked back down to the food to recover.

She thought then that the woman spoke to another on her own right. Mattie could see only that it was a very small person, perhaps a child. But turning back, Mattie looked for the first time at the fourth woman, diagonally across from her. She recognized the long neck and asymmetrical face. The Golden Goose Girl.

Mattie almost greeted her. Was the name . . . Elizabeth?

The woman was looking right at her and yet had given no sign of recognition. So then Mattie's disguise, the blank face and the native clothes, worked. Yet it was more likely, from what Mattie had seen of them so far, that the native women's powers of observation were no greater than their attention spans or their linguistic skills.

The one with the haunting face turned back to Mattie. Her black eyes reflected the light of the distant torch.

"Sing a . . . an Earth story," she said.

Mattie laughed. They knew her. They had recognized her from the first. Next they would call her witch.

"You are a doctor?" It was the little one, leaning to look

round at Mattie. She was the red-haired woman that Parn had so admired.

"I am a doctor. I'm Doctor Mattine Manan."

There was silence.

"You are not a father," Elizabeth said.

"No. . . . And not a witch." Casually Mattie bit into her bread.

"Where are your fathers?" Elizabeth asked then.

"On the ship," Mattie said.

"Sing a story of the Ark," the dark-eyed one said. Mattie was startled by memory every time she looked at her.

"What is your name?" she asked her.

She said nothing.

"She doesn't understand your speech, Doctor," Elizabeth said. "She came from Fian. She is Ariella."

"Ariella Bren," Mattie said, and studied Ariella's face.

The tall woman was Rebekah and the small one Erin.

"And Lucilla is not here," Elizabeth said.

"Do you all live here? Are you all members . . . all Brensdaughters?"

The story-telling had ceased at the other end of the room. One woman left and two others entered from a door at the rear. All of them had light skin and dark eyes and hair like Ariella's—and Mattie's. None seemed to be paying any attention to Mattie.

Mattie learned from Elizabeth that daughters came and went to neighboring familyhouses with fathers and losos, as the men worked together harvesting or sowing. There were often strange daughters in the daughterrooms. No one noticed.

"But sometimes they sing a new angelstory," Ariella said.

Mattie could hear no difference between her accent and Elizabeth's.

"But I came alone," Elizabeth said. "I escaped."

Ariella nodded.

They were all silent for awhile.

"Eastcountry," Mattie said then, "I want to go to Eastcountry."

"I . . . want to go to Eastcountry," Rebekah said, speaking for the first time. Mattie thought she was mimicking her.

"They sent Lucilla to Eastcountry," Elizabeth said.

"We think so," Erin said.

"Tell me about Eastcountrymen," Mattie said. "Losos . . ."

"Sing an earthstory," Ariella said. She seemed angry.

"A . . . a skystory?" Elizabeth asked.

Mattie suddenly understood. They wanted her to tell them her own story. She had said nothing about herself.

She did not yet know enough about them to translate her history into experiences they could understand. She tried to tell them about the mission and her own reasons for being on it but it was hopeless. Ariella looked distressed and Rebekah was not listening at all. Erin and Elizabeth watched her face closely but it may have been politeness or some other kind of interest.

"What is the matter?"

"It is hard when you don't sing," Elizabeth said.

"I can't chant it. I haven't memorized it either. . . . I . . . I have escaped from the men on the ship," she said very slowly, very flatly. Ariella looked eager again.

Mattie told them about running away and needing to find Eastcountry, glossing over her reasons. She said that if she were discovered she would be imprisoned on the ship and never be on Dagda again.

"Can one walk there?" she asked them.

Across the table Rebekah and Elizabeth nodded. Ariella said yes. Mattie couldn't see Erin.

"Tomorrow morning will one of you show me the way?"

"Very early," Elizabeth said. "Before losos or fathers see."

When the losos came to clean the table and urge them into sleep rooms, Mattie followed the women and copied everything they did. She finally fell gratefully onto a narrow wooden bunk with a noisy, straw-filled pad for a mattress and a wonderful woven cotton-and-hemp blanket for a cover.

Cabin

Again, Elizabeth is walking along a furrow in a newly plowed field in early white light. This time she carries water and food as well as her paints and dictionary. And this time she is not alone.

The turned earth is soft and walking is difficult. Elizabeth watches her feet in order not to stumble and not to look into the rising white sun. Each time she looks up she sees the earthdaughter walking before her. The doctor's dress doesn't seem to fit. The skirts hang not quite right and lift and swing awkwardly with her uneven steps.

The doctor's short hair is covered by a hat, and her too-white skin is shaded under its brim. Sometimes she and Ariella look just alike. But when she looks a certain way, a way that a daughter never looks, her face is like a father's or an Eastcountrydoctor's. Then, at other times she will speak or frown or smile, and she is not like any Dagdan at all; her mouth and her eyes and her whole body move too much and too fast. Elizabeth does not know how to see her.

"How far is Eastcountry?" the doctor asks. She has asked them several times before. They do not answer.

They walk from first white light to afternoon, with many rests, and then they come to a cabin; Erin says it is a long-house for storage of goods. Sometimes Erin knows things.

They stumble into the cabin. Ariella pours the last of her water over her face and Erin's. Elizabeth rubs her eyes and scratches dry clumps of soil from the back of her neck. Rebekah lies down with her back to the others. The earthdaughter mutters in pain with her new red skin and has no water left at all to wet it.

* * *

Elizabeth wakes in the dark. She is lying on something hard and rough. She cannot move or breathe. Her skirts are twisted and knotted around her legs and her collars are stuck to her neck. It is as hot as noon although it is black night.

There is a sudden rustle. Only a losobit. But there is no loso to eat it. Elizabeth remembers that she is alone in a lost place with only daughters. No losos. No fathers or tallbrothers. Only daughters. And perhaps a witch.

Ariella stirs, whines, and Rebekah, beyond her, moves but is silent. Erin's eyes are open, her face just touched in one spot by the light of Venus coming through a crack in the door.

Elizabeth can barely see the daughterdoctor on the other side of the room. She seems to be lying on her stomach, a lump, as *vulnerable* as any daughter. Then she groans and turns herself. She cannot be a witch.

"We'll have to go back," the doctor says.

Fever

"We have to go back," Mattie told them again.

They were leaning together against the west side of the longhouse, out of the morning sun. The fields around glared, empty. In this place not one green shoot yet disturbed the planet's textured, light brown surface.

"I had no idea how impossible this plan was. I thought Eastcountry was close, a section of Plain. And I didn't know how little you knew about—about anything."

Mattie looked at each silent, blank face. Why did they stand there, staring? What did they want from her?

"This is a game for you," she went on. "Of course, your fa . . . your men may be angry with you when you go back, but any real danger is make-believe. You will certainly be better off than starving or dying of thirst in this desert."

"The fathers do not become angry," Elizabeth said.

Mattie slid to the ground still leaning against the longhouse wall. She was weary and helpless.

Elizabeth said, looking down at her uncritically, "I know that you are vulnerable, too."

Mattie laughed. "Good," she said, and, thinking of Sylvia, added, "Then you know that I am not a witch. I have no magic to transport us all. I am a real woman just like you."

"But you have a ship that came through the sky," Erin said. "Your fathers allowed you to . . . to talk. I mean your men."

"But my fathers will not help me now. They want to please your fathers. They want me to stay on the ship, and I seem to have no choice. I will be imprisoned for two years here and two more returning to Earth. Locked on that ship—not being able to do my work!"

"I understand," Elizabeth said.

"Lucilla told us we were women, not children," Erin said.

"Who is Lucilla? Where . . .?"

"Lucilla is . . . my . . . friend," Rebekah said, speaking for the first time.

"She has been stolen," Ariella said.

"No, not stolen," Erin said. "Her fathers have . . . taken . . . sent her. Maybe to Eastcountry."

"Why?" Mattie asked.

"Because . . . because she talks and laughs. She is not serene," Elizabeth said. "And because she is . . . Rebekah's friend."

"We are going to find her," Rebekah stated flatly.

"She—Lucilla is—special. She told us that Erin, Ariella and I are special, too. Erin is smart, and Ariella is a singer and story player, and I paint and read. That is why I have to run away," Elizabeth said. "Tallbrother Lucius . . . *Father* Lucius heard me reading and told Pater that I am turning into a witch."

"I am not a witch," Mattie said again. "And you are not a witch. There are no witches. And we will not survive on our own. We will die if we don't go back."

"I know what to die is," Elizabeth whispered. She sat down and leaned toward Mattie. "The others do not. They do not understand. They will be afraid."

"Please explain, Elizabeth. I mean . . . I'm the one who doesn't understand now."

"I read so I know things. About death. About birth. They will . . . I don't know. Take me away. Maybe I will . . . die, like Lucilla."

Mattie stared into Elizabeth's gray eyes and shivered in the dry, hot dust. She decided to continue the journey.

First, was Eastcountry really east of Plain and how far?

Only the delicate one, the always-blushing Erin, seemed to have any practical knowledge. She knew that "waterbushes," were one source of water and that "unchanged" native life, animal and vegetable, could not be eaten by human beings. She also knew that the train took a right turn and continued on to Eastcountry after its last halt in Plain and that the same train came back to Plain in a few days.

They would travel only by night to avoid the heat of direct sun. The planets—Bethlehem and Venus they told her—were bright enough to see by. So bright in fact, that Mattie worried that the light pastels of their huge dresses would be too visible, white flags signaling across the dark fields. She had them rub soil into the material and on their hats and faces, but she noted, as they struggled awkwardly and ineffectively with the task, it didn't much matter since they were already filthy, five brown figures, paper dolls cut out from an old, wrinkled, brown bag. Caricatures of caricatures. Only their eye color sharpened in contrast to the dust and told them apart.

The furrows were clear dark streaks, easy to follow in planet light. As they walked along, Ariella sang stories. Mattie realized that singing meant reciting, not even chanting as the men did their holywords. It was the monotonous droning she had heard at Brens. She found it both unpleasant and almost incomprehensible at first. Then, reluctantly, she began to recognize individual words: monsters, dragons, Eastcountry, castles, deep, dangerous moats.

"Angelstories are all they know," Elizabeth told Mattie privately.

Fairytales. Mattie was impatient. Mythology was Kyly's business.

"We are such inept fugitives," she said later as they rested, "that they should have found us by now."

Elizabeth reached for her dictionary. *"Inapt?"*

"I mean why are they not finding us? Surely we left an obvious trail."

"They . . . don't know," Ariella said.

"How is that possible?"

"They don't . . . they can't think we could be gone. They never thought of it," Elizabeth said. "I think they will search when they call for me."

"It is true, Doctor," Erin added. "They wait. I think they talk to other fathers and Eastcountrymen about it first."

"What about your loso animals? Why aren't they after you?"

"When we hide they don't know!" Ariella laughed.

"But won't they warn the men . . .?"

"They can't talk," Elizabeth said. Mattie was less satisfied than ever.

"Are they intelligent?" she asked.

They didn't understand the question.

They walked on slowly, with many rests. The daughters watched for signs of Eastcountry. Ariella sang. Mattie did not tell them that they had covered very little distance. They stopped and sat for a longer time in a newly plowed field—perhaps the same field—at the first white light in the eastern sky.

"This field is to be planted," Mattie said. "Will there be houses nearby? Do your people cultivate at great distances from their living places and barns?" She expected no answer and got none.

It should be Rachel here, not she, Mattie thought. Healing and nurturing the young was Rachel's profession and her pleasure, or so she always claimed. Mattie's profession was genetics, hard science. ("You are a hard woman," the OC had said.)

"We are going to have to steal food," she told them.

They only watched her and waited.

"One of you . . . I cannot do it. I don't know where things are kept in your houses. I would give myself away."

"I! I know how to be a thief." Ariella sang. "I will steal away the jewels. A magic ring."

"Elizabeth will do it," Erin said. "She has been stealing things for a long time. She can trick loso and fathers."

"You are a thief, Elizabeth?" Mattie asked.

"Books. I take them but not to keep. Except for the holybook and the dictionary, I returned them." She leaned her back against the side of the furrow. The earth was so loose that her motion disrupted a great clump, turning it into a stream that poured down over their legs and laps.

"How did you learn to read, Elizabeth?" Mattie asked.

"The letters on my paint jars said the colors. I learned the letters, and then I found a reading book for verysmallbrothers in the fathers' bookroom—*library*."

"And she found books with new angelstories, and she read them to us, not sang them, read them," Erin said.

"Old stories. Old Earth books," Elizabeth said.

How many other Elizabeths might there be in this population? Mattie yearned to study the gene pool.

She tried to wipe and shake the dirt off her skirt; the others paid no attention. They sky whitened.

"Can we hide in a barn or silo while we wait for Elizabeth to bring us food?" Mattie asked.

"They are full from harvest. We can make a secret hideaway," Erin said. "We always make a secret place in the hay after harvest when all our old places are gone."

"So then, let's go now before someone discovers us lying here like lumps of sod."

They found buildings, a farm. They spent two days on the lower, cooler level of a haybarn, burrowed into a cave of their own making. Cooler but not cool. Dry heat, dust, stiff, scratchy straw scraping, pricking Mattie's raw, innocent skin, recently irradiated by a new sun.

The inside of her nose was coated thick with a mixture of soil and grain, and she was unable to rub her sore eyelids with filthy, encrusted fingers. She remembered her webbed hammock suspended in air whose temperature and moisture were carefully measured to respond to her needs. But the water she fantasized was not recycled, reconstituted ship water; it was on Earth, great ocean waves, icy spring-fed creeks, just plain ice. Ice cubes, ice chips, crushed ice. Ice cream!

Elizabeth had managed two trips to the familyhouse. She was even able to identify the family by name. The others were disappointed to discover themselves still so close to home, still in Plain. Had they traveled in circles? No. Mattie had kept the bright planets of the night always on her right. They had moved very slowly, that was all.

Elizabeth brought food, mostly cereals.

"Couldn't you find anything . . . anything wetter?" Mattie asked.

They drank some light, tepid, tealike liquid, the little that Elizabeth was able to carry in a heavy earthenware jug. It did its job effectively, with greater benefit than some freezing spring water, but Mattie could not relish it.

"Elizabeth, there must be water," Mattie insisted. "You bathed, washed your clothes. There is not enough in those bushes. Find water. A stream. A brook?"

The concept was too difficult for an answer. How could it be then, Mattie wondered, that they droned on so easily about deep moats? What images were in their strange brains?

They sprawled exhausted for two days. Mattie could understand her own paralysis—the unaccustomed gravity, new climate, the life-burning white sun, the excess yards of heavy clothing, and fear. But what was wrong with these native women?

On her third trip to the farmhouse Elizabeth had to take an indirect route to avoid losos working in the field. "They almost saw me," she said.

"And if they had?" Mattie asked.

"I'd—I'd be caught."

"Who teaches losos? When they are small?" Mattie asked. "How are they trained to . . . to care for you?"

"They are not small," said Erin.

"They just know how," Elizabeth said. "Are Earth losos different?"

"There are no losos on Earth."

"Then where do they come from?"

"Earth," Mattie said.

Mattie wondered if the losos "belonged" to a particular master of the family and tended the females like a dog herding sheep or cattle. Or were the things loyal to the females themselves? And how was this behavior instilled in the first place? Could they be reimpressed, reattach themselves?

She tried to elicit stories of aberrant loso behavior on which she could base some theory.

"Once two losos were at our house that were not the same color as losos are," Erin said, "and they didn't take care of things. Fathers sent them back."

"Back where?" Mattie asked.

"Eastcountry," Erin said.

Mattie took a long drink of lukewarm tea.

"Let's see if we can catch a loso for ourselves," she said.

A brown figure was standing in the field.

Mattie and Ariella walked toward it. Erin, Rebekah, and Elizabeth watched from a distance.

"Why doesn't it look at us?" Mattie asked.

"Wait," Ariella said, almost impatient with the doctor. There was a slight breeze. "Now it smells us."

It stood taller, ears erect, distinguishable points. And then, slowly, it came toward them. The dragging shuffle of the foot movement was not apparent in the distance and the loose soil of the newly tilled field. No need for Mattie to run.

Then suddenly, unexpectedly, it was upon her. The heavy motions were not, after all, slow; only deliberate. Mattie was caught in the middle of the open field, caught, hoisted, and carried toward the farmhouse.

She kicked and punched, made herself a difficult squirming weight, tried to slither through the creature's grip.

Ariella turned and ran the other way, yelling back over her shoulder. Beyond her the other daughters cried aloud.

The loso turned and carried Mattie to them and finally let her down. Mattie looked up at its blank face. Not enigmatic, or unreadable, but a nonface even in pet terms. Less "face" than any Earth dog or cat. Or bear.

They tied themselves together with ribbons so that the loso could not carry any one of them back. It might follow them. Might.

They marched off that night—eastward—across the interminable field, five women abreast, each walking in her own plowed furrow, linked with ribbons knotted from arm to arm, followed by a tall brown animal.

Forest

Now they must be far away. There are no more fields. Just open land with thin brush and sparse grasses of the type that grow near the city. Elizabeth wonders if they have traveled toward the city by mistake. But the doctor says no.

Elizabeth is afraid of the strange land, afraid of being lost forever.

One late white morning they see a little roughness on the line where the earth meets the sky. Doctor says that it is a forest. The next day it appears flat and solid, a thing one can go around, perhaps behind, but certainly not into. Only when they are very close, can Elizabeth see that it is made of separate trees.

And when they pass between two, they are in another place, a strange cool place; it is like being in the city pavilion or in the gazebo, both indoors and out at the same time.

Standing exactly between the two trees, they can see far down the rows until the stems meet at a distant point. Doctor says it is too *symmetrical* and cannot be a natural forest. Human *geometry*.

And then Elizabeth sees that it is like a cornfield just before harvest only there is much more room among the stalks, and the leaf canopy is much higher. Elizabeth loves the long narrow leaves, which form a roof far overhead, protecting them from the sun.

They stay in the forest and eat all the food and then drink the water.

"Why doesn't Rachel help us?" the doctor asks.

The doctor calls loso Rachel. It is cot. Loso is loso. How can loso be Rachel?

Then Doctor says, never mind; it is her own *irrational*

feminine anthropomorphism. Elizabeth finds the words in her dictionary.

Loso goes away and they hope that it will find them water, but it doesn't come back. Soon they are very thirsty. Maybe they are going to die.

"Someone planted these trees," the doctor says. "There must be a source of water. I'm going after loso. I'll walk the perimeter of this field."

Doctor takes Erin and they turn out of sight. Elizabeth is too sick to care.

"We cannot go back," Ariella says. "It's too far." Elizabeth sees that Ariella's eyes are small and her lips cracked and peeling.

Now Elizabeth hates the snakeplant leaves covering the white sky above their heads; their green is too bright and sharp. There is a cruel smell of damp earth under the trees; Elizabeth remembers it from when loso poured wastewater on the plants around the house. She falls asleep and dreams loso is pouring water on her.

The water sound is loud and then soft. Elizabeth's eyes open and she sits up in one motion. There is nothing. Just the strange green light from the leaf roof.

"Let us go find it!' Ariella says. She has raised herself on an elbow and is staring through the trees as though she can see their end.

Rebekah has not moved, but when Elizabeth leans toward her, she sees that her eyes are open, staring only at the bark of the tree a few inches in front of her face.

Ariella stands up, shaking soil and leaves from her skirts. "Let's find it."

"We have to wait for Doctor and Erin."

"We'll come back for them."

"Don't be cot, Ariella. We'll be lost."

But Doctor and Erin might never come back. Like loso. Rebekah rises and follows when they tell her to.

They walk with difficulty crosswise through the rows of trees. They seem to hear the sound just ahead, perhaps behind the next tree, but when they get there, it is gone. They hear it again in the distance. They never seem to be able to catch up to it. They walk for a long, long time.

Then—almost at once—the forest changes. The trees are no longer in straight lines, the paths between no longer even, and then there are no paths at all. There is no pattern. The sun comes in here and there. And the trees themselves are different. Some still seem to be tall thin driwood, but others have fatter trunks, rougher bark, darker leaves. There are all kinds of bushes again—including waterbushes!

The sound of flowing water is loud, and there in front of them is a house. Next to it is a tall waterbush with a spout through which water is pouring into a wooden basin. The basin itself is full and overflowing into a stream that runs through a garden of growing food, good changed food. Sweet cooked foods are set on a windowsill.

Standing before the doorway is a very, very old old-daughter.

Water Witch

The loso was standing by a bush half as tall as the line of trees. In its snaky dark brown fingers was a Y-shaped piece of wood, the wood the forest was made of, "driwood," Mattie suspected. It concentrated on the point of the long straight branch.

"Is it our loso?" Mattie asked.

At first, Erin didn't answer. Suddenly she nodded. "Oh. I see what you think. You don't know that all losos are one loso."

Mattie understood then and stopped thinking "*the* loso."

Loso walked away from the first bush to another growing closer to the edge of the tree field. Suddenly, the branch tilted, point downward. Loso dropped down on fours and groped in the high grass between bush and tree. When it reared, it held an object, an artifact, a simple pump with a spout and a handle. A stiff, pointed wooden pipe or tube protruded from its base.

Loso pushed the sharp end of the tube into the plant stalk and worked the pump handle. After a minute liquid trickled through the spout.

Mattie and Erin knelt before it, like pilgrims worshipping at a shrine; they cupped the water in their hands, drinking, wetting their eyes. Mattie lowered her head and let it run over the back of her neck and then raised her face to drink again. Prayer became debauchery. Erin lay flat on her back in the puddly mud they had made, while Mattie let the wet mud slide through her fingers and liked it so much she smeared her toes, face, neck. Loso kept pumping. The stream was soon only a trickle.

"Quick. Fill the jars before it stops."

Mattie and Erin held the heavy clay jars under the spout. Loso carried a wooden container, amazingly light, which Mattie also filled. There was no water left to wash the mud off. Three dark brown figures walked back into the forest field the way they had come, one looming tall and hairy over two smaller shadows of their former selves.

Mattie cursed aloud when she saw the empty place. There was no mistake. Ariella and Elizabeth had left so much behind: baskets, jugs, hats, shawls that stolen loso had stolen in turn. Not left behind, of course, were Elizabeth's paints and dictionary.

Perhaps they had been captured. But no. Their feet had left clear impressions in the soft soil of the untouched rows.

Damned Dagdan daughters! Irrational. Illogical!

Mattie turned to say these things aloud to Erin, not remembering who she was.

But Erin was ahead of her, already loading loso with the abandoned baggage. "If we could be sure to find more waterbushes, we would not need to carry all this heavy water," she said. She draped a shawl over loso's shoulder like a child dressing a big, dark snowman. "But their tracks lead deeper into the wood and the bushes seem to always be in the open—on the edges of fields." She hung the last basket on the animal's left arm.

A logical Dagdan daughter! Mattie followed the leader.

They walked so long through the planted woodland that Mattie began to believe they were following the wrong footsteps. Those three could never have come so far.

They lost the trail when the symmetrical field gave way to natural disorder. In spite of the strangeness of individual trees and vegetation, the overall picture was less alien than anything Mattie had seen on Dagda so far. Yet there were few such forests left on Earth.

Flying things, silent, winged losobits, swooped and darted into the cultivated part of the woodland and quickly out again into the wild.

The lovely mud had become a dry and tight mask on Mattie's face and throat. Her caked fingers were rigid claws sorely gripping the handles of buckets and jugs, but she couldn't bend to rest them on the ground.

Why not let them go? Was she the daughters' keeper? Erin and she alone with the loso would fare better. They might actually get to Eastcountry—or somewhere.

"Loso smells something. Can it find their trail?" Mattie asked.

Loso began to shuffle away. Mattie and Erin followed it.

Soon Mattie heard running water and then, around the next clump of trees, saw an unlikely little house. It was surely a mirage, a hallucination of the sensually deprived, a delicate, ornate whim on this planet of plain, bare brown functionalism, like a daughter in her finery in the middle of a fallow field.

There were a tiny waterfall, curtained windows, plants growing in the "kitchen garden." Sweeps of tall flowers, vines on trellises and on the house itself, short colorful "ground covers" seemed to flow and swirl in an elaborate ballet. It was a living map of someone's unconscious mind. The door frame and verandah roof were carved in complicated patterns. Decorative, useless pieces of wood overhung the windows, eaves, and steps. Gingerbread. Fussy. What man on this machineless planet would bother with such a tedious job?

Mattie walked up the crooked little dirt path, zigzagging and curving through the madness of vegetation, and stepped into a room as busy and wild as the gardens. It was parlor, kitchen, laundry, pantry, and waiting room.

Ariella, Rebekah, and Elizabeth sat in a row on a bench against a wall, like wallflowers. Standing near them was the oldest female Mattie had seen on Dagda—and perhaps on Earth. She was as dry as the land, but unlike the land, narrow and crooked.

"What are you doing?" Mattie asked Elizabeth. "Why are you sitting there?"

Elizabeth shook her head, cautioning, but did not speak.

The woman threw back her head and laughed loudly, raucously. "Dese are my dottas," she said. She jabbed Mattie's shoulder so suddenly and strongly that she almost fell back onto Ariella.

"She has great power," Ariella whispered. The woman's laughter came in long waves of hooting, each cresting in a nerve-destroying screech.

"This old woman has no power." Mattie stepped firmly toward the woman. "Stop it. Who are you?"

"No!" Ariella cried. "Watch out. She has magic."

A sharp, spicy smell filled Mattie's nose, and she was on her knees. The floor floated, rocked. The woman leaned down, something in her hand, something in Mattie's face.

Mattie did not lose consciousness, but could not move. She was aware of the smells, which were suddenly much stronger and very unpleasant. She was aware of the daughters watching her. But her mind, which had remained clear and rational, had somehow become disconnected from her body and its sensations.

She knew it was a drug, was fairly certain what type, could list its effects, thought to tell Elizabeth that it was science not magic, but her mouth wouldn't work.

She raised her fingers.

"Don't move, Doctor, or the crone will give you more of the potion," Elizabeth said.

"This is an enchantment," Ariella added.

Mattie tried and failed to shake her head.

The woman's wavelike laughter began again. "*Ich bin* Gudrun. *Eine mutter.*"

Mattie felt no time pass, yet the room suddenly turned blue into evening shade. The woman was no longer standing above her, but the daughters still sat on the bench. Mattie shook her head and realized she was rid of the drug.

She saw then, across the room, the old woman sitting at a table. Paler light from the tiny square windows touched her features, her crooked fingers and bunioned knuckles, and small hills of shredded leaves and powders before her. On a long counter behind her, something wet glittered. Tiny droplets of liquid beaded a large jar.

The woman paid no attention to the fact that Mattie was getting up and moving.

Mattie walked across the room to her and sat herself at the table. She watched the woman work, making tiny bundles of various mixtures of herbs. The gray head nodded a quick dart. It might have been a bowcurtsy for Mattie or just a muscle spasm. Her fingers twitched, and she seemed to have a slight tic on the right side of her mouth. The lips themselves held a faint smile.

"What are you making, daughter?" Mattie asked carefully.

"Medicines, fader."

"I'm not . . ." Mattie stopped. Perhaps the woman would obey a man. Would she use the "potion" on a father?

"I must have pricklystem to treat my dottas. To heal my little ones."

"What is their illness, daughter?"

"Der minds are unfit, fader. A disease has softened dem. Die Eastelves have made a plague in Deech. *Krankeit.* All Anu is sick."

Anu!

"And fathers? Are fathers sick, too?"

The ancient woman looked up under her heavy white eyebrows slyly. She gave no answer.

Gudrun brushed together a bunch of leaves. "Here is only bindweed, *gar nicht*," she said. "I must have pricklystem. Medicine does not work without pricklystem."

"What medicine are you making?" Mattie asked.

"I am a doctor," said Gudrun. She cackled, threatening the manic laughter.

"Why are you here, Doctor Gudrun?" Mattie asked. "Why are you alone?"

"I need lily buds and pricklystem."

"Tell me where you came from? What happened . . . ?"

"Please, daughter, Gudrun, please sing us a story," Ariella said.

Gudrun's vague smile widened into a lopsided grin. One

side of her mouth, lower than the other, showed missing teeth.

"Once upon a time," Gudrun began to intone, "a serene daughter had twelve olderbruders who were turned into black birds. De daughter had to live in forest for fourteen harvests and never speak."

"Why?" asked Mattie.

"For speaking. For talking too much," Gudrun said in real language. And then she added, "She was a doctor."

"But what about the brothers? Why . . . ?"

"De bruders went wid her. Dey all ran away because she spoke. She was a doctor. Dey were turned into birds by de wizards. De elves. If she did not speak for seven years, her bruders would come back and become men. But dey didn't. De elves lied. Dey are evil Eastelves." Gudrun touched her forehead and then her chest with the tips of her fingers, a gesture Mattie had never seen.

"Did this doctorsister come from Deech?" Mattie asked Gudrun.

"I . . . know this story," Ariella said. She began to recite in a singsong style: "The daughter had to sit in a tree for fourteen harvests. Then a wickedwitch tied her to a stake. Then she burned her with fire. Then the brothers came and put out the fire with their wings. Then they turned into fathers again except for one who always had one wing and one arm because the daughter spoke one word before the time was up.

"And Gudrun is the wickedwitch," Ariella added in normal voice.

"No, she is the princess, the daughter, in the story, not the witch. Don't you see?" Mattie said.

"But she became a witch," Elizabeth whispered, almost inaudibly. "Afterwards."

Mattie shook her head but kept her eyes on Gudrun's eyes and gently grasped her arm, wrapped her fingers around the thin, bony elbow. "Deech is far away. How did you get to this place?"

"De elves took me. De elves left me here. I did not speak

but dey never came back," Gudrun said. Her mouth reeked of odd plant life. "Your face is an elf face."

"Are elves wizards? What are they?"

"Dey are doctors who make sickness."

"Do you ever see them now? Do you ever see anyone?"

"My bruder, Hans. Sometimes elves."

"Where is Hans?"

"On de water. He is ferryboat man."

"But you have lived here alone since you were a youngdaughter?"

"*Ja.* I was alone. Now I am not alone. I found dottas. Dese are my dottas."

While they spoke, Ariella and Elizabeth had been slowly moving to the door. Suddenly, they turned and scrambled through it.

Gudrun jumped from her chair and cried out, "My dottas!" She started after them, stumbled and almost fell. Mattie caught her arms and tried to hold her back and stop her violent quaking. She managed, finally, to sit her calmly on the bench next to Rebekah.

Mattie was embarrassed to find herself holding the old woman tenderly as if she were a frightened child. She stroked back wisps of thin hair. Some stuck to the wall behind them. The thin, parched skin wrinkled over thick cords of Gudrun's throat. Her breasts showed small and narrow through the tattered cotton of her colorless dress as the material stretched uncomfortably, caught on protruding splinters and small wooden nails beneath her.

Mattie wondered vaguely why Gudrun fussed so over every detail of the house and garden and yet remained drab, barely dressed in remnants of rags. Was it the common symptom of mental illness? Or just no mirrors or persons to reflect her image?

Gudrun turned her face to look directly at Mattie. All madness seemed gone.

"Fader in a frock?" she said and touched Mattie's cheek curiously. "Dottadoctor."

Craft

The trees are fat and misshapen, crooked and bent. Against the sky they are people, oldfathers and elves. Olddaughters—bent and crooked women. Where is loso?

No loso and now no doctor.

A long screech comes from somewhere or is just around them. Perhaps Gudrun is coming after them. Or elves.

"It is a sked," Ariella says. "A different kind of sked that lives in the dark and screams in this country. Elizabeth, you said that magic wasn't real."

Elizabeth does not answer.

"You said that there is nothing on Dagda but fathers and daughters and fields, nothing bad and nothing good," Ariella adds. Elizabeth cannot see her in the dark.

"The doctor is a witch," Elizabeth says. She hears Ariella breathe fast. She thinks so, too, but she does not want Elizabeth to say it.

They curl together against the trunk of a tree, looking up at the narrow leaves writing horrible things on the sky. Messages from the holybook, parts that Elizabeth hasn't gotten to yet.

Cottage

Elizabeth and Ariella returned to Gudrun's cottage in the morning.

"I ran away because I was afraid," Elizabeth said to Mattie.

"Afraid of Gudrun?"

"Gudrun . . . and you . . ."

"Me! Why?"

"You said you were not a witch, but you are. Just like Gudrun. You call it science, but science is just magic. What is the difference? You both make potions and spells. Your 'oldness' is . . . a kind of spell. You cast a spell on your fathers . . ."

"I'm not . . ."

"I came back because I'm a witch, too, now. It's too late to save me."

"It's better to be a witch than a daughter," Mattie said, "so you are saved."

Gudrun hated Ioso, and it hated her. Both were adamant, and Gudrun's reasons were no clearer than Ioso's.

When Erin had decided at last to come into the cottage after Mattie, Ioso stayed out. It did not go away, but it would never come inside.

In the weeks that followed it busied itself in the gardens. It collected things—tools, bowls, indefinite articles. Once Mattie was forcibly washed in the waterfall as she passed. She wished the animal would wash Gudrun! And put her in fresh clothes.

Mattie studied Gudrun's medicines—or potions—as best she could without laboratory equipment. Gudrun seemed to enjoy the attention. She tried to show and explain her work.

Mattie asked Gudrun how she changed the native flora for Earth people. Where did she get the seeds for her gardens? Did she add, delete, modify at some point during the process?

At these times Gudrun was emotionally stable if not rational. She smiled her asymmetrical grin and nodded, pointed, and spoke half Deech.

At other times her rage returned. They learned to wait for it to pass.

Because of her there was water, shelter, and enough to eat. For the first time the daughters lived on products of a woman's labor, and Mattie, at last, had time to study a small bit of Anu.

She longed for her laboratory instruments. The finger-cube's functions were limited so far from the ship's computers. She used her hand tools and a primitive magnification cube. Even an antique microscope would have helped. Mattie cursed the fathers, all the fathers.

She was lonely, isolated from her kind. She needed to discuss her discoveries and speculations, to share the wonders.

"Elizabeth, Erin, look. Loso's feet are so different from its hands. It has primate teeth. And see its ear. Canine. Loso is more than a hybrid. Someone on Dagda is able to open cell walls of . . . no recombinant molecular methods could . . . it's all genes," Mattie said and sighed as Elizabeth started to open her mouth. "I know, 'What is a gene?' "

Elizabeth gestured vaguely to the dictionary in her pocket.

"Never mind the dictionary," Mattie said. "Genes make a baby what it is. They come from the parents. They are a kind of code . . ."

"Seeds," Elizabeth said. " 'The sons of God came in unto the daughters of men.' Before I read the holybook I thought skeds dropped the seeds in the fields and they grew into smallbrothers and daughters."

"I always knew people are not made in dirt," Erin said. "I thought God made babies. I thought . . . maybe they came down to the landing field from heaven. That was cotton. They came out of Noah's Ark . . . 'male and female.' "

"The Bible says that Adam put seeds . . . genes? . . . unto Eve and she conceived and bare Cain. Babies come from daughters' bodies," said Elizabeth.

"That's true," said Mattie.

"But many daughters believe that familyfathers get babies in the hospital from Eastcountrydoctors," said Elizabeth.

"That's not true," said Mattie.

Erin had an incredible mechanical or engineering ability, saw the structure and logic of devices at once, and built "contraptions" for Mattie's laboratory.

Ariella continued to sing stories and sometimes acted them out. She was never blank-faced anymore.

Only Rebekah remained faceless, not from emptiness, but from distraction, as if she had some purpose or pain so consuming that there was no energy left for expression.

Elizabeth was the most changeable. One moment she was a perceptive adult and the next, father's guilty little daughter. Cynical irony gave way to childish doubt without warning. Mattie wondered what Elizabeth's paintings were like.

"You have to work," Mattie told them.

"Why? There is plenty."

"Plenty must be replenished. Do you think these things grow by themselves?"

It was not easy for them to work. They didn't know how to work. When they were given a task, they began willingly enough, but soon forgot what it was they were doing. Mattie often found one of them, sitting beside her work, singing a story or just dreaming.

One day Mattie returned to the cottage from a bio-scavenging trip by herself to hear clapping and laughter coming from the side yard. There was a kind of guilty delight in the sounds. Even Gudrun's voice was a gentle chuckle.

Mattie did not exactly sneak up on the group—nor did she make any unnecessary noise.

They were all sitting in a loose half circle except Ariella, who was standing in the middle dressed in Mattie's ship suit.

But the face was not Ariella's. Nor was it the blank, wit-less, docile mask Ariella and all Dagdan women wore with their fathers. It was intelligent and stern, rather than immo-bile. Maybe arrogant. A little cold. It was definitely some-one Mattie knew. It was her own face!

Ariella had put on her suit and her person.

A wave of cold anger came and went before Mattie saw how funny it all was.

Ariella saw her first and dropped the face. The others turned and waited. When Mattie laughed, they all laughed together, and Ariella was just Ariella again—posturing in a dark blue pants suit.

Rebekah was the only one who did not change. She learned to work the water pump, to identify edible "wild" plants—descendants of Earth germ, Mattie discovered in her makeshift laboratory—and to cook. She learned but did not change. She was competent at everything she tried, but not proud of her accomplishments as the others were.

"Doctor," she said one day, approaching Mattie where she was cutting samples of a tree ear from the side of a dead stump, "we ... have ... to go on now. We have to find Lucilla."

"We will. I've told you that. But if we leave before we are ready, we won't make it. We still have much to learn."

It was exceptionally dark early night. Only Bethlehem was in the southern sky, and its single light did not penetrate Gud-run's tiny, plant-cluttered windows. Mattie tried to lie still on her noisy mat. Gudrun's snoring came irregularly from her small alcove. One of the daughters moved and sighed.

Mattie tried to force sleep before the white late night came. Hay crunched beneath her hip as she shifted position. Its odor, the ubiquitous smell of dried vegetation, had a sound and texture. She scratched her head and felt the dry, uneven strands of ill-grown hair.

Losobits were noisy outside. Maybe it was loso scratching or catching the losobit. The thought of loso was comforting. Mattie fell a little toward sleep.

But it wasn't loso. It was a step.

There were no animals on Dagda larger than losobits.

Another step and then two more. They were close, just outside the door.

Mattie sat up. Elizabeth was already sitting, staring at the doorway.

Men walked in.

There were more than two large figures, darker than the sky behind their heads. Hulking, they were apparent giants from Mattie's angle on the floor; they stood still. They couldn't see her yet in the dark, Mattie realized. Move! But it was too late. There was a flash; real light shone painfully in her eyes. Blinded, she knew in the flash that this was not a lantern, not candlelight, and not a sconce or burning fagots. This must be a product of Eastcountry, electronic or chemical. So they did have an advanced technology.

The light moved away from Mattie's face and searched the rest of the area. Its spot, as it picked out the others one by one, was at first all Mattie could see besides the painful afterimage burning the backs of her eyeballs. Outside, a fagot torch flickered and then burst into a wave of flame, a dim sweep of orange next to the pure intensity of the artificial spotlight.

She was blind again as it moved back to her own eyes. It skipped down over her body, rigid on the small mat, and then back to her face.

"Mattie."

She couldn't see. She tried to brush the light out of her eyes with her fingers. He knew her name. She knew his dry voice.

"Kyly?"

"You look a mess."

"What! Take that light away! Kyly. Kyly, damn it!"

"Quiet . . . quiet, Doctor," Erin whispered urgently, protectively, behind her. The others said nothing, but Mattie felt their panicked breathing. But it was only Kyly.

It was not only Kyly. Which others were with him?

"Kyly, move the damn light." Mattie managed to get to her knees. Kyly switched the power to general from spot, and Gudrun's kitchen was flooded with light as it never had been before.

The other men were not her shipmates but Plainsmen. They stood with their elderly bowed necks and patient postures looking sadly down at the daughters. But not one of them was genuinely old.

"Lucius," whispered Elizabeth. One of the men, the only fat one, smiled. Mattie felt the crawl of hayseed between her shoulder blades and shivered.

She awkwardly struggled to her feet, patting her hair and straightening her tunic, a comfortable thing Gudrun had sewn together for her out of the remnants of her dress.

"What are you doing here? Did the OC send . . . did you decide to . . .? Have the fa—the natives changed their minds about me? Who else is with you?"

Kyly smiled but Mattie was not reassured. He seemed wary, almost afraid of her. He moved back imperceptibly.

"Now, Mattie."

She had heard that before. That tone. It was not good.

"What is it? Where *are* the others?"

He didn't answer. His posture slumped and he stared vaguely to the side. She waited.

"Ah," one of the Plainsmen muttered. "Oh," a low grumble from both. "Horror." They were staring across the room to Gudrun's alcove. She stood small and crooked in her rags, wrinkled skin a yellow-brown in the artificial light, tiny blue eyes as wild as the wisps of thin white hair that stood out around her small head. She was not looking at them but at the doorway where another male figure, still holding the orange, flaming torch, had appeared.

"Elf," Gudrun said.

It was the Eastcountryman.

He looked at Mattie directly and nodded, smiling. Then he paused for a second and raised one eyebrow. She knew that at that moment he had recognized her from the train. He laughed aloud as he backed out the door.

Men

"The OC?"

"He doesn't know. The OC doesn't understand the importance of our relationship with the Dagdans. There was only one way to deal with the problem . . . of you. A couple of us have been meeting in private with representatives of the more enlightened community of Eastcountry. They think the best . . ."

"Wait a minute. Slow down. Aren't you describing treason?"

"Ha! And what was your walking off the ship against orders?"

"That's different; I had no choice. But just tell me everything. What's going on between you—all of you on the ship—and the natives? What have you found out about Eastcountry? Tell me!"

"Well, I really don't feel free to . . ."

"So you don't know either. I'd hoped they were different, less ignorant."

"They are. Not that my Plain friends are ignorant. It's a matter of cultural values. They cannot compromise certain basic . . ."

"You mean they haven't been persuaded to change their minds?"

"Hardly." Kyly smiled his dry wisp of a smile. He and Mattie sat beside Gudrun's little waterfall in the early morning, with the long white light beginning to yellow.

On the other side of the front yard the Plainsmen slept rolled in roughly woven blankets. The Eastcountryman was not among them.

"Have you worked on it? Did Delt really try? The OC?"

"Yes, of course. But you know, Mattie, that the whole thing is very tricky. These people are fascinating. The chance of studying the folkways that have developed over the centuries cannot be lost. Surely you'll understand that, as just one person, you can't be allowed to jeopardize my— our work."

"Folkways! The way they abuse their women is folkways? Kyly, maybe you just don't know. I've been among them all this time—I really don't know how long it's been—not isolated on the ship as you have been. It is much worse than we thought. There is a perversion whose nature I don't yet understand. The ignorance and immaturity of the females is so extreme and so uniformly maintained that they are like—like psychotic children, especially the intelligent ones because . . ."

"I have not been isolated at all," Kyly said. He had stopped hearing her beyond the isolation comment which she saw he took as competitive. He shut his eyes and leaned his back, permanently curved to fit the ship's hull, or a pre-figuration of it from an earlier time in his life, against the trunk of the waterbush. Mattie watched the smile, a smirk of badly cracked, dried-out lips in the middle of his painfully sunburned face. Smug bastard. Locust brain. He was *cotton*.

"These men from Eastcountry have been surprisingly accepting, appreciative actually, of me and . . ." He stopped, eyes still closed. When they suddenly snapped open, Mattie found herself staring too closely into the washed-out green irises, vague and filmy like the rest of him. "They have invited me to their Eastcountry! They have not been willing even to confer with Delt Marker or . . . or others. We are going there now."

"What we?"

"All of us. You. And those women that you have led away from their homes and families."

"Those women" had remained indoors, awake, silent, and almost motionless. Aside from Elizabeth's involuntary naming of Lucius, there had been no exchange of greeting or answering of questions either way between the male and female family members. Mattie had expected the fathers to scold the daughters, or the daughters to show fear or apology or defiance. But there had been nothing. For the few minutes the men had remained inside Gudrun's cottage the women, except for Gudrun herself, had expressed nothing physically or verbally. No language.

"Mattie, I appreciate that you are not a social scientist, so you may not have realized the damage you can do culturally to these people with your misguided intervention into their social evolution. It is always ignorant to judge an alien society by one's personal standards. There are mores and customs whose significance may be beyond your understanding."

"All right, Kyly, all right. But while we have time, tell me what's been going on. What has Rol learned about the crops? I'm sure the colonists established somehow—amazing as it seems—a symbiont relationship between the native wild grasses and imported Earth . . ."

"I'm afraid it's quite awhile since . . . since we left the others. But at that time Addle was still trying to get near the domesticated plantings but was meeting with curious resistance. Again your actions . . ."

"What do you mean? This place cannot be so far. Where have you been? Who from the ship is with you? How did you know where to find me?"

"Now, Mattie, these men don't stand around talking to their daughters like this, don't you see?"

"What do I—or you—care what they do?"

"I care because we need their favor to get the most benefit out of this expedition, and you know it."

"These Plainsmen only think they have authority. Real power lies in Eastcountry, and you know it."

"Well, that's where we're going."

"Why? And why me?"

"They want you."

"For what?"

"I suppose—well, you're—they think they may be able to work out something, some compromise maybe, with the fathers. Maybe it's your profession. The Eastcountryman with us, Gabriel, said something, asked me something about biology. You're some kind of biologist and he—they seem rather interested in it."

"Then they know about my being off the ship! But how do they know about me at all? Who told them anything about any of us from Earth? The OC permitted this exchange?"

"Now, Mattie, the men are listening to you being so irrational." Kyly smiled toward the Plainsmen, who were sitting awake and obviously observing closely, but Mattie was certain they could follow little of the quick, idiomatic Earth talk.

"I am angry and completely rational, far more rational than you. The word 'exchange' was not right. Obviously the information has flowed one way only—from you to them. You have no idea what their motives are. Or their capabilities."

"Come on, Mattie." Kyly lowered his voice. "Their capabilities are almost nothing. I mean, look around you. Have you observed nothing all these weeks? There is no technology on Anu—Dagda—at all. The Eastcountry people are philosophers. They have handed down a tradition of being scientists and at most practice a rather primitive form of medicine."

"Kyly," she said, controlling her anger, trying to sound respectful of his wisdom, his manhood, "I am more than a biologist; I am a geneticist. Have you noticed the animals, losos? They are evidence that . . ."

"Mattie, you are looking for things. Just because the men are clever and trained native animals for work as we on Earth did horses, doesn't make them great biologists."

She gave up. The Eastcountryman might return, and she had to find out more.

"What about the dau—women with me? What will happen to them?"

"These men—their kinsmen—yes, their kinsmen," Kyly repeated, pleased to have found the phrase, "will conduct them, accompany them to Eastcountry for awhile—for some counseling, no doubt—and them, I assume, home to whatever farms they came from. You see, Mattie, these Eastcountrymen serve as advisers and mediators to the simpler Plainsmen. In their way they, too, are psychologists." Here he coughed modestly.

Mattie found herself unable to do more than gape blankly at Kyly the psychologist. She pictured the face of the Eastcountryman. The first time, he had been looking down at her from the train car that early night only weeks ago; he had been a deep blue shadow with only his glittering eyes and taunting, low laugh clear to her. And, again, he had looked down at her from far above, just a few hours ago, his face naked in the flood of unflattering artificial illumination. Deep laugh-lines around the smiling lips and tiny lines sharpening the eyes: lines not of age, but of exposure to the white sun's radiation. It should not have been a handsome face, but it was, and it should have been pleasant, but it was not.

"You might say they act as priests, ministering, advising, acting even as informal judges in disputes among the Plains and Fian families," Kyly was saying.

"Kyly, you're gullible," Mattie said.

He was offended and withdrew into vagueness.

"Kyly, you have got to listen to me, really listen. These men are dangerous. They are highly skilled geneticists—in some ways ahead of us on Earth. My latest researches were only beginning to approach some of . . . Kyly! Will you listen?"

But Kyly had shut his eyes again and reassumed the patient smile. She realized that he was still trying on roles with her that would preserve his self-esteem: first, stern authority, then wiser colleague, now patient, sorely tried martyr. Had life among Dagdans done this to him, or had Kyly always adopted personnae? Mattie had rather avoided him privately because of his hobbyhorse and his irritating, unsatisfying manner in communicating information, his constant distraction inward. Parn playacted, too, but his motives were not defensive or offensive. He was more like Ariella, dramatic for the love of it.

"Kyly, please. I understand your motives. I think your research into Dagdan culture and social evolution is wonderful," Mattie lied, "and more important than—I mean you are probably observing behaviors and developing theories on the effects of adaptation and isolation that will revolutionize your discipline. Your name and Dagda's will go down together in history." The last may have been too much. But no. His smile broadened.

"But, please. Indulge me. I have evidence if you will just listen . . . Okay, listen and tell me how I am wrong. The Eastcountrymen seem to create or at least to promote this unnatural . . . All right, wrong word. There is no such thing to an anthropologist. This deviant social pattern, the intellectual and psychological retardation of one sex and, although I've been exposed to it less, the precocious aging of the other. No, wait. Let me finish. These odd 'doctors' . . ."

"Hardly deviant, Mattie. For most of history, even and most extremely for the first years after the Wars, women were protected from harsher realities. I have pointed out often to our shipmates, both before and after your hysterical flight, that female innocence was a great value in many societies. Nuns for example were to the clergymen as these daughters . . ."

"Kyly!" Mattie started to shout but remembered his self-esteem. Time, if only she had more time with him. Patience, Mattie had never been known for patience. "The point is, those Eastcountrydoctors create sickness; they do not cure it." (She couldn't believe she was quoting Gudrun. This was hardly scientific language.) "They may even brainwash, or harm in some way, the females who deviate from the pattern. Perhaps kill them. I don't know. Girls and women disappear there."

"Poor Mattie. I suppose dramatic stories and childish fairytales are basic to the female psyche, even to you, a supposedly educated woman. These long suppressed propensities have been liberated and exaggerated by your time among these girls. An interesting phenomenon that I might include in my final report."

Kyly was watching her face.

"What are you laughing at? On the ship you were always serious. I think you've lost your mind. Maybe that's what happens when the hard scientists—inflexible personalities— are under stress. They break—badly. Or maybe a female trying to adopt . . ."

Mattie pushed him backwards into the liquid flowing from the waterbush. His shoulder slid into the muddy stream, his face upward under the spout. She was up on her knees, considering another shove, when the Eastcountryman came through the tree with four losos.

Wait

From Gudrun's cottage they had walked for two days to the tracks where they all climbed onto a single flatcar, which losos and men moved with pedals and a long bar. They had ridden then—very slowly—for another two days and had finally stopped at this place. It is not a regular halt like those in Plain and the city. There is no longhouse, no shed, not even a platform, and the forest is wild. Each tree is different from the other. The fat trunks and thin branches twist and curl.

As the flatcar grinds to a stop, Elizabeth sees a youngfather and a daughter tied to two of the trees and guarded by several Plainsfathers. They both wear the strange Fian robes and the daughter a dark hood instead of a hat. Ariella knows what family they belong to in Fian. Its ways are said to be wicked, wilder than those of her own Fian Brens family.

The men and losos raise three canopies. Two are for sleeping and one for eating. The earthdoctor is outside the daughters' canopy. She too is tied to a tree, but far from the Fian prisoners. Loso cares for her.

Elizabeth hears that they will all wait for the real train, with an engine, which will pass in another day. The others have been already waiting by the empty tracks for a day and a half.

Ariella, Rebekah, and Erin wear their empty faces. Elizabeth feels like a tired foot back in an old straw shoe, worn to its shape.

She recognized the fathers. There are fathers from Erin and Rebekah's families, a veryyoungfather, Jack from Ain's family, and Lucius, of course. Yet they are all strange. They have all changed somehow. They are not so old as she remembered, not so still, and not *invulnerable*.

Their speech, too, has changed. Now Elizabeth and Erin can hear the meaning as well as the words.

The fathers say that Gudrun and Mattie are witches. They were afraid of Gudrun and left her behind, alone in her cottage. Gudrun had no magic and her potions were medicine. And Mattie cannot free herself. They are not witches.

The fathers also tell one another that the Fianfather is a sinner and has corrupted his familydaughter in an unspeakable way. They never look at her or at Mattie. Elizabeth does look at her and sees under the hood glittering angry eyes and a thin red mouth. She tosses her head. She is not serene.

There is only one Eastcountryman. He watches everyone and smiles, but he says nothing to the two earthpeople or to the other Dagdans.

Before they left Gudrun's, Mattie dressed herself in the blue shipsuit again; it is just like the one her earthfather wears. She looks like a youngfather again.

The next day Elizabeth hears men say that the train has been detained in the city because of something wrong with its engine. She walks serenely to Mattie's tree to tell her.

Rebekah, Ariella, and Erin are there waiting. They seem to sit as they always sat, doing nothing, waiting for nothing. This time they wait for something, and this time they talk.

"Perhaps some of my other shipmates will come along before the train. They must be looking for both me and Kyly by now. Surely Parn or Rol. Nat Smythy is a mapmaker. Or the OC. He won't let this happen to me," Mattie says.

"It is Eastcountrymen who knew where we were, not your fathers or ours," Elizabeth says. "They will not tell your shipfather."

"The OC is not my father," Mattie says, "but maybe he is the shipfather."

"The doctor expects a handsome youngfather from her ship to come and save her," Ariella sings.

"Nonsense," Mattie says.

"Maybe the one from the pavilion. He was Parn," Erin says. "I think they're all doctors."

"None of them will find her," Elizabeth says.

She and Ariella try again to untie the ropes that bind Mattie. Even Erin has not been able to loosen them. They are not just knotted rope; there is some kind of chemical, an Eastcountry invention, holding them together.

Suddenly, there are footsteps behind them, and Ariella disappears around the tree trunk. Rebekah does not move. Elizabeth and Erin slump and gaze at nothing.

"Doctor Manan? May I speak with you?"

The Eastcountryman stands before Mattie like an angel-story prince. But his smile is not polite.

"You may," Mattie says. She sounds like a great doctor or a veryoldfamilyfather and not like a daughter sitting on the ground.

Elizabeth thinks something is suddenly wrong with the Eastcountryman. He doesn't speak for a moment, and he stops smiling. "I am very unused to addressing a—a woman," he says.

"Surely you speak to the farmers' daughters often," Mattie says, very slowly as if she is talking to a smallbrother.

Elizabeth thinks he is angry until she sees that he is smiling again.

"I thought," he says, "you would like to come to our laboratories and share knowledge with us. Your fathers said as much. What is the purpose or meaning of this resistance?"

"What do you have to share? You are five hundred years behind us. You are primitive witchdoctors. You are ignorant peasants."

Elizabeth is afraid. Why is Mattie talking this way to him? With *contempt*.

And still Mattie does not stop. Even though his face is frozen in its laugh, she does not stop.

"I am Earthstates' leading biological engineer. Your best 'doctors,' not to speak of a common worker, an agent, like you, would not be capable of receiving—[a word Elizabeth cannot understand]. We have offered to help you. Hardly can we share."

But she has often told Elizabeth that the Eastcountrymen are very good doctors. They practice *genetics*. Erin listened to these things; Elizabeth did not.

"Daughter," the Eastcountryman is saying, as if his throat hurts, "we not only manipulate genes, fuse variant species, we create new genes synthetically. We— No. No more from me. From you. It will all be from you, daughter. If you are possibly what you claim to be."

"Why do you doubt me? If you are such masters of molecular biology, you know that female intellectual inferiority is a myth."

At that moment Lucius walks toward them.

"On earth. It is a myth on earth but not here. Or soon it will be true all over Dagda. We are learning now to modify the code to control undesirable female traits." The Eastcountryman no longer sounds angry.

And Mattie is serene. She seems to have forgotten everything but what the Eastcountryman is saying. He, too, forgets to laugh or to mock. They say things to each other that Elizabeth does not understand. Sometimes they do not understand the words either and have to make definitions for each other. Elizabeth tries to remember the words, "sex-linked properties" (Isn't that like her paints? Belongings?), "linguistic-intellectual poly-something," and "zygote," but she soon gives up.

Now Mattie seems afraid. She sits quietly, looking at nothing. Elizabeth guesses that the Eastcountryman has said something terrible. He still wants to talk. He asks Mattie things about her work on earth, but she does not answer.

Lucius laughs down at Mattie and then smiles more slowly at Elizabeth. "Doctor Gabriel," he says to the Eastcountryman close to his ear but so the women can hear, "daughters spoiled are like fruit that . . ."

"Leave us," the Eastcountryman says to him.

Lucius looks back quickly to Elizabeth and turns away to

the eating tent. Elizabeth watches his wide back and narrow legs as he walks away.

"Daughter," the Eastcountryman says, "I can tell by your understanding that what you say of yourself is true. You will tell us all in Eastcountry. Better then. I ask now only from my dedication to my science which I see you share in spite of being a—a woman."

"Why do you say that when you admit females are not—at least not yet . . . ?"

"We have lived with a reality we have promoted, if not created, for so long that we believe it ourselves."

"But your own women!" Mattie startles Elizabeth who cannot understand her sudden sharpness. "Your mothers, your—daughters?"

"In a way, you will see," the Eastcountryman says and laughs again. "And now I must go and pacify that fool, or I will have no peace for this whole trip."

He turns and walks the way that Lucius went.

"Where is that scalpel?" Mattie says when he is gone. "It is all much worse than I ever imagined. I cannot go to Eastcountry as a prisoner, and you must not go ever."

Ariella comes out from where she had hidden behind the tree with Mattie's bundle of instruments. Elizabeth goes for her paints and dictionary even though she knows they cannot escape.

Mattie takes out the sharp metal instrument. "They are going to hurt you," she says, "and make me help them."

Instead of cutting the rope, Mattie slips the blade to her arm and slashes her own flesh. She cries out loudly and starts to slice the other wrist just next to the knot.

Ariella runs to her and pulls at the hand with the knife. Mattie lets her take it away but continues to cry until loso comes. Loso tears at the ropes, tries the knots, pulls again, and Mattie continues to moan and cry, but not loudly enough for the men to hear.

Finally loso finds a weak spot against the tree trunk and takes the scalpel itself and saws through the rope. Mattie slumps forward. Loso drops the instrument and reaches for her. It carries her, rope dangling, to the waterbush.

"Get the scalpel," Mattie says, "and run." Her voice is weak. It is not make-believe.

Loso puts her down next to the bush and turns for water and clothes. Mattie jumps to her feet and takes her scalpel back from Erin.

"Run. Hurry. All run. Make it follow." Rebekah does not move. The others cry and run, Mattie stumbling with them. There is no chance that loso will not catch her right away.

When they are beyond a thick stand of trees and far from the eating tent, Elizabeth cries as loudly and as pitifully as she can, but loso knows Mattie is hurt and is not distracted.

When it catches Mattie, will it follow them, or take her back to the railroad camp? Ariella runs ahead and pretends to fall. She moans as though in pain, but loso pays no attention.

Erin supports Mattie and they run together, but loso is already upon them. It sweeps Mattie up onto its shoulders while Erin sits on its foot and drags. Ariella moans and Elizabeth cries, calling loso away from camp.

"Here, what is this? Daughters, what . . . ?" One of the Plainsmen, the veryyoungfather Jack, has been walking in the forest with a single loso, away from the other men. He calls to them. Loso with Mattie turns back toward camp.

Mattie drives the point of the scalpel into the back of loso's head and it falls. Dead.

Elizabeth sees a dead thing.

They all see it. The youngfather, Ariella, Erin, Elizabeth, and Mattie look at it. Only still-living loso doesn't notice. It waits for the men, looking at nothing at all.

Then the youngfather raises his arms and his mouth opens by itself but that is all. The daughters stand the same way, but their mouths are closed. Elizabeth thinks nothing at all. Mattie is bleeding.

When she walks toward the youngfather, he doesn't move.

"No!"

"No, Doctor."

"Mattie, wait."

The youngfather moves then, turns, maybe to run or to fight. Can he fight a daughter?

"Hold him, and I will not hurt him."

How can they hold a father? But they do. They hold him just the way they tried to hold loso. He is easier than loso.

Mattie goes up behind him and does something with her scalpel and he falls.

"But you said—!" they cry.

"He is not dead," Mattie says and wipes only loso blood off the blade.

They tie him to living loso's back with the rope from Mattie. Much of it is still stuck to her bloody arms. Elizabeth wonders if the chemical is a forever potion. She sees Mattie with ropes permanently hanging from her wrists. Foolish, empty thought. They must run. But Mattie cannot.

"You must ride on loso, too," Ariella tells her.

Mattie climbs up behind the limp youngfather, but after a few steps she falls off and lies still on the ground.

"We have to bind her wounds," Erin says.

"What is that? How do you know?" Ariella asks.

"I don't know. I think it is what Gudrun would do." Erin kneels beside Mattie and rips strips off her skirt.

"They will come after us. They will follow us easily," Elizabeth says.

"I am going back," Ariella says. "Give me her suit."

They take off Mattie's shipclothes and put her in Ariella's dress. Ariella dresses herself—right in front of them—in everything Mattie was wearing.

"Now cut off my hair with her knife," she says to Erin. "Make it just like hers." She makes a disgusted face and Elizabeth laughs.

After that, she looks just like Mattie; she even looks old.

Ariella walks back the way they have come and says, "I am not going to talk for seven years."

They do not know what a year is.

"A long time. Until we meet in Eastcountry."

* * *

They tie Mattie on behind the youngfather and they walk. They worry that they may not be traveling in a straight line without Mattie to tell them.

"This terrain is much too rough," Erin says.

"Terrain?" Elizabeth is learning words from Erin. "Terra is earth," she says.

When Mattie doesn't wake up through dark night and then in late white night, Elizabeth is afraid. The blood on Mattie's arms is hard and black. Her face is too cold.

They keep walking.

The youngfather starts to mumble and talk. Elizabeth and Erin don't know what to do with him. They ask Mattie, but she doesn't answer.

When white light becomes sunrise, Elizabeth thinks Mattie is dead. She doesn't tell Erin.

Although they are both much stronger since they left home and have more *endurance*, finally, they have to rest. They sit on a raised root and take off their shoes.

"Loso is walking away," Erin says. It has gone ahead and suddenly turned right. They jump up and run after it barefoot.

It stops before a thick clump of trees and moves slowly, smelling. But there is nothing there. Trees and vines.

Loso, with Mattie and the youngfather on its back, disappears. Swallowed.

Elizabeth is afraid of wild vegetation; even Gudrun's methodical madness made her uneasy. This is beyond endurance.

"Come on, Elizabeth," Erin says.

Elizabeth cannot go into that thicket, that waiting monster. Better to lose Mattie.

"Look. A chimney. And see, through there, is a door. It's a hidden house. You'd never know it was here if you weren't right on top of it. Without loso we would never have . . ." Erin stops as a draped vine brushes her face. She pulls Elizabeth after her through a tunnel of leaves.

Inside is a house of the best driwood. It has several tiny rooms on the first floor and one open room on the second where someone has only started to erect dividing walls. The furnishings are also incomplete, but there are odd beds with barred sides upstairs and food downstairs.

They help loso untie Mattie and the youngfather and, while loso cares for them, eat. Elizabeth sits in a small rocker, determined to wait until Mattie wakes, but when one of its runners collapses, she realizes she has fallen asleep. She climbs the tiny staircase, opens a little gate, and throws herself onto a bed. It is the first bed she has been in since leaving Brens. There is a rough but light quilt. She dreams she is sleeping—in her own familydaughterrooms. Then she dreams she has been dreaming and is now awake at home.

"Look! She's sleeping in my bed."

Elizabeth hears smallbrother Thomas's voice. Why is he yelling? She opens her eyes and sees at the foot of the bed a smallloso. It is a dream; there are no smalllosos.

"What are you doing in my pen?" it asks.

Losos

Mattie awoke during late white light. She might have been back on the ship, in space, weightless, floating, but it was a horrible, moving kind of freefall. They were spinning; something had gone wrong with the engines. The life-support fluids were pulsing, surging out of control. And too much blood, pumping in tidal waves, was trying to break through the outer tissues of her left arm; the rhythm made her seasick. She started to vomit and loso brought a small newood bowl.

She fell back onto pillows, bags of dry hay, which crack-led under her heavy head. Loso washed her face. Her neck and shoulders ached, her legs felt like they had been pulled off and reattached at wrong angles, and her skin was sore and scraped. Then she remembered; she had ridden loso's back; she had been tied to loso—behind a Plainsman. A long ride.

And before that she had killed someone.

She sat up.

Killed someone. No. Only loso. Mattie had had to destroy an animal. A painless surgical procedure. She had done it often.

Loso had saved her earlier, released her from the tree. She shivered, colder and sick.

Loso wiped her forehead again and she looked at it for the first time. An animal without a face.

When loso walked away from the bed, Mattie saw that it was pregnant. She?

Mattie also saw that her bed was a kind of enclosed slab in a large open attic. Foliage covered the windows so densely that she could see nothing of the outside world.

Dim green light filtered through onto Elizabeth sitting on a similar bed, or crib with gates, on the other side of the room. There were wooden planks, nails, and studs lying about.

"Mattie, you're awake. You're not dead."

"Loso is pregnant," Mattie said.

Elizabeth said nothing.

"Where are we? Where are the others? I remember . . ." A new wave of nausea swooned over Mattie and she lay back. Loso shuffled back to her.

"We are in *the* losos' house. It is a secret house."

Elizabeth had just spoken nonsense but it made no difference in the face of Mattie's empty retching. She leaned too hard on the worst arm and the pain stabbed back, making her cry out.

Another loso appeared with a bowl and spoon. "Sip this," it—he—said. "It will calm the sickness."

Human genes! Goddammit, they had human genes too! And so Mattie was a murderer.

Loso—*the* loso?—held the bowl out to her.

"Is your pain great?" he asked.

"Are there others? Did your parents talk? Where do you come from?" Perhaps the animal—person?—animal worked for Eastcountry. Elizabeth seemed to be in a cage. Mattie and Elizabeth might be his prisoners. Mattie stirred.

"Rest," he said. "We all hide here. Losos have no parents. No loso talks but smallloso and I.

"The female?"

"Pregnant loso does not have speech."

There was hope. The killed loso, all other losos, were just . . . just losos. Not "human." Perhaps this creature was a result of some kind of advanced surgery or, if gene manipulation, then not a germ-line change but simply a direct interference with the DNA of a single individual at an early embryonic . . .

Impossible. She was fooling herself. Anyone could see—except Kyly and some other Earth fools—that all losos were symbiotic. There was no way to deny that the Eastcountrymen had opened cell walls and fused cells of different species, including homo sapiens. Mattie had to face the horror of the technology and of the men who owned it.

Was there a difference in the nature of intelligence of the talking and nontalking losos, a difference understood in any way by the Eastcountrymen? Is there a necessary kind and level of mind that goes with speech?

Mattie closed her eyes. Tired. She pictured the Eastcountryman standing before her like a humble student in the presence of the "great man." Posing, the ironic bastard. He had spoken of genomes. Earth geneticists themselves had long surmised that no one gene was responsible for "single" traits like intelligence or language. He had said they were linguistic-intellectual polygenic strings. (It had taken a while for her to understand his technical vocabulary; in some ways it was archaic—familiar from the shreds of written scientific history which had survived the Wars—and in others, new and strange as were the concepts it labeled.) He had claimed that his people were now able to turn them off or on and alter their normal chronology. But how could such a complexity of relationships be controlled? Did they actually know what they were doing beyond haphazard interference? Perhaps he was merely bragging to impress the Earth biologist.

Mattie forced her eyes open to look again at the loso.

Did he know who she was? She knew what he was. She studied the lips and throat. There seemed no outer structural difference between him and any other loso she had seen. It would be interesting to compare the tongue and mouth roof.

She shuddered and the loso stepped back. Was it—he—offended? Were emotional reactions another intrinsic component of linguistic ability?

Her eyes had to close. She still wanted to reject the possibility that the Eastcountry scientists could know so much. Even if their ancestors had emigrated with such a technology, a technology which Earth biologists had not begun to rediscover, even then, how could they have preserved it on this mineral-barren world and among such an ignorant, backward population?

Mattie slept for another day and then she learned the losos' story.

The three, the talking adult male, the talking male child, and the pregnant, mute, adult female, had escaped the Eastcountry laboratories only half a harvest before. They were not a family, not related at all.

(As far as they knew. Mattie guessed the genetic pool must be limited. How many animals of any one species had come with the original colonists? How much germ plasm? How great a variety? The first hybrids and the subsequent variations must have been created through both species combining and recombining of the existent code in one or more contributing species—ursine, canine, primate, including human; and the numbers of individual organisms were probably the result of cloning.)

Unlike Gudrun, the losos seemed truly hidden—so far. Until their escape and long journey they had never left the "safety" of the laboratory where they had been born. They had re-created home as they knew it. The beds and food tables were more like laboratory pens and cages and animal feeding stations than human or Plainsloso furniture but the little chairs were copies of those the Eastcountrydoctors and attendants sat on. The losos had never strayed from the site of their choice in this, the wildest part of the forest. They ate losobits and "unchanged" native vegetation.

(Which meant, Mattie realized, that they had been "Dagdan-fixed," genetically modified to adapt to the alien ecosystem. It was still the other way around for the human Dagdans who had to eat only direct descendants of Earth foodstock or genetically altered indigenous crops. Still more evidence that the Eastcountryman had not been merely bragging. Their molecular biologists were capable of mutagenesis on a grand scale. The direct addition of DNA to individual developing plant embryos was too laborious to consider. Mattie guessed at some kind of symbiosis here, too, between Earth and Dagdan vegetation. She wondered how far Rol Addle had gotten with the subject. According to Kyly, nowhere.)

They sat at a table in a "kitchen" area, Mattie, Elizabeth, Erin, and three losos. Mattie ate her porridge, not tasting the bland cereal, and yearned to be in Eastcountry, to have access to all its technology. If she had gone along with her captor, she might have had it all—and freedom from the ship. Might.

Might. Not likely. Not with the attitude of the only Eastcountryman she had encountered. She was the object of curiosity. An object, not a subject, as long as she held out from them her and Earth's state of the science. And the daughters were "preparations."

She suddenly remembered the young Plainsman. Where was he?

"We have not seen him," Erin answered. "Losos put him in a room below, alone."

"Sequestered," Elizabeth said.

"Have you . . . has he heard you speak?" Mattie asked the loso.

"No. No. I don't know what he will do. What will happen to us? I must care for pregnant loso and smallloso. And now I must care for daughters. He asks to be let out. He sometimes shouts. I do not answer. It is difficult not to do what he asks."

Was this a compulsion, biologically imbued, to obey the male human, or mere training? Whatever the nature of the urge, this creature had defied it at least once before in running from Eastcountry and his original masters. The motive must have been powerful. All the more reason she and the daughters had been wise to escape. What would this loso think if he knew she had killed a loso to do so? The one that witnessed the act seemed not to have perceived it. Or had it seen and been indifferent?

"What happened to loso-that-carried-me?" she asked.

"It is here. It cares for daughters and brings food to the youngfather," the loso answered. "It was tired."

The next day when Mattie was well enough she visited the young Plainsman in his room. He looked at her and by her without interest or recognition.

"Where are your fathers?" he asked.

"There are no men here," she said. No human men.

He did not look into her face or answer in any way. He watched the door through which she had entered. She hoped he would not move toward it to escape but wondered why he did not.

He was extremely young, a teenager. She had learned from the daughters that his name was Jack; he was a familyfather of someone called Ain, and had reached the status of father only a harvest before.

"Where are your fathers?" he asked again, not impatiently but as if it were the first time.

"Don't you remember me? I am the Earth woman. I was your prisoner."

He glanced at her, frowned, and looked back to the door, a sliding panel. "Fetch one of your fathers."

Was it her dress—Ariella's—or damage she herself had done to his head?

"Don't you remember, Jack? I am the Earth doctor. Look at me."

He would not. His face reddened. It might have been an attractive, boyish face in other circumstances. Studying him at close range in daylight—filtered green though it was— Mattie had even more strongly the impression of a young boy cast in the role of an elderly man for a school play. He might be a ten-year-old playing Joseph or an ancient shepherd.

"Jack, do you understand?" She moved in front of him so he had to look at her but he averted his eyes, this time to the leaves covering the tiny window. She understood that he would not see her, could not see her or hear her or understand her meaning. It was not the dress or the blow on the head.

For a second she pitied him—until she remembered the daughters.

"You are the prisoner now." His Adam's apple moved. Her satisfaction was childish and perhaps the information dangerous. She decided not to tell him again, yet, that he was the only human male in the house.

Loso-that-had-carried-them came into the room with water. It shuffled to her and fussed at her face with a cloth. As Jack watched, the lines of his face relaxed. She was a daughter. Just a daughter.

"My fathers are Earth fathers," she said, pushing loso off as automatically as any real Dagdan daughter would. "My fathers flew through space from Earth. You know that." She stopped and looked at him as if waiting.

He shifted but did not look at her.

"My fathers know about Plain and Eastcountrydoctors. My fathers have more to give you than the Eastcountrymen. You met Doctor Kyly. He is a . . . only a smallfather. He has disobeyed the leadingshipfathers."

"Where are your fathers?"

Mattie could not tell by his inflections whether he was listening to her now or merely repeating his earlier question.

"They are . . . above. Outside. They are coming after me. You are to help me. Their daughter."

At last he looked directly into her eyes. Now, she thought, now she had reached him. "Jack, talk to me."

"You are a witch," he said. "An abomination."

Elizabeth called the smallloso Thomas, but she gave the others no names.

Mattie learned about Eastcountry from the losos. The adult answered her questions willingly but never offered much spontaneously. He spoke slowly and never went beyond the scope of the question or continued to talk without urging. Mattie was never satisfied about the level of his intelligence or the emotional quotient of his personality—if he had a personality.

Thomas, on the other hand, seemed to have a personality and to be personal. He responded to Elizabeth's angelstories and Bible readings, sympathized with Mattie's pains. His face, feature by feature, was as immobile and indistinguishable as that of any other loso, yet one sensed intense and changing expression.

His experience in Eastcountry had unfortunately been limited to that of a baby laboratory animal. He had not been taught to read, had talked to no one but the doctors. He had played and exercised in controlled circumstances with mute losos and other experimental animals.

Were the mute losos like all the others on Dagda? Were they being raised to care for the daughters or to do other work?

Thomas could not answer. Loso-that-carried-Mattie-and-Jack was the only one he had ever seen outside of Eastcountry. No, they were not alike at all. Some were tall and some fat. Some had great muscles, biceps, while others were slender and nimble. Some smiled. No others talked. Some were pregnant.

Erin and Elizabeth were more amazed at his information than Mattie. Except for the size of a few field-workers, losos were identical, interchangeable.

But Thomas was bored with the subject of losos. Losos were dull. There were other creatures. Large skeds with faces and hairless monkeys that danced.

Mattie looked to the older loso to see if this were true, but he gave no clue.

Mattie wished Kyly and all the other Earth people could hear Thomas's descriptions of the laboratories, pens, dormitories (The distinction between the last two was not clear.) and other physical facilities—and the machinery and instruments therein.

"And daughters?" she asked. "Are there human females—or males—in the laboratories?"

"Like you?" Thomas asked.

"Or smaller," Elizabeth said. "Or older."

"Yes," Thomas said.

They were gathered in the kitchen area. The older losos were doing something over the fire. Mattie was never sure if the male actually listened to their talk.

It was time to eat porridge again. It was always time for porridge, and they were always hungry, but it was as dull as losos in Eastcountry.

"Porridge hot," Elizabeth sang, "porridge cold. Peas porridge. What are peas, Mattie, some Earth vegetable? Interminable, ubiquitous, infinite porridge."

"Isn't there anything else?" Mattie asked.

"Not that you can eat," the loso said.

"Look at what smallbrother Thomas is eating," Erin said. "That isn't porridge."

Smallbrother! Their *brother* was eating mashed losobits, Mattie guessed.

"Do you know what anthropomorphism is?" she asked.

Elizabeth looked it up in her dictionary.

In a few more days pregnant loso went into labor. Mattie had delivered thousands of laboratory animals and needed no help but asked Elizabeth and Erin if they would assist.

Elizabeth at first said no.

"This may be the most important thing you can do now," Mattie told her. "It will give you strength. Maturity."

She was eager now. This was a moment to teach. She thought they would be astonished and delighted. She did not consider that they might be revolted and terrified at the sight.

But that was not the problem. There was no gore, no pain for loso, almost nothing to see. The tiny wet thing that slipped into the world from undefined furry dark between thick loso thighs was white and hairless. A human being.

Mattie staggered back in order not to fall, holding the infant dangerously, almost absently, wet and screaming in her hands. She wanted to drop it, to throw it away, as if it were the beast, a mutant to be destroyed, and not the perfect human being it obviously was.

It was Erin who took it from her, held it in her arms, and then cradled it against her neck.

And Mattie saw that its thin fuzz of red hair matched Erin's own, and she started to scream.

Elizabeth came to Mattie and held her arms to stop their shaking.

"It's a horror, Elizabeth," Mattie said.

Loso took the baby away from Erin and held it to its nipple. Erin watched, staring, oblivious to the dripping mess of her neck and dress front. Elizabeth turned from Mattie to stare. And Mattie finally looked too. There was silence in the room except for the sound of the baby's sucking.

Jack

"My familyoldfathers hide from sun," Erin said. "They have bad skin sores. Their faces are scarred and purple. Even some olddaughters, who never go outside after early white light, get burns that never heal. They are treated by the doctors in the city. But smallbrothers go out into the fields at midday with hats only and, though their skin turns red, it no longer blisters, and soon it grows darker and golden. My skin is like that."

Erin's complexion seemed as uncorrupted as the baby's. Eastcountry genetics, thought Mattie. Her own skin had already become dry, dark, and cracked from exposure to Dagdan sunlight.

"It is hard for me to understand how reproduction was for your families," she said. "How you saw it. How those 'elves' managed. You never saw an infant before. It is still incredible to me."

"We wondered. Some of us. When new verysmallbrothers and daughters were brought to our families."

"And they shared family genetic characteristics? You must have seen that they were biologically related . . ."

"I don't know what that means," Elizabeth said.

"Traits like the baby's red hair or your gray eyes," Mattie said.

"Your familyfather Lucius has the same gray eyes," Erin said to Elizabeth.

"The zygote implanted in loso uterus," Mattie said aloud. "Human genes but 'doctored' who knows how." A Fanatick had once shouted at her: "Did you *doctor* them, Doctor?" But those were baboon genes she had been working on, not human. It wasn't the same thing at all.

"And," she continued to herself, "think what a feat of engineering loso itself is to sustain and nourish the fetus of another species. And yet they have adapted it to the Dagdan ecosystem, the food chain . . ."

"I do not look like Lucius," Elizabeth said.

"Well . . ." said Erin.

Elizabeth flicked her paintbrush in Erin's direction.

"You're getting it on the baby," Erin said.

Mattie leaned back against the tree trunk to which she was tied only by the bond of her promise to pose for Elizabeth.

"This happened before," Elizabeth said.

"Déjà vu?" Mattie asked. "That's a feeling you are living an experience or a single moment for the second time. Or more."

"No. I did paint this portrait before. In a way I am finishing what I started. I had no model then. It was Ariella—and you—from memory. This is better . . . but oh cot. The red is all dried up! Half my jars of paints are ruined. Or just lost."

"You should have painted the baby," Erin said, holding her high for viewing and pulling her down again to kiss.

"Not interesting," said Elizabeth. "Besides, I have no red."

Loso brought them water and took the baby to nurse. Perhaps life with losos on Dagda was not all bad for females.

Mattie saw them all as in a painting, a pastoral scene from a preindustrial period on Earth. They might be females of the leisure class in a "civilized" nation posing in the park of some manor house. Their long, full dresses, loso-clean, were designed to grace nonfunctional figures. Erin held their one remaining parasol over her and the baby.

Up close the picture failed. The parasol and dresses were tattered and torn, Elizabeth was less than pretty and her painting obviously more, the servants were huge, hairy animals, and one of them was nursing the baby.

Instead of a mansion, behind them stood the house that

losos built and Jack was a prisoner within. What to do with Jack?

But the moist air was Earthlike; ever since they had come away from Gudrun's place Mattie kept thinking she smelled rain.

"Mattie, your head is dropping. Please keep your eyes open."

" 'Kay."

"We'll bring youngfather out to us. To the kitchen. When he is hungry, very hungry. We'll be eating. Daughters and doctors and losos and child losos. And loso will be nursing the baby. Except for the baby and loso, we'll all be talking. That ought to do something to him. There is nothing to lose."

"I cannot let him be hungry," adult-talking-loso said.

"You must."

"I cannot."

"That is too bad because then I must kill him. To save myself and the daughters."

Mattie read horror on Thomas's face but nothing on the adult. Should she force a choice now and learn the nature of genetic loyalty as conceived and executed by Eastcountrymen?

"All right," he said.

"Don't tremble," Mattie told Thomas. "Be the way you always are with us."

"Is he a doctor? Maybe he will take my speech away."

Mattie tried to imagine that smallloso had seen no man outside of Eastcountry.

"And you . . ." She could not call him just loso. He was more or other. "Thomas's father, will you talk in the presence of the man?"

It must have been right; he might have smiled. "Yes," he said. He was T.F. from then on.

It was Elizabeth and Erin who were not the way they always were, who did not talk in the presence of the man.

He half-stalked, half-staggered through the door. It was not hunger alone that gave him the gray, wild-eyed look. He had never known a variable. A talking-woman-who-killed-loso had done him in.

"Please, sit and eat with us," Mattie said with a wide, welcoming gesture of her arm. As she moved she saw that Erin was bowing curtsy. On her other side Elizabeth started to move and stopped herself. Her eyes met Mattie's and she shrugged, and then stared downward at her plate of porridge.

Mattie laughed to her then and Elizabeth laughed back, but then both she and Erin fell into a glum, blank silence.

Jack stopped halfway and gestured to any loso toward the food. He looked beyond them all.

When he came closer to the board that still served as table, Mattie turned significantly to T.F.

He spoke: "We have hot porridge, father."

Jack almost cried then and even Mattie the Earth woman sympathized. She too had almost cried when the loso first spoke to her and she had not lived with their silence all her life. How would she feel if some Earth animal, a pet, suddenly began to speak?

And then Jack saw the baby nursing and shouted.

"We didn't do this," Mattie shouted back at him. "Your Eastcountrydoctors have been doctoring all of you."

He was hysterical and Mattie let loso give him some food a few hours after it had led him back to his room. But not enough food.

The next day she went into his room with a very little food. She bowedcurtsy, smiled humbly, said losos were cooking good food for him tonight, and left quickly.

That night he was brought again into the kitchen/dining room with all of them waiting. He sat and began to eat. When baby nursed he stood and bellowed.

"Eastcountrymen!" Mattie shouted. "They have abused you."

After five days of this he sat with them and ate.

* * *

"He has changed," Mattie said to Elizabeth.

Elizabeth did not answer. She frowned at her palette and touched the tip of her brush. The cerulean blue had a green caste and it must be Mattie's fault. The frown said it all.

"Elizabeth, is he smarter—and—faster than you? He can change with so little time and you, with so much, still bowcurtsy and remain silent in his presence? Is his family simply genetically superior—to yours for example?"

"No! Ain is his . . . only a daughter. My pater and my other fathers and brothers are all brighter than that . . . You have trapped me. 'Ain is only a daughter.' I said it."

"I didn't mean it. I was only teasing—challenging you. But it is true that he has already accepted . . ."

"You taught me yourself that the fathers are not smarter. You said that knowledge is not intelligence. You said the fa—our brothers were given a chance to learn. You said daughters were rewarded when they were stupid and ignorant. You said it was not our fault and now you think dumb Ain's dumb brother is smarter because he knows more!"

Elizabeth slapped her brush at the stretched fabric that was her new "canvas," spattering the tainted, wrong blue in a trail like a meteor tail across the gray blankness.

"I'm not talking about information. He is as ignorant as you were about . . . important things. I mean that when he finally broke, he was able to adapt, to change, to . . . He has tried to learn quickly. Don't you notice the difference in the way he talks to us—all three of us?"

"Erin and I have changed too."

"I'm sorry," Mattie said. "But when he is around, it is as though you haven't changed at all. You and Erin are other people from the ones you had become. I understand but I don't anticipate. You're gone somehow."

Mattie, Jack and loso-that-had-carried-them trudged over rough, knolled ground. Everything came in clumps: turf, odd raised roots, six-inch shrubs. The trees themselves were bunched unevenly, the batches close enough together to obscure their view but far enough apart that the humans had to wear hats against the sun.

But the heat was different. Their sweat did not evaporate.

Jack pulled off his hat and wiped his forehead with his sleeve. Mattie saw his damp, brown hair move. A breeze. And then she felt it herself. It raised the hairs on the back of her neck, lifted her hat brim slightly, cool-dried her face. It smelled of water.

There were a number of natural, nonhybrid waterbushes, but they had not planned to travel so far and had not brought pumps. Yet, although it was late in the day, they decided to go on toward an odd sound that they had begun to hear in the east. They took turns riding loso. They rested and they ran. Yet the sound grew no louder.

"Tell me again about the sea," Mattie said.

"I've never seen it," he told her. "No one I know but Eastcountrymen have seen the water. They call it the water, not—sea."

"But how far from Plain is it? Eastcountry isn't all that far if the train goes there. The Eastcountrymen travel back and forth frequently and the losos could not have made the trip if it were on the other side of Dagda. I would give anything for a map!"

"It is not that it is far. I think it is part of Eastcountry and we from Plain do not go there." Jack mumbled the last part in wise-old-man ones. As if it were their choice, Mattie thought but did not press him with the observation. He had done too well and didn't deserve humiliation.

"It seems," she said instead, "that all of Dagda except Plain and Fian, really very small places in population and geography, is Eastcountry."

"There is Deech," he said.

"Is there? The dau—the women seem to think it might be an angelstory. Of course, Gudrun . . . but it may not exist anymore. She might be a survivor. One that the Eastcountry 'elves' let survive for whatever reasons of their own."

"No. It is there. Very far. They come to trade. I saw two of them once myself when I was young on a trip to the city.

The trip from Deech takes more than a harvest, they say. It is also said their daughters used to come with them, but no more.

"And, oh, yes, Mattie, they cross water, two or three waters. And that is not daughters' nonsense but the truth."

He had gone too far and she chastised him with a frown.

They were forced to turn back. Mattie determined to prepare next time for a longer expedition. They would bring changed food, water pumps, and sleeping bags.

Elizabeth had put aside her first two paintings unfinished. She was not satisfied with the portrait of Mattie and Mattie felt that she blamed her somehow for its imperfection. It looked wonderful to Mattie. Grudgingly she admitted that her respect for Elizabeth had increased because of it—which meant, of course, that that respect had not been complete.

The other painting was of a certain crooked tree next to the losos' house. Elizabeth said her paints were inadequate for the job.

Now she worked at stretching an old underskirt across a frame for her next attempt. The material was so worn that it tore with each increase in tension. Elizabeth ignored Erin's suggestion that she just paint on wood.

Erin spent most of her time with the baby. And when she did work with and for Mattie in setting up another makeshift lab, she sat the baby nearby so she too could learn.

"She is only five weeks old," Mattie said. But Erin wasn't taking any chances. There would be no innocence or serenity for this baby.

The baby had as yet no name. They were waiting to find the perfect one. They all agreed that angelstory names were out: no Cinderella, Rapunzel, Snow White, Gwenivere, Griselda. Elizabeth offered a Biblical list: Naomi, Rachel (Mattie vetoed this one firmly), Ruth, Sarah; many of these belonged to Dagdan daughters already.

Jack suggested a traditional name from the Fergus family. Why should the circumstances change convention? The baby was a Fergus. The familyfathers would be expecting her in a couple of years.

Jack worked more and more with Mattie and Erin in the laboratory. He followed complex new theories and seemed to understand when wonder and delight were appropriate. Finally he seemed to feel these things for himself as he began to see how the universe was made. Mattie felt like a scientist again and a teacher.

Every once in a while a bit of abysmal ignorance would rise to the surface, be exposed, and burst. He thought in the very beginning that sperm was a poison that had to be changed and in contradiction that each sperm contained a complete, miniature person. But with him at least she did not have to start from a scratch in the dirt.

He knew that—at least until now!—women bore children. In some remote, heathen, primitive places, such as Deech—and maybe in some not so primitive, certain Fian families, the prisoners at the Halt—it was rumored that the daughters were aware of the act of impregnation.

How? How could they not be aware?

In the hospital in the city when their health was checked—all examinations by the doctors were done under anesthesia—anything else would be cruel, corrupting, sinful. Fathers of course were strong enough to endure the process of—of sperm extraction.

"Artificial insemination." But for how long and where?

Not always. Not everywhere. He could not look at her. He blushed. "The other way," he said, and turning encountered Erin's blush and waiting. He spun back to Mattie. "I cannot say these things before daughters. Even among fathers we no longer . . ."

"On Earth there is only the other way," Mattie said, not quite truthfully.

He knew astronomy, solar system astronomy and early stellar. The books in his family library were old; they had come from Earth. (If the Eastcountrymen had means or knowledge of printing, they were not sharing it.) Yet from what Mattie could tell, the discrepancy between the theories he described and those she had been taught was not five hundred years. The Wars had undone more than biology. She was learning how much further ahead the preWar world had been than they had suspected. Less credit then to Eastcountry. Their ancestors had come to Dagda with an advanced technology.

"The books in your libraries will be a treasure trove to Earth historians," she said. No doubt Kyly had already been into them. They would make him famous. Why couldn't he be content with that?

Mattie, Jack, and Erin, on another expedition, lay in sleeping blankets in early dark night watching Bethlehem and Venus in the southern sky. Mattie described for Jack the difference in appearance of Earth's Venus. She tried to make him see the moon and a black sky full of distant stars.

"How do you—calculate the distances?" Erin asked.

Mattie had forgotten she was there.

"It's too complicated. I learned once and probably can remember but I'm not an astronomer."

The next day they found that the ground rose. It was a hill, an end to the endless flatness. When they came to a relatively treeless area, Mattie saw that it was not a hill they were climbing but the side of a long ridge, extending as far as she could see to the north and south. But straight ahead was nothing, just white sky meeting a very close, slightly raised, tree-lined horizon.

The climb was not steep but longer than it had seemed. Mattie felt chilled and realized that the sun had disappeared. The world was white-gray everywhere and no longer had an edge. Ghosts of dark, narrow trees emerged one by one and faded in turn as they passed. Erin shivered and slowed her steps. Jack hesitated but, glancing at Mattie, pushed on ahead.

Except for the brush of their own steps, there was silence.

And then, with a grunt, Jack was gone. Completely and all at once. And Mattie heard the sound of crashing brush ahead—below, and Erin said, "Wait," but Mattie's forward foot had already gone over, and was taking her with it. "Oh," she said and tumbled after Jack.

She didn't fall far through air. She hit ground and rolled and then slid. Stalks and sharp brush scraped her legs and one hip. She felt hard soil rasp her cheek and tear her ear and then she was horizontal—on her back.

"Jack?" Mattie shouted.

Erin's voice came down from above.

"Erin, I'm here—somewhere. There's a ledge. I don't think I fell far. I . . . Jack, are you anywhere? Jack! Erin, I don't hear him. I don't know where he is."

"Mattie," Erin shouted down at her through the fog, "are you hurt? I can't see anything."

"Be careful. Don't move. Move back. Don't . . . ."

"I'm holding on to a tree. We should have brought loso! How are we going to get you out? Up?"

"I don't know."

Mattie sat up. It hurt but she knew she wasn't broken. She shouted Jack's name as loudly as she could. Erin tried too but there was no answer.

"Erin, I think I'm all right. I can see a little ways around me, but not well enough to climb. It seemed very steep as I fell. Even if this mist ever evaporates, I may not be able to get out. There is only one thing to do."

"I know. I have to go back to the losos' house and bring losos and rope. It will take days—if I don't get lost—and you'll be . . ." Erin dropped her voice. "You will be dead."

"What? I can't hear you."

"Mattie, do you have your pack?"

"No. Yes. Yes, I can reach it."

"I'm throwing down one of my blankets and one food bag."

"No. Don't. You'll need the food. And the . . . Erin, wait. It won't land in the right place and—"

But it was too late. Mattie heard the sond of the bundle falling past her. How far below it went she could not tell.

"I'll be all right," Erin said. "I'm going now while it's still morning. Just stay there. Don't fall anymore."

Mattie laughed. " 'Kay. Remember where the sun should be in the day and the planets at night and ..."

"I know. I know. Good-bye, Mattie."

Chasm

Mattie strained her eyes as if to force the mist to clear by her will to see. She fixed a certain bush at the limits of visibility and taught herself to see beyond it. But when she looked away and back again, the bush itself had been erased.

Later—it must have been afternoon—she closed her eyes for just a moment. When she opened them, the mist was gone.

She was on some kind of narrow platform suspended in air, half a mile above a river.

Vertigo. She flattened facedown and tried to grab hold of the ground with clawed hands and feet.

When she recovered from disbelief and convinced her body that the platform was not tipping, rolling her off, she was able to look again to verify what logic told her must be so. She was on a ledge, a firm, horizontal notch in the apparently vertical face of a cliff.

Upward and outward, across an immense gulf, were palisades running as far as she could see in each direction. She understood that she had come upon one of the ravines or fiords that traced the entire planet. This was one of Anu's veins.

Below, the white-gold water moved fast, flowing from north to south in tiny brilliant ripples, miniaturized from her distant point of view. So too must the width of the waterway be deceptive; it must be far more than a river.

Southward the water seemed to narrow to a stream and then to a needle point where the cliffs on each side finally merged. Mattie could not guess how many miles she was seeing. A bulge or bend in the cliffs on her left cut off some of her view to the north.

Jack could not be alive. Mattie forced herself to peer over and down. There was no possibility she could make out anything as small as a man at the bottom but she saw that the cliff side was not really perpendicular or smooth after all. There were other ledges, crevices, irregular grassy patches that sloped at less precipitous angles, and roughly horizontal "shelves," strata, whose counterparts on the cliff face of the opposite shore looked like high-water marks.

Mattie scanned all the places close enough to see which might have caught a falling body. There was nothing. He must have fallen too far, out of sight, all the way down to the bottom.

Mattie's face hurt. The sun was burning the salt of her tears into her skin.

The sun was still high and hot, and Mattie's hat was gone. She was too near the top of the ravine for the cliffs themselves to shade her. Even for a person with a hat the Dagdan sun was poison in the middle of the day.

She searched the walls above and behind for protection. There was no projection directly above her perch but a few yards to the left a line of shade seemed to be widening. A lidlike irregularity, actually another ledge, served as a half roof. But between Mattie and the shade her little balcony narrowed.

On hands and knees she crawled, rolling her sack before her. When she came to the bottleneck, she tried to push the sack all the way over at once so that she could get herself across unimpeded. And it got there nicely and then bumped into the wall and bounced off and down. Mattie watched it arch and jump and land and tumble out of sight.

She reeled, almost toppled after it, caught hold of the edge of the little overhang she had been heading for. She knelt for awhile, hanging on, forehead pressed against her arm. Then she turned sideways and sidled the two remaining feet, inching along on her knees. Only as she moved onto the wider, partially shaded section of the ledge could she raise her head and see Jack sprawled on her little roof.

He was half on his side, half on his stomach, face toward the cliff. His pack was still on his back.

"Jack?"

There was no answer. He didn't move.

She repeated his name several times, but he never responded.

Mattie stood up, slowly, not letting go of the overhang's edge, not looking back where a few inches behind her heels the cliff dropped away. She put a knee up onto the higher ledge but could find no handhold from which to pull herself up. Finally she grasped Jack's leg but was afraid of dragging him back over with her. She stood in this awkward position for some time.

She tried to see if his chest moved but the angle was wrong. His leg felt warm but the sun was hot. In fact, if he was alive, she decided he must be protected from it. She was just able to reach his sack, take out his blanket, and toss it over him. She took a small sip of water from his flask, and then, balancing herself with both hands, she moved down onto the lower shelf which was then all shade.

He could be alive. He had not fallen as far as she had. But it had been hours. If not dead, he might be in a permanent coma, seriously injured.

Mattie remembered Jack's glance at her just before striding bravely ahead. Men. Boys. Her fault. He was showing his strength, showing off. A child. Worse, a newborn. And that was her responsibility too. She brought him life and, by doing so, killed him.

Mattie's muscles were trembling. Her whole body began to quake. The sore places in her arms were refired, but she looked at the scarring tissue indifferently.

The water below had turned black-blue, and although she was still looking across at bright afternoon light on the opposite cliff wall, Mattie knew that the night shadow was already climbing up her side of the canyon as the sun moved west behind her. The darkness would well like blood to fill this great cut in the surface.

Mattie got back onto her knees and crawled farther left. The shelf narrowed again but continued around the bulge that had obstructed the view to the north. It finally met a stony culvert which zigzagged below and above at a less treacherous angle than the rest of the cliff side. Mattie turned on to it, or into it, and climbed. She slipped back a foot only once as loose sand or stones slid out from under her.

When she reached Jack's ledge, she took another left turn, and crawled back parallel to the way she had come.

He was sitting up, watching her progress. His stare was so blank that she thought for a moment that he was unconscious with his eyes open.

Suddenly, just before she reached him, he stood up, took a step toward her, almost missing the ledge, smiled, and swayed dangerously.

"Jack, stop. Sit down. Don't move!" Mattie couldn't imagine such fearlessness, such carelessness. But it wasn't that. He didn't see the drop, didn't know where they were. He hadn't recognized depth, which he had never seen before.

"Sit," Mattie said again, as strongly as she could. "Just do it. Please."

He sat too casually, close to the edge. She crawled the rest of the way, took his arm and urged him back to the wall with her. When finally they sat side by side, Raggedy Ann and Andy, legs straight out before them, backs leaning safely against the cliff side, she breathed again and told him what they were looking at.

They could not spend dark night on the narrow ledge and so climbed, crawled, slid their way down the crevice as far as they could. At one point they had to travel horizontally when their original chute steepened; at another, a small grassy place, they were able to walk down a few hundred yards.

Mattie's scraped flesh, aching arms, and torn ear throbbed, and thirst and then hunger were increasing.

Jack's only visible physical damage was the large, vividly discolored bump on his forehead. He showed no signs of dizziness or nausea and his pupils remained normal so Mattie assumed he would be all right in spite of having been unconscious for several hours.

Soon the "river" began to look like a tidal ocean as the opposite shore disappeared and the ripples grew into currents and waves.

They found the blanket but not the food Erin had thrown down or Mattie's backpack. Mattie told Jack the river water would be drinkable because Dagda was mineral scarce. She hoped she was right as they shared the little remaining water and food from Jack's pack.

The line of darkness came almost perceptibly up to meet them as they walked down toward it. Mattie decided they should stop for the night on a second grassy, relatively flat, plot. They rolled themselves in their blankets and slept until first white light—which was a dim pearl reflection of itself this far below the surface.

The heavy mist returned with the morning and they had to wait for several hours.

"Tell me about the families," Mattie said. "There must have been intermarriage in the early days, before your ancestors stopped doing it the 'other way.' "

Jack knew nothing of the subject. They did say that some families were "cousins" to others, but he didn't know why. The children brought to each family looked like members of that family.

"They share inherited characteristics," Mattie said, "just as you and Ain—whoever she is—are both stupid according to Elizabeth."

He looked angry for a moment before he saw that she was joking. "Is my daughter Ain stupid?" he seemed to ask himself rather than Mattie. "I have never spoken to her."

"It is hard for me to hear you call her daughter. She must be older than you are."

"It is hard for me to think of daughters as any kind of old," he said. He was improving.

"Are the men in Elizabeth's family artistic? Creative I mean?" Mattie asked. "That pig Lucius seems an unimaginative lout."

"Oh, Lucius," Jack said, making a gesture of spitting, a strong, uncourtly behavior on Dagda. "Lucius reported us for laughing during city lessons when we were all smallbrothers. He has never changed. There are rumors of things he has done that I cannot believe. Is Elizabeth a daughter in his family? I am sorry for her then. What is 'pig'?"

"You mean you don't know one dau—female—from another? You must have seen Elizabeth a thousand times. You know every male. Your population is so small—"

"We do not look at them. Of course, when the looks are so close like the baby and . . ."

"Erin. You know her name! But it is true. The baby might be her own. Probably is her own."

Even when the mist lifted, literally moved upward, it blocked the light from above. Mattie told Jack about thunderstorms on Earth, the strange "indoor" darkness just before the storm broke.

Jack told her about tornadoes, how they could be seen coming long before they arrived, a small disturbance in the distance. Mattie tried to picture the speck of change in the blankness. Until now Jack had known only flat, open distance, vast empty sky, yet he seemed not to be claustrophobic under the pressure of these low, thick clouds any more than he had been acrophobic when they began their descent. Mattie wondered if he was insensible from his upbringing or hiding his fear under masculine—no, fatherly—dignity.

When the mist had risen and thinned enough to be translucent, they continued down to the water.

The last hour was most painful and frustrating. The edge of the water seemed to grow nearer and then unaccountably to recede. Their passage was not straight, and although the way was not as steep, they were often blocked and had to backtrack. The only passable culverts zigzagged and the flat places grew fewer.

The sound of water grew louder, pleasant, painfully wonderful to Mattie who was suddenly and for the first time desperately homesick. Water. It was both ocean and river. Rushing wet water. She laughed and, starting to run, looked to Jack to share her pleasure.

But now he showed all the feeling, all the reaction she had looked for earlier. Height had not done it. A lowering, enclosing sky and ravine had not done it. Water. So much water. Water moving with a life of its own. Water out of control. (Out of Eastcountry measures and doles and means.)

He shied like a horse. He looked away from it like a cat she once owned who denied the existence of the beach waves by refusing to face in their direction and licking its paws instead. Jack stopped and looked at his feet and then back to the cliff, steep again behind them.

Suddenly Mattie thought of the daughters and was wrenched to know that it should, would, might have been their reactions she experienced. Taught. Led them to. Then she was ashamed of her arrogance. She had not created this waterway nor had she discovered or recovered it.

Jack was looking at her face, gauging her reaction. She smiled, laughed, took his hand, and ran forward over what might, with much imagination, have been a narrow beach. He hesitated. A look of elderly disapproval came and went like a shadow. Then he laughed open-mouthed and—now it was he who was somehow holding her hand—ran forward to the water's edge and stopped. His laugh was loud; it came in shouts seldom heard on Dagda.

Her own need of the water was greater now than the fun of watching him. She pulled away from him and waded in, giving only passing thought to the possibility that all this liquid might not be "water," might be harmful to an Earth organism. Why else would it be unknown to a Plainsman? It was far from Plain but not that far. Why forbidden?

Mattie dove and forgot the danger and forgot Jack. First

it was cold and then it was freefall, but better than freefall because it fought back. The pleasure of battle. Mattie dove, fought her way underwater against the current, gave in and let it return her to the starting place. Again she turned, dove, and swam upstream and again surrendered and let the tide carry her back.

But this time she was not back. There was a strong undertow pulling at right angles to the north-south flow. Mattie had to swim strongly toward shore to resist being dragged out.

She touched bottom with some relief, straightened up to look into Jack's horrified face. He was standing waist-deep, with the smaller currents near the shore rushing around him, his tissue-thin, jacket-shaped shirt clinging to his chest and upper arms in torn sheets. His hair for the first time looked like it belonged to a boy instead of an old man as it flopped in wet tendrils over his forehead. His mouth was open as though he had been calling or shouting to her. She had not heard.

She tried to smile, to reassure him. She managed to wave as she struggled up the sharp incline of the bottom. She reached for his hand and he hauled her in. Then he was angry.

"I couldn't reach you," he said. "What if you could not come back? It is not serene! It is the behavior of a foolish youngbrother. We have no loso."

She stood before him, still panting, dripping, and shivering. She had gone into unknown, treacherous water in her only garment, a simple tunic dress provided by loso, and had nothing dry to change into. He was right, this weird boy/father. She had behaved like a foolish child. Not a bit serene!

Just as she started to speak, not to chastise him for treating her like a mindless daughter but to agree and to calm his panic and fear, his anger changed to something else. He reddened and turned quickly away from her.

She looked down at her wet, one-layered dress sticking to her breasts, caught between her legs, torn off her shoulders.

"Jack, it's ... I ..."

He walked away from her without looking back.

He returned later with a shirtful of tiny fishlike things and told her they were edible. He knew them well. They were traded to the fathers in dried form in the city and transported by train to Plain and Fian where they were ground by brothers and losos into the inevitable grain meals. He had never known or wondered where they came from.

Mattie was surprised he had recognized them in their living form but all she said was, "Protein. This must be one of the ways you get protein."

She was wrapped in her blanket, sitting in the sun, waiting for him, thinking like a responsible adult again about food and rescue. How would Erin find them? They would have to get themselves back up the escarpment and return to the losos' house, perhaps missing Erin along the way—if she had found the way. All without food except for these fish—if Jack was right and they really were Eastcountry-changed.

Jack stood before her naked to the waist. His thin, loose trousers were beginning to dry in the legs but still hung damply over his flat belly, He was beautiful, strong, muscled, lean. The only defect was the elderly stoop they all affected. In a few years he would have a permanent hump.

She looked up at his face and he colored again. She smiled wickedly, amused at his embarrassment. He was so young. Except for the dry facts he was as innocent as the daughters had been. Perhaps more so since they had had their underground secrets, their sharing and stories that were more than stories. Her students on Earth—as immature as she had often found them—were far older in years and every other way. In experience this young man before her was a child.

And that appealed to her. He appealed to her.

He turned his face from hers and twisted to reach for his blanket. Mattie watched the muscles in the stretch of his leg, the long, tight thigh and perfect, round buttocks. Not like the OC's bulk.

It amazed her still, again, that they—who? the older fathers? Eascountrydoctors?—controlled the sex drive of such apparently normal men—young men. But as he turned back to her she saw that they had not controlled it at all.

He covered himself with the blanket and put on a fatherly face as he sat down a few feet away from her.

She had feared at times that the Eastcountrydoctors had played with their hormones as well as their genes, or maybe redirected their desires to something other than living, conscious, human females. Now she realized it was only mind control and that she knew how to undo.

She rolled over to him, blanket and all. He was not so rude as to move away but shifted position slightly, averting his head, turning a shoulder, a cold shoulder.

"Cold?" she asked and reached for the damp hair on the back of his neck. She smiled to feel him tremble. He neither looked nor moved.

Mattie slid her hand, sun-warmed on his still chilled-wet flesh, under the blanket down over his shoulder, caressed his upper arm, slipped her fingers over his ribs. As she moved to find the flat of his belly, he pulled with a growl out of her reach and rewrapped his blanket.

"Jack," she said, "come back to me."

"No," he said, voice muffled in cotton.

"Come let me touch you. Don't you see that I need you? You are so handsome. Your body is . . . your body excites me."

"It's not right," he whispered, hoarse. "You're a daughter."

"Don't you see? That makes it right. You know that. I've taught you that." Mattie spoke into his ear, lay her hand on his thigh, pressed her fingers against the cloth of the blanket.

"But you're a doctor!" This made no sense to Mattie. He said it as one of her students might have addressed the school chancellor. She sat upright behind him, letting her blanket drop.

"I'm afraid," he said and turned to face her. He stared at her naked breasts. "I'm afraid of you."

But he lay back when she urged and let her open the blanket. He cried out when she touched him. She dropped her own blanket and knelt above him to let him look at her. It was he who pulled her down onto him.

Mattie decided that there was no need to try to climb back up the escarpment the next day. It was wiser to stay longer where they were and search along the base of the cliff for an easier path. They made a fire on a flat open place near the edge of the water, far enough out from the base of the cliff that Erin might see it from above, and then they cooked and ate the fish.

Fire

"Mattie and Jack have fallen. Fallen into a place or off the world. I don't know. . . . Where is the baby?"

Elizabeth stops her work, painting, not a picture but the wall of the eating area, with a stain she has made from sourberries. She stares at Erin's wild face.

"Fallen? Are they . . . are they alive? Where? Far?"

"Yes. Mattie is alive. Was. I came back in one day and night. It took us two to get there. Where is the baby? After I see the baby, I'll take losos and go back."

"How did you know Mattie was all right? Why . . . ?"

"We talked but I couldn't get to her. Oh, Elizabeth, it was so terrible! They just disappeared. She can't be all right. Poor Mattie. I have to go right back with ropes and food and water. She's probably dying right now. And Jack . . ."

" 'Kay. I'll come too." Elizabeth drops her whisk brush on the floor and follows Erin upstairs to losos and the baby.

Elizabeth, Erin, loso-that-carried-Mattie-and-Jack, and T.F. set out east toward the edge of the world prepared for a long trek, but before they have gone a mile, there is the most horrible sound Elizabeth has ever heard coming from the sky somewhere behind them. It rattles and groans and grows louder until it pains her ears.

They look back at the place where the losos' house is hidden in its dense stand of trees and at first see nothing although the clacking and whirring grows ever louder. They stand, all four, deafened and mute with fear.

Then into the open place, the "parkland," between them and the house a huge, graceless structure with some kind of halo or thin parasol lowers itself. It hits the ground with a jolt. The halo becomes spinning, fat wooden blades, the largest fan Elizabeth has ever seen, and as they stop so does the hideous noise.

"This must be a machine of the earthmen," Erin says.

"Yes," Elizabeth says, fear almost gone, "they must have come looking for Mattie."

"No, wait," says T.F. "It is a thing of Eastcountry. I have seen it before."

The lank, straight-backed figure of an Eastcountryman is distinguishable even at that distance. There are two of them climbing out of the flying box. T.F. crouches and pulls loso to the ground with him. Elizabeth and Erin step back to the nearest tree trunk.

"Is it so old then," Elizabeth asks, "that it came from earth with the grandfathers? Have the Eastcountrymen kept secret . . .?"

"No, they have just made it," T.F. tells her. "Or perhaps made some of it and used old parts for the rest. They cry to each other that they have not enough metal. But when I was there the machine never stayed up in the sky. It fell and killed one of them. Now they have made it work."

"They are going to the house!" Erin cries loudly and leaps forward "The baby!"

"They saw the roof from above," says T.F.

"Wait. Quiet," Elizabeth says.

"No. Let me go," Erin says, trying to pull free.

"Think, Erin. You can't fight them. They'll just capture you too."

"Elizabeth, you are the Eastcountry monster. You would let them take the baby and do horrible things to her, all the genetic experiments Mattie does on losobits. All you care about is yourself and your damn paints! I wish they had you instead. I wish . . ."

"They'll just let her grow more and then take her to your family as they would have if pregnant loso had not run away."

"Not all of them," says T.F. "Some they keep and work on, even humanborns."

Erin cries out again and Elizabeth groans. Speechless loso tries to touch them to fix whatever is wrong.

" 'Kay," Elizabeth says, sounding like Mattie in tone and word. "But let's plan. We'll go back to the house through the trees, around the open space. I wonder if they know we are here. Were they looking for us? Or just for runaway losos?"

Elizabeth rides on T.F.'s back. She asks him if he can fight an Eastcountryman. He doesn't know.

Will loso-that-carried-Mattie-and-Jack, who is now carrying Erin, will its take orders from the men? Most likely.

Elizabeth sighs and wonders what to do, and she worries for Erin, who is so fierce now that her face has less expression than loso's.

Silently they slip between the shrubs and trees and look through the tiny windows of the losos' house. They hear Thomas calling out.

"Cut out its tongue," says one man. He has smallloso Thomas pinned down on the eating table. When he laughs he sounds like the Eastcountryman who first captured them, but he is not that one, that Gabriel.

The other is opening a straw satchel, removing instruments, real metal; Elizabeth sees a scalpel like Mattie's.

T.F. roars beneath her, a sound of pain in no human language. As he runs around to the door, branches and twigs slap Elizabeth's face. Erin races behind on her own feet.

T.F. shouts, "Stop!" but it is too late. The forepart of a small pink tongue lies in a wash of blood on the floor next to the table. Elizabeth watches the blood run into the puddles of her forgotten sourberry stain, and mix in marbled swirls of red and purple. She notes the ugliness of the colors while T.F. breaks the Eastcountryman's neck and throws him down into it.

Erin is pressing the material of her skirts into Thomas's mouth, trying to staunch the blood, the endless flowing blood.

But the other man is moving, must have been moving, because he has already crossed the room away from the eating area. There, lying on the floor, still, is female loso and beside it the baby. The man is shouting commands at T.F.

T.F. ignores him, watches little Thomas dying, but speechless loso hears from outside and heeds. It comes in through the passageway and heads first for Erin who is covered in blood.

But the man calls loso, gives it the baby. Before they get to the door Erin has attacked. She punches and kicks loso. Loso ignores her but the man takes her up in his arms. He continues to stare with fear at T.F. but "Thomas's father" remains by the table. The talking loso is speechless.

Elizabeth has picked up the scalpel. Carrying it casually by her skirt, she runs over as if she too would attack loso with fists and feet. But she jumps up into riding position on its back and holds the blade at its throat. It pays no attention.

"Tell it to stop and give Erin the baby," she says to the Eastcountryman.

"Serene. Be serene, daughter. The beast does not know. It does not fear you. This is folly."

"I will cut its throat and then T.F.—the loso that talks— will kill you. We will all kill you."

He sees her now, listens. Erin has ceased struggling. T.F. now also watches and waits from across the room.

"Daughter!" the Eastcountryman roars but there is more of fear than of anger in the cords of his neck.

Elizabeth starts to draw the blade through the beast's flesh. Its blood begins to run. T.F. moves toward them, stalking slowly. The man's eyes shift to his companion dead on the floor.

He drops Erin and signals loso to give up the baby.

But T.F. keeps on coming.

"Stop, loso," the man commands, backing against the wall.

"Don't kill him," Elizabeth says.

"We need him," Erin says.

"I will tear out his tongue, not kill him." T.F. curls long dark fingers around the Eastcountryman's neck. Elizabeth stares at loso fingers, more familiar than humans', so commonplace that they have never been worthy of notice.

"No! No, T.F." Erin speaks like a father. "We need his tongue to tell us how to . . . how to win. Tie him. Unless he gives one wrong command to losos."

They bind his arms behind his back, tend to little loso who has stopped bleeding but still breaths. The female loso is alive, unconscious. T.F. sits by them silently. Loso is sent to the room above with the baby, away from any kind of signal the Eastcountryman might give.

Elizabeth stands near him later with the scalpel.

"Daughter," he says, "you cannot harm me. Perhaps you might, having been somehow corrupted, bewitched, actually damage the animal, but your serene nature, your innocence—"

"*Patricide.* No. You are only pretending to be a father. You do not believe what you are saying. I have heard an Eastcountrydoctor explaining to . . ." Elizabeth stops. The man seems not to know who she is. But surely he has come to find them, Mattie and the deranged Dagdan daughters.

"Why are you here?" Elizabeth asks him.

When he sneers and makes some remark about curiosity, she holds the blade against his face and repeats the question.

"You cannot understand these things," he says, this time matter-of-factly, without contempt.

Elizabeth finds herself tracing a line across his cheek with the edge of the blade. She sees Thomas's tiny tongue tip in its blood-and-berry puddle. This one did not do the cutting but he urged it. Were all Eastcountrymen so evil? Were these two—like Lucius—exceptions, sick ones? (Even Lucius would not do this.) She pulls her hand back so she will not be sick too.

"These animals are the results of a series of experiments which we have discontinued," he says in a monotone, as if to himself, complying rotely with her order. "Speech goes along with undesirable traits which the doctors could not eliminate. I am not a doctor. He," he nods his head in the direction of the body on the floor, "was a doctor."

"But why—?"

"The subjects got loose, took the host female with them. We had to get them back. That's all. And it's been the devil. The damn things are clever. That came with the tongue. They hid their tracks, disappeared completely. We had no chance until the copters were workable."

"Why did you do it?" Erin has come over to listen. "Why did you hurt little Thomas?"

"Thomas! A preparation with a name. It was calling to someone. It had to be silenced. The doctors were going to remove its speech anyway."

"Then he didn't come here after Mattie," Erin says.

"Sssh. Doctor, can you fix the smallloso?"

"No. I'm not a doctor, I told you. Look, you had better stop all this. Others are on their way here now."

"Is that true? How do they know where you are? How did you find the house?"

"We have ways. You are not able to understand these things . . . Where are your fathers? I wish to question them."

Elizabeth laughs aloud.

"Do you think he is telling the truth?" she asks Erin out of his hearing. "Or is it deceit? Are other Eastcountrymen coming here?"

"We have to leave. Even if he lies, they will search for them. For the—coppa?—the flying thing. And we have to find Mattie. Poor Mattie is lying there, hurt and starving. She is waiting, thinking I've just abandoned her. She probably thinks I've forgotten because we are empty and cot, not smart like Jack."

"No, she doesn't. She's the one who says—"

"She talks to him all the time, teaches him the things she used to teach me. You don't notice because you're not interested in most of it."

"We can't leave. What about female loso? The baby needs its milk. And little—"

"We'll all go this time," Erin says. "I'll drive the coppa. The Eastcountryman will show me how."

T.F. and loso will follow on foot. The others will ride, little Thomas, female loso, which is awake now, the baby, and Elizabeth with the scalpel to coerce the Eastcountryman's cooperation.

The Eastcountryman took much coercion to begin with and none at all after.

"Cut my throat directly," he tells Elizabeth. "I may as well be killed that way as to let this daughter fly the copter. Look. Let me loose and I'll fly you wherever you want to go."

They do not answer him. Elizabeth ties the cords to the base of one of the little stools and stands behind the man, scalpel ready. They lay Thomas at her feet behind the pilot's seat, baby squeezed in beside him while female loso sits on the floor in front of the man, feet dangling through the opening.

Erin studies the controls. If she has second thoughts, Elizabeth cannot tell. Elizabeth herself has second, third, and fourth thoughts. There are meaningless knobs, sticks, bentwood circles, all made of the newood except for some gauges or dials which appear to be real metal. She saw more pattern and purpose in the abstractions on the globes in Pater's library.

Erin apparently sees a design; she turns a knob, pulls a stick. When she reaches for a second, smaller knob, the Eastcountryman yells out, pleads, and then explains how to work the controls.

Elizabeth is glad it is Erin who must listen to all of it and not she. She thinks about skeds flying through the air. The ship of the earthpeople seemed another matter; they dropped from the sky.

The huge fan above suddenly bursts into noise. How will Erin hear the man's instructions?

Suddenly they are off the ground, rising up at an angle. Sweeping up, being pulled up and swinging sidewards at the same time, tipping. Elizabeth looks out and down and freezes in terror. They are all being poured out through the left-hand opening, but the thing rights itself with a sickening swing.

Elizabeth curses the moment she climbed into it. She curses the moment she left home, curses all of life's moments leading to this one.

The Eastcountryman is shouting into Erin's ear. His hands strain their bonds. Erin lets go of the stick she is holding and points toward the east. The man screams at her and the copter lurches and drops. Erin herself cries out but grabs the stick. They bounce and leap like losobits.

Then the copter turns or, Elizabeth hopes, Erin has turned it. They face a purple darkness rising toward them from the east. It is a deeper evening than Elizabeth has ever seen. And there is no horizon. To the south Venus and Bethlehem are brightening and directly down, now that Elizabeth dares to look, she sees the tiny trees and barren open spaces moving beneath them. Fear is enriched with beauty. And when she looks back she sees two fires, one is the setting sun and the other is the losos' house.

"Bring us down, daughter! Before dark." The Eastcountryman is pleading.

"Yes," Erin says, but they fly on. Elizabeth squats behind them, staring out, forward and down, hands vaguely checking Thomas, restraining the baby. Female loso sits, legs dangling, exactly as it was before they left the ground.

"See up there," Erin says. "That is the open space before the edge."

"Yes," the man shouts, "do not go over it! That is the great waterway. Stop. Go down, daughter."

"Is this the stick to move down . . . oh, I remember. The knob must always work with it . . . to the left?" Erin asks as they tilt suddenly face downwards and then as abruptly skyward.

"No! No!" he cries, trying to break his bonds. "We are going right over the edge. We can't make the other side. Go back! Turn, turn."

Elizabeth cannot imagine an edge. Straight below is blackness, while ahead is the normal evening blue and behind dim white light fading in the west.

As Erin tips them steeply in a huge arc and heads back the way they came, Elizabeth sees directly downwards a speck of orange, one spot in an immense swath of black. A tiny candle.

In a second it is gone and then the blackness with it has disappeared and they are low over a pale bare place and they are hitting and whacking the ground. Elizabeth is wrapped around the baby and little Thomas.

"Pull the rod! That one or you'll run us into the trees. Yes. Yes. Good," the Eastcountryman says.

There is a silence as mute and impenetrable as the blackness they escaped.

It is only hours later that Elizabeth makes any graphic sense of what she has seen. The Eastcountryman called it a waterway. Mattie and Jack fell into a gray emptiness, according to Erin. As they lie in their blankets with little Thomas between them, Elizabeth tells Erin about the globes, balls that are models of earths and the blue veins that trace yellow Dagda.

The Eastcountryman, tied to the large wooden leg of the copter, at first refuses to answer their questions. He grunts and curses in a language unknown to them.

When Thomas cries out in pain, Elizabeth says, "Now that you know how to fly the copter, Erin, we may as well take out the Eastcountryman's tongue.'

"And then cut his throat," Erin says.

"We are next to the great waterway," the Eastcountryman says. "Around here it runs half a mile below ground level. If you walk near the palisade in early white light, and some days at any time before afternoon, you will be in danger of falling off the edge which is obscured in mist."

"What was the bright orange dot we saw?"

"A fire. It may be Hans, the ropeferrry man. Someone has built a bonfire on the shore."

Waterway

Mattie thought she heard a sound. Beyond Jack's breathing, beyond the hissing and cracking of the fire, and beyond the swallowing and turning of the water, a tiny, mechanical sound, artificial. Machinery. It was gone. She must have been dreaming of Earth.

She shifted carefully to look at the fire. The darkness seemed to be just behind the flames. They slashed at it but could not cut into it. Its totality was more appalling on Dagda with its pallid night sky than on Earth where clouds often cover moon and stars. But down here in the bottom of the fiord, night was hours early and dense. The other system planets were too low in the southern sky to penetrate this fissure in the planet's surface.

Mattie imagined the sheer side of the escarpment rising close beside them, imagined the weight and height of the black atmosphere sitting on her chest and face. It was like the return of weight after freefall, burying and smothering. She forgot the tremendous width of the waterway and saw herself and Jack tunneled at the bottom of a narrow shaft, the bottom of the rabbit hole.

She tried not to tremble against him. Let sleeping lovers lie. Especially a lover who had discovered lovemaking only two days before and had since been trying to recover years of lost passion for himself and perhaps all his kind.

Mattie watched a trace of leaping light play against his lower lip. The jaw and mouth were wide and firm for such a boy. His Adam's apple was a cotty thing jutting up into the light, and his nose cast a crooked shadow. The upper part of his face was in shade but the bump on his forehead and the curls of hair above seemed to move with the fire.

The shadow of the cliff receded from her spirit and she smiled and stretched her feet in pleasure.

He woke her in early white light. The dark pearl air around them seemed to illuminate everything from within. Their skins were saintly white and even the gray water breaking along the shore beyond their feet was luminescent.

He touched her face, studied her throat as he stroked her jaw and felt the skin of her shoulder, and stopped to wonder at the shape and texture of her wrist.

She lay still, eased, watching him study and touch. She was not the teacher now but the lesson. His eyes still apologized as his hands followed the shape of the waist and hip and caressed her thighs. But when suddenly his fingers slipped between her legs, she gasped and arched her back. Now, she saw, he was watching her face.

Too late for a mask. Rueful, she had no choice but to move in pleasure to his hand and let him see her real nakedness. She was aware of his look, stern, too objective, until he made some sound himself and put his face down onto her.

Later they swam, tied to bushes on the shore with cord from Mattie's pack which they had spied and retrieved not far back up the cliff side. After that they ate more fish and the last of the pack food. And after that they made love again. And slept again.

Mattie decided that looking for a path back up the cliff could wait.

The sun, for the few hours at midday that it lit the bottom of the ravine, was too hot. They had to sit—and lie—shaded by a blanket draped from one of the scrubby trees, away from the banked fire which they needed so badly at night. She told him about the Frazan Wars while he counted and measured the toes on her left foot.

The machine noise, ugly and rough, was back, not a dream, growing louder. It came from above.

Mattie and Jack jumped to their feet and ran out from

under the trees, trying to see up into the white, bright sunlight.

"What is it?" Jack asked.

Mattie couldn't tell him. She hoped it was from the ship, her fathers ... her people come to find her. It seemed impossible. Could Kyly had been found out and then found? Perhaps his confederate—whoever it was and if Kyly had been telling the truth when he said a shipmate was working with him—had turned against him. Would they have been able to trace her through the forest in any case? With or without the help of the Dagdans?

The sound was too rough, crude and painful to the ears, no Earthmade thing. "Eastcountry!" Mattie said aloud. "We should hide. Run. They must have seen the blankets. Last night the fire. Why didn't you tell me they had flying machines?"

Jack looked at her blankly, pained, uncomprehending. "Mattie," he said, "is it something of Eastcountry?"

Too brightly backlit to be seen as more than a blurred silhouette, the machine grew larger overhead, its noise deafening as it reverberated from the cliff sides.

Jack stood gaping, awkward. Mattie was unaccountably annoyed with him. She realized that she did not know if he had been in the city and seen the Earth ship land. She had never thought to ask him.

She saw then that the thing was a helicopter, a crude, lopsided, wooden helicopter. The wind from the propeller whirled dust into their faces.

The pilot had red hair—and was Erin.

Picnic

The evening shadow has already reached the water's edge, covering and cooling them only two hours after noon, two hours after Erin landed the copter on one of the flat, grassy areas. Erin is angry with Mattie and will not speak. It is up to Elizabeth to tell her all, but Elizabeth is hypnotized by the water; she watches it, listens to it, but she has not approached it.

Jack lies close to Mattie, too close. He looks often toward the place where the Eastcountryman is tied and then back to Mattie's face. In spite of the cooling shade, Jack is sweating. The Eastcountryman looks at him and laughs loud, with heavy disgust. He has attempted to rouse Jack to help him, to free him from his contemptible captors. It seems to help Jack resist that the man's physical position is without fatherly or doctorly dignity.

Thomas lies awake but quiet. Mattie cursed and pounded the ground when she saw him. She wept that she had no medical or surgical supplies, no painkiller. It was then that the Eastcountryman looked at her, frowned. He said nothing.

"He is not an important person in Eastcountry," Erin said, not looking at Mattie, talking perhaps to the water. "Not a doctor. Just a mechanic. He does not understand even the simplist scientific principles."

It was then that Mattie began to laugh.

Elizabeth thinks it curious that Jack takes Mattie's hand—which Mattie quickly pulls away—but she has no mind or eyes for anything but the water. She cannot think to tell Mattie—and Jack—all that has happened. Each time she begins, the rush and roar swallow her thoughts. The water is so close and running and surging so powerfully that she cannot see what holds it back from swallowing her and the others on the shore. What controls and directs it? The seas and moats of her imagination did not look like this. But when Elizabeth tries to bring them back to her mind's eye, images she had held up until only two hours ago, she finds they are gone. *Obliterated* by the reality.

Still staring at the water, holding it away from them by her attention, Elizabeth tells all. Her own wielding of the scalpel is presented in the same abstract tone as the description of the dead Eastcountrydoctor and the fire far behind and below the fleeing copter where T.F. was burning his house.

Erin speaks finally to tell about the copter, its fuel supply, why they all had to land together in the ravine, why Ioso and T.F. will come on foot to meet them.

"Oh, yes, there is more fuel," she answers Mattie's question, "but not an excessive amount. According to the gauge and to him." Erin nods her head toward the Eastcountryman.

"What kind of fuel?" Mattie asks. "It must be some kind of vegetable fermentation . . . Perhaps an oil of . . ." She redirects her question, calling over to the Eastcountryman. "What is your fuel?"

He merely snorts but his expression belies his tone. He seems afraid of Mattie. But Elizabeth knows from what he said at the Iosos' house that he was not searching for her. His business was only to retrieve three loose lab animals.

"Do you know who I am?" Mattie asks him.

Again he snorts but he looks away from her, down at his bound wrists.

"Let Elizabeth encourage an answer with the scalpel," Erin says.

Jack scrambles to his fee. "No!" He moves toward the place where the man is tied as if to defend or free him.

"Stop, Jack," Mattie says.

Jack slows but does not stop. His face is torment. Elizabeth feels sympathy for him. It is the first time she has ever seen a man as an object of pity.

Elizabeth knows that Jack feels at the sight of daughters rising up against a man, especially an Eastcountryman, the way she feels at the sight of the water.

When Mattie stands and walks toward him, Jack stops, then turns down toward the water away from them all. They watch him walk north along the shore until he dwindles out of sight.

Erin laughs and, when Mattie glares at her, looks angry again. She rises and goes to the copter, her copter, and becomes preoccupied in adjusting instruments and straightening seats.

Together Mattie, Elizabeth, and the scalpel persuade the Eastcountryman to help Elizabeth draw two maps: one of their immediate location and the other of a overview of Plain, Fian, Eastcountry, the waterways, and the railroad. "He may not know 'scientific principles,' " Mattie says, "but as pilot, he ought to be an excellent cartographer."

"Damn," she adds, "Eastcountry is more north than east."

Mattie questions the pilot further about all sorts of things, only some of which have meaning for Elizabeth. She can tell, however, that they are not the doctor things, genetics and biology, that Mattie discussed with that other Eastcountryman, the always-smiling Gabriel, when she was the captive, back at the forest station.

"Gabriel? How do daughters know of the great doctor?" the man asks, expressing his first open curiosity. He had until now covered his helplessness and loss of power with a variety of postures: indifferent patience, outraged disbelief, patronizing weariness, and sometimes amused contempt.

"Don't you know who I am?" Mattie asks him.

He shakes his head.

"I'm the doctor from the earthship. The 'woman' doctor."

"I know better than that, witch. The earthdaughter is in Eastcountry. We have her. You'll not trick me."

"Then how do you account for me? Us?" Mattie glances at Elizabeth.

"I don't account for you. The doctors have to account. They let some females go. Some from Deech, others. It's their business."

"Gudrun?" Mattie asks.

"Her nephew is the ropeferry man. He should be along soon."

Mattie and Elizabeth look at each other inquiringly. And Mattie questions the man more about other Eastcountrymen. Are they searching? Where? How? Did he say there was more than one of the helicopters?

What is happening between Eastcountry and the earthpeople? He says only that there are meetings, arrangements. What is it to some wild daughters and a deranged farmerson? Where? In the city? In Eastcountry? Is the earthman Kyly in Eastcountry? Any other earthperson? Yes and yes and yes.

They trust none of his answers nor the accuracy or validity of the maps. Tricksters. All Eastcountrymen are elves, Gudrun said. And this man may, as Erin said, be no one, not a doctor, politically unimportant and uninformed.

As they walk away from him, female loso approaches to tend to him. They see Erin holding the baby, showing her the water—from a distance.

Mattie urges Elizabeth to the water's edge. Elizabeth holds back. Every time she forgets the water or believes she has grown accustomed to it, it takes her by surprise with a rush of sound and motion as though it had gone away and suddenly come back.

But now there is pleasure in it.

"I'm immunized to further shock," Elizabeth tells Mattie as they wade into the water.

But it isn't true.

The next early white light is not very light or white. The eerie dimness is a color Elizabeth has never seen before and is stained by the embers of the banked fire. Elizabeth unwraps her blanket quietly so as not to disturb the baby or Thomas, stands and walks around the fire and away from the camp to go to the water again and to think what colors to paint it. As if she will ever paint again.

To her surprise, she sees another, small fire at the water's edge.

Elizabeth crosses the grassy plain, climbs and stumbles over a rough incline, and walks along the narrow stretch that passes for a beach.

Someone is lying on a blanket near the fire. Two people. One is on top of the other. Jack. Jack is on someone. Mattie moans. What is he doing to Mattie! Elizabeth starts forward.

"Wait." A whisper from the dark behind her. Erin grabs Elizabeth's arm, holds her back.

"Erin! Erin, Jack is . . ."

"She likes it. She's doing it too."

"How do you know?"

"Ssh. I've been watching them . . . for awhile."

When Elizabeth wakes a second time that day, the mist is light white, just changing from opaque to translucent. The sun is burning deep into the shaft in the earth, drying up the vapors. The brightness hurts her eyes while the palisades far across the water loom dark as night.

There is a good smell. Jack is nearby pulling cooked fish out of the fire. He puts one on a bread cake Erin and Elizabeth brought from the losos' house and takes a huge bite. Elizabeth studies him for awhile, watching his large, lean shape, his mouth as he chews. He pays no attention to her at all, doesn't notice if she wakes or sleeps. But when Mattie approaches, his face glows.

"I have food here, Mattie," he says. "Come eat with me." He pats the ground next to him.

But Mattie only frowns and shakes her head.

"Let me try to feed Thomas," she says and busies herself preparing some kind of meal that he can swallow with little pain.

Farther around the fire Erin is trying to feed the baby some mushed fish and grain, a gruel that is almost liquid. She offers some to Mattie for Thomas and smiles at her.

Elizabeth sees that Erin is no longer angry with Mattie and she knows it has everything to do with what they saw last night. ". . . The sons of God came in unto the daughters of men . . ." Sperm and ova and DNA and genetic something. Why would Mattie want a baby now?

Female loso has disappeared somewhere, perhaps to find losobits.

The Eastcountryman walks in arcs, back and forth at the end of his rope. He does not face their way, misses the looks of hate Mattie sends him as she tries to get food into Thomas and avoid the horrible stump of his tongue.

The fish Elizabeth is eating does not taste good anymore.

"Look!" Erin cries. "I think I see something near the top. It must be losos coming. T.F."

Elizabeth sees two small moving figures about a fourth of the way down the cliff side. It is not the place Mattie said she and Jack descended. It appears less *precipitous*.

It is strange to bend one's neck and look so high up at something.

"They are men, not losos," Elizabeth says.

They put all their food and most important supplies into the copter and climb in themselves and wait. Jack is nervous and seems about to jump out but looks constantly toward Mattie and stays. The Eastcountryman laughs over and up at them from where they have left him tied and awaiting rescue. Erin's fingers play over the controls. They remind Elizabeth of her own empty, idle twitching for her brushes.

"Wait, Erin," Mattie says. "Let's see who they are."

"There is no man that it can be who will not imprison us," Elizabeth says.

"Except the Eastcountryman who is our prisoner and Jack, who is yours, Mattie," Erin adds.

Mattie does not answer and Jack seems only confused. It grows hot in the copter. The baby cries. Thomas makes no sound or movement but they know he suffers. They climb out of the copter and lay some blankets in the shade.

When they take out some food and eat again, the figures

are still small, halfway down the escarpment. The evening shadow is crossing the water.

The two men grow in size. They are tied together with long ropes, carry pickaxes, and wear large backpacks. One of them has only one arm.

Then Mattie is shouting, jumping to her feet. "Parn!"

They watch her race across the grassy place and a distance up the culvert to one of the strangers. She throws her arms around him, jumps and shrieks and laughs.

The rest follow Mattie more slowly and meet her and the visitor halfway. By this time, blue dark has arrived.

Mattie tells them that Parn, her colleague, has come searching for her with a "native" guide, Hans, the ropeferry man. (Erin and I are Mattie's native guides, Elizabeth thinks.)

"These are Elizabeth, Erin, Jack, and the baby, my friends," Mattie says.

Erin and Elizabeth do not bowcurtsy. Elizabeth remembers his face, the dark eyes. HIs skin looks red and sore now.

"I think I remember you," he says to Erin and looks at her seriously. "It that a helicopter? How . . ."

"Parn, tell me how you found me. Kyly said . . . What has been happening with our mission? How have you come this far?"

Doctor Parn laughs and puts his arm around Mattie's shoulder. She looks merely uncomfortable now and does not hug him again.

"Parn, please. What is the worst? Am I a wanted criminal among my own people and the Dagdans? Are you—we—working with Eastcountry? I don't know how much you know about them. Kyly thinks . . . Parn, will you talk?"

"How can I?" Parn smiles at Jack who does not smile back.

Mattie waits silently then.

"We have had great difficulty all around," Parn says, serious finally. He looks around the circle of faces in the deepening dark, Erin, Jack, Elizabeth, even the baby, watching him wide-eyed. Hans has moved over to the fire and is adding wood to it. "Look, Mattie, shouldn't we talk privately?"

"No. They have been with me. There is nothing they cannot hear." Elizabeth has doubts about Jack.

"Mattie this is delicate stuff. Let's talk alone first."

"No." Mattie is angry now. "Tell me what I want to know," she shouts. Jack reaches for her hand, frowns at Parn. Parn frowns back.

"There's the official version and the private version. Privately we're all on your side. The OC, Delt Marker, everyone."

"So you're not here to take me back, lock me up?"

"Well, that's the private version. Officially we have to 'assume another posture,' as Delt Marker says. Only if we claim that you have disobeyed us, are acting on your own against orders, will the natives cooperate with us at all."

"Damn! Nothing has changed. What the hell have you being doing all this time? Sitting in the dumb ship. Everything and everyone the same. It seems impossible. How long has it been?"

"Look, Mattie, it's because of you that our work has been held up. The natives won't trust us. Until—"

"Hah! You cotton-headed losobit! Don't you know that that's just an excuse? They—Eastcountry elves—are using me. They would not cooperate even if I had never existed. If you had no women with you, don't you see? They don't want earth anywhere near their real work."

"It's not Eastcountry. It's the Plainsmen. The Eastcountrydoctors are acting as mediators, trying to conciliate, to move the farmers from their rock-hard position. Without them . . ."

Mattie howls and then laughs. She grabs Parn's wrist and pulls him after her.

"I'll show you an Eastcountryman, an enlightened spiritual adviser. Over here."

Just as she turns around there is a horrible noise, nerve-and-ear-destroying. The propellers are spinning, the helicopter body shuddering. The Eastcountryman sits in the pilot's seat. The thing rises up and slides away sidewards at the same time. They all stand stupidly in its wind.

"My copter!" Erin screams.

Elizabeth listens to them talk all night. Mattie tells Parn many of the things that have happened to them. The early parts interest Elizabeth most, before Mattie joined the daughters, and even more, when they first left Brens, when Elizabeth had not yet understood things. She is amused when Mattie's view of what happened differs from her own, and she notices that Mattie sometimes strongly edits and even lies.

Most important, Mattie argues, illustrates, pleads her case against the Eastcountrydoctors. Parn is first amazed and then believing when she tells him about Kyly and the doctor called Gabriel. She shows Parn Thomas's tongue.

Parn is disgusted. "They did this without anesthetizing the animal? Why? What was the purpose of the procedure anyway?"

Mattie says that he is missing the horror of it but he still cannot believe that the loso ever spoke.

"You mean animal-like noises that communicate some basic types of meaning? You always did anthropo—"

"No," Elizabeth interrupts from the darkness, "real language. He spoke exactly as we do and so does T.F."

Anthropomorphism. Delicious word. Elizabeth heard it once before from Mattie.

Jack and Erin, with her losoless baby, are invisible in the nearby darkness, wrapped individually in blankets, but Elizabeth knows they are listening.

"I believe you, Mattie," Parn says several times even while he argues evidence with her. "It's just that our experience with these people has been so different. We see the Plainsmen all the time. We try to barter with them using technology as the goods. We coddle, cajole, go so far as to assume their piety and creed. Pretend to be as righteous as they are."

There is a vague sound from Jack.

"We seem to be getting somewhere and then it all comes to nothing.

"They do not try to stop us from investigating the uncultivated areas, the natural wilderness. Rol and I have learned a great deal about the indigenous plant systems. And of course, Sem the Doc has been out in the field most of the time too. The first thing we did was to put together the land vehicles. Sem the Doc twice brought specimens back to the ship's labs but you weren't there to—"

"And have you found the answer to our first and most important question," Mattie asks, "how earth life survives in this alien biosystem?"

"Yes and no."

"Changed food," Erin says.

"Yes. Yes, of course, we were able to 'appropriate' some of the cultivated crops. They could not watch all the fields," Parn says. "We identified some of them as variations of earth plants, of course; we expected that. With traits adoptive to the native soil and fixed for the specific elements of this system, crossbreeding seems to have been possible. They were incredibly lucky."

"It wasn't luck. It was Eastcountry," Mattie says. "They *fused* imported earthplant crops and native Dagdan. They fixed some of the wild Dagdan plants to be adaptive to the needs of earth life-forms, and they changed the DNA—"

"I can't believe they could have the manpower to add DNA to all the developing plant embryos!"

"Parn, you are not listening to me. They are far beyond that. They have created new species by genetic manipulation."

"But they are so primitive. Except for the train and . . ."

"Has any one of us been to Eastcountry?"

"No," Parn says. "We meet the Eastcountrymen semiformally, with and without the Plainsmen, always in the city. They act as moderators, referees in a way. Intellectually and socially they are head and shoulders above the farmers, but technologically? If anything they are a kind of nonreligious priest class . . ."

"I know. I know. Kyly told me all that. It is pure bull."

Bull, Elizabeth later discovers in her dictionary, is a male earth animal.

"Well, Kyly has learned the truth by now. We know he is in Eastcountry—studying their 'folkways.' "

They lie in silence for awhile. The man Hans snores from around the fire. Jack raises himself on an elbow and stares across too big a space to Mattie. In the light of the flames, his features are as young and beautiful as a child's. The baby whimpers and a dark figure suddenly blocks the light. Long arms reach to Erin. It is female loso returned to nurse. Parn jumps.

"It's just loso," Erin says and smiles at him.

Ferry

"I work for myself," Hans said. "Eastcountry uses my services; they cross over the water both ways. When their bridge is finished, they won't need me."

"But do you ferry anyone else, anyone but Eastcountrymen? It seems you really do work for them."

"Nuh. Sometimes, once a year or two, a pair of my countrymen, Deechmen, come to Plain, to the city and to the farms to trade—when Eastcountry lets them. Them I ferry across."

"Do they go to Eastcountry too?" Mattie asked.

"Hah. No. No one goes to Eastcountry." Hans looked back at Mattie over his left shoulder, the one with the empty sleeve, and winked.

"And your aunt, Gudrun . . . ?"

"My great-great-aunt. She thinks I'm her brother. He was probably my great-grandfather. It was in his time she came here. Exiled from Deech."

"Exiled," Elizabeth whispered.

"Why?" Mattie asked.

"Who's Gudrun?" Parn asked.

"An elderly doctor, a healer," said Elizabeth.

"A good witch," said Erin.

"A crazy old Deechwoman," said Hans.

"An excellent host," said Mattie. "You remember, Parn, I told you about the old woman in the forest. We stayed in her cottage for awhile. Hans, is she an enemy of Eastcountry or their tool?"

Hans was silent for awhile. He climbed over a pile of earth and reached back with his only arm to help the others after him. It was their second day walking, climbing, struggling northward along the water's edge to Hans's ropeferry.

They were all on foot, strung together, the baby on Parn's back.

"You might be asking the same question of me," Hans said finally.

It had occurred to Mattie that Hans might be an Eastcountry agent. And not the unwitting and unwilling tool that Gudrun probably was. Why had he told Parn nothing of the real nature of the Eastcountrymen during the days he had guided him through the driwood and then the wild forest bordering the water? Why had he not warned Parn that the train ride the Eastcountrymen had so generously offered, that took him so many miles north and east in the right direction, was without a doubt a means to a very ungenerous end? She wondered what the plan was. To capture both her and Parn? But they thought they had her already. They thought Ariella was Mattie, at least they had thought so up until the time the pilot and doctor had left in the helicopter seeking the escaped losos. Mattie was certain the man had not been lying about that. And the map he had helped them draw was accurate according to Hans. Unless, of course, Hans was lying.

He was taciturn; his friendly face, misleading. His accent was not as strong as Gudrun's but his speech was guttural, sometimes unintelligible. He seemed unused to conversing. The Eastcountrymen rarely spoke to him beyond simple requests and directions.

When they camped for the night, Mattie asked him more questions about Deech. Since his youth he had visited his home only once. It was more than a harvest away.

And that's what had saved it—only somewhat and only so far—from Eastcountry. Distance. Hans shook his head over Eastcountry's latest invention, the helicopter. That would change everything. Somehow he didn't see the Earth people, with their star ship and incomprehensible technology, as threatening to Deech's autonomy and way of life as this primitive, wooden, inefficient, mechanical flying machine. Maybe he didn't believe in them. Maybe they were so alien as to be practically irrelevant.

But Eastcountry had for the last century increasing

control—even long-distance. They had the ability to change food, to produce sufficient crops, to obtain goods, technological devices like the driwood and now newood, water pumps, and medicine.

Through the first four centuries of its history, independently of the far more advanced Eastcountrydoctors, Deech had kept and developed some knowledge of medicine brought to Dagda with its own emigrant ancestors. Women like Gudrun were "healers," and the descendents of healers. But a couple of generations ago Eastcountry had put an end to it—an end to independent doctoring. They withheld necessary life-support technology and goods. They never shared the ability to change food. Now they took away the ancestral changed seeds and plasma. Deechmen had to succumb. Only distance prevented total submission.

So too with their females. Not so bad as in Plain and Fian but going in the same direction. Three generations ago women had come too to this side of the world.

Gudrun, in her own time, had been a holdout, both as a doctor and as an autonomous woman. At least that was how the story went. It was already becoming a whispered legend in Han's time. Gudrun's many brothers had tried to protect her but others, afraid of what measures Eastcountry might take against them, had given her up to the elves.

No, Deechwomen were not like the daughters. They were still . . . Hans could not go on with this subject in front of Mattie, Elizabeth, and Erin. He had been a long time in this part of the world.

His own position? He shrugged his shoulders. He thought of himself as an independent operator, taking people from one side of the water to the other. That's all.

The decision to go with Hans to his ferry place had been unanimous. The helicopter was gone—with much of their supplies. They had been living on the fish, some packed food that Parn and Hans had left, and a bit of changed food that they had taken back out of the helicopter before the Eastcountryman repossessed it. They had only a few blankets. Everything else was gone. Hans said he had plenty of food and supplies in his cabin.

They had to leave their place on the water in any case. The Eastcountryman had escaped. Erin doubted the copter had enough fuel to get the man all the way back to Eastcountry, and, since it was such a new invention, perhaps they had not yet placed fuel stations around the country. But they couldn't count on that. They had to get away, to hide.

Parn was convinced. He wanted to warn the OC immediately, but he saw that to go back the way he had come was impossible.

At one point the edge of the water became impassable for a few miles and Hans led them up and around that stretch. So on their second night, they made camp on a wide, flat step a fourth of the way up the cliff side. They kept themselves loosely roped together. They made no fire for fear of being seen either from the air—unlikely yet—or from the top of the cliff. They ate the little dry food they had left. Except for the baby, who had loso to nurse, they were all hungry.

In the unrelieved dark, they lay silent for a while in spite of still having so much left untold, so much yet to discuss, to decide. With Parn's arrival Erin and Elizabeth had returned to serenity and daughterly quiet, not quite the dumb obliteration they had undergone when they were among the men who took them from Gudrun's cottage, or the sulky silence when Jack had first become human and left his cell in the losos' house. Mattie did not understand their silent anger during that time, nor why they had suddenly—overnight—become friendly to her again. Yet she realized, lying there tied to all of them, they had changed toward her. They seemed not so awed, not so humble . . . That wasn't it; they had never been humble.

With Parn they were shy but not blank. Erin, Mattie thought, might even be flirting.

Jack was a problem. Mattie did not understand his silence. Whenever he had to speak to Parn or Hans, he resumed his fatherly manner, was polite but brief, in content said nothing at all. He ignored Elizabeth and Erin almost as completely as he did Ioso. He looked often and long at Mattie but said nothing in front of the others and they were always now in front of the others, day—and night.

Since they were always together, except of course when one or two of the males or females went into the water or behind a bend, she could not tell Parn about them. She could not say, "Jack is wonderfully smart, quick to learn, eager and alive, not the solemn figure he presents." Or "Elizabeth creates worlds in paint and is in love with language. She has a mind made of different stuff from yours and mine." Or "Erin will be a master engineer. She can understand any mechanical or physical thing. Her logic—her reasoning is incredible."

Once, as she walked close behind Parn over particularly difficult terrain, she had said a little of it.

"They're just children," he said, interrupting her, "especially the boy. You've been alone with them too long and have lost perspective. Do you see yourself as their mother or is it as their teacher?"

She had not tried again.

"When we get back to the ship," Parn said in the dark, "we'll be able to deal with the whole thing. By 'we' I mean all of us, the OC, Delt Marker, you, me. You didn't waste your time, Mattie. You learned the truth. That changes everything.

"You know I'm the last person to be a company man, a member of the crew."

It was strange to listen to Parn in a dark so complete that not even his eyes might glisten meaningfully, without seeing his dramatic posturing, his dark, lost-poet looks. Was this the voice and mind of the person she had shared a small lab with for two years and a hammock for two nights? He had liked to see himself as an alien among his peers, the isolate, misunderstood, sensitive one. But now he sounded like an Earth man.

"You know how angry I get when they spoil my research

with their cowardly regulations. Most scientists, even the good ones, are as lacking in spirit, as unimaginative about everything but the particulars of their own fields, as these farmers."

Jack sat up. "Father," he said.

"I'm sorry," Parn said. "I really am, Jack. I'm tired and frustrated. I feel like a prisoner. It's ironic, Mattie; you escaped from prison and the rest of us became prisoners. Oh, yes, we get off the ship. In fact, we've set up a camp in the landing field to stretch and move away from each other. We go as far as we like in the uncultivated areas. For me that's been the good part. My work. But we may as well be studying an uninhabited planet. We go into the city, meet the natives—men, all men—except for old Racey I haven't seen one woman until now. We meet again and again. We approach their farms. We ask questions. But except for Kyly we get no answers. And Kyly stopped telling us his. Now I know why."

"You're asking the wrong people," Mattie said.

"Don't think we didn't try subterfuge. With and without official sanction. The OC, as I started telling you before, isn't so bad."

"I always thought so. I had thought so . . ." Mattie was glad they couldn't see her face in the dark.

"Huh. Why not? He's doted on you from the beginning."

"That's ridiculous. He's . . . he's old. He could be my . . ."

"It's funny, Mattie," Elizabeth said. "Ariella said you hoped a prince would come, your shipfather."

"You do not understand any of this, Elizabeth!" Elizabeth was instantly quiet and Mattie sorry.

"Kyly began to strike out on his own right after you left. He disappeared for longer and longer periods. We thought he had somehow insinuated himself with the fa—the Plainsmen and we really didn't care that he was operating behind our backs. I mean we resented his supercilious attitude, so knowing and at the same time so damned unaware of what was right before his face, but we hoped any breakthrough he made would be a chance for all of us. He didn't seem to be with Eastcountrymen any more than we were. But then we didn't know where he was when he was away. We just couldn't understand why they accepted him and not the rest of us."

"Who was he working with?"

"What? Eastcountry. You've shown me that."

"No. I mean . . ." Mattie stopped, listened for Hans's snores. "I mean on the ship. One of us."

"No one. What do you mean?"

"He told me that he and another person contracted with Eastcountry. I said it was treason."

"You didn't tell me this." Parn's voice became cold in the dark.

"There's been so much to tell and ask. We have hardly covered anything. I just didn't think of it before. He may have been lying."

"And he gave you no clue as to who it is?"

"No."

Erin dangled the baby's feet in the water. Early sun, which had just burned through the vapors, touched her red hair and the baby's tufts of red curls. Erin's skin still had the pure tones of a woman shielded all her life from harsh rays. Parn was watching her. Mattie started to tell him Erin's story of her family's genetically changed skin. What greater evidence that in the biological sciences the Eastcountrydoctors were centuries beyond Earth's physical engineering technologies?

"She is so beautiful," Parn said. "And her baby. Lovely, gentle person. Delicate—female."

"You should see her fly a helicopter after a one-minute lesson and kick and punch the Eastcountryman. And I told you again and again the nature of the baby's birth."

"What insane bastards they must be," Parn said.

Hans said they were a half day south of his ropeferry. They would make it easily the next day. They stopped early at a rough, crooked place on the shore so they could cook fish in a daytime, invisible fire and then swim, wash their clothes, and do nothing.

When they compared maps, Parn's turned out to be wrong—according to Hans. Naturally the ship's maps of the geographical planet had the plateaus and waterways right, and the historical preWar maps of the landing places and early Anunne settlements were no doubt valid. But the one of current human populations and places, designed for him by the Eastcountrymen, was just wrong enough to confuse and deceive. The map Elizabeth had drawn was almost perfect. Hans nodded at it but refused to add any more details.

Mattie saw Jack watching Parn as he scrutinized the maps. She couldn't read his expression, but it definitely wasn't the benign oldfather. He looked both angry and puzzled. She remembered the young men at Brens greeting each other with the bland, polite indifference of elderly functionaries.

She rose, stretched, walked over to him, whispered with her lips. When he rose the others seemed not to notice. Erin was bringing Parn more fish—Mattie shook her head at that—Elizabeth drew pictures in the sand for little Thomas, and baby slept at Ioso's nipple.

As soon as they turned out of sight around an uneven jut in the cliff wall, he reached for her. Pulled her against him, leaned with her against the wall, pressed himself hard length on her length, hard his thighs on hers. She felt the width of his rib cage, his breath in it, put her mouth on the roughness of his throat, moved up to take his mouth. But he was already pulling her down to the ground, hands under her ragged tunic. She helped slide off the things that passed as his trousers with her feet, left her feet high on his hips, like hands walking up the wall. She had meant to go into the water first, to play wet first, but it was too late.

Why did Jack have to be so awkward and inarticulate in front of Parn? His attempts to hide in the oldfather role exaggerated his clumsiness and insecurity. Whenever Mattie tried to bring him out, encourage him, ask him questions she knew he knew the answers to, he stumbled verbally, blushed and then sulked.

She sometimes thought Parn deliberately tried to make a fool of him. Yet she had no evidence. He was extremely polite to Jack, deferred to his judgment—but on subjects on which Jack had no basis for judgment.

The ropeferry had been built where the distance from shore to shore was narrowest. Farther north the ravine was as wide as it had been at their original campsite. It almost made an hourglass figure on the map.

But if narrower, it was also steeper on both sides. The relative hardness of the geologic material accounted for both conditions.

So it was that Hans's cabins, one on each shore, were cut into the cliff face, handmade caves with wooden façades. The steps leading up from the water (there was no beach at all here) and down from the planet surface above were concave, each sloping toward the center from centuries of feet.

In addition there were a great number of ropes hanging down from above on both sides of the cabin. Most hung away from the cliff and were held away by wooden arms intermittently placed as far up as they could see. There were several wooden platforms, each tied to four ropes, primitive elevators, probably operated with tackles and pulleys from above.

On the water below the cabin was the ferry, a huge raft floating among a number of smaller odd craft, dingies, boxes, great cups, normal-sized rafts. On the main raft were sails, folded but upright, ready. The whole flotilla was hooked to the thick multiple ropes, draped incredibly from this shore extending, presumably, to the opposite.

Mattie was glad to be inside a real structure again. It seemed luxurious to everyone but Parn. There were many bunks with cotton mats, real cotton sheets, blankets; the larder contained a great supply of dried foods, a kind of soap—Parn sniffed at it in disgust—paper napkins, cups, plates. And books—in Deech. There was not a fireplace but a place for a fire, far back where the floor became part of the cliff.

There were shelves full of clothes, trousers and tunic tops and the imitation formal jackets the native men wore—Plainsmen and Eastcountry. And straw slippers and wooden clogs.

People were wet on the crossing, Hans explained. These were communal things. For all travelers, for him himself, and, yes, primarily for the Eastcountrymen as they went back and forth from their homes and laboratories to the fields and newood forests on the other side of the water and wherever else they went; Hans didn't really know. Who else was there to use them? One or two of his own countrymen. No one else. The men of Plains and Fian had no means or reason to come so far. They did not know of the existence of the water.

"We do," Jack insisted, a rare occasion when he spoke in front of Parn. "It is . . . unseemly, unnecessary . . . Our obligations to our work . . . Childish indulgence of . . ."

Parn's laughter cut him off.

"Try these pants, Jack," Mattie said. "They seem long enough for you." Parn was shorter than Jack.

Elizabeth and Mattie dressed themselves in tunic tops that reached below their knees and long socks for their lower legs. Erin found the only small trousers in the batch and tucked into them a too-large, pale gray shirt. Parn said she looked like a redheaded mushroom and she threw slippers at him although she didn't know what a mushroom was.

Jack and Elizabeth froze then, open-mouthed. Erin blushed as she had not in a very long time and Mattie was annoyed with every one of them.

"If we march all together, openly," Mattie said, "right into Eastcountry, what can they do? I wish there were more of us from the ship, but what can we do? I wish that we could send a message to the OC . . . to the ship, but we can't. Your fingercube is worthless from this distance. We have no choice. We can't both just disappear. They wouldn't dare. We'll go 'boldly together'—'stouthearted men.' "

"Mattie," Parn was whispering so that the others in the inner room, near the fire, might not hear. "We'll go back to the ship. Yes, we'll take your friends. Nothing will happen to them. And then we can come back stronger, protected. When the OC learns—"

"He'll never let me come with you. And I have to go there. I have to. I have to see their work."

"You could have gone with Kyly."

"Don't you believe me even now? I was tied. By Kyly. That Eastcountrydoctor—Gabriel." Mattie hid her shudder from Parn.

"Look, Mattie . . ."

"I forgot how often you guys—you fathers!—said, 'Look, Mattie.' "

"Lo—Mattie, you're not being rational. You'll finally know everything they know whether you actually go there in person or not. There is no reason to take this risk. And what about the girls—Erin . . ."

"That's another reason. I promised. Lucilla."

"Who the hell is Lucilla?"

"I don't know."

They laughed then so that the others came to look in on them through the door.

"It's Ariella," Mattie said finally. "She took my place. Who knows what they are doing to her? She's wearing my fingercube but she doesn't know what it is or how to use it . . .

"Parn? Have the Eastcountrymen been in the ship? In the control room? Have they seen our equipment?"

"Yes. It was part of a bargain. The OC and some of the rest of us were against it, but Delt Marker thought it was a good idea. He consulted Kyly . . . this was before Kyly disappeared for good . . . and they decided that psychologically or morally or some damn way it would show our trust and good intentions. What harm could it do? They would understand none of it and maybe be impressed, all right—intimidated. Kyly assured us that, from his professional observations, their stage of cultural and religious development and the social stability inherent in the political balance between Eastcountry and the others protected them from any serious dislocation or something like that."

"They need metal," Mattie said. "They have been crippled without it. They have been recycling so little so long."

"But the rest, our software . . ."

"That too. But they have much of it already. You underestimate what their ancestors came here with. Blueprints. The programs. The knowledge and concept. Some old equipment, instruments, paneling, gauges, tools, other stuff from all the original ships, theirs and the other colonists'. But it's wearing out and used up. The controls on the helicopter had to have come off something else. They have the word but not the flesh. Yes, they have been getting there without us. Look at the newood. It seems to have more flexibility than metal and no more porosity, but how heat-resistant can it be? How durable? Think what our ship would mean to them."

"It's not logical. They could get so much more by working with us. All of Earthstates' materials and technology."

"And biology . . . I don't think that's what they want . . . What did they do in the ship? What did they say? What did they look at?"

"Nothing. They didn't know what they were looking at. At least that's what I thought then . . . damn Kyly! He had us thinking our nervousness was paranoia. Anyway I wasn't in the control room with the Eastcountrymen. Just Kyly and the OC."

"Did they come into our lab? Did they look at my things?"

Parn shut his eyes. " 'Kay. Let me picture it. I told them a little about the botany; one of them seemed to follow. Anyway he listened, appeared interested. And then I noticed the other guy over on your side. I don't know what he had been doing. He was near old Barney's cage.

"By God, Mattie! The cabin boy said the female was missing. But that might have been some other time, maybe earlier. Maybe not. I never put it together."

"When was this?"

"A week or so after you left. One of the parts of the bargain was that they would help us get you back. That they would keep the Plainsmen calm and as ignorant as possible of your being somewhere on planet."

"So did they? How? Why did it take so long?"

"They gave us many leads, false I see now, and excuses. I really think they didn't know where you were themselves for a long time. Even now they weren't sure. They told us you were in this area somewhere, that Hans might be able to pick up your traces."

"You see that they thought they were making a fool of you? They believed, maybe still do, that they had me. That's why it was safe to help you look at last. I wonder if Rebekah and Ariella still have them fooled.

"And what about the natives who have been running with me? Kyly said I was disturbing some basic cultural mores. Endangering a natural societal evolution—that might have values that we cannot now understand but that some day we might adopt to our benefit."

They laughed again and Mattie watched Parn in the dim light coming through the front entrance and tiny windows of Hans's cabin. The backpack was gone; he was no longer upright and ready for marching or climbing, or wrapped compactly in a blanket. With his head thrown back, the dark lock over one eye, and his legs thrust out and all the way across a little table, he looked as he had so often in freefall, that space was his to fill and he filled it lightly, with the grace and consciousness of a water-ballet dancer.

Erin alone came through the doorway from the inner room and she too watched Parn. Mattie wondered what he looked like to her after the stiff, immobile dignity of all the men and boys she had ever known.

Boat

The sun shone directly down from overhead. For two hours the water in front of the cabin would be ultramarine, instead of its usual cobalt blue. There were glints of aqua near the shore and true green in places where the eddies and current were so rough the small waves jumped up and folded back upon themselves. The sky that showed itself between the palisades north and south of them was a real "sky" blue, not the blank, whitewashed vague color it appeared from the planet surface.

The colors of Earth oceans and Earth skies. Mattie was homesick. It was a pain that gave her some pleasure to poke.

Elizabeth had found some charcoal sticks among the cabin's supplies and was sketching the prospect from a perch next to Mattie and Jack on the small deck attached to the cabin. She scowled as she failed to catch the three dimensions. Mattie looked from the drawing to the reality and could not help.

"There are techniques you can learn for things like this," she told Elizabeth. "It has nothing to do with your talent."

But Mattie knew that Elizabeth knew that Mattie didn't know what she was talking about.

Jack looked only at Mattie but he obeyed her earlier injunction not to touch her in front of anyone else and later not to touch her at all without warning.

Parn appeared and disappeared as he poked about among the ropes and tackle on the ferry below. He shouted questions to Hans who was out of sight, doing something at the base of the "elevator."

Mattie thought Parn was studying the workings of the ferry until she saw him scrape something off the side of the raft and realized he was plying his trade, the study of plant life. It was Erin, down there with him, who was trying to unfurl the sail. Hans came running out to tell her to stop and then whirled about and went back the way he had come. Parn and Erin turned and stood like statues staring after him.

"What do you suppose is going on?"

"Get ready!" Parn shouted up at them. He waved and continued to shout. "They're coming down. Many of them."

Parn ran after Erin out of sight toward the steps. By the time they had reached the cabin, all the gear was rolled and packed. Jack was putting food into baskets and Mattie and Elizabeth were pulling on stronger shoes and trousers. Only Ioso was doing nothing; Thomas held the baby.

"Come on. Run," Parn shouted.

"They're coming down the rope lift," Erin said. She urged Ioso to move but it wouldn't until Jack ordered it.

"Hans is signaled through some coded movements of the ropes. First there is a noise to call him, something drops through a cable, and then—"

"Why do they let him know at all?"

"I don't know," Parn said.

"They have no choice. They can't operate the thing easily without his doing something from below," Erin said.

"Tie yourselves together," Hans called to them as they neared the foot of the steps.

"Don't let them come down, Hans," Mattie said. "Just don't do whatever it is—"

"I didn't daughter, I didn't. Two can come by one small platform anyway; the rest will walk the steps."

Mattie wasn't sure she believed him but asked how much time they had. Several hours. But it would take more than an hour for him to get the ferry ready.

She didn't trust him. Why not walk north or south on foot as they had been doing? With such a head start, with Ioso to run with the baby, they could evade the Eastcountrymen.

"This is their place, close to Eastcountry." It was Erin who explained as if she were talking to a child. "They can travel quickly on the surface above and come down anywhere they choose; they know the less precipitous places. They may have ways of detecting us below. And they might have my helicopter." Mattie smiled in spite of everything.

They all worked together, loading, hauling, uncoiling and feeding rope, unfurling sails, heeding Hans's every direction. Mattie took a sharp knife from Parn's pack—her scalpel was long gone—and dug a hole in the small raft and tore the huge floating bucket. She pulled a small canoelike thing up onto the large raft with them. There was nothing left for pursuers. She looked to Erin for approval.

They pulled away from shore, Hans winding the great pulley, its cords attached by a long pole to the bridging ropes like an ancient electric trolley car to the cables above. When the wind caught the sail, the thing wound itself faster than even a two-armed man could do.

They saw them then, the Eastcountrymen, a dozen or more, halfway down the escarpment behind them. The two on the elevator were already on a level with the cabin. Mattie imagined that one of them was Gabriel but knew this was foolish. The man was only a dot in the distance. But such a definite dot. A laughing dot. Mattie was not whimsical.

The ferry seemed not to be moving at all when Mattie looked at either shore, but when she watched the wooden edge of the raft, it seemed to be speeding, flying over the water, but then that could have been an illusion of the motion of the water. They might be stationary. Hans, the-traitor-at-the-tiller, was frowning into the spray.

Parn had his arms around Erin. They stood together near the mainmast almost in the exact center of the raft.

Small Thomas stood close to Mattie, looking out to the side. Had she ever thought his face had expression? Anthropomorphism.

Farther away from shore the water grew rougher. Mattie had not expected the slow swells in addition to the choppy whacks and slaps of the little waves. Elizabeth had flattened herself, facedown, the way Mattie had when the mist cleared on the cliff side. Jack was sitting, bent over, face hidden, very close to baby and Ioso.

Mattie had to admit now that they were indeed moving. She could hardly see the cabin. They were in the middle of a cat's cradle, the palisades on either side of giant hands holding the strings.

The raft rose and then, as though the water under it had been removed, fell. The three Dagdans and Thomas groaned aloud.

Then someone was shouting: "They're on the other side, too. Look!"

They were trapped like losobits. On either shore were men. Tied. Tied again. Like the toy monkey between sticks.

"You're not tied together," Hans shouted. "Tie yourselves together."

"What are you going to do?" Parn yelled back at him. "Why ... Mattie, Mattie, let's just give ourselves up to them. A thing like this will be known everywhere. We'll be all right. Elizabeth!"

"Elizabeth was helping Hans cut the ropes.

"Won't they follow us in ... some better vessel?" Parn asked.

"Nah," Hans grunted. "Can't. This waterway's not navigable."

Mattie and Erin were making the last connections; the baby had her own several loops, bound both to loso and Erin, Erin to Mattie and to Parn, and Parn to Hans and Thomas and—they were all tied together, all-in-together then, and untied from shore, from the ropeferry. Cut loose.

Like a discus hurled without aim, they were whipped away by the current, shot out on the surge of water.

The raft skipped over the surface, slapped, rose, hit again. The tiller and sails were useless. They choked on the centrifugal pull of the ropes from the spin and whirl; their bodies wanted to fly out.

After an unmeasurable time length, the raft steadied. Its speed was still incredible, but it held to the water and maintained a relatively straight line—south.

Hans was doing something with the tiller. The small sail was fully open and taut.

"It might work if I keep her in the middle. Nearer the shores the water turns and pulls. Bad," he said.

"Then how in hell do we ever land?" Parn shouted. Mattie thought he held Erin in his arms again, but then they were all in each others' arms, jumbled in a heap. Loso seemed to be the central, stabile fixture toward which they all leaned now that they were no longer pulled outward away from the center.

The raft suddenly leaped and belly flopped again, and Mattie could not imagine worse turbulence nearer shore or anywhere else. Again Hans seemed to lose control; they tilted almost vertically and then righted only to tip the other way. The ropes cut brutally into flesh, across bellies and breasts. Hans muttered.

Then they were upright behind the rip, racing along horizontally to it or with it. Only Hans moved his hand and talked to himself in his own language. The rest of them locked into motionless silence, as though any stir would provoke retaliation, remind the current of what it could do.

Mattie cursed as every minute pulled her backward, back the miles over which they had been crawling for months.

But the water flowed directly south, not southwest, according to the ship maps of the local geography. If they kept going they would pass miles east of the city and then go where? Most of Dagda was blank. The choices seemed to be to starve, drown, or be smashed onto the shore. Parn had been right in choosing Eastcountry.

They saw then the edge of the dark appear on the top of the western palisade like a narrow black margin of sympathy for the dead. In less than an hour night would reach the foot of the cliff and then begin to move across the water.

There was nothing to discuss. Hans motioned Jack to his side, showed him how to move and hold the tiller. He got himself to the mast and pulled against it. When Erin tried to help he brushed her aside with a growl. Even Parn was almost no good, his slight form at first dangling from the yardarm. It was Ioso's added force which finally made the difference.

The raft turned toward the western shore, cut into a cross-current, almost capsized, righted, shuddered, threatening to break apart.

Hans managed to find an angle; they worked their way in obliquely, jogging and zigzagging when they had to. In some places they made no headway, lost ground. The dark was almost at water's edge. They searched for a flat wide place, hoped they could urge the raft to it.

But it didn't matter; they were towed out of control by the strength of an almost invisible swell, lifted and thrown hard onto the shore like something the water did not want.

There was silence and then the baby, who had been quiet through the entire voyage, started to scream, angry and insulted. And they all agreed with her.

It was a bad night. In spite of a reluctant fire, their clothes and blankets never dried. Only body warmth kept them from freezing.

Since they could climb the escarpment only during sunlight hours, it took them three days to reach the surface of the planet.

Parn took Mattie away from the others.

"As we neared the top," he said, "my fingercube began picking up something, a signal from or to the ship."

"Really! But what does it mean? Who ... Why are you telling me alone? Is there something wrong?"

"Look, Mattie, it's really our business. Yours alone actually. Though I don't see you have any choice."

Mattie moved back from him, alarmed, as if to call the others.

"I don't mean it that way. Do what you want. I won't interfere. But what else can you do but go back to the ship? I'm sure you won't be a prisoner now, now that we can both tell Delt and the OC the truth about Eastcountry."

"They might send Elizabeth back to her family. The baby—Erin's family has never seen a child that young, unless perhaps the very old men ... Erin might survive ..."

"Things will change ..."

"For the worse. There will be a backlash of fear." Mattie remembered the glint in Lucius's fat-narrowed eyes.

"We have never seen any sign of active abuse of the females . . . All right, all right! I promise I'll try. Kyly's absence, I mean of course, what Kyly did to you, will work for us."

"Parn, we have to ask them what they want us to do. They have the right. Jack too."

"But look at the signal," Parn said. "I don't see how we can be close enough. And just look at the map. We could be anyplace along this whole length; I have no idea how far down the water we were carried. I don't think Hans does either though he claims to know this whole area. Though how can you tell one place from another on this planet is beyond me. It's all flat and faceless—just like the people."

"Except Erin," Mattie said.

"Now, look, Mattie . . ."

"She may look like a grown-up person, Parn. And she's far more intelligent than most of us. But you didn't know her two months ago. In experience, in personal experience, she's a child. Maybe a person can grow up intellectually in a couple of months, but not psychologically, not emotionally."

"But what do you want her to be like? I mean how does a woman grow emotionally? I'm trying to say, what kind of grown-up do you mean she should be? What are the prerequisites for 'adult' experiences?"

"She has never seen a couple, lovers, among her people. She has seen only fathers and female children."

"What about you and Jack? A mother and a male child?"

Mattie blanked. She could not hear what he had said. Only she was suddenly very angry about his treatment of Erin, much angrier than she had been a few seconds earlier.

"Men," she said. "Everyone thinks the old man picks the young girl for her uncorrupted skin. That's not the real reason. It's so he can play master, teacher; the child is a blank canvas that he can fill in with any shapes and colors he wants. Unformed, his for the creating. He draws her to fill his personal fantasy. Pygmalion."

"Men! What the hell do you think you've been doing?

Running all over this planet playing Pygmalion, playing God the creator."

"Wrong," Mattie said. "I have not forced any one of them into a preshaped mold. I let them develop as they should have long ago, like individual flowers."

Parn laughed at her.

"And what else am I doing with Erin?" he asked. "She is more a flower than Jack. Jack's more like a . . ."

"That's a blind and prejudiced, stupid, fatherly attitude."

"Fatherly?"

"It's the worst name I can think of. What you want from her is adoration. Every new idea you introduce she'll credit you with instead of Plato. Every sexual and emotional experience she learns from you for the first time, she'll believe is because of you alone, most wonderful of men. Bigger daddy than all her big daddies."

"Wait a minute. What sexual . . . ?"

"An experienced woman has something to compare you with. She'll see your weaknesses, inferiorities, your place in the wonderful human-being chain. She won't help you tell yourself the big lie about . . ."

"Look, Mattie, I don't think you're talking about me. I'm not . . . I haven't done more than flirt with Erin. And in spite of my calling her a flower, she's much tougher and wiser than that dog who follows you around, drooling. Talk about adoration. You haven't taught Jack to value females; you've taught him to worship you alone."

"But . . . How can you say that? I don't have those needs. I . . . don't flirt and play seductive games. I'm direct and hon—"

A hairy arm reached for Mattie, firmly carried her away from Parn. Long brown fingers wiped the sweat from her face. It was loso taking care of a daughter in need, upset.

Parn gaped as Mattie submitted absently, half gratefully, to its ministrations. He had not seen this before. Loso had been totally occupied with the baby and trying to stop the rest of them from jeopardizing her welfare—that is if loso thought anything at all.

* * *

When they marched directly west the signal stayed the same. When they moved northwest it grew stronger. It was not coming from the ship. Hans had finally decided they were somewhere west and south of Plain, not as far south as the city. So someone was doing fieldwork somewhere between Plain and the waterway. The signal must be coming from one of the land vehicles, with instrumentation more powerful than a fingercube.

They were sick, hungry, bruised, without extra clothes or enough blankets to cover them in the night. Most of their hats had been lost in the water. During the day they had been draping rags torn from their clothing over their heads to survive the sun.

Their food was limited to the supplies of dry stuff—now wet and growing moldy—that Hans had stocked in built-in compartments in the raft. The fish had rotted halfway up the cliff.

As soon as they left the area of the waterway and its trees, there would be no more water.

Were losobits common everywhere on Dagda or would loso, and then the baby, starve too?

They stumbled along for two days and lay exhausted at night, hungry, cold, and aching. There were no farmhouses or fields to steal from. Their bruises, cuts, and sprains from the raft ride and climb did not heal. Loso could hardly carry the baby alone, never mind an adult. Finally they all fell as silent as Thomas who trudged beside them; in their quiet his grew louder and became an accusation.

Accused were all doctors, scientists, fixers, and creators. Doctors, not healers like Gudrun. Eastcountrydoctors and Earth doctors. Human beings.

Parn kept his fingercube on all the time to pick up any signal from the vehicle to the ship. For a day and more there were none and they were uneasy about their direction. Perhaps the vehicle was moving to another place and they were wasting painful, precious steps.

Then it came in loud, stronger than it had ever been. Parn tried to contact it with his cube but still the distance was too great. Fingercubes were meant only for confined communications, and their other functions were completely useless this far away from the ship's frames.

Mattie and Parn said, tomorrow. A few more miles and they would surely be within range.

But in early white light Elizabeth could not be awakened. Mattie treated her for shock; they waited while her respiration increased, her body warmed. When she opened her eyes, Mattie and Erin cried.

Jack, by far the strongest and most durable of them all, carried her for awhile, but even he had grown weak.

They drank the last of the water before late bright morning and did not think about noon.

Mattie limped and saw Erin limping ahead of her. Her foot twisted outward with each step and when Mattie examined it, she discovered huge, raw sores and patches without skin. Almost as bad, Mattie noticed then, were her own feet.

Parn stood blinking into the sunrise, oblivious. He was never careful to remember to keep his head covered and the skin on his forehead was an evil maroon. Mattie watched him sway and fall in slow motion and she was helpless even to call out a warning. Thomas went to him first and pulled his shirttail up over his face.

Jack lowered Elizabeth but remained standing, the last one, a tall blur against the sky. Around in every direction was nothing but painful, yellow distance, flat, blank, infinite, and in the east, behind them, the hideous white sun.

Erin tried to get up and fell back. She turned over then onto her knees, crawled to Parn, and lay against his side, face on his chest.

Mattie sighed but wasn't angry. She found herself looking instead at Elizabeth who was still, even in the heat, a cold dead white. There was something left to do but Mattie couldn't think what it was. She couldn't think.

"What was it, Elizabeth?" The color of Elizabeth's gray eyes in the thin white face made Mattie want to cry.

"Parn's fingercube," Elizabeth said. "We have to try it again."

"Yes."

Jack took it off Parn's finger and brought it to Mattie. He sat down next to them and watched her without expression.

Would he be the last one left alive or would it be Thomas or Ioso, both designed for endurance on Dagda? Or perhaps Ioso would keep the baby alive last. Would it do that or would it kill the baby when it knew it was going to die first? Mattie hoped so. She wished she had something to give them all now so no one would be last.

"Mattie," Elizabeth said, "use the cube. Signal."

"Maybe Jack can go with Ioso still and save the baby," Erin said. Parn did not stir at the sound of her voice so close to his ear. "Can you, Jack? Will you try?"

"I can't leave Mattie," he said. "I'm sorry, Erin." It was the most and the most directly he had spoken to one of the daughters.

"Mattie, signal," Elizabeth said.

Mattie signaled and got an answer. She stared at the cube. She tried to think, codes. Help codes. He would know where—whoever he was—but hurry.

"Elizabeth," she said, "keep doing this so he can find us."

Mattie started to feel cold underneath the heat. She couldn't see very well. Elizabeth took the fingercube.

"Mattie, wake up! Mattie, look. A thing is coming."

The sun was low in the western sky now. Their bodies made blue shadows. Mattie tried to raise her head. Thirst was pain. Ioso had stood up and was walking away to the west with the baby.

"Mattie, do you see? A thing is coming to us. A thing that walks. See it? Just against the sun?"

"Maybe it has water."

"Yes, maybe. Water."

"It must have water."

It took a very long time to get there. The blue-purple line of dark from the east almost reached them first. But the ship's land vehicle won.

"Sem the Doc," Mattie said. "Oh, Sem the Doc."

Field

They travel only a few hours at a time three times a day, white morning, late afternoon, and the middle of the night. The vehicle has lights, artificial lights like those the Kyly man shone into Gudrun's cottage that horrid night. And Venus and Bethlehem, now on their left and somewhat behind them, are bright every night at this time.

Elizabeth's ability to recall in her mind's eye the precise image of an absent person, the ability that enabled her to work in secret without a model, has been failing. She can no longer visualize the faces of the people with whom she spent most of her life. She remembers them as information but cannot see them clearly. They have faded and lost shape. Slipped from center. Been superimposed with others. Even her dreams are cast with the new people, Mattie, Parn, Gudrun, Jack. Instead of smallbrother Thomas she sees their Thomas, furry and silent.

From her past life only Pater's features are sharp and clear, but they are smeared with red wax, ripped through.

Right now, three days after Sem the Doc found them, Elizabeth is studying his astonished face in her mind and in fact, as he listens to Parn and Mattie tell him about the Eastcountrydoctors and what they can do. This is the first earthdoctor who is as old as a doctor should be. His skin is old dark gold and there are wrinkles around his eyes and mouth, which move and change direction as he listens. When he smiles his eyeballs disappear completely and the brows bunch together over his nose. When he is astonished, as he seems to be now, and as he was when he first saw Mattie through the window of the land vehicle, his brows and lids move up in half circles, an arc repeated twice more in the deep lines of his forehead. It will be amusing to draw him with the pens he had "lent" her from his shirt pocket.

"You alone must have suspected," Mattie is saying. They are examining Ioso outside the vehicle. Mattie has instruments again, more than she ever carried in her long lost bundle. Small metal things—including scalpels of all sizes. Thin cylinders that emit slivers of light, glass that magnifies what is seen through it, boxes that look like they are doing nothing at all, and large oculars and scopes and small moleglasses and other things to look through. Sometimes the doctor put some part of Ioso or Thomas or some food right under a microscope or a molescope, and other times they cut a bit of fur or scrape some skin and put that on the slide. They take hair from the people too and examine it or put it into a larger machine that seems to be part of the vehicle. Attached to it is a window that lights from behind, a *monitor*, and letters and number appear in it and move. Mattie, Parn, and Sem the Doc exclaim and argue over it.

Elizabeth cannot look up "monitor" in her dictionary since it was soaked in the waterway. It may always be just white porridge, Mattie warns, but Elizabeth puts it out to dry every day that they are not traveling.

Two days before, when they began to work on Ioso, Sem the Doc brought out a long needle and a tray of scalpels and scissors and Mattie grew very angry. Parn agreed with her. Sem the Doc looked confused and apologized.

Ioso allows them to prod it and poke it everywhere. Then suddenly it will knock them away and find the baby to nurse or sometimes try to tend to Erin, Elizabeth, and even Mattie.

"It doesn't discriminate between native daughters and important earth scientists," Parn tells Sem the Doc. "It has no respect for female doctors." Mattie laughs and says he is jealous because he has to wash his own face.

What wonderful things pads of paper and pens and pencils are! Even the simple pens that do not narrow and widen or turn colors at a touch, are marvels of utility. The stubby things Elizabeth hid in her pockets and plied hastily—

sketchily—when no man observed, were dull and blunt, lost their point with each stroke. These are metal. Metal. The weight and balance is a pleasure to her fingers.

Elizabeth draws the doctors at work, the land vehicle from a distance with all the others under the awning next to it, eating and resting, the baby's face—to please Erin at last, and Erin and Parn mating.

The truth is that Parn and Erin have not mated with their bodies and Elizabeth knows it. It is difficult to mate in the middle of an endless, treeless plain in the constant company of four other people. Mattie and Jack cannot do it. (Elizabeth does not know if Sem the Doc suspects at all that they ever did do it. Mattie tries to teach Jack what they are finding and learning, but Parn talks to him in much the same way.)

Erin and Parn sit in early dark among the others and they do not touch or look right at each other. But Elizabeth sees that it is with them exactly as it was with Mattie and Jack who thought they were alone behind their small fire by the water.

So she draws it that way and for the first time since she left Plain is pleased with what she has made. It is good as a black-on-white drawing but it will be better in color. She sees Erin's white body sharply shadowed where Parn blocks her from the fire. The reds and oranges of hair and fire will work fiercely together and Parn's loose dark hair will fall through the other colors as if from outside the frame of the canvas.

Elizabeth sees again the pater painting, the red wax from outside, a color she did not add, giving the portrait a meaning she had not conceived or intended.

Elizabeth will not think of Plain. She looks back at the drawing and wonders when Erin and Parn will manage to mate and if it will be like Erin's dream of riding the merry-go-round.

Elizabeth remembers suddenly the face of the Fian daughter at the train halt—its fierce anger—and she understands then that the prisoners were lovers.

And then there is no time to wonder because they must all pack up again and move on as the hottest part of the day passes. All the equipment goes back into the vehicle with Jack and Erin whose turn it is to ride inside. One more, Parn this time, sits on the top and the rest walk along.

Mattie is happier than Elizabeth has ever seen her. She talks about what will happen when the rest of the earth-people learn the truth about life on Dagda, about how they must be cautious so that Eastcountrymen won't know until too late that their secrets have been discovered. "They must not be allowed to hide or destroy their work," she says often.

But mostly she talks about genetics—*molecular biology*. She is so eager, talks so fast, uses only the scientific terminology, that Elizabeth cannot understand at all. Poor Mattie must have been so frustrated with only her and Erin and then Jack to talk to. Sem the Doc, not Parn, shares Mattie's field, but even he, Elizabeth can tell, does not know or understand as much. He questions her, frowns his deep-line frown, shakes his head, and asks again. Mattie is so excited that she is sometimes impatient with him—an *exozoologist*.

A daughter impatient with a father. It still has the power to startle, unexpectedly, every once in awhile even long after one has adjusted to it, even when the father is a child like Jack or an actor like Parn who moves about without dignity. Sem the Doc is both old and dignified and yet Mattie lectures him condescendingly and without serenity.

"The incredible discrepancy between their genetics and the development of any hard technology is not just the result of the paucity and inaccessibility of metal, though that, of course, is now their main handicap; their forefathers were mostly organic chemists, botanists. Survival—for all the colonists—depended on the quick development of a symbiont agronomy, even before the Wars cut them off from earth resources. The Eastcountrymen had the upper hand from the beginning but they needed all the starships, all their metal and tools."

"But, Mattie, did this doctor . . . ?"

"Gabriel. Elf, tallest, slyest elf. A wise old woman, a doctor, calls them elves. His great-aunt." Mattie gestures toward Hans who, as always, walks along silently unless directly questioned.

"Did this Gabriel say why? What Parn said yesterday—cooperation with us would get them so much more. Why kidnap you?"

"He told me very little, mostly technical things. Most of what I've been saying I've put together from Kyly and from what I've seen, from what these people have told me." Mattie smiles at Elizabeth and Sem the Doc winks at her. The lines of his face all skew to the left.

"But to eliminate the function of one of the sexes," he says.

"Well, one function. Actually the function*ing* of both sexes is . . . You know, Sem, I wonder if all our colleagues would believe me if I didn't have evidence—Ioso, Thomas, the baby. Will they believe anyway? The nonscientists, the OC?"

"They'll believe you," Sem the Doc says.

"I'll fix poor Thomas."

"What is wrong with it?"

"He—never mind. I think Parn still doesn't quite believe yet."

Mattie does not tell Sem the Doc about the tongue or T.F.'s killing of the Eastcountryman.

"The genetic makeup of such a hybrid can be comprehended if we imagine a model like Markson's graphs," she says instead and Elizabeth stops listening as the conversation grows technical again. She watches Jack peek through the vehicle window from time to time to watch Mattie. Poor Jack.

That night Jack gets to walk with Mattie and it is Sem the Doc and Hans's turn to ride. They make Ioso take a turn sitting on the top.

Mattie asks Sem the Doc to stop the vehicle after half an hour. When he climbs down to her, she tells him that the system's planets seem to be behind them rather than to the left. Should they not be traveling directly west to the city and the ship?

He tells her that they are moving due west. Bethlehem and Venus have moved in the night sky in the last month.

"They do not move in the sky the way he said," Jack tells Mattie after they are all walking again. "Bethlehem and Venus are sometimes higher in the sky and sometimes they disappear below the horizon, but they are always directly south."

"Well, Jack," Mattie says, "I'll ask Hans about it in the morning."

"Mattie. I do know this." Jack's voice is cold and he says nothing else for a long time even though he believes he is alone with Mattie for once. Erin and Parn have walked far ahead together and he does not count Elizabeth and Thomas.

"Look," Jack says at last, "we are coming to the railroad. See, the tracks lie beyond this field. We are in an area fallow now but sometimes cultivated."

"How can you tell so much? It all seems the same. There is nothing but empty wild plain, just as it has been since we left the watershed trees."

"Don't you think I know what I am looking at? I work these fields. I load our crops into the train wagons for Eastcountry and the city."

"How can we have come so far? Hans? Sem the Doc, stop for a moment."

Parn and Erin see the tracks only as they actually step upon them. They turn back to the group around the vehicle.

Sem the Doc makes his puzzled face and shakes his head.

"We are far north of the city," Hans says. "We were not carried as far down the water as I first thought. The tracks go northeast. If we turn and follow them south, we come to the city but first to Plain."

"Why didn't you tell us this sooner, when you realized it?" Parn asks.

Hans had no reason. What good would it do?

"We can't go to Plain," Elizabeth says. Some part of her wishes to go to Plain.

"We can take the train," Jack says.

Mattie brushes him aside. "How far from the ship must we be for cube contact?" she asks. "Why should we travel such a great distance—all the way south and west to the city and the ship—when we intend to come back to Eastcountry anyway?"

"Right," Parn says. "Maybe this mistake was for the best. We contact them and wait somewhere. Where? We'll need water, food. Hans?"

"I know you have to be a lot closer than this to communicate," Sem the Doc says.

"But you were signaling. We picked it up on Parn's fingercube," Mattie says.

"I was trying. I could read them but they didn't hear me."

"Maybe Sem the Doc can go alone to where he can signal," Erin says, "and the rest of us can hide and wait." She looks at Parn.

"Let's camp now," Sem the Doc says, "until we decide. I think Jack may be right."

Venus and Bethlehem are so bright that it seems like white morning although it is only late night. Elizabeth feels close to Plain, her familyhouse. This very track they lie next to goes straight there; it links her to it, to home. She wonders if Erin and Jack are feeling the same way. But no. They are feeling others things, fear of losing mating and hope of starting mating. Elizabeth wonders what Rebekah is feeling now, linked to them at the opposite end of the tracks, in Eastcountry. Is she with Lucilla? Dead together?

Elizabeth dreams that the ropes from shore to shore across the waterway are the tracks from Eastcountry to Plain and the city. They are hanging in the middle again.

Tracks

"Only two regular Eastcountrymen run the train. But groups sometimes travel on it to the farms or the city," Hans told them.

"When we load crops in boxcars, we do all the work at our end. There's always just the two engineers," Jack said. "They must unload for themselves in Eastcountry."

"No losos?" Mattie asked.

"Losos. Of course, losos. There's always losos."

"The train always has an enclosed car? The one I rode was flat—open."

"So if we're lucky, there'll be only two of them and at least one closed car," Sem the Doc said.

"But they'll see us sitting here by the track waiting for them," Parn said.

"Nothing wrong with that. The people often wait to get the train," Hans said. "That's how they go anywhere."

"With the land vehicle? Look at the clothes the women are wearing."

"Don't worry. They'll stop to see what it's about and then we'll have them," said Sem the Doc.

"They have weapons," Mattie said. "I've seen them. And some kind of long distance communication, a radio or telegraph perhaps using the tracks. They knew the train was late the time they held us. That was with Kyly," she added to Parn and Sem the Doc.

"I was there," Jack said.

"We didn't see you," Erin said.

"They can send themselves messages, I know," Jack said. "They are mental communications that only Eastcountrymen have the power to do." He laughed. "I believed that."

"Another reason you remained dependent," Mattie said.

"And no one ever told me about it at all," Erin said. "Had I heard of such magical powers belonging only to the elves, I would have seen how illogical it was."

Jack withdrew into dignity and it was decided that they would hijack the next train to come along in either direction and take it to the city. Parn and Sem the Doc would dress in the engineers' clothing and the rest would hide inside the car until they reached the city.

"You will have to stop and let people on and off," Jack said. He was stiff, distant. Trying to be an old man again, Mattie thought. How would he be, back among his own kind? How long before he would disappear into form?

"Great," said Parn. "I always wanted to be an engineer. Locomotive, not genetic."

The first train came a day later, traveling south from Eastcountry. It stopped, and Sem the Doc climbed aboard and moved over to the two Eastcountrymen with his surgical gun in hand. The others handed up the equipment and supplies and, with the help of losos, lifted the stripped land vehicle onto the flatcar.

When they were done and every person and loso aboard, Mattie and Jack walked over to slide open the door of the enclosed car. There were seven Eastcountrymen inside.

Mattie spun around to see Sem the Doc pointing the gun, not at the two Eastcountry engineers, but at her.

Gabriel

Mattie had been alone since the train stopped sometime and somewhere in early dark night. The room they had led her to was as bare and wooden and humble as any she had seen on Dagda. It was not a cell or sleeping chamber; there was no bed or cage that losos knew as bed places. It had one long, simple wooden table, benches, empty open-shelved cabinets, a rocking chair. Two candles burned on the table while fagots of native material remained unlighted in the single wall sconce.

Mattie's heartbeat and the faint hiss of the candles were the only sounds. She waited. Her body was sore from sitting bound for so many hours of cranking, jolting motion of the train, but she resisted the rocker's comfort.

She had been taken away by herself. The other captives were left staring after her helplessly from inside the boxcar. Jack had struggled against his ropes futilely, and Parn had hours earlier given up trying to reason with Eastcountrymen as silent and unresponsive as their losos.

She paced the room, sat on the bench, paced again. There was nothing to look at. No decoration relieved the bareness of walls and floor. Could this be Eastcountry? Mattie thought perhaps the train had stopped to let her off at a farm somewhere on the way.

She sat longer at the table staring at the candle flame and finally surrendered to the passivity of the rocker. She almost slept. She might have dreamed of betrayal, of Sem the Doc's wrinkled face, which she had not seen since morning. And then the laugh-lines of the Eastcountryman, Gabriel, took its place. But there, above her, in the candlelight, it was real, smiling as it had in planet light on the train, in bright artificial light in Gudrun's cottage, and in white sunlight by the tree to which she was tied. And now as always she was looking up at him from below, powerless, caught like one of her own lab animals.

"Fallen again, daughter?" he asked and waited, head tipped politely down.

Mattie said nothing.

Gabriel reached for the candle and held it up before Mattie's face. He laughed.

"I see the difference now," he said. "That Earth fool Kyly saw it. Female faces. The daughter who couldn't talk and the daughter who wouldn't talk."

Had they discovered Ariella's impersonation before or after Sem the Doc "rescued" the real Mattie Manan? What had they done with her? Mattie would not ask. In silence she watched the tiny orange images of candle flame flicker in his eyes; the laugh-lines around them were frozen.

"The game will not work for you, daughter. Your own fathers have identified you and turned you over to us. We have waited too long for your knowledge."

Still Mattie said nothing.

"You will speak," he said.

Mattie allowed herself to rock the chair.

The long face tightened into a narrower smile.

"When *she* wouldn't speak," he said, "we waited. We did not know then that you—or she—had not communicated with your shipfathers, and we were not yet certain that they were as stupid as our people. So do not think our patience was weakness. You will speak."

He spoke evenly and quietly. Compared to an Earth person there was little emotion in his body or face—beyond the constant smile—but his was not the solemn canted monotone or rigid posture of the Plainsmen.

Mattie had no reason not to speak. Her identity was not in question. Her only strategy was to give nothing without a bargain or purpose. And perhaps to irritate by imitating Ariella's silence and remind Gabriel of his own stupidity. He had met and talked with Mattie and yet had not seen the difference. A mere Dagdan daughter had tricked him with her ultimate serenity.

So Mattie waited.

For awhile he did not go on. He walked to the table, replaced the candle, and sat on the bench with his back to it. His face was dark and Mattie's only dimly lit.

"You will tell us all you know and, according to Doctor Sem the Doc, that is all Earth knows of molecular biology and genetic ... 'engineering,' he calls it. You will perform your miracles for us. You will do this because you have to find out what we know. Even though you are ... female. You have to make this trade."

He was right. Mattie had to know. But he didn't know the strength of her control, of her resistence to her own compulsiveness and to outside coercion.

"Also," he added, "there might be another reason that you will speak. Doctor Sem the Doc assures us that you have some phobia—incredible in a scientist of your stature and supposed capabilities as a surgeon, but perhaps it is a female trait—against certain kinds of surgical procedures."

The room grew cold.

"We never cut out tongues," he went on. "What can be learned from it? Removing speech can be done genetically to any adult animal. But in this case ... if we must ... not your tongue! What would that get us? The tongue of someone of no consequence. Dr. Ramsay is not yet expendable. Kyly ... but I see you are relieved. Not Kyly.

"Then perhaps one of our own. Perhaps Lorddaughter."

Mattie could not think. What was he saying? Who ... ?

"And Fergus. The family thanks us still for the radiation-resistant skin of its younger generation. The Fergus-daughter—they call it Erin. These daughters need care and treatment anyway. They have been so long with witches. Serenity. Permanent serenity."

Let him not see her reaction! He must not have that power. Say nothing yet. Rock the chair. Serenely.

His expression changed. It might have been disappointment. She had fooled him.

"One of our ancestors was obsessed with birds," he said. "He read and studied the old books. Skeds are losobits engineered many generations ago—to fly."

Mattie let him see that she took this bait. She looked toward his shaded features with undisguised curiosity.

"Have you found," he asked, "that the Y chromosome is largely inert and that the differences between the sexes seem to be a matter of certain genes being switched on and off rather than a matter of the individual's actually possessing different genes?

"Language," he said, "is the product of six genes and another developmental circuit—a set of lower genes we have not yet isolated—which also involve other apparently unrelated traits, emotional and apprehensive."

"Take me to Eastcountry," Mattie said.

"We are in Eastcountry," Gabriel said.

Mattie followed Gabriel through several rooms all on one level, all as low-ceilinged and as simple as the inside of any house on Dagda. In fact they were more barren; there were none of the attempts to decorate or create comfort: no woven carpets, no wall hangings, no baskets of dried flowers. Wall sconces, tables, open shelving with pottery and wooden utensils, benches, dry sinks, all were totally plain and utilitarian.

One large square room seemed a kind of study or common meeting hall. There were many chairs and benches, several long tables, some with slant tops, which held stacks of crude paper on which Mattie saw print—one of the technologies Eastcountry did not share with the other Dagdans.

Four men sat at the end of one of the tables, one had been reading, perhaps aloud. He stopped and they all looked up at Mattie and nodded at Gabriel. He looked back at them but did not appear to respond.

Late dark night was just changing to early white light. Mattie could distinguish a little of the outside landscape through the windows. It seemed as flat and empty as the rest of Dagda. Somehow she was more surprised and disappointed at this than at the crude simplicity of the housing. Yet what else could it have been?

They encountered several other men eating or also walking through the rooms. There was one male child.

They passed through a small enclosed courtyard where three losos were laying a walk of some kind of clay tiles. They were shorter and broader-backed than losos Mattie had seen, and the arms were longer and more muscular, more apelike.

She and Gabriel entered a windowless corridor with doors opening on either side. The sconces on the walls were lit and blazing eerily, making the night seem earlier and darker. Then Mattie was startled as bright artificial light came on suddenly in a room to her right. She saw that Gabriel had pressed a button on the side of the door.

They walked into a large laboratory. There were machines, instrument panels, scopes, sinks, enclosed heavy-doored cabinets, perhaps refrigerators. Gabriel turned and grinned at Mattie.

It was not as wonderful to her as he supposed. It was like any well-equipped Earth laboratory. Her amazement was that it was there at all in the middle of a primitive organic world.

As she looked more closely, she saw that it was not like the Earth labs after all. The machines and other equipment were just different enough to seem wrong. And the smoothness and gleam were not of metal but polished newood. Even some of the smaller instruments were wood, light, springy, obviously strong when Mattie touched them. Flexible. One could do things with these that perhaps were impossible with metal, alloys, or even plasticols. But the disadvantages far outweighed any benefit.

Gabriel was watching, smile fading. He led her to a cabinet on the other side of the room, took a key from his pocket, and unlocked and pulled out a drawer. In it lay scalpels and other small instruments, all metal. It did not shine as the newood did. Tired metal.

All this time she asked no questions, and he did not talk.

He led her through several more rooms and partitioned areas of the laboratory/operating complex. She saw refrigerated storage units, culture containers; watched men working silently in compartments whose purpose she couldn't understand with tools whose purpose she did not know.

Mattie listened and looked all the time for the experimental females and losos and other animals Thomas had described. Where were these kennels or dormitories? Perhaps in another building? But would they be so inconveniently far from the labs? She must not ask Elizabeth and Erin, or Jack and Parn. Gabriel must remain convinced that they were not important to her.

He showed her the small-animal room last.

And there in a strangely built cage was Barney. Mattie did not hide her reaction. She ran over to him. Gabriel started; Dagdans did not move suddenly or quickly.

It wasn't Barney and it wasn't just one hamster. There were several identical copies of the unnamed female from Mattie's lab on the ship.

"You have stolen her from the ship!" she said.

Gabriel laughed. "Borrowed," he said. "You can have her, any number of her that you want. But not the original."

"I can take her back to the ship?"

"No," Gabriel said. "Of course not. But we will send three of them to your . . . commander. Later."

It didn't make sense. The OC would find out that his Eastcountry guests had stolen from the ship. But then, Mattie thought suddenly, what else had they stolen? Viruses? She had had cultures for cell fusion, retroviruses.

"Bacterial cultures," she said to Gabriel. "In my lab were dangerous . . ."

"Yes. We have them. Your methods are primitive. Perhaps we have not so much to learn from you after all."

Mattie thought of the baby's birth and believed he was right. Still she did not want him to know this.

"I witnessed the birth of a human child from one of your beasts," she said.

"And it is not done on Earth?" he asked.

She said nothing, and he led her from the small-animal room back to the long dark corridor or one exactly like it. They walked to the end and turned left into the more primitive areas of the compound. There was no chemical or electronic lighting or machinery of any kind. There were tiers of bed/cages, tables, rockers with men sitting in them, and the sound and smell of living beings. It was white morning and Mattie could see clearly, but at first she recognized only the familiar common loso.

"Are they clones then?" she asked, thinking of her multiplied hamster.

"Not quite," Gabriel said. "They are made with identical DNA patterns. Except of course for . . . for the exceptions."

The daughters were right! Losos were all one loso; there was no definite article.

"Abdiel," Gabriel called suddenly. A younger man came through an open doorway and nodded. "Take the daughter through the animal quarters and then back to my offices."

Gabriel turned back to the corridor without another word to Mattie.

"Follow through this door to the hostlosos," Abdiel said.

They entered an adjoining room. There were nine or ten losos and two human women in different stages of pregnancy. Mattie took the wrist of one woman and looked into her face to ask a question. But she wasn't a person! There were eyes, a nose, a mouth, but no face. It wasn't the blankness Mattie had encountered everywhere; there was no conscious mind in the human-looking head.

"What have you done to her?" she screamed to Abdiel. He frowned and shook his head.

"What kind of hideous surgery . . . ?"

"No surgery. Be serene, daughter," he said sharply. "Earthdaughter," he added, modifying his tone slightly.

"Doctor," Mattie said, "You may call me Doctor Manan." Careful, she told herself. People who would perform such a mutilation on this poor woman really would cut out Elizabeth and Erin's tongues.

Mattie looked for scars on the woman's head to see how the operation might have been done.

"No surgery," Abdiel said again. "It was made this way, not changed. Losoborn."

The baby, Mattie thought. But the baby cried and laughed. She had a mind, emotions. But she didn't talk.

"Are all losoborns without . . . You are saying this

woman is not a human being and never was? You must tell me if all losoborns are in some way inhuman."

"Follow, daughter. I am to show you other rooms."

In the next room were nine or ten young women; they were not mindless nonhumans like the pregnant . . . thing with the hostlosos. The vacant faces, the listless postures, the motionlessness spoke not of low intelligence, but perhaps an experiment gone wrong in yet another direction; all emotion, animation, will was gone. They all looked more alike than any other group Mattie had seen and yet they were different in height, face shape, hair color. But the hair was limp and lifeless, stuck to pasty white necks in thin streaks; one did not notice the color. Losos fed them; they did not lift spoon to mouth on their own. Not that they could not, but that they cared not enough about the food or life to bother. Yet there was not enough volition for suicide. They did not resist the food when it was brought to their mouths.

In the next, much larger room, were smalllosos, small girls, adult losos nursing infant losos and human beings, human at least in outward appearance. There were no adult human females. Mattie looked around for loso and a red-headed baby but they were not there.

"Where," she asked Abdiel, "do you keep . . . other women?"

"Everywhere. Here and there. There are many rooms in this area. Doctor Gabriel did not ask me to show you all that," he said.

She hardly heard. Coming toward her from among the small ones was Thomas. Mattie knelt and put her arms around him.

She felt another arm around her shoulder and turned to see a six- or seven-year-old human girl looking sweetly into her face. The child smiled and hugged her and Thomas together.

"What is your name?" Mattie asked.

The child nodded a little bowcurtsy.

"It doesn't speak," Abdiel said and turned to leave the compartment.

Mattie whispered a word to Thomas and rose to follow Abdiel.

DNA

Mattie stared at Gabriel across the small meeting room attached to the main laboratory. On the wall behind his long narrow head hung large sheets of coarse paper with doodle-like notations and diagrams scribbled in various colors. Bulky wooden pens filled with some kind of vegetable stains lay on the table before him. Next to them were strewn the fine, metal pens, pencils and laser writing implements that Sem the Doc always carried with him and which had so delighted Elizabeth.

Sem the Doc himself sat between Abdiel and another Eastcountrydoctor against the far wall to Mattie's right.

"For us it is easily possible," Gabriel said. "We have the skills to directly modify the code so that the central regulatory master genes and the lower genes and time sequences of gene activity stop, start, or change their functioning. If it is a male zygote, the cells are directed to ignore the modification. If female, the signal is given, and the modified circuitry acts to suppress the intelligence sequence."

They are insane, Mattie thought. All of them. Insane. But she had to concentrate on what he was saying, on their methods. She leaned forward, narrowed her eyes.

"So it is sex-linked," she said, "and does come out only in the male—but what comes out is the gene which says go ahead with intelligence?"

"But how can a characteristic show up in the phenotype of the females only?" Sem the Doc asked. "Most sex-linked properties show up in the male."

"You have not understood," Gabriel said, shaking his head slowly at Sem the Doc, "but your daughter has understood. We attach a recessive gene but *not* for stupidity or intelligence, which, as you, daughter ... Doctor, must know, is polygenic. In fact, the number and kinds of genes involved and the hypercritical timing of their interaction which produces capability of internal symbolization, abstraction, is so complex that it is yet not entirely known to us. And its interdependence with spoken language still surprises and puzzles us. As you say, we cannot control its heredity.

"The gene we do attach controls the code for turning on or off the linguistic-intellectual polygenic complex. In other words, we turn off all the intelligence genes in the species. Then we attach another gene, a recessive gene, to the X chromosome which signals the intelligence genes to function. This gene, like that for hemophilia, is passed on through the females to the males. In the female it is recessive and so never activates the intelligence. It is masked by the dominant gene with which it is paired. There is no such matching gene on the Y."

"But then," Mattie asked, "wouldn't some women also be intelligent when they happen to inherit a matched pair of the recessive signal genes in both their X chromosomes? And how can you be sure the male will not inherit the dominant X signal gene?"

"Ah. We have also spliced into the Y chromosome another signal. It is able to alter the nature of the X gene if it should not have the recessive signal gene and turn off. If the recessive signal gene should not be inherited by a female, in the absence of this Y signal, it will not function."

"But Dagdan women can speak. You haven't done this," Mattie said.

"We have begun. Our subjects are still here in Eastcountry. In the past we tried the direct addition of DNA only to somatic cells so the desired changes were not passed on to progeny. Recently we have altered the germ line of the newly fertilized female embryonic cell before implantation in loso uterus. The oldest of these daughters are almost ready for replacement in the general population."

"Do the people . . . the men know? Do they want . . ."

"Serenity is the highest quality a daughter can have . . . next to . . . modesty. The fathers understand very little else of the matter."

The alien scientific scribbles clashed and fought on the paper behind Gabriel. Mattie shut her eyes.

"Yes," she said. "Yes, I want to see how these things are done . . . But . . . why?"

Gabriel stood and his smile was gone. "We are improving the human race on Dagda. Perfecting mankind."

He walked to the door and turned. "You will talk with me in the morning after you have rested and every morning after until I am satisfied that we have learned all of Earth biology."

"But I am not satisfied," Mattie said. "You have shown me nothing, given me only theories."

"Michael will show you and tell you anything you want about our science." Gabriel's smile returned. "There is no harm you can do with it.

"And," he went on as if an afterthought, "the cart you loaded on the train for us. You will demonstrate the uses and functions of its laboratory equipment. I am beginning to guess that it is Earth's machinery and instruments rather than its science that we lack."

"Cart? . . . The ship's land vehicle? No."

"In that case we will show you nothing. And we will learn to understand your machines anyway. It is a matter of time that you might have saved us. Doctor Sem the Doc is ignorant but has knowledge of some of it."

"All right. I will demonstrate the equipment through a surgical procedure, the restoration of the smallloso tongue."

Gabriel frowned. "The animal we found with you? They tell me it speaks no more. But how? Did you remove its tongue?"

So he didn't know that his men had done it, or that T.F. had killed the doctor. That meant that the copter pilot had not gotten back to Eastcountry. Erin had predicted that he would run out of fuel. Maybe he had crashed and would never come back.

Had Mattie, or Erin and Elizabeth themselves, told Sem the Doc all the circumstances of the attack on Thomas? Mattie thought not, but if so he had obviously not repeated the story.

Gabriel grinned and nodded without waiting for an answer. "Michael will work with you and Abdiel assist."

Speech

The daughter on the other side of the table eats her cereal with a large, clumsy wooden spoon. Elizabeth looks down into her own bowl. The stuff is tasteless, blander than the losos' porridge.

"Remember the fish," she says to Erin.

Erin does not answer. She has not noticed Elizabeth speak. Her spoon lies on the table where she dropped it.

Silence. It has been a meal of silence. The daughters who are eating in this room do not speak, and Erin, who is sad, doesn't care.

"What is your name, daughter?" Elizabeth asks the woman eating her cereal.

She raises her head and looks at Elizabeth. She is not deaf, but Elizabeth cannot tell if she understands the words. Perhaps her tongue has been cut out like Thomas's.

"Why don't you speak?" Elizabeth asks.

The woman says nothing. The one on Elizabeth's left is watching, perhaps listening.

"Erin," Elizabeth says, "they don't talk. I think they can't speak at all."

"Do you think Eastcountrydoctors will harm the baby?" Erin asks. She stands and walks over to a small window. She looked through this same window when they were first brought by loso into the eating room.

Elizabeth says nothing. Erin has asked her this question twelve times since the men took Thomas, nursing loso, and the baby down a different corridor as they were all led away from the train. Erin cried out then and tried to go after them, but they paid no attention. Parn had been left on the train and could not help.

Elizabeth follows Erin to the window. There is still nothing to see but a long building with plain doors and windows across a large empty space.

Erin sticks her head out and looks right and left.

"This is a big courtyard," she says. "The building goes all around it. There are some people, smallbrothers, down that way. Where do you think they took the baby? Where did the train go with Parn? Aren't we already in Eastcountry?"

"I don't know," Elizabeth says. She stands behind Erin, looking out over her shoulder.

"Maybe we can get out through this window," Erin says.

"It is too small for me," Elizabeth says. "Erin, there is something wrong with these daughters."

They turn together and walk back to the table, but they do not sit. Loso brings more food and cold tea, and Elizabeth takes some tea and bread to dip in it. A daughter pours herself tea and drinks it. They all continue to eat in silence.

"I will sing a story," Elizabeth says. She starts to sing Brer Rabbit. Two of the daughters look up at her and then back to their food. They all continue eating. One daughter rises and follows loso out of the room and another comes in. She glances vaguely at Elizabeth and sits with her back to her.

"Oh, stop, Elizabeth," Erin says. She turns back to the window. "Do you think the baby . . ."

Elizabeth does not listen. Two daughters have come in through the door without loso. They are Lucilla and Rebekah.

"Erin! Look," Elizabeth cries, and she runs to Lucilla.

Lucilla is not dead. She smiles her old smile and her blue eyes crinkle at Elizabeth. Elizabeth throws her arms around her.

"Lucilla. I'm so glad. Oh, Lucilla, we have found you. You are all right."

Erin runs across the room. "Lucilla!"

They look at Rebekah whose face is as solemn as ever

but is not empty anymore. Suddenly there are tears in her eyes. Elizabeth hugs her, too.

"Where is Ariella?" Elizabeth and Erin ask together.

Rebekah says nothing.

"The Eastcountrymen have Mattie," Elizabeth says to Rebekah. "They know who she is now. What did they do with Ariella?"

"They have the baby and Parn," Erin says but, of course, Rebekah does not know who they are.

"Doc . . . doctor is . . . hiding," Rebekah whispers, looking at the door behind her. Only losos are nearby. "Doctor . . . Ari . . . Ariella, I mean . . . is hiding."

"Where?"

Rebekah shakes her head.

Lucilla, holding Elizabeth's hand, walks over to the table. She smiles at Elizabeth and reaches for the tea pitcher.

"Oh, Lucilla, it is so good to see you," Elizabeth says. "Tell us what happened."

"She cannot speak," Rebekah says.

Operations

Mattie's cot was suspiciously like the bed/cages of the experimental subjects, but it was at least in a private room or cell, about the size of her cabin on the ship.

Loso came with water and clean but worn clothes.

Mattie lay stretched flat for the first time in two days. She turned her head comfortably to look through the crib bars at a small window only a few feet away. It was a blank, gray square. She rose and walked over to it and saw that she had been looking through it over a small courtyard to another wall of the compound. It was an intolerable, faceless wooden wall, a wall worse than the sides of the boxcar or the escarpment of the waterway.

Mattie dreamed she was on the ship, locked in her cell, shut in from the plains, the horizon, the huge planet-lit sky. She was in Barney's cage; someone was coming into the lab to perform oral surgery on one of them. The person was Ariella dressed in Mattie's lab suit.

"What happened to my Earth suit that the daughter wore?" Mattie asked Michael the next day.

He told her that it had begun to disintegrate, and they had "borrowed" what was left to study its mineral content. Nothing was said of Ariella's fate.

"Tell me about the pregnant woman," Mattie said.

"What woman?"

"With the hostlosos."

"Ah."

"She ... it is more than lack of speech, isn't it? She is not a real human being?"

"It is human to some extent. Human genetic information

dominates. We learned much from that error. How much material can be removed or exchanged without loss of essential function."

"Then all losoborn human beings are not necessarily defective? It depends on what genetic experiments you were doing with the cell before implanting it in the surrogate mother?"

"Mother?"

"Hostloso."

"Yes," he said and offered no more. She could not ask about the baby, but there was no reason not to ask about Thomas.

"Smallloso that I will work on. He . . . it could speak."

"It was a failed experiment. There were several attempts to give speech to the animals; it would have been a convenience. Unfortunately, we cannot do it successfully yet. We are still not able to isolate linguistic ability. Three were given too much intelligence and other concomitant traits accidentally . . . a byproduct. There was a loss of docility and dependence. Smallloso was one of two that left Eastcountry and were able to survive in the wilderness independently."

"So none of the others, 'regular' losos, are intelligent?" she asked.

"We know less of the genes for intelligence than language although we can control many of their effects. In some loso embryos we include the human genome which we believe controls some forms of problem-solving."

"And what about the surrogates, the . . . hosts?" she asked. "How are they engineered?"

"Well, of course, with enough human DNA patterning to carry and nourish a human fetus. No nonphysical human genes. High primate intelligence, not human. Very limited maternal characteristics. Beaver."

"Beaver? Why these choices?"

"Obviously they must be protective of the young physically, resourceful and single-'minded,' but not . . . not personal."

What kind of personality would develop in any human being raised from birth by a nameless, faceless, speechless, unresponsive, indistinguishable animal? Mattie had once thought the lumpish silence of the Dagdan daughters resulted from physical abuse.

"Are your women losoborn and losoraised?" she asked Michael.

"Most daughters and brothers are now losoborn and all daughters losoraised. Except in Deech. But now with the copters . . ."

"No, I mean your own familydaughters, Eastcountry-women."

Michael stared. Abdiel, at a bench on the other side of the laboratory, dropped a plasticol beaker they had taken from the land vehicle.

The surgery on Thomas was over. Losos were taking him back to a recovery area, Gabriel and two other doctors had moved up to inspect the land vehicle equipment Mattie had used, and Michael was directing Abdiel and loso in the replacing of metal instruments and new chemicals. Mattie watched them absently; it had occurred to her that whoever had anesthetized Thomas before bringing him into the surgical lab would not have told him why. She was wondering if he had felt human fear.

Mattie realized suddenly that she was looking at T.F.! There was no doubt at all that loso pushing a wooden cart with Earth instruments was T.F. He had been there near her throughout the operation.

He gave no sign. He was identical outwardly to all others of his physical type. Yet Mattie knew him.

And she saw, looking quickly around, the Eastcountrydoctors did not. They could not distinguish their own creation.

Mattie ate and rested during the day by herself close to the surgery in a small room that had obviously been a private study. It had a desk/table, the ubiquitous rocker, and a good window for reading.

Mattie returned there after the surgery and another long talk with Gabriel in which she managed to tell him little and leave him with the impression that there was much more to know.

He had seemed at one point more interested in machines and instruments than methods and theories. Again and again together they went over the contents of the land vehicle. He—and the other doctors—had touched the materials with a kind of reverence.

Mattie shuddered and walked over to the window. On the table behind her were reading materials, models, charts, labeled samples. It was all very difficult. The written language was familiar but archaic, and the technical and scientific terms and symbols had no relationship at all to Earth notation.

She looked through the window at the glare of white late afternoon light. The inside of the room was turning blue around her. Again, the feeling of being closed in, trapped, became overwhelming. On Earth Mattie had never been claustrophobic and during the flight she had borne the ship's small quarters as well as anyone else, until she had been threatened with being locked in for another two years. What had this flat, wide-open planet done to her?

She walked to the unlocked door and out into the corridor that divided the two worlds and two ages that composed the Eastcountry science compound. Perhaps this building or collection of buildings was all of Eastcountry. Hans had said the doctors had stations on the other side of the waterway. There were certainly cabins like those at the ropeferry, and sheds, various storage buildings, temporary quarters for losos and men near the experimental fields, but were there houses for families? Did the Eastcountrymen live anywhere but here?

Where were their women? Mattie was braced every time she entered a new area to encounter some horrible form of female. None she had seen so far had the long, narrow faces or the unusual height or sharp eyes of the Eastcountrymen.

Mattie knew her way back to the most central of the laboratories and surgeries. This time she turned the other way, to the "medieval" areas.

She found herself again near the hostloso rooms and then the compartments where she had first seen Thomas, but he was, of course, not yet returned. And there too were the empty women, the ones without will. It was as though someone had forgotten to turn them on. Mattie had forgotten them.

There seemed to be no locks anywhere. The locks were "mind-forg'd," she supposed.

Men were working here and there among the animals. They all looked at Mattie directly, but none spoke to her or tried to stop her. She passed Abdiel or someone who looked just like him, but he did not greet her.

She looked at loso every time she passed one, but none was T.F.

There was finally the large "nursery" that Mattie had expected, and at first she thought she must have come at a sleep time; it was so quiet. But no. As she walked by rows of cradles—real wooden cradles—she saw the open eyes of the infants. None seemed to look back at her. Even the older ones in the next room rocked in their little chairs absently and vacantly. Little girls. There was one with Fergus-red hair, but she was too old to be the baby. Mattie saw Elizabeth's gray eyes in another little one, but they had not the light that animated Elizabeth.

So many duplicated traits throughout the planet's population was, Mattie knew, the result of a population so much larger than the original immigrants whose genes they all shared—with or without Eastcountry intervention.

Through a large open door on the right wall of this children's room—it could not be called "playroom"—Mattie heard the wonderful sound of childish voices, not as noisy as those of Earth children, but flowing and overlapping lightly, almost normally.

Eagerly, Mattie moved toward the sounds and came out into a huge courtyard, as large as an open sports arena, surrounded by the building itself. In the little area near the door were children walking and talking, almost playing.

They were all boys, verysmallbrothers, dressed in the drab brown, loose, square-cut suits worn by all the men of Dagda. Two Eastcountrymen looked at Mattie.

Without stopping, Mattie walked through the group and cut across an arc of the great courtyard thinking to reenter the building at another point.

There was a small garden in front of one entrance with

what looked like vegetable vines growing on trellises against the walls on either side. All the rest of the walls surrounding this immense yard were as bare and plain as the one facing Mattie's sleep cell.

Mattie smelled the dampness of freshly moistened soil as she walked through the garden to the open door. It took Eastcountry bacterial strains for Dagdan soil to grow edible food, Gabriel had said. That was their secret and most potent control. Had Gudrun needed it too or did she have her own ways?

Just as Mattie thought "Gudrun," she stepped across the threshold into the cottage, Gudrun's cottage.

There were the drying herbs hanging from the ceiling, the clay vessels and pipes, the little hills of powder and seeds on counters along the walls, the combination of odd, familiar, almost pleasant smells. And there, sitting at her table, was Gudrun.

"Dotter," she said, "de lily buds are not good."

"No, I suppose not," Mattie said and sat at the other end of the table.

Mattie moved in with Gudrun. She accomplished this by simply walking diagonally across the great yard directly from the laboratories at each day's end instead of to her sleep cell with its horrible window. It took only a few minutes longer. Since she had no belongings it mattered not at all. Loso brought her clothes and grooming things just as it—or some loso—had in the other place.

She could not find out why or when Gudrun had been brought to Eastcountry until several days later when Gabriel returned from wherever he had gone. Michael never discussed any matter with Mattie not directly covered by the subjects Gabriel had prescribed, and Gudrun herself made no sense on the subject. She cursed the elves with renewed anger sometimes and at others seemed to believe she was still in her cottage in the forest.

From Gabriel Mattie learned Gudrun was a repository of the lore and wisdom, called witchcraft by Plainsmen, of generations of Deech. This included medical and pharmacological knowledge that had been brought from Earth with the original colonists and all that had been learned since. Eastcountrydoctors wanted any information or skill, no matter how primitive. These women—there were others allowed to live here and there in different areas of Dagda—had ways of their own, not orthodox according to Eastcountry methods, of learning the uses and powers of Dagdan flora. They could, though in a very inefficient way, sample by sample, adapt certain plants to human physiology.

Why not just leave them where they were in Deech among their own families, and trade for their skills?

"Female doctors? Witches." Gabriel looked at Mattie and laughed. "It is not just a matter of sex. Deech must be completely dependent upon Eastcountry for everything."

"Why?" Mattie asked. "Will you finally tell me the reason for such destruction?"

"How dare you accuse us, daughter? Eastcountry alone is responsible for the survival of the colonies. Without us the other Dagdans would have destroyed themselves. Ignorant inbreeding was already having disastrous effects. For all the generations Eastcountry has selflessly devoted itself to keeping the gene pool as large and healthy as possible in spite of the small original population.

"At first our ancestors controlled procreation by selective, scientific breeding. And it was never easy. According to our early records, the people, in their ignorance, resisted. We had to connect our rules to certain of their religious and cultural values. Some of those beliefs had to be reinforced and reshaped.

"Now of course all breeding is done here *in vitro*. Almost all. There is still Deech . . . and certain families in Fian but very few now. Fians are a wild, emotional strain. Impervious to threat, discipline, or reason. And deceptive. Some have been able to hide their destructive practices right before our eyes. But I am certain now that we have eliminated most of it and removed some of the youngdaughters from the worst families to healthier environments."

Ariella had been moved from Fian to Plain, Mattie remembered.

"Why not the natural way?" she asked. "With strict laws you could . . ."

"We do better than nature. We remove defective pairs of recessives and alter nonadaptive gene linkages. We compose, each time, an organism optimally adaptive and disease-resistant. And each retains a degree of recognizable individuality, and at the same time conforms to the traits of the family to·which it will belong. Usually that is the same family which contributed the majority of its genetic information. The children are never completely the offspring of the families who take them, and sometimes it is healthier for us to mix distant donor families. But the fathers do not know this, and we try, as I said, to include at least one visible family trait in every family member.

"Most often we may use and alter an ovum of a single female family member; that is still the most expedient method if we are not trying to create something more original.

"We actually augmented the color of the Fergus hair when we rid them of their sun-sensitivity. They have no more skin cancers."

Gabriel's smile was without its irony now. Mattie thought he was feeling genuine pride, a kind of strange joy.

"We have strengthened the composition of the teeth of all the population of Plain born in the last twenty harvests. It is now being noticed in the city hospital examinations of the children.

"Digestion—the intestinal track—has always been a problem because of the nature of the planet's food supplies. We do not have enough of a selection yet. The gene pool lacks a good . . . Ah, but perhaps that will change with the arrival now of new individuals from Earth."

"If you want us to contribute our cells to your banks, you will have to change your . . ." But he paid no attention.

"We adapted native waterplants to grow deeper away from the waterways. We have mutated the plant fibers, the wood, so that it is stronger for pipes, irrigation, their houses and furnishings and tools.

"We changed varieties of Earth trees and bushes to be drought-resistant.

"And, most important, the food supplies. We spliced Earth-crop genes, making them adaptive. And we give the fathers an Earth bacteria to put into the soil that adapts the indigenous nutrients to Earth crops and makes edible the Dagdan vegetation.

"It must be reapplied every second or third harvest. We grow the culture in our laboratories." He smiled here almost to himself. "It will be our hold over Deech. They cannot survive without it; we have removed their own doctors and chemists. They will finally follow our rules."

But it wasn't enough, Mattie thought later. Dependence on Eastcountry for survival, old "religious and cultural values" brought with them from Earth, the male drive for power and control, none of it was enough to explain the perversion of the people of Plain and Fian.

It must be fear of incest, not between individuals, but between generations. On some "collective unconscious" level they must have known that they were becoming one family. Copulation, gestation, birth could no longer be accepted as human functions.

They divided themselves into parent and child in order to forbid the sexuality of the relationship between male and female. In that way, any sexual act had to be labeled incest, and so, ironically, Mattie thought, it was a way of avoiding incest.

Sex had to be obliterated the way we deny death. In ancient times there was the laying out of the dead one, touching the body in one's home. Then external institutions took over that function. And now we no longer even look at the body in our funeral ritual. It is cremated and gone before we mourn. We refuse to look at death; the Dagdans refuse to look at both death and sex.

Hiding

Elizabeth knows now that Lucilla is not like Thomas. They have done nothing to her tongue or her ears. She can hear but she cannot understand the words. She has no speech in her mind.

In her familyhouse Elizabeth sat outside in the gazebo or painted and read in her studio. Her familysisters did nothing. Daughters usually stayed wherever they were. Sometimes smalldaughters played in the fields and went to their hiding places, but they were soon very tired and sat and sang stories or just sat. When Elizabeth walked over the fields to Brens, she fell with exhaustion, and when they all started out with Mattie, they could cover very little distance without resting.

The daughters in the Eastcountry building are more tired than the daughters in Plain. The first group Elizabeth and Erin met, the mute daughters, walks back and forth between their group sleep hall and the eating room. Another smaller group stays in the eating room most of the time; they are slightly older than the others and can speak, but they do not do so often, and they do not sing stories. There are some who never move at all; they sit in one room next to the smallloso area unless losos carry them.

Elizabeth and Erin walk around all the rooms, pens, sleep rooms, eating rooms, animal exercise rooms, even some places where doctors are doing tests with short losos. If they move slowly and do not look at them, men pay no attention.

Once when they wander into an unfamiliar dormitory area, Elizabeth sees a face she has seen before. She cannot think where. The eyes are without expression, fixed on the opposite wall; the mouth is open, lower lip loose. The woman moves her head slightly, hardly a toss at all, but Elizabeth knows. It is the Fiandaughter—the prisoner at the halt.

Elizabeth says nothing to Erin. She hopes Erin has not noticed. They continue their search.

Rebekah will not walk with them, and she does not want them to take Lucilla. She says Lucilla is tired and that is true. Lucilla has not moved in a very long time. But Elizabeth knows that Rebekah is afraid the doctors will take Lucilla away again. She stays with her in a sleep cell except when they must go into an eating room. Lucilla smiles and holds Rebekah's hand and follows her—like a very serene verylittledaughter.

Erin looks for the baby everywhere. When they first found a large nursery with rows of cradles, Erin was very excited, but the baby was not there. The next day they go back and Erin insists on looking again into each cradle and there she is. Someone has put a tag on her foot with a notation on it. Erin is very angry and Elizabeth cannot convince her that the symbol is not a name.

The baby is happy and holds Erin and cries when she puts her back in the cradle. Loso hears the baby and comes to nurse, but the baby continues to cry and pulls her head away from loso nipple to look after Erin and Elizabeth.

"Where are they hiding Thomas?" Elizabeth asks later. The men took him with the baby and nursing loso. They look again in the rooms where they first saw smalllosos, but Thomas is not there.

They look often through the many windows and doors onto the large courtyard. It would be easy to go out and walk across it, but it is encircled with walls. There is nowhere to hide. Elizabeth would explore but Erin will not go so far from the baby.

"Maybe Parn or Mattie are on the other sides," Elizabeth says.

"They took Mattie off the train at another halt," Erin says. "She is hidden in another place altogether. She cannot help us."

Erin says nothing about Parn. She never mentions him.

They try to make Rebekah talk about Ariella. How can she be hiding? Are there secret hiding places here in Eastcountry? There are no cornfields or barns of hay. And what happened when the doctors tried to question Ariella? Did they really think she was Mattie? They want to hear the whole story.

Rebekah says that Ariella was so like Mattie that Rebekah believed it.

"That's cot," Erin said. "Where is she? Did they . . . Where have they hidden her?"

"Hiding," Rebekah says.

"Did they do something to Rebekah's speech, too?" Erin asks Elizabeth later.

"No. She is exactly the same."

"She won't help us," Erin says.

"I know. Now that she has found Lucilla she will stay forever right here hiding with her in that little room. I think she wishes we would go away or that we had never come."

Plans

"They want me to see their fields to the north," Parn said. "They have had me in their labs day and night now since we've been here. Some of these botonists are obsessive."

Mattie had returned from her latest meeting with Gabriel to find Parn waiting in her little study. He had insisted upon seeing her, had refused to work any longer otherwise.

"In a way it's been wonderful," he said. "I've seen things I never imagined possible. Rol would sell his soul for this chance."

"How about his genes?"

"We could change the Earth. The food problem . . ."

"Not their way," Mattie said. "Have you seen the . . . the experiments?"

"Only vegetable."

"Try animal—and human. It amounts to the same thing."

"Well, I haven't seen any talking losos," Parn said.

"Are you doubting me?" She told him the highlights of Eastcountry's genetic plans for the Dagdan population, described the mutants she had seen.

"I believe they can do it," he said after awhile, "if their biology techniques are anything like their botany. But why?"

"I don't know why. I asked. I don't know if they know."

"Mattie, what have they done with . . . with the women?"

"You mean Erin?"

He nodded.

"I don't know." Mattie told him about Gabriel's bribes and threats. "I couldn't show any interest in them at all. If I ask where they are or how they are, Gabriel will use them to control us."

"God!" Parn whispered. "I'm glad I asked to see you and not her . . . them."

"But then how did they force you to work? What weapons did they think they were using?"

For awhile Parn didn't answer or look at Mattie.

"None?" she said.

"I couldn't see any reason not to talk to them. Earth will probably benefit more than they will. Scarcity and necessity have forced them to achieve at an astounding pace. The state of botanical engineering on Earth is primitive compared. What we take home . . ."

"They are not going to let us take anything home."

Mattie described the doctors' fascination with the land vehicle and all its contents.

"But if they deal with us, they can have much more than that—and our genes. That costs nothing."

"Dealing with Earthstates would mean loss of Eastcountry's absolute power on Dagda," Mattie said. "According to Gabriel, they have spent almost five centuries attaining that control. They haven't quite got it all yet, but with the helicopters it won't be long."

She lit the candle on the desk. They had been talking in almost total blue darkness.

They both sat then in silence looking at the flame.

"Jack," she said suddenly. "Have you seen Jack?" She had forgotten him.

"Yes," he said. "He and another young one, the only fat native male I've ever seen, are housed near me. There are two or three older Plainsmen around somewhere but that's all."

"They keep them well away from the biology sections, wisely. But how does Jack act?" Mattie asked. "I'm surprised they have not imprisoned or isolated him. After all, he's been contaminated by witches, too."

"Contaminated?" Parn asked. "That's an interesting way to put it."

"I don't mean that. Well, yes, that, too. I mean the ideas. He changed so much."

"Did he? If so, Mattie, I'm afraid the Eastcountrymen don't know it. Maybe it's fortunate . . . for Jack anyway. He behaves no differently from any other young Plainsman. I think they assume he was your prisoner . . ."

"For such a long time! Impossible," Mattie said.

". . . or just that he doesn't have enough sense."

"But how does he act? Does he ask you about me? What . . . ?"

"No. He acts as though he doesn't know me. He looks and acts like all of them. Not there."

Mattie remembered to tell Parn about Sem the Doc. "He seems to be treated just like we are," she said. "No particular respect even though he is a collaborator.

"In fact, none of us seem very well guarded."

"There really aren't that many of them," Parn said. "And they all have professions; they're doctors, technicians, mechanics of sorts, agricultural engineers. None seem to function primarily as guards or soldiers."

"Eastcountry never needed guards. Losos and women offer no resistance. And where would we go anyway? There's no way out except the train."

Together they drew a rough, composite blueprint of the Eastcountry compound as each of them had perceived it. All the buildings faced the large central courtyard in a closed circle. The train tracks, they discovered, must partially encircle the whole thing on the outside, stopping for access at different places. The botany rooms and storage areas were adjacent to the laboratories on the west side as biology was on the east. Finished, it looked like an antique clock dial: the laboratories were twelve o'clock; the dormitories and pens, two; Gudrun's rooms, six; and the botany building, ten.

Parn put an "X" where he thought his sleep room lay in the great circle.

"It's like living in a granary," he said. "They warehouse every new thing they grow. They are working on some hybrid barley and have stockpiled samples from each experimental stage."

Mattie sketched some details of Gudrun's quarters and the pens and dormitories—where the samples of biological experiments were stockpiled.

"I think," Mattie said when Parn was at the door, "that the Eastcountrymen plan to take the ship."

Sem the Doc was in the laboratory the next day. He was wired into a contraption somewhat like the crude birthing chair for hostlosos in the next compartment. This one, too, was wooden but smaller, and attached to it were wires and disks made from precious old metal. There were gauges and machines connected to it and, Mattie noticed, one of the landing vehicle monitors was actually in use, revealing something, perhaps vital signs. Mattie had not shown the doctors how to use it. Sem the Doc must have done so himself.

Metal from the very body of the vehicle, and from other places where it had not been part of an essential tool, was already in use here and there in the labs and work cubicles. The elves were vultures. Mattie imagined what they could do with the whole ship.

Sem the Doc smiled at Mattie, turning his wrinkled face into crushed parchment, benign, delighted to see her, his "very favorite person," as if he had not handed her over bodily to a deadly enemy.

Why was it that Mattie was loose and he bound? Or was that only in appearance?

She did not smile and did not attack though she was tempted to do some random testing of his equipment.

Abdiel came in from the adjacent storage room with newood vials and plasticol containers from the vehicle mixed together on a wooden tray. It didn't take long for technologies to mate.

Michael and three other doctors came in from the corridor. Gabriel was not among them.

"What are you doing?"

It was Sem the Doc who answered from behind the additional apparatus they were putting in place. "Longevity genes," he said. "Eastcountry has been working for generations on age-resistance. They say it is a question of modifying the time sequence rather than the addition of new genes. They are going to interfere directly with the regulatory clock. Reverse the action of the developmental circuits. Splice in new instructions not to turn off."

"What?" It sounded like nonsense, but that could be because Sem the Doc had misunderstood Eastcountry scientific language. Yet Mattie had heard none of these great achievements from Gabriel.

"Michael," she said, "would you tell me what . . ."

Michael did not answer right away.

Losos came in but one was not T.F.

Mattie tried to understand the working of the equipment, but there was too much of it and doctors and losos were in the way.

"Go into the other laboratory, daughter," Michael said. "Gabriel will tell you about this experiment himself."

"Experiment?" Mattie asked.

"Experiment!" Sem the Doc's voice was muffled by a mask of some kind.

Mattie went into the next room, but Gabriel was not there, nor, when she did see him an hour later in his study, was he willing to answer her question.

"I know his explanation was nonsense," she said.

"Not really," Gabriel said. "Once we know the sequences . . ."

"You can't reverse time by reversing a process."

"True, but perhaps we will retard its effects. Radiation-resistance, drought-resistance are all ways of obstructing time's damage."

" 'Perhaps.' Sometime in the future. You know that Sem the Doc thinks you are doing some kind of youth process on him now. Not that I care what you really do to him."

Gabriel's smile never left his face. He stood up and walked around the room, picked up one of the wooden pens from the table and drew a line in orange on the sheet of paper hanging on the wall. Then he dropped that pen and took

Sem the Doc's laser marker from his pocket and doodled light designs around the original mark.

"His age and his particular new genes are just what we want," he told Mattie and punched another series of tiny dots onto the paper. "And his sex. Yes, his sex is very important."

Mattie watched and waited.

"We have tried with male infants, children, elderly fathers, ourselves. Very successful. But there is more we have to know.

"We have not lied to him. We may have given him a new self, younger in a sense, a body beyond his imagining. There was no way to tell him that he could have accepted. . . . Nor is there a way to tell you.

"Know only that the plans you so object to for the daughters are nothing, only a first step toward our ultimate goal. And I have told you what that goal is—the perfection of mankind."

"You have said the words but I do not see."

"The elimination of the female sex."

"Genocide?"

"We are not eliminating persons."

"Women are persons."

"We are not eliminating women. We are eliminating the female sex, gender."

"Preventing the birth of half the race then?" Mattie asked.

"No, not at all. We neither murder persons nor prevent the existence of persons to be.

"All individuals are the result of genetic information, a particular combination of particular genes, whether engineered by an outside planner or not. The same persons who would have been will be but none of them will be female. Those who would have been 'born' female will be 'born' male."

"How can that perfect the human race? How can the race even go on?" Mattie spoke in a soft monotone, not to distract him.

"Wouldn't you prevent the inheritance of a disease like

diabetes? Should we not eliminate genetic imperfections when we can? Any human form less than optimal is imperfect. We aim for excellence, efficiency, and the ability to achieve total expression without impediment. And beauty."

"How is the female form . . . inefficient?"

"Its design is based on one function, reproduction. Without that function, its structure is a useless impediment to all other human expression.

"It is not only the body: breasts, womb, protruding belly, cushions of fatty tissue . . ."

Mattie held her neck rigid in order not to look down at her body. She felt that someone was telling her a particularly obscene and degrading joke, not sadistically but indifferently.

Since she could not look into his smiling face, she stared instead at his stiff, angular shoulders. The long, loose-hanging jacket and trousers hid details of his shape. He was not stooped like the fathers, but his face and large hands and narrow wrists in their too-short sleeves suggested his body was as tight and fleshless as theirs.

"The problem is to isolate and eliminate the behavioral traits that are sex-linked, that are functions of the reproductive process. Go and look at the P-group of females . . ."

"I have seen them all," Mattie said. She was no longer humiliated. The man and his whole society were mad. That was all. She wanted to hear no more of his experiments.

"Then the whole human race on Dagda will be male?" she asked.

"Based on what is now the male form, yes. But vastly changed, perfected. The augmentation of organs . . . Your Doctor Sem the Doc, for example . . ."

Mattie laughed aloud. "You are augmenting his . . . Oh, wonderful. But why not do yourselves since it's such an improvement?"

He looked away from her for a moment and then back. He, the ironist, ignored her irony. He was not smiling.

"We, the men of Eastcountry, are already the second generation to have been transformed. Our fathers and grandfathers engineered us with new structures and new chemistries. But we are still only an intermediate stage. It will be half a century before our offspring will be perfect, and they will change all the men conceived on Dagda."

"So you are planning a race of homosexual supermen whose offspring will be created from their genes in the laboratory? Is that it?" Mattie sounded bored.

"Homosexual? Would we substitute one barbaric and impure form of sexual contact for another? No, daughter, we are self-mating. Like the phoenix, we are self-creative, self-reproducing. But for us it is more. We have within ourselves total procreative and orgasmic capability. With the organs capable of this singularity, it is the greatest sexual experience imaginable, mating with oneself."

Spaces

"You live like spayed cats," Mattie once said. The only cat Elizabeth knows is Puss from "Puss in Boots"; there was a drawing in the old, paper earth book. That cat had boots and a shirt and pants. A-n-t-h-r-o-p-o- . . .

"Erin," Elizabeth calls across the area. "Erin, will we just be like these cats, these daughters, forever?"

"We always were," Erin says.

"We were never like these daughters," Elizabeth says. "We sang stories. We played stories."

"We just sat most of all," Erin says.

They are just sitting now in an eating room watching silent women eat tasteless porridge.

"The copters," Erin says. "Didn't the pilot say there were more than one? Or maybe he got back. Where do they keep the copters?"

"If he got back and told them what we did, they wouldn't just . . . just leave us alone here."

"What would they do?"

"What did they do to Lucilla?"

Erin shakes her head at Elizabeth and they stare at each other across the low table.

"We'll be experiments," Elizabeth says after awhile and laughs. "They'll grow loso fur on you, Erin. Red fur."

"The baby?" Erin says.

"They won't change her. She is already a—an experiment. She's theirs."

"She's mine! Ours. My family genes."

"Theirs. They made her."

"But—out of me."

"Yes. Of course," Elizabeth says. If Erin cares so much, let it be however she wants it.

Lucilla and Rebekah are coming into the room. Elizabeth waves and smiles. "Come sit with us, Lucilla."

Lucilla's face is smiling. She does not move. Rebekah frowns.

"Sit here," Elizabeth says and pats the chair next to her. Lucilla, still smiling, moves over. Rebekah follows. Elizabeth cannot tell if Lucilla remembers their past lives or is just responding like an animal.

Does Lucilla "know" Rebekah, in fact? Elizabeth does not ask the question aloud.

Rebekah scowls aside at Erin for no reason Elizabeth can see and hands Lucilla the wooden cup of tea Ioso has put down.

"We cannot take them with us," Erin says. "You see that, don't you, Elizabeth?" She speaks as if Rebekah, too, is unable to understand language.

Irony. They came to Eastcountry to rescue Lucilla, to save her from monsters. Yet, they will leave without her—if they can leave at all.

Erin stands and walks to the small square window where she often looks out over the courtyard. One woman glances at her vaguely and goes back to her porridge. Rebekah offers Lucilla a piece of bread.

"They may never do anything to us at all—ever," Elizabeth says. "If I had paints, I'd paint Lucilla's blue eyes." Lucilla seems to smile back at her, as she chews on the bread. This is Lucilla who encouraged Elizabeth to read, who said Erin was a great builder, who applauded Ariella's play-singing, who said they were all special, Lucilla, now most serene of daughters—most innocent.

"I wonder what they are doing to Mattie," Elizabeth says. She imagines that someday soon it will be Mattie who comes in, her face smiling just like Lucilla's, Mattie, without her pride, without her impatience, without her curiosity about all those genes, with nothing behind her eyes.

"Elizabeth!" Erin cries. "There's Parn! Across the yard. It's Parn!"

Elizabeth runs to the window but sees only indistinguishable male figures in front of the opposite building.

"You can't tell that . . ."

"Yes, I can. Parn is totally unlike any other . . ." Erin is already in the next room where there is a door onto the courtyard. Elizabeth runs after her.

As they begin to race across the great open area, Elizabeth sees to her left the small boys at their lessons whom she has seen and heard from the nursery windows. At the far end, in front of the building that forms the bottom of the enclosure, there seems to be a small plot of some kind of garden. Otherwise the courtyard is empty. There is nothing to the right or directly across, where Erin saw Parn.

"Loso is coming," Elizabeth says. If they run they will reach the building ahead before it catches them.

The odor of hay and other dried vegetation comes through the wide-open door and windows. It smells like home. It must be a barn or silo.

As they leap up the small ramp onto the doorsill, Elizabeth hears voices. Someone is talking just inside. It is an unpleasant hissing—very familiar. Not Parn. Lucius.

"Parn?" Erin calls as she and Elizabeth almost fall into the building.

Lucius is standing at the end of a long narrow hallway on their right, staring at Elizabeth, mouth open. Slowly he smiles. The man next to him is a Plainsman, tall, old, solemn and blank—but he is Jack. Or he was Jack.

Erin has started up a staircase just in front of the door; loso has reached the ramp behind them. "Hurry," Erin says. "We'll just have time to see what's up there. Maybe Parn. Parn?" she calls again.

Elizabeth is only halfway up when loso catches her. Erin is already standing in the hallway above.

It is no use struggling to get away from loso so Elizabeth tries to get it to go up with her. "Erin, cry so it will come up," she says.

"Let it take you back, Elizabeth," Erin says very softly. Then Elizabeth hears Parn's voice and Erin's steps moving away from the stairs.

Elizabeth goes back to the compound, a mindless lump, with loso. She has lost Lucilla, Ariella, Mattie, and now Erin.

But then she finds someone. In one of the pen rooms, one that holds mostly smalllosos, where she and Erin sometimes sit—away from the silent daughters, by himself in a large cage is Thomas.

Elizabeth tries to turn the handle but it is locked. She presses her face against the bars. Thomas touches her forehead softly with the tips of his long, dark-brown fingers.

"Speak," he says. "You used to talk to me, Elizabeth, but when I couldn't talk anymore, you all stopped talking to me—even you."

"Your tongue! How—? Did the doctors fix it?"

"I don't know. They must have. They put me to sleep."

"I thought all these doctors do is take away tongues," Elizabeth says. "Maybe they want . . ." She stops.

"Maybe they want to do more experiments with me," Thomas finishes.

"We won't let them," Elizabeth says. "We'll take you with us when we fly away." If she and Erin aren't experiments themselves first.

"I saw Mattie," Thomas says. "Once. Before they fixed my tongue."

"Where?"

"Here in these rooms."

"Then where is she now? Where have they put her?"

Hours later Erin comes into the area where she and Elizabeth usually sleep.

"I found room after room filled with dried stuff, like barns we used to hide in," she whispers. "I also found Parn."

"You were with him a long time," Elizabeth says. "What were you doing?"

Then Elizabeth sees that Erin's face is red even in the dark blue night, and she knows that Erin was mating.

"Was it like the merry-go-round?" she asks her.

"Yes."

Donors

Something had gone wrong. Sem the Doc was alive, but things had not worked out as hoped. Abdiel looked frightened, Michael, more taciturn than usual. He had no time for Mattie.

"But where is he?" Mattie asked. "Can I see him?"

"Why?" Michael asked. He had never questioned her about anything but science. While he knew she had intelligence, it never occurred to him—unlike Gabriel—that she might have "motives" any more than would loso, a piece of furniture, or any other object that was not an Eastcountryman.

Mattie did not pretend to care for Sem the Doc's welfare. "I am curious," she said.

"Your interest is of a doubtful and unwelcome nature," Michael said and turned to his work.

There were several other young doctors in the laboratory that morning. All busied themselves in silence while Mattie went to her side bench and the bacterial cultures, both Earth—from the land vehicle—and Eastcountry, which she used to access the work of the Eastcountrydoctors. Michael had been teaching Mattie—reluctantly—Eastcountry methods but refused to let her experiment with their machines on her own. She, of course, pretended indifference, never letting him see that she coveted their technology, nor did she tell him that Earth had only recently begun——with Mattie and one or two other molecular surgeons——to use enhancement and wave techniques.

Michael sneered at retroviral methods. He said they were not only inefficient and slow, but almost impossible to control. Dangerous.

The Fanaticks on Earth used to fear the escape of materials from the labs. Accidental metamorphoses.

Things could escape, Mattie thought. They might escape right here in the Eastcountry laboratory. Correcting genes.

Yes, her methods were primitive, awkward, uncontrollable, dangerous.

"Daughter," Michael said perhaps an hour later. He had come suddenly, quietly, to stand next to her. "Go to d-surgery. Follow Abdiel."

"Why? For what?"

"Gabriel wants you there."

Michael could have told her in the beginning that Gabriel wanted to see her at a certain time. Instead he had waited. Waited and then given the directive. "Now," it said. "Jump." So he was angry at her, not with her as a problem any longer. So she was no longer just an irritation. She had become an enemy. At least an enemy is a person. But why?

Mattie stood and followed Abdiel although she knew the way as well as he. In that surgery, which was as much a study and office as "treatment" area, Gabriel stood looking into one of the scopes they had taken from the land vehicle, his back to the entrance.

Mattie waited, standing. She would not sit and look up at him again.

When he turned, he was, of course, smiling.

"Wonderful, wonderful instrument this!" he said. "If we had had the like, the metal, other materials, we would have done so much more these many years. The ship, your Earth ship, must have more, larger, better? You will show us, Doctor? The exquisite workings of these tools? Teach us 'ignorant peasants'?"

His questions were not questions so she said nothing. "You are ashamed," he said, "because your people have done so little with so much, and we, who have had nothing, empty dirt, have done more, all. So, now we begin, you and I."

"Let me go," Mattie said. "Let me negotiate for you. Delt Marker. He's the official ambassador. Earthstates' Official

Ambassador. That's—that's important. I—look—you'll have far more than the contents of a ship, or of just a single mind like mine. You'll have all the scientists, all the newest and oldest Earth hardware. And people. An almost infinite gene pool. Trade with Earthstates will . . ."

"And how do you think they will like our plans for mankind?" He did not laugh aloud.

"Not well," she said. And she laughed.

He turned again to the scope and seemed to study it, to forget her presence.

"I admire you, daughter—Doctor Manan," he said, not looking at her. "It's not your Earth science." He turned and looked down at her, down but without hostility.

"It is you, yourself," he whispered. "We all find you, in several ways, an optimum individual. You have mental and physical characteristics like our own in spite of your obvious handicap. Unfortunate but not irreparable. You may not know that we have had some chance to study your genes. We'll know more after we extract ova. One ovum. You will grant . . ."

"What? Nothing! What are you saying?"

"You will submit now to a procedure," he said.

"I will submit to nothing."

"You have chosen to rest at night in the rooms of the Deech witch," he said.

So Mattie's activities were worthy of his notice.

"The old female is not of much use to us now. We have her nephew bring any plants she wants, but her work is no longer productive. Perhaps she worked better in isolation or perhaps she is just too old. In any case, an examination of her brain tissues might reveal more than . . ."

"All right. You win. What procedure?" Mattie asked.

"The removal of an ovum, just a single cell—this time."

"Where? Who will do it?"

"In the surgery." Gabriel frowned. "What matter? We are all capable—do you suppose that any one of us will have pleasure in the sight or handling of your body? Quite the contrary."

* * *

If they experienced displeasure, they did not show it. Mattie scanned the faces for any emotion, any eagerness beyond the professional, but the young doctors were impervious, as solemn as always, remote, neither kind nor cruel. Even Michael whom she had suspected of pleasure, not sexual but power, appeared as objective as Mattie herself when she operated surgically on any animal preparation. Complete personal disinterest.

Yet Mattie felt more violated, exploited, humiliated, more naked than if her surgeons had been lurid Earth voyeurs. She was stripped of humanity as well as sexuality.

Then when Michael and the others were finished and crossed with their prize to the opposite workbench, she felt tender fingers loosen the straps from her arms. A human touch. As the hand reached to pull the coarse cotton sheet over her body, Mattie saw that it was not human but loso. She turned to look into T.F.'s face and quickly away and mumbled as though muttering to herself from the drug, "You bring my things to where I live. Can you? Can you be loso who comes to Gudrun's rooms instead of . . . loso?"

T.F. gave no sign of having heard or understood. If, in fact, it was T.F.

Gabriel seemed pleased about something the next day. He also seemed pleased with Mattie. She thought it related somehow to her ovum removal, but he mentioned instead a method she had demonstrated to some of the doctors a few days earlier.

"The technique you taught Abdiel will be of great benefit to us," he said. "Mitochondrial information has been inaccessible until now. Tomorrow we'll test it on another subject. If we can induce a minor change in . . ."

"What subject?" Mattie asked.

"What does it matter?" Gabriel looked at her curiously, smiling less pleasantly. "Not the witchdoctor. She's too old. She might not live through the surgery."

"I will not work on women," Mattie said, "human women."

"We are not cruel," Gabriel said. "We anesthetize. In many cases we give serenity where there was anguish and pain."

"Are your subject females being punished for—misbehavior or not obeying the men of their families?"

"You continue to misunderstand and misjudge us. First, we cannot allow a female who belies the necessary pattern to remain among the others. Such an example might impede the progress of the race toward perfection.

"Second, we never punish. Our purpose is not vengeance. At this point, we cannot waste genes or wombs. If the case is minor, simple removal from family and community suffices. They can do no harm here and add to our pool of subjects. In cases of extreme maladjustment, or when the subjects are troublesome to contain, we must induce permanent serenity for the creature's sake as well as ours.

"And often we are curious about the genetic makeup of such a variant. It might be some optimal combination of traits, a particular combination we might do well to preserve and to reuse if none of them are gender dependent. Yours, for example."

Mime

Instead of going through the laboratory door and cutting across the courtyard to Gudrun's rooms, Mattie crossed the dividing corridor to the dorms and pens. Her purpose, she had told Abdiel, was to check Thomas in the smallloso area. Her other purpose was to find Elizabeth and Erin. She must warn them to be serene, to hide any interesting "combinations of traits." Erin must not invent or fix anything. Elizabeth must not read or find paints.

Mattie glanced casually into an eating room, walked through the area with all the pregnant things, and stopped in the doorway of what turned out to be a sleep room. In a larger room a little girl stood staring at Mattie, longingly it seemed. Mattie had encountered this one before. She was mute. Mattie remembered, and wondered if this gift of serenity was the result of genetics, surgery, or chemistry. She stroked the child's head.

"Doctor," a female voice said.

Mattie leaped. It was not the child. There was no one. Only losos and the women without will.

Mattie looked at that group. They slumped as ever, flaccid and forgettable. Mattie started to turn away.

"Doctor Mattie!" the voice called again. Mattie knew whose it was. It came from among those women.

"Where? Which . . . ? Ariella?" Mattie ran over to stand before the group. They were dull, drab, expressionless, slumped lifelessly on their benches. Indistinguishable. Mattie looked for the familiar features. And found them!

Ariella burst into laughter and sat up straight. There was no question who she was, and Mattie could not now believe that she had failed to recognize her.

"Upstairs, downstairs, in my lady's chamber," Ariella sang.

The woman next to her began to turn her head toward the sound and stopped.

"I was here once before," Mattie said. "I didn't see you." Mattie was still amazed that Ariella looked just like herself, and not at all like the others.

"There was an Eastcountryman with you," Ariella said. She stood and stretched and scratched slowly and fully. "There were men when Elizabeth and Erin came in, too. Every time."

"Elizabeth and Erin! Are they all right? I thought they might have been put away somewhere . . ."

"We are all put away—here. Doctor, did I save you? I never spoke to the men. Never."

"Ariella, you were wonderful. They thought they had me all along." While she had been playing on the shore of the waterway with Jack, Mattie remembered.

"But they caught you anyway, Doctor? How . . .?" Ariella started to ask. There were footsteps and then a voice in the corridor. Mattie turned to glance at the doorway. When she looked back, there was no Ariella. Just a group of torpid women.

No one came in. The sounds faded.

"Ariella," Mattie whispered. She knew which one she was now.

"I can't stand it anymore," Ariella said, straightening up again. "Every part of me hurts. Is everything all right now? Am I out of hiding?"

"No. Just out of this disguise. Nothing is all right yet. Hurry. Follow me quietly. If we encounter men, don't look . . ."

"I know how to look," Ariella said.

"I'm sure you do."

Mattie did not risk going out through the play area. Instead they walked on through the interior for awhile, but even that was dangerous because they couldn't see into the rooms ahead. She finally led Ariella out into the courtyard through the next convenient exit and continued around the long way, hugging the walls of the buildings.

Only when they were in the garden did Mattie tell Ariella where they were. Ariella, who had once feared and mythologized Gudrun, was delighted.

"It feels so good to move again, Doctor," she said. "And to talk. I can sing stories again."

"Sssh. Someone might hear. Come in."

Gudrun accepted Ariella's presence as she had Mattie's. It was as if she had been away for only an hour.

They sat at her table, elbows in her spills of flakes and seeds and powders. She brought them food.

"Oh, it's good, good, good," Ariella said. "They feed those daughters porridge with nothing in it. When I was you, they gave me better food."

'It isn't all good yet," Mattie said. "We are still prisoners."

Ariella, swinging her legs and gobbling pudding, looked doubtful. Mattie tried to tell her some of what had been happening and Ariella tried to listen, but in that way she had not changed.

"They are going to alter the human race on Dagda," Mattie said. "Dagdan women . . ."

"The doctors did not put me with any women," Ariella said. "I stayed in a little place alone. There was a window and then a wall." She shuddered and Mattie remembered her own feelings in that first small sleep room.

"Did they hurt you?" Mattie asked.

"They talked to me. Men kept talking to me. They asked me things. I didn't answer. I just looked—" Ariella put on a face of such contemptuous superiority that Mattie laughed.

"Do I look like that?"

"Yes. No. You did before. Sometimes."

It was already blue dark in Gudrun's rooms, whose small windows faced north. Mattie got up and looked out over the courtyard toward the lab building at the far end. Artificial light suddenly appeared in three or four of its windows as otherworldly, thin bright spots, and everything else was instantaneously darker.

"Come here and look, Ariella," Mattie said. Ariella liked a show better than lengthy verbal explanations. "As you said when I found you, this whole place is our prison. We can't get out even though there are no bars or locks."

Gudrun had come to the window with Ariella. She too stood staring at the distant lights. She seemed to be listening. Mattie had no idea what she made of any of it. She must see that they were not in the forest.

Here and there on the right and left, windows and doors glowed with dull orange torchlight. Mattie gestured toward the dorms and pens. "That's where you were. That's where Erin and Elizabeth probably are. They might be experiments for the doctors. You too if they find you."

"They won't find me. They don't know me."

"Just like T.F.," Mattie said. But of course Ariella had never met T.F. or Thomas.

"Are you an experiment too, Doctor?"

"A different kind, I think. They won't destroy my mind or tongue—at least not for awhile. They need me to show them how to work the ship's laboratory equipment—when they capture it." Mattie did not expect Ariella to understand. Ariella had never seen the ship either.

"Will they lay siege? Storm the gates?" Ariella sang the words.

"No," Mattie said, "they'll take it from within. My shipmates don't know they're in danger."

"Why don't you tell them?"

Mattie was impatient finally with such simplicity. Had Ariella understood so little of their predicament?

"I can't get to them, Ariella," she said. It was no use trying anymore with her. Her acting took all her genius. Mattie missed Erin.

"We can get out the same way we got in," Ariella said. "The train."

Mattie didn't say anything. She thought about the map

she and Parn had drawn. The locations of the halts. Could Ariella do it again?

"I can't go but maybe you can."

"Shall I be you again? Or what I was?" Ariella let her face turn to soup.

"No. You can't be a daughter at all, especially not one who is a failed experiment without the will to move."

"I can be an Eastcountrydaughter—but I've never seen one."

"There are none," Mattie said. "You have to be a boy; you are too small to be a man. You will be a smallbrother from Plain. Or Fian."

"Oh, good!" Ariella started trying on smallbrother faces—solemn, then vacant, then smug.

"This isn't a game, Mattie almost said. But no. Let it be a game, a story for Ariella to play. "You'll need clothes, a costume. And we'll need a guide," she said instead. "I'll talk to T.F. And Parn."

Losos have an aversion to witches, even T.F. He would not come inside the apartment any more than loso—regular-loso-that-brought-clothes-and-supplies to Mattie and Gudrun. T.F., too, left things on a bench at the far end of her garden.

The first day he almost walked away before Mattie could reach him.

"T.F.," she called. "It is you, isn't it?"

"Someone will see me talking," he said.

"Then come inside."

"I cannot." He wiped at her face. Mattie guessed that it wasn't only to disguise their conversation from near and distant watchers—there were windows all around the courtyard, even on the floor above Gudrun's rooms—but that she really was smeared with the dark and grainy powders Gudrun had been mixing that day.

"T.F., will you go to the city with a daughter?" Mattie asked, trying not to move her lips.

"No." He started to turn away.

"T.F.! Please. It is to save daughters. To help me." Mattie sat suddenly on the bench and held up her foot to him as if it hurt or there were something wrong with her shoe. He responded by squatting before her and taking it in his hands.

"I cannot help you. I must protect Thomas and some others and daughters. I must stay here and, when I can, kill doctors."

"We can stop them all, protect everyone, if you will work with me."

"I'll stay here," he said. He pulled her shoe off and held it up to look at the sole. "Loso will go."

"Who? What loso?"

T.F. picked at the shoe sole.

"Will you at least help me get the daughter onto the train?"

"Yes."

"Can you find out when the next train leaves?"

"In two days. Early white light. The train goes every fifth day. Third loso will go on the train with the daughter." T.F. put the shoe back on Mattie's foot. "Cluster-F, the farthest room to the west, next to the copter place." He turned and shuffled back across the quad.

The next day Mattie went boldly and openly at midday to the botany building. She had even made a point of asking Abdiel publicly for directions, although she knew it was the structure immediately to the right as one came out of the labs.

The air inside was heavy, thick with dust and flakes. Mattie thought she smelled mold, an uncommon odor on dry Dagda. The "front" door opened into a long hallway apparently running the length of the building. Mattie climbed the staircase at the far end.

On the second floor was an identical corridor with several windows on the courtyard side and smaller hallways at right angles on the other.

"Parn," Mattie called.

There were sudden footsteps in one of the side passages,

but when Mattie looked down there was no one. She opened doors to find rooms filled with dried plants from floor to ceiling like a barn.

Parn had said he was surrounded by barley and other plants.

"Parn!" she called more loudly and thought again she heard movement. Losobits. Perhaps Parn was in the botany labs or fields.

"Mattie?" Parn's head appeared on the stairway. Behind him were two Eastcountrymen and losos. She thought for a moment he was a prisoner, but he had a sheaf of paper under one arm and some kind of writing implement behind an ear. One of the men and losos carried stuffed burlap sacks.

"Hello, Mattie! These are Ith and his assistant Seraf. We are trying to check this strain of barley. You'd be amazed at the plasm variations."

Both Eastcountrymen looked uncomfortable. Only the one named Seraf nodded curtly in Mattie's direction, eyes down.

So Parn was still working with them—happily it seemed. But then so was she—but not so happily. At least the botanists weren't interested in Parn's body.

"Can we . . . ?" Mattie gestured.

"Let me show you the way they bring in this stuff, ramps and pulleys, all wood, pre-electronic, unbelievably primitive given the state of their biotechnology. Come to the back."

The Eastcountrymen did not follow them.

Mattie waited until they were far enough away, looking out the open back of the building down at other storage areas, long platforms, silos, narrow train tracks barely visible here and there among the bins, more holding fences and moving equipment, and beyond, diminishing the whole into a small and insignificant jumble, were the fields, the open flat land and distant horizon that Mattie had not seen since she was carried to Eastcountry. She felt diminished too, their plans pathetic.

And Parn seemed to think so too when she told him about them. "This Ariella will travel alone, unquestioned, all the way through Plain to the city, and then somehow make her way to the ship with no Eastcountryman or Plainsman questioning her."

"She'll be dressed as a smallbrother—a boy. It would be better if an adult male were with her, but what other choice do we have, Parn? Unless you want to go yourself? You might dress as a native? You could . . ."

"They would miss me immediately. I work with them all day every day."

"I see."

"Really, Mattie. Don't you think you might be worrying more than we need—or sooner than we need? These men— the ones I work with anyway—are extremely rational, objective scientists, not crazed . . ."

"Since I spoke with you they performed minor surgery on me. They removed an ovum. Also you may have noticed that these rational, competent scientists you work with so compatibly are not physically, sexually, exactly Earth normal. Oh, I see you haven't noticed." Mattie told him the plans for the improvement of the human race on Dagda. "But of course, you can't go. If there were any chance you might talk to our people before the Eastcountrymen capture the ship, they would never let me see you now. Or Gabriel would not have told me those things."

"If this girl is caught, what will happen to her, to us?"

"If we don't do something, things will happen to us. I'm worried about Elizabeth and Erin. Now they may only be simple experimental material. If the Eastcountrymen find out about the helicopter pilot . . ."

"Uh—I saw Erin."

"What?"

The sun, just moving into the western sky, shone in Mattie's eyes; Parn's face was a blur.

"She—she came over here. We— Really, Mattie, it's none of your business."

"My business! I'm trying to save her life, her mind—her

person, and you are . . . having sex with her. The farmer's daughter in the hayloft! Do you know what they'll do to her?"

"Nothing. Why should they? What did they do to Jack, speaking of farmers? I'd think you were jealous—if you weren't the one who ended our . . ."

"They don't know about Jack and me. And daughters are completely different to them. Did anyone see?"

"I don't know. Maybe. That fat one was around somewhere. It was daytime— Oh god. I guess you're right. But remember I didn't know until now about their—gender plans. It still seems . . ."

"But they captured us—you were there! And you know they have been lying since we landed."

"But that's far different from . . ."

"From blanking Erin's mind? 'Permanent serenity' Gabriel calls it."

"She did say something about a friend—Drucilla?—being mute. I didn't really listen. We— All right. When she comes again, I'll send her back. Tell her to stay away."

"So at last they found the wondrous Lucilla," Mattie said. "Let's go ahead with the Ariella plan. Get me some men's clothes, the smallest possible size you can steal. Bring them to my study—today. Where is Cluster-F?"

Parn pointed out and down toward some longhouses off to the right.

"We'll meet you here early dark morning."

Mattie walked down the stairs and out into the courtyard. As she started toward the labs, she sensed a movement in the corridor window above and turned to see Jack staring down at her.

After dark, Mattie walked across the courtyard with an innocuous bundle under her arm, the clothing Parn had left in her study.

Mattie gave Gudrun the Plainsman's suit and asked her to adjust it to fit Ariella. Gudrun understood and started immediately tearing the jacket seams apart and resewing them with needles made of some thin, hard, plant material. Mattie wrote the words for Ariella to learn. Then as she read them aloud over and over, Ariella intoned each line.

Ariella learned easily. Mattie warned her against making any improvements on her own to turn it into a better story.

"Gudrun," Mattie said, "I want some of your drug. The stuff you paralyzed us with."

Gudrun did not understand. She offered Mattie some new concoction she had been brewing by steeping seeds.

"The magic potion?" Ariella asked. "Why?"

"Just in case," Mattie said. "I don't like killing."

She poked about in the storage area trying to locate the drug by smell. There were too many odors, and she was afraid to remove any stoppers from containers and take a whiff.

Suddenly, Ariella gasped and fell on the floor, where she lay rigidly staring at the ceiling.

Mattie turned in horror and Gudrun stared. Ariella stood up and said again, "The magic potion."

"Hah," Gudrun said and took a clay bottle with a corklike stopper from a shelf.

Mattie put it in the little bundle she carried back and forth to the laboratory.

It was still late dark night when Mattie tapped on the open door of Parn's airless room. Ariella waited behind her.

Parn got up from his cot and tried through the darkness to see Ariella in her smallbrother disguise.

He led the way down a rear staircase again, and this time turned left into a small courtyard, more like an alley, and into another building, Cluster-F.

They walked a narrow aisle between stacks of wooden boxes on the right and open bins of some kind of root crop on the left. When they reached an open area at the end, it had begun to grow light. Parn turned around.

"Which room did the loso say . . . My God! Mattie, she looks just like you."

"No, she doesn't," Mattie said. "She . . . he looks just like a smallbrother from Plain." And it was true.

They found the room that looked out at the tracks. Losos were there. Two.

"T.F.," Mattie said. Neither loso looked at her or moved.

"Parn is an Earth man. My friend," Mattie continued.

"Doctor," Ariella said, reassuming her own personality, "you are speaking to loso."

"He will lead us to the halt. Is this the other loso, third loso, T.F.?"

T.F. inclined his head. It might have been a nod.

"Look. You can see the sheds around the loading area from here." Parn stood at the window.

This halt was unlike others Mattie had seen, even in the city, simple platforms or nothing at all. This was where many of the crops from Plain and Fian were unloaded and stored and where Eastcountry products and "gifts" waited to be shipped the other way. The tracks were hidden among the storage buildings.

"We'll probably be lost and stumble into the men and be caught," Mattie said to T.F.

He and the other loso moved to the door on their right.

"Come on," Mattie said to Parn and Ariella, and she went after them.

T.F. walked ahead through a series of aisles in an open, well-stocked warehouse. They went out through a small stock door on the side, circled the rest of the building, and stopped before rounding the last corner. They could hear the voices of Eastcountrymen. In an open space to their right, under a huge torn tarpaulin, was a crooked or broken helicopter. Mattie thought first that the pilot must have returned, but then saw that it was not the same one. This must be the place where they built and tested the copters, where one Eastcountryman had crashed and been killed. There was no sign of Erin's copter.

Mattie wanted to ask T.F. but already he had turned the other way and they went after him through a smaller building and out. Again they stopped. They found themselves standing behind the last car of the train. Far down to the left the men they had heard could be seen loading the first cars.

"This is it," Mattie said. "Which car would a smallbrother alone be on?"

"I never saw one alone," Ariella said.

T.F. became himself for a moment and gestured to the back of the second car, a flatcar with a platform in the center like the one Mattie had ridden to Plain on. He lifted Ariella and placed her on the floor with her back against the side of the platform. Her large straw hat tilted forward. She straightened her back, bent one knee, and crossed her ankles as no daughter ever would. She was a brother.

Just as T.F. was jumping down again, he and Mattie heard a noise. Someone was standing behind the last car just where they had been. Someone had been watching and listening.

Whoever it was started to run.

Mattie and T.F. went after him. It was Lucius. He saw they would catch him and started to shout to the men down the tracks, but T.F. was on him, strangling him with his long, dark fingers.

"Wait! Stop, T.F." Mattie was afraid she couldn't stop him. "I have a better idea."

She had the drug out and open. She poured some onto the cloth and clamped it over Lucius's nose and gagging mouth.

"He'll go with her," Mattie said. "The smallbrother will travel with his familyfather."

The stuff was so strong that Mattie started to feel it herself, and so fortunately did T.F. He let go of Lucius's throat but stayed in a squat position next to Mattie. Neither of them moved. Parn and Ioso stood above them.

Then Mattie forced herself to rise and recap the bottle.

"Have you killed him?" Parn was asking her, but he was looking at T.F. rather oddly.

"Maybe," she said. "Did those men see or hear anything?"

"It doesn't look like it."

They could see only slight movement now near the first car.

"Let's get him up," Mattie said.

All four worked at it, but T.F. and loso did the most work. They lifted Lucius's dead weight onto the car and sat him in position next to Ariella. He was a dead weight but not dead. He was breathing and his eyes were open. Mattie remembered how it was. Awake but paralyzed.

Mattie gave Ariella the bottle with the drug and cloths and tried to tell her how to use it. "Whenever he starts to stir, give him more. Try not to kill him but don't let him trick you. If he doesn't stir for awhile, give him more anyway."

"I know," Ariella said.

They heard the unpleasant sound of the train's engine, and Parn, T.F., and Mattie jumped down and backed off to the corner of the nearest shed. They watched as the whole train jerked forward. The other loso had stayed aboard. On the second-to-last car two Plainsmen sat with quiet dignity, as all Dagdans do, and the smaller one waved good-bye.

Offering

"We have been studying your genes. The ovum, the little blood and urine samples we took when you first arrived. We still have difficulty in isolating the circuits and sequences as well as the loci which determine what we call intelligence, and the characteristics we admire in you are more complex than simple intelligence.

"In other words . . . Doctor, you'll be happy to know that we value you as an individual organism and wish not to lose you."

Did Gabriel mean it as a compliment? Mattie was valued by madmen? But perhaps their view of the female sex had changed because of her.

"We have decided to free you of those obstructive and useless reproduction-dependent traits. Why should the accidental inheritance of genetic imperfection impede the expression of an individual of such unique composition when we have the skills and technology to correct it?

"It will, of course, be impossible for us to endow you completely with our singularity. But at least we can free you from a structure without function or beauty.

"I see you are afraid. There is no danger even though you will be the first so honored. It is nothing like the procedure we did with Doctor Sem the Doc which was at best experimental. It is only a matter of reinstructing your genetic code and some macrosurgery.

"When? Are you asking me when? We must take more ova, for stocking, fertilization, implantation in hosts, of course, before we can begin. And then the process will be done in two, at most three, stages. But right now we need more blood, other specimens. Go into the lab with Michael here. As soon as he does some tests and if the outcome is satisfactory—I know it will be—we will prepare the materials.

"Congratulations, Doctor. We are going to make you one of us."

"Zephon's found," Abdiel said, coming in from the corridor.

Michael looked up from the chair in which Sem the Doc had had his unfortunate surgery. He had been fussing over its wiring, old wires made of old metal, while one of his younger assistants mixed a specimen of Mattie's blood with some chemicals she could not identify.

Mattie did not listen, though the unusual excitement in Abdiel's voice should have alerted her. The gift Gabriel promised supplanted any other thought. Metamorphosis. A kind of death.

She started to work again with the cultures, her primitive and dangerous methods.

"What? What about Uzziel?" Michael was asking.

"Uzziel's dead, Zephon says, killed by loso."

"What! . . . Not possible."

"Zephon's alone. They found him on the tracks waiting for the train. He says he had to leave the copter and walk miles. It ran out of fuel."

"What happened to Uzziel? How . . . ?"

"They say it's a horrible story. Plains females—" Abdiel hesitated, looking over at Mattie. "I don't know the whole story. Anyway, Zephon's in poor condition—dehydration, exhaustion. They're trying to talk to him at Halt One."

"I'm going," Michael said. "Clear up this mess."

"Aren't you going to tell Gabriel? Shall I?"

But Michael was already gone.

Mattie stood slowly and moved casually to the interior door. They had never coerced her physically. And neither Abdiel or the other young doctor seemed to have the authority to command her.

"Tell me what you heard, Abdiel. Loso killed—killed

Uzziel on purpose?" the assistant was asking as she went out into the connecting corridor.

Mattie crossed into the pens and dorms and began a calculated search, scanning quickly every room and area. Time—time, if only she had more time. She ignored the few Eastcountrymen working in the test areas. In the smallloso room she looked for and found Thomas in his cage. She cautioned silence and went to open it. Locked.

"Hanging on the wall by the door," he whispered.

Mattie found them, a bunch of massive wooden keys, and opened the bulky wooden lock. She carried Thomas in her arms out of the room, through a wide hall, stopped to look into a daughter sleep room, and went on to an empty loso testing area. If anyone saw her, she was examining her patient, checking the result of experimental surgery.

"That pilot has come back," she said, standing Thomas on a bench. "They are now learning what T.F. and the daughters did. They'll be after them and you."

"But they fixed my tongue?" he said.

"I did," Mattie said. "Hurry. Hide. Keep your mouth shut."

Thomas wrapped his arms around her neck for a moment, then jumped to the floor and ran out of the room.

If only Elizabeth, Erin, and Mattie could lose themselves as easily. Don't think about it and don't panic. Just search—efficiently, quickly.

There were no daughters older than six harvests in the playroom or nursery. Each eating room was a disappointment. The daughters with their shared genes and colorless dresses all looked familiar for the first half-second. It wasn't until she entered a small, dark, sleep room that Mattie found someone she really knew. Rebekah. It had been a long time since they had left her at the camp near the tracks. Mattie was glad to see her.

But Rebekah did not seem glad at all to see Mattie. She stood up and glared at her. Her broad face was not sad as it had always been since Mattie had known her but tense, almost angry. There was someone sitting behind her.

"Rebekah!" Mattie said. Perhaps Rebekah had been changed or abused in some other way. Perhaps she didn't recognize Mattie. "It's me, Mattie. Doctor Mattie. Are you all right?"

"You're not—not Ariella?"

"No, I'm the real me."

Rebekah's ferocity did not change. If anything, she seemed more suspicious. As Mattie stepped farther into the room, she moved as if trying to block her way. Mattie craned to see the woman behind her.

"Go away, Doctor," Rebekah said.

"What's the matter? I'm not going to hurt you—or her. It's Lucilla, isn't it? Your friend."

Rebekah said nothing.

"Let me see her, Rebekah. You know I'm a doctor. Maybe I can help. I can fix tongues sometimes."

"You cannot take her away."

"This is a miserable place, but I promise I won't if you don't want me to. I have no time now. Just let me look quickly."

When Rebekah stood reluctantly aside, Mattie saw a small white face. When Mattie smiled the mouth and very blue eyes smiled back, but Mattie knew at once that there was no conscious intelligence behind them. There was nothing to fix.

Mattie leaned sickly again the wall. This was worse than the other mindless creatures she had seen. This one had been a person, had been a leader of the daughters.

"I take . . . take care of her," Rebekah said. As if to demonstrate, she brushed Lucilla's hair back, like loso, and kissed the bared forehead, unlike loso.

"Rebekah, where are Erin and Elizabeth?"

Rebekah sat again and did not answer.

"Please, Rebekah. Bad things will happen to them if I don't find them—fast."

No answer.

"I promised to leave you and Lucilla alone but you must help me now."

"Leave us alone. Elizabeth does not leave us alone. They are in this eating room," Rebekah pointed to the left, "or other places. We don't go with them. Lucilla is tired."

It was the most Mattie had ever heard Rebekah say at one time.

Elizabeth and Erin were not in the eating room. Mattie stood for a moment leaning against the long table. Loso wiped her face. Loso gave her tea. She must have looked bad, very needy. She took the tea, walked to the unusually large window, and looked over to botany.

Parn—maybe Erin was there. She didn't know where else to look.

Then Mattie saw men, men crossing the courtyard from the Eastcountry living quarters on her left, some almost straight across to the labs, others coming toward this area, and two turning toward the building were Gudrun lived. She had never seen so many at once.

In spite of the infinitely long day it was only midafternoon. Mattie could not cross the courtyard or even circle it hugging the walls as she had done with Ariella. She made her way instead from room to room on the inside.

She passed through a large empty area, apparently disused, and then encountered a blank wall. She had to come out into the courtyard to continue. But she found herself only a few yards from Gudrun's garden and some small screening. She knew there was no passage from the little apartment to other parts of that building, but she dreaded leaving the half-protected area. The entire courtyard was an empty, bright stage with only a narrow margin of dark blue like a floorboard on its western edge.

There was a faint sound of voices. Men had come out from the building on Mattie's right. She leapt behind a vined trellis and then into Gudrun's front room.

She found Gudrun cowering in the far corner of a small storage area in the rear.

"De elves was here," she told Mattie.

* * *

Mattie chanced the yard again and prayed all eyes were busy inside while she raced to the next entrance. That building offered some passage and she tried to find a rear exit, hoping to continue to circle the compound in the rear, or outside, but there was no way or she didn't find it. There was no sense, no hope going on. Just as she decided to wait in this place until dark, she heard the voices of searchers approaching from the rooms to the rear. She had to come out again to the open yard.

She had run only a few yards toward botany when she saw the three doctors coming toward her from the labs. Without losos. The leader was Michael.

She could make the ramp. But then what? Lead them to Parn, to Elizabeth and Erin if they were inside. And the men would get her finally anyway. She decided to let them take her out here and turned as though she had meant all along to go to the labs.

She walked slowly toward Michael. There was a surgical gun in his hand.

She heard the other searchers coming out of the empty building behind her. They started running and in a few seconds one grabbed her from the back.

At the same time another man appeared from the botany building door. He was running down the ramp. Someone tall.

When he reached them, he knocked one of the men to the ground and the others backed away. He turned toward Michael, and Mattie saw that he was Jack, Jack blocking her as Rebekah had Lucilla. Mattie saw his narrow hips and broader back in its discolored drab brown shirt, his foolish hat.

"No," she said. "Jack, no."

Michael raised his arm and shot. Jack fell dead. The hat rolled away and the dark, loose curls that made him a boy instead of an old man spilled around his head on the dry sand.

Storage

Jack is a dead person on the ground below the windows of Parn's building. The blue edge of shadow seems to cut off the hand from his outstretched arm. Except for his dark head his body looks transparent. His faded clothes and half-bared legs match the dry soil and weeds around him. Elizabeth is glad she cannot see his face. A dead person's face.

Mattie is walking away from the place where Jack lies, back over the courtyard with Eastcountrymen all around her. She moves as evenly as they do and looks straight ahead. But it is not the way Mattie usually walks, not the way she ever looks. Suddenly she stumbles.

"Mattie is falling," Erin says.

The men stop and wait. The one who killed Jack is saying something. Mattie stands up by herself, and they all go into the end building.

Erin is crying, her face on the baby's head, and Parn is as faded as when the earthpeople first came to Dagda. He is still looking through the window. They do not speak. When Elizabeth looks out again, the shadow already covers Jack's shoulder and losos are coming across the yard toward him. She will not look any longer.

"Hurry," Parn says suddenly, loudly. "Before they look here."

Earlier he said that Erin and Elizabeth had been foolish to come across the yard in daylight with the baby.

Elizabeth told Parn that Thomas had found her in the eating room. He said Mattie wanted them to hide. The pilot had come back. There was no time to wait for dark.

"Quiet," Parn says as he leads them to a small hall off the long corridor.

"Where is Lucius?" Elizabeth whispers.

"Gone," Parn says. "Both Plainsmen are gone, one on a train, one dead."

Parn opens a door on the right. "All these rooms are filled with variations of a barley hybrid," he says. "They are so full, I don't see how you can get through or behind the stuff."

"We will," Elizabeth says. "After harvest that's how we made new secret passages in the barns." The words sound childish to her. "Secret passages."

There are sounds of men somewhere inside the building. Parn must go back to his room so the searchers will find him there alone. The baby must not cry.

It is very hard to tunnel through the hay. Elizabeth goes first. She bores with her head and tears and digs with her hands. Erin follows with the baby wrapped in a hat.

The brush scratches Elizabeth's face and neck, and the dust fills her eyes and throat. She arches her back to make a higher ceiling for Erin and the baby. Near the rear wall the barley is thinner, and they are able to create a space in front of a single small window.

Erin manages to push the window halfway up. Although it is open it provides little air and no light. Elizabeth imagines that the blue shadow has covered all of Jack's body now, that he matches it, belongs to it.

The men come into the hallway and open the room door. Let the baby sleep and not cry.

"Waste of time," one man says. The baby stirs and Erin coos a whisper and rocks.

"They probably have them and don't know which ones they are."

The door shuts and the men can be heard opening the next door, and then, more faintly, the next. Only when the sounds disappear completely, do Elizabeth and Erin move or take a deep breath of the terrible thick air.

They hear Parn come with water and food. He thinks he is in the wrong room when he faces the same solid wall of dried leaves. "Erin?" he says, his voice strange and muffled.

"Erin, I've brought food and water. They're already looking for me again. I'll be back tonight."

Later, lying in the breathless, black air, they talk about Jack.

"Jack and Mattie were the only mating people we ever saw," Elizabeth says.

" 'Lovers,' not 'mating people,' " Erin tells her.

As the hours pass they strain to hear Parn's footsteps, but he does not come back—that night or in the morning. The baby cries with hunger. And finally when they do hear steps, they are not Parn's. It is the men back again—with losos. Elizabeth can hear doors opening but not closing. And then there are voices calling to one another in the other rooms, but the words are muffled by the hay.

Then their door opens.

"We'll have to unload this one, I fear," says an Eastcountry voice. "It's packed bottom to top and all the way to the front. We can never poke through it all and the poles aren't long enough to reach the back."

"No one can be hidden in here," another voice says. There are small thuds of something hitting the hay. "It's a solid wall."

"We have to, Seraf. The doctors think they have to be on this side. Where else? The earthman knew them. He might have helped them. He lived in this building," the first speaker says.

"Rot," the one called Seraf says. "I've been working with Ramsay in the plasm bank. He knows what he's doing. What does he care for daughters?"

"Michael says he does, says the earthpeople imagine females are like themselves," the second man says and raises his voice. "Are losos done in the other room? We need them in here."

Anthropomorphism, Elizabeth thinks, anthropomorphism to think that females are persons. It is so dark behind the hay, even with the little window on the air shaft, that she cannot see Erin's face. She cannot hear her breathe. The baby is quietly sleeping. Elizabeth might be alone.

"Seraf," a new voice calls from somewhere farther away. Elizabeth cannot distinguish every word. It seems to be asking for some kind of help.

"It is one distraction after another," one of the technicians says. "How can I do my work? We'll never finish here as it is."

Elizabeth hears something drop and voices and footsteps moving away quickly. She says nothing and takes shallow, soundless breaths even after the sounds have faded completely.

"Let's go," Erin whispers.

As they emerge from the haymow there is fresh air; the men have left the door open.

In the corridor are long poles lying on the floor and propped against the wall. There are no losos or men.

They move down the small hall to the long corridor. After all the people and animals in the other building, this one—Parn calls it botany—seems strangely empty and silent. They walk warily through the corridors, knowing from barns that stored food and forage muffle sound. And there is no crowd here to lose themselves in.

As they pass the window in the long corridor, Elizabeth looks to see that Jack is not still lying in the yard. She imagines he has become so transparent that he is invisible. But then she asks herself what fathers really do with dead bodies?

There are steps on the stairs just ahead, and they turn quickly down one of the side halls. This one is not a dead end; it jogs and continues to what appears to be open space. The building simply stops; it's as if it has no rear wall. There in front of them is the horizon. They stand and feel the space and sun.

Then Elizabeth looks below and sees the ramps to the first floor, the longhouses, the bins, and the tracks. Men and losos, small in the distance, are loading or unloading a single flatcar. Others in a square yard to the right are working on some kind of machine. It's the copter. That pilot must have brought it back.

"No, it's the other copter," Erin says. "Not mine. They are fixing it."

Below, losos walk from the building down the ramp. One looks up at them, then another. They move back from the edge. They must leave—quickly. But there behind them is loso coming from a side room. They are trapped between it and open space.

They walk toward it with the flat, slow motion of all Dagdan daughters and do not resist its care. It takes the baby and pulls Elizabeth by her arm back to the long corridor and then to the far stairway. It ignores Erin who tries to distract it. As they start down Elizabeth smells food and hears voices, Eastcountry voices. She squirms to get away from loso even though a lifetime has taught her that it is impossible. Will it really bring them into a doctors' eating room?

At the bottom of the stairs loso carts them toward an open door. At the same time two losos come from the rear of the building. One starts to walk fast. It is T.F.

He takes Elizabeth and the baby from loso and turns back the way he came. He seems to shuffle at usual loso pace, but Erin has to run to keep up. Almost at once they are in another place, a very large room full of boxes and bins of alfalfa and grain. He puts Elizabeth down, and she and Erin follow him through narrow aisles. Only his head shows above the goods. Straight ahead are the open side of the building and the tops of the ramps they saw from above. T.F. draws them into a side aisle.

"The doctors are searching for us," Elizabeth says. "They have taken Mattie and maybe Parn. They have—have killed Jack."

T.F. nods and Elizabeth cannot tell if he knew these things already.

"Do you know where they are?" Erin asks.

"Mattie is in the surgery."

"Have you seen her? Is she . . .?" Elizabeth asks.

"No. Not yet."

"And where is Parn?" Erin asks.

"The earthman is not caged. He goes where he wishes."

"Then why didn't he come back to us?"

"I did not speak to him," T.F. says. "There were doctors with him."

"He isn't free," Elizabeth says. "He knows they will follow him wherever he goes, hoping to find us. Remember what the men said?"

"I saw Thomas. They fixed his tongue. Mattie set him free."

"Mattie fixed his tongue," T.F. says.

They ask T.F. about the copter. He says it is not the pilot's—Zephon—but the other one that had been built at the same time. The men are working on it now, attaching the metal parts Zephon brought with him from the other copter.

"Will it fly?" they ask.

"It is the one that crashed and killed a man."

"Fuel?" Erin asks.

"Men run its motor," T.F. says.

"So then," Erin says, "we will leave in that copter."

They say that they will get into it just before the end of dark night—and it is very dark with both Bethlehem and Venus set—and fly with the very first of early white light.

"You will take Thomas," T.F. says.

"And Parn and Mattie and you," Elizabeth says, but T.F. shakes his head.

"You have to tell Parn," Erin says.

"I cannot speak to him," T.F. says. "The men are always there."

"A message," Erin says. "Give him a message."

They will write a message to Parn and T.F. will pass it to him secretly. But who will write it? Who can write? No one.

"I can't," Elizabeth says. "I have never written. I don't know how."

"Paint the words," Erin tells Elizabeth. "Paint a picture of what we want to tell him. Isn't that what writing is?"

No, it isn't, Elizabeth thinks, but there is no way to tell Erin why. But she will try. She has still hidden in her skirt one of Sem the Doc's metal pens. But what to draw—no, not draw—write on? Hanging at the end of bins are sheets of rough paper with symbols, like the ones on the baby's toe. The reverse side is naked.

Elizabeth tries to see things in her mind, as she did her smallbrother Thomas's face when she painted his portrait. First she does the easy thing: the copter. Then the bare letters—the shapes and their sounds. She copies *D* and *A* and *K* for *dark*, and *K* and *N* and *I* and *T* and *E* for *night* from the images in her mind. They look like the Bible. And then she writes *NOW* all at once because she sees the whole word all together.

Preparation

The men brought Mattie into the large surgery and secured her to the bars of an animal bed at the side of the room. When one of the younger doctors approached her with an injector, she kicked it out of his hand.

She said, "Let me talk to Gabriel."

He shook his head and left the room.

It was Michael who came in then with another injector.

"I want Gabriel," she said. "I have to tell him what I have been doing. You will destroy yourselves and your future."

Michael measured by eye the fluid in his injector.

"What is it? I don't want to be sedated."

"It is stage one, Doctor. Prepared by me," Michael said.

"Michael, do not do this. I have done what you have feared. In this laboratory, in other places all over the compound, are bacteria cultures, unstable. I have injected your . . ."

Michael reacted to her words no more than he would have done the squeak of her hamster.

"Gabriel had believed that you understood the honor and welcomed this operation," he said, leaning close over Mattie and speaking so the others would not hear. He held the injector out of her reach. "I knew you had tricked him with your acquiescence and that you would try to escape. I sent men to intercept you."

"You acted against Gabriel's orders?" she asked loudly, hoping to betray his disloyalty to the others. "Gabriel will understand what I have been doing. I alone can stop the process."

He stood and directed the young doctors to leave the surgery.

"I understand you better than Gabriel does. If I were not a man of science, I might believe with the stupid fathers that you have witched him. He believes that you transcend your reproductive function. I know that you do not. He refuses to be convinced that you have somehow removed the two insane daughters to prevent their necessary destruction.

"That same weakness in your character which provoked you to repair Ioso tongue prevents your appreciation of the gift Gabriel offers and you so little deserve."

"Then why are you proceeding with it?"

"Obedience. And curiosity."

"The microbes I have put among your stocks carry a gene that is lethal to your—"

He raised the injector. Mattie, tied to the bars of a cage, tried to kick at him and then to shrink away, to grow too small for him to reach. She thought again of all her laboratory "preparations." Anthropomorphism.

Michael pushed up her skirts. He was staring down at her—in some kind of trance. His eyes seemed to grow larger as he stabbed the instrument into her belly. The eyes began strangely to protrude and his tongue, too, protruded. A fat, protruding pink muscle.

Then Mattie saw the long, brown fingers around the throat, fingers squeezing and squeezing, and releasing. Michael dropped to the floor. And T.F. was standing there instead.

Mattie reached to pull out the injector and saw that it was half-empty.

Flight

The sun is low in the western sky and shines blinding white onto them through the open rear wall of the building.

They wait there for T.F. to return. The baby sleeps and wakes twice. They have no water for her but Elizabeth has the cloth bag with leftover food tied to her waist. They eat some of it and are all thirsty.

Men and losos walk through the room along the main aisles from time to time, but none stay. Soon the shadows of crates and bins and boxes grow wider and darker blue until the aisles themselves are narrow inky caverns while the tops of mounds of dried grasses glow white. And then even their fuzzy halos fade and drab.

"We'll do it alone," Erin says, "if he doesn't come back. If no one comes."

A head appears, small and dark with tiny ears, way above them. Thomas is there, sitting on a bin of alfalfa. It takes a second for Elizabeth's stomach to calm even after she recognizes him.

"T.F. sent me," he says. "We are going to fly again."

"Where is he?" Erin asks.

"In the surgery," Thomas says, as he climbs down to them. He has a jug of water.

Men come up the ramp from outside and walk through the warehouse area of the botany building. They are talking about the copter, but Elizabeth cannot follow what they are saying. She hopes they have fixed it so it will fly without crashing.

Then more men, almost a stream of men, are walking up the ramps into the building. It is too dark to work outside now. It must be time for Eastcountrymen to eat.

After awhile no one comes through the room and the dark in the west is almost as thick as it was in the waterway. T.F. does not return.

Men can be heard again somewhere behind them. Elizabeth fears they are searching. Thomas crawls to the corner and looks back along the main aisle, but he sees nothing; the men are gone.

T.F. comes at last and tells them that he gave Parn the message in spite of the men watching him. And it is time to go.

"But what about Mattie?" they ask.

T.F. does not answer. He takes the baby from Erin and turns back to the main aisle. They follow him, not to the ramp, but to a small stock door to its right. They go out into an alley and around a large low building. It is so dark they believe they are still indoors. T.F. turns right and leads them along the side of some other structure and then stops. They wait.

"What's the matter?" Erin whispers.

"Here is the copter," T.F. says.

Elizabeth sees nothing at first. How will Erin fly a copter if it is too dark to see? But the plan was to get here just before early white light. Elizabeth turns, but the botany building, all the Eastcountry compound, blocks the eastern sky.

When she looks back she can make out the shape of the copter. She can almost see Erin climbing up into it. T.F. stands holding the baby. Suddenly there is a sound of movement from behind. Human feet running. Elizabeth can feel the air move, a person coming toward them and then total light as bright as day. The copter, Erin almost sitting, Thomas behind her, T.F. handing up he baby, all jump into existence, all caught and frozen in the act. Parn crashes into the picture, shattering it into motion. A man shouts. Parn is running to the copter, pulling Elizabeth with him. Everyone is moving.

And the light itself jumps and bobs and sways as an Eastcountryman runs forward. There are losos and perhaps a second man, but Elizabeth has no time to see them as she climbs into the copter.

Erin is touching the controls, moving sticks and knobs, frowning in the glare. Nothing is happening.

T.F. has not come in. Elizabeth starts to call to him but stops herself in time. Two men and Iosos have reached the copter and T.F., one carrying the source of the painful light, both shouting.

The familiar hideous roar mutes the men. Their mouths are open, hands reaching upward, when suddenly their clothes and hair start blowing wildly and the copter lurches upward. The circle of light narrows into a bright artificial spot on the darkness below.

Elizabeth tries to see T.F. but she cannot distinguish him from Iosos where the copter was. Maybe the men won't distinguish him either.

She cannot think about him any longer because there is a sudden silence far more horrible than the noise. The copter motor has stopped. They fall. Erin works and pulls and still they drop. There is a sputter and silence. She pulls again and the motor moans and bursts on.

They have come so low that Elizabeth can read the faces watching them from the roof of one of the buildings. They are like ghosts in early white light. One man raises a surgical gun. It will kill them like Jack, she thinks. But the copter suddenly tips sidewards and she is looking straight up at the empty sky, and when they are level again, they have left the compound behind. On their left is the waterway, a straight blue-black line cutting through the gray land. And directly below and ahead the faint trace of the train tracks leading them to Plain and the city.

Skypeople

They have turned away from the waterway and there are no more forests. From so far above, the native wild grasses give the land only a matte finish, miles and miles of empty wash that move slowly under the copter. Sometimes when everything everywhere is exactly the same, it is as if they are not moving forward at all. Flying is not frightening anymore and not exciting either. Even Parn can sit up and talk again. (Elizabeth wonders how someone who flew through space in a great, all-metal ship can be so sick in a little, wooden copter.)

He tells them about misleading the doctors after T.F. slipped Elizabeth's letter into his hand. "I thought all three of us were doomed," he says. Then he lowers his voice, but Elizabeth can still hear him. "But I wanted to be with you whether we crashed in the copter or were taken apart for tissue supplies and chromosome information." Erin blushes and the copter moves slower for a second.

Elizabeth looks away from them and sees that the land is changing. It is becoming a neatly sewn patchwork of squares and rectangles all in shades of green. The new planting is already tall since harvest when they left.

Then, far ahead, there is a dot, which slowly grows into a single, low building, a longhouse. A few miles more and a farm appears, tiny barns, a silo, and a miniature familyhouse. Elizabeth thinks about her paints.

There are more farms, closer together. They are coming to Plain.

"Thomas," Elizabeth says, "this is our home. And over there—look, Erin—Jack's familyfarm."

And then her stomach hurts—and her throat, too—

because she sees that the farm directly below is Lords. There is the gazebo and the barn. There are fathers and losos, and no way to recognize an individual of either species.

If they landed, who would greet her? No one. What person does she wish to see? No one. Smallbrother Thomas was no longer a person even before she left. Already he had learned not to see her or other daughters, already he was assuming the shape and face of a miniature oldfather. There is no one else but Pater.

But Erin turns the copter again and flies to her own familyfarm, and then, to the horror and fear of her passengers and the unspeakable anguish and confusion of people on the ground, Erin lowers the copter almost vertically until it hovers below roof level. Tall red-haired fathers bend in fear and red-haired youngbrothers leap away and run toward the familyhouse. Even losos move from their path.

We are the tornado, Elizabeth thinks, as the new corn bends like the fathers in their wind. The only things that don't move are two red-haired lumps—familydaughters— who sit and gape blankly up.

Standing alone at the end of the housefield is one tall figure, arms raised to the sky above the copter. His hair is more white than red and his face is a ruin of scars and sores. Erin's veryoldfamilyfather.

Erin flies toward him, but when he remains straight and unmoving, she turns the copter sharply away and up. "Let's get away," she says.

"I saw that man when we landed," Parn says. "He spoke that day."

"I hope I can find the tracks," Erin says.

But, of course, Elizabeth knows, she has never lost them. In fact, as soon as the copter rises, there they are just to the right, and there they pass through the center of Plain. The three Plain halts can be seen all at once. Such a tiny place is Plain, Elizabeth sees, on the vastness of Dagda. She does not try to think of that greater vastness through which the earthship has come.

In a few minutes they fly over the train moving north to Plain. They persuade Erin not to fly low over it, not because they fear being seen—Eastcountrymen know where they are and where they are going.

In late afternoon a tiny spot, an inch of roughness, appears on the horizon. The city.

They laugh together and point it out to Thomas.

And then the copter noise worsens. It chokes and gags and growls.

"Land, Erin," Parn says. "It must be the fuel. Bring us down." But Erin is already lowering the copter.

The noise lessens as the big fan above them slows to an irregular clopping. They drop hard onto the tracks, and there is a loud crack.

Then incredible total silence. No one moves.

"Well," Erin says, and sighs, "we walk."

"We lived," Elizabeth says.

Their shadows move narrow and long, streaks of ink, as they walk beside the tracks. Again they are silent. Parn strides as smoothly and solemnly as any Dagdan father or loso, but he carries the baby in one arm and the other is around Erin's shoulders. Elizabeth and Thomas follow, hand in hand.

Thomas hears the sound first. The points of his ears sharpen. He tips back his head and sniffs.

The others cannot hear it, but they see it before Thomas does. There is something moving on the tracks ahead, far ahead, something coming toward them from the city.

Before they can make out what it is, there is another noise behind. The train. It has reversed itself and is coming south.

They are caught between some kind of train car moving up from the city and the whole train coming down from Plain. The Eastcountrymen have trapped them in the middle again, Elizabeth thinks.

They angle away from the tracks, walking fast, running.

"If I had my fingercube!" Parn says. "We are so close."

They can see now that the thing coming from the city is

a single flatcar, like the one they rode after the Eastcountry-men took them from Gudrun's cottage. They can hear the cranking sound of the pedals turning the wheels. There are several losos working the mechanism and tall men handling the long bar.

Everything is suddenly slow. The noise of the train engine is growing slowly louder and the day slowly darker as they stumble through the stubble of this wild field. Yet it seems to Elizabeth that they do not move at all. They are still close to the tracks. This time they will not be captured. The Eastcountrymen will kill them like Jack.

Thomas is faster than human beings; he can escape. Elizabeth lets go of his hand and pushes him to run ahead, away, when a sharp, small artificial light appears on the flatcar.

Close behind them, the train's engine roars and stops with a grinding and whining of wheels. Then they can hear the quiet cold voices of Eastcountrymen giving orders to losos and Plainsmen and, farther away, the sound of the flatcar, its pedals and wheels rhythmically turning.

"Go, Thomas," Elizabeth says, pushing him.

"Parn!" a voice calls loudly from behind the light on the flatcar.

They stop and turn, stumbling against one another, holding one another.

"Parn. Parn, get over here," a man calls.

"Nat?" Parn shouts, pulling Erin toward the flatcar.

But earthmen can be traitors, Elizabeth thinks. Sem the Doc. Kyly.

The flatcar stops on the tracks a short distance from the front of the train. The light moves to shine on several Eastcountrymen standing on the platform just behind the engine. They stare back at it.

"We have powerful weapons aimed at you, Doctors." It was Nat's voice. "Do not interfere with us."

"These are our daughters," an Eastcountryman answers. "They have been taken from their homes. They have no understanding. Let us have them. And your man who has misled them. We must talk to him."

"Do not move," Nat says. "Restrain your losos."

Parn walks silently and directly toward the flatcar, urging Elizabeth and Erin to run ahead of him. Only the baby in his arms makes any sound and stretches toward Erin. Thomas is moving fast, pulling Elizabeth along.

"You misunderstand us," the Eastcountryman says. "We are attempting to conciliate the fathers, to convince them to work with you. If you take this traitor and these daughters now, you will destroy forever any chance of gaining what you have come here for. We can mediate between you and our primitive countrymen. As their advisers—"

While he talks another Eastcountryman and loso have been moving to the edge of the platform. There is a sudden flash of green light and a hiss and one of the train's wooden wheels collapses.

"That was a warning. I will destroy you if you move again," Nat says.

It is still early enough to see the two earthmen and losos as Elizabeth climbs up onto the flatcar behind the light. One with a very dark face holds a metal box in his hand and keeps his eyes fixed on the train. The other helps her up and reaches to take the baby from Parn. Loso lifts Erin and begins to brush her.

Parn throws his arms around one man and slaps the back of the other. A strange behavior for fathers. The lighter man smiles and almost shouts. "Ay, Parn! What have you brought—"

"Sssh, Rol," the dark one whispers.

The men and losos start to pedal the flatcar back to the city, but the dark one, Nat, keeps the light and weapon pointed back toward the train. The Eastcountrymen and losos do not move. Only later, just before they reach the city halt, Elizabeth thinks she hears the train engine start.

"I thought we were dead," Parn says then. "How did you know? When did—"

"We didn't—for sure," Nat says. "You sent the message.

That child with her story. Woman really. First we thought she was an odd boy, and then we would've sworn she was Mattie."

"But what about the loso and the fat one we put on the train with her?"

"She was alone. Not on the train. We met her coming across the field from the city. Alone."

"But—"

"She sort of sang it," the one called Rol says. "Something about a princess and a prince locked in a tower by evil elves. We thought it was all nonsense until she started singing about DNA and genetic codes. So, prince Parn, what was there? The plants—"

"Enough, Rol, even for you. More than you've dreamed of. Here, have some barley." Elizabeth hears Parn scratching through a fold in his Eastcountry jacket. He puts something in Rol's hand.

"Wow! What's this? Is it—"

"I'll tell you all about it—later. I still don't understand how you knew we were coming, Nat."

"After we heard the woman's story and finally understood that she was talking about Eastcountry and that the message was from Mattie, we started checking. We broke into the inner recesses of their hospital here—that Kyly said was a primitive 'healing' temple—and found medical labs so sophisticated we knew we'd been had. We tapped their telegraph system. It, on the other hand, was so simple we had never considered its existence before. It runs through the tracks. No code. Who was ever capable or curious until now?

"Anyway we heard their alarms and messages to the ones in the city and we just took their stuff. That's all. Did you really fly some kind of machine, Parn? I thought you were afraid of—"

"I am," Parn says. "Erin flew the copter. Where's Kyly?"

"Away again," Rol says. "In the field!"

They leave the flatcar at the city halt and walk in the dark across the field, past the pavilion to the landing place. That is, the men and losos walk. Losos carry Erin, Elizabeth, and the baby.

They are halfway across the landing field when lights come on near the bottom of the ship.

Elizabeth tries to remember the earthmen as they looked coming out of the ship and then in the pavilion that first day. They were all different colors, but looked alike at the same time, faded somehow, washed out. She cannot recall any individual one of them now except those she met again, Parn, Kyly, Sem the Doc—and Mattie.

She sees now in the light that while Nat is tall, he is not narrow like an Eastcountryman or even a Plainsman, but broad and curved. His skin is dark, darker than any Dagdan, even one who spent his life in the fields, and it shines. On his neck is a metal rope or braid, gold in color—of course, it is gold itself! Most remarkable is his hair which stands up straight and goes from black to white.

Another earthman comes out, waves, and comes to meet them with a cart and other equipment, while several more watch from the door above the place where the stairs are now lowering themselves.

Yet when they climb up to the door, there is only one earthperson waiting inside, an earthdaughter.

"I am Rachel," she says. Her face is a warm brown, lighter than Nat's, and her eyes are brown, too, very round and soft. "Nat said there were women and a baby. So I came alone first to ... Oh, what a beautiful baby! What is its name?"

She takes the baby from loso, not noticing a quick fierce look from Erin. Parn and the other earthmen disappear through an inner door.

First Erin lost control of the copter, then Parn was lost to his friends, and now the baby is out of her control, too.

When Thomas climbs through the opening behind them, this Rachel daughter ignores him. Earthpeople don't know there are not supposed to be any smalllosos.

Rachel is excited, however, as she looks from the baby to Erin. "I see you are the mother," she says very, very slowly and loudly, pronouncing each syllable with care. "I will take care of you both. I hope you can understand what I am saying." She smiles at the baby. "This is the first baby I've seen in*—three years."

"She is the first one I've ever seen," Elizabeth says.

"What?"

"Do you remember, Erin, that time Mattie gave loso a name?" Elizabeth adds as a little gift to Erin. "It was Rachel."

Then, by itself, the entry at the top of the ramp slides shut behind them, and Elizabeth wants to turn and run back out. There is metal above and around and under them and the air is wrong, strange. It has no dust, no smell of vegetation. And it is damp, wet. This is a terrible place. Mattie lived here for many harvests without ever going outside. No wonder she ran away.

It is worse when they enter a room filled with earthmen. Elizabeth cannot breathe. She is going to be sick.

These people are a blur of motion, jumping about, jerking with quick and aimless movements like verysmallbrothers. They talk all at the same time, and they look alike again. In the small room there seem to be many more of them than she remembered.

It is worse than the wild forest near Gudrun's the first night, worse than the Eastcountry pens. Elizabeth turns to run away.

And there is Ariella in a shipsuit.

"Elizabeth, you look so old. You looked old in Eastcountry. I watched you walk by," Ariella says and then she sings, "Upstairs, downstairs, in my lady's chamber. Silly goose."

"Tell us about Mattie," a man says, and all the earthpeople are quiet. He is looking at Parn. His face is dark gold and his hair and brows and mustache white. Elizabeth knows he is Mattie's shipfather, who made her so angry.

But Parn does not look back. All the noisy earthpeople wait silently.

"They have changed her and killed her," Elizabeth says. Her voice is too loud and clangs rudely against the closed metal. After she stops, she can still hear her words, loud and awful. There is nowhere for the sound to go, no distance to thin it.

Suddenly Elizabeth is angry at these people who made Mattie run away, who did not save her, who believed the Eastcountrydoctors.

Their faces are all around her, too close, too big, staring, ranging from Nat's black through all kinds of gold and tan to one almost white but darker than Mattie's, faces strange, inhuman in the artificial light, light coming from everywhere and nowhere, pretending to be sunlight, but red and dull, like no light Elizabeth ever saw.

"Parn, what does she mean?" the shipfather asks. "Is this true?"

Parn nods. He tells them all he knows, more than Elizabeth knows. He talks for a long time.

The shippeople sit on odd seats and benches and some sink to the floor to listen to Parn. They do not talk but they are not still. They move their fingers, scratch their chins, frown and unfrown, cross and uncross their legs. Someone hands Elizabeth a cold liquid, and someone else gives Erin strange food for the baby, but no one interrupts Parn's story.

He asks Ariella where Lucius and the third loso are, and she says, "Fian." She sent them on the branch track to Fian as they passed through Plain.

Parn goes on, stopping only to ask Elizabeth and Erin to add things they know or saw themselves. They tell about the Eastcountryman and the copter and the losos' house. They tell about the baby.

Doctor Rachel looks at the "beautiful baby" in horror as though she were an alien thing.

"But you said you were the mother," she says to Erin.

"What's a mother?" Erin asks. "Loso is her mother. Or I am. My family genes—" Erin is about to explain bioengineering to these genetic engineers.

"Did you see this for yourself, Parn?" someone asks.

"No, but Mattie—"

"We were there," Erin says.

"I was there," Thomas says.

The earthpeople stare at him as dumbly mute as any Dagdan daughter.

They listen quietly again as Parn goes on with the story. When he tells them about Sem the Doc's betrayal they make noises.

Parn talks about plants and vegetables. He says things that Elizabeth cannot quite understand and that are surely not as interesting or urgent as the parts about people, but the other earthmen, especially the one called Rol, who was on the flatcar, seem very excited. He keeps looking at the barley seeds Parn gave him.

They are all talking again and Elizabeth is tired. She sees Erin's head nod, the baby is asleep in spite of all the noise, and, on the other side of the room, Ariella sits, dreaming her stories. But the earthpeople are making plans. Elizabeth tries to listen.

"We can just take off," Nat is saying.

"You mean go into orbit and . . ." Rol asks.

"I mean go home. With Mattie—gone. Sem the Doc and Kyly made their own choice."

"What!" Several people are shouting.

"They can't get away with it," someone says.

"Go back without what we came for? What about the crops?" Rol shouts. "Parn says those Eastcountrypeople have enough to solve the food prob—"

"What about us?" Erin asks. "Mattie said . . ."

"You can come with us. There's no problem with the life support with two of us gone—"

"I meant us—us Dagdans," Erin says.

"Can't fit all of you."

"Nat, you're not serious," Parn says.

"Colleagues and welcome guests," another man says and stands up slowly, almost as a leadingveryoldfather would. "Let me make it clear as ambassador that my official duties behoove me to . . ."

"Marker, stop! No lecture. I wasn't serious. I just had to mention it as an option."

"We are going after them," the shipfather says and everyone is quiet. He has sat in silence since he learned Mattie is dead.

"Diplomatic policy unfortunately determines a contrary decision," the one called Marker says. "It is my responsibility as delegate to these colonies to ensure that physical intervention does not precede diplomatic . . ."

The others pay no attention. They all agree with the shipfather. Now that they know the truth the ship is no longer in danger. Surprise and stealth were the only weapons Eastcountry had.

The shipfather bends his large head to the group and does not talk anymore. He is different in every way from graceful, dark Parn and even more from Dagdan men, both Plains and Eastcountry, young and old. He is broad where they are narrow. His skin is not dry and tight. He is not a venerable oldfather.

At first Elizabeth thought they would fly the earthship to Eastcountry. She imagined their landing in the great courtyard in the middle of the compound just as they did in the landing field. What could Eastcountry do against them with surgical guns?

But as the earthpeople talk, she understands that for some reason this cannot be done. The ship must stay where it is until they leave for earth. They must make other plans.

Elizabeth cannot sleep inside the earthship. She discovers that Ariella too could not stay at night in a metal cell no matter how much she tries to be an earthdaughter. She has been sleeping out in the field, "camping" with earth supplies. Elizabeth, Erin, the baby, and Thomas join her, and, of course, Parn must watch over them, and Nat stays too to keep Parn company.

Venus and Bethlehem are low. There are stars in the northern half of the sky. It is good to be out again.

If Mattie were with them.

Nat and Parn talk about Kyly. Why would he betray his

own people? What loyalty does he have to the Eastcountry-men?

"He's just stupid, a fool," Nat says.

"Obsessive," Parn says. "Monomania. Addiction."

If Kyly is a traitor to earth and his shipfamily, then are Erin and Elizabeth traitors to Dagda and their families?

"I actually showed those Eastcountry bastards the control room, how the system works," Nat says. "Kyly said they had no hope of understanding but would be honored with the respect I was showing them."

"I know," Parn says. "I worked with them too even after I should have known better. Mattie warned me but I thought—I don't know. I didn't see the animal side of it. And now—" Parn's voice is tight. He takes Erin's hand in front of Nat. Elizabeth sees that Parn has changed.

Then Nat says: "Since this little animal has human genes, then—I mean, have they introduced animal genes into human lines too?"

Elizabeth can see only the glint of white at the top of his sweep of hair and the whites of his eyes. She realizes that he is looking at her as he asks the question.

"In their compound, yes, according to Mattie," Parn says. "Whether in the general population yet, I don't know."

Mutagenesis

Mattie dreamed she was by the waterway again, lying next to Jack. She heard Erin flying the copter, taking it up to the planet's surface. Mattie turned to look at Jack's face and remembered he was dead.

She woke to find she was looking through bars, not at gleaming newood cabinets and surgical tables, but at a small window cut into a plain wooden wall. She was back in the small sleep cell, lying in the crib bed—alone.

She was not bound to the bars. She swung her legs to the floor and stood. There were no aches. That meant they must have moved her right away from the cage to this bed. She must have slept long and well. Perhaps the injector had held a narcotic and not some chemical initiating her "change." Michael had lied.

He was dead, too. She remembered the bulging eyes, the tongue. T.F.'s fingers. And then no more. Surely it had been only some sleep-inducing drug.

How long had she slept? Elizabeth and Erin must surely have been caught.

The door was locked. Mattie stood with her hand on its latch. Someone had put her in a loose simple tunic, which hung only to her ankles. Its sleeves were much shorter than those of the work dresses she had been wearing, and she noticed that the old scars on her arms from the scalpel cuts and rope burns had faded. The deepest, the one she had inflicted herself above her left wrist, was only a faint white line.

The latch moved under her fingers and Ioso came in with porridge, tea, and shoes. Mattie grabbed the porridge and ate all of it. She was so hungry that she knew it must have been a long time that she had slept. She drank the whole pitcher of tea sitting on the side of the bed while Ioso put the shoes on her feet.

Abdiel came when Ioso had finished tending Mattie and led her, not down the narrow corridor to the labs and surgery, but out into a side yard near botany and then into a large open warehouse. They went into an alcove, a kind of office area. Gabriel stood beside a desk. Mattie was struck first by the slack in his posture, the slope of his shoulders. His smile seemed no longer to belong to his face, and the face itself seemed to have aged. Could Michael's death have meant so much?

She stood before him waiting for the accusation—and the sentence.

"Earth has another science, far higher than its primitive biology, a science which you and your Earth fathers have carefully hidden from me."

"Our space technologies are clearly . . ."

He waves her words away. "It is a science of the mind. It is the power to control the wills of other beings. What I do not know is whether it belongs to all Earth females or only certain individuals."

Mattie didn't understand the accusation. She thought it was a metaphor or another irony. But mocking what?

"Plainsdaughters leave their families and follow you over the empty wilderness, our Iosos murder us, a simple lout of a youngfather attacks us and dies in your defense, Hans gives up his livelihood to help you escape our pursuit and now has removed the old Deech female from us. All native Dagdans, male and female, human and animal. All have been in close company with you for some period of time. All behave in ways contrary to their nature and do your will. I didn't see it sooner because I had not thought your shipfathers capable of such subtlety. Keeping such a power hidden from us has been a careful and devious strategy, one to match our own."

"So you do believe in witchcraft," Mattie said.

"Not at all, daughter. Do not try to deceive me further. It

may be what the ignorant call witchcraft. Perhaps the Deech female doctors have some small amount which they use to control native vegetable and animal life. That would explain why your males allow you such an important position. We may learn more once we complete your change."

"You won't find anything. You will discover nothing like this, no matter how long you study my DNA. It is not there. Nor is it in my training. Your logic is based on incomplete and false data. The loso's behavior was a result of intelligence you yourselves accidentally gave him. Hans must have acted on his own to protect his kinswoman. That is not unnatural. But the Plainsdaughters are indeed innocent. In their case I accept all the blame. I coerced them but not by any mind powers. You must not do anything to—to change them. They will remain serene. In fact, if you harm them . . ."

"Do you attempt to mock me? You and loso arranged their escape. Only you could cause the ignorant female to fly a machine she cannot understand. You made them fly your wretched Ramsay in our copter to warn the Earth ship."

He had no more hostages!

"They—these daughters—and Parn and T.F. are all gone? And Gudrun, too?"

He narrowed his eyes as if suspecting for a second that her surprise was genuine. "You have always dissembled," he said. "Michael warned me; I did not listen. Because I would not hear the truth, we may lose the Earth ship. Because of you."

"I am free," she said.

"Not quite." He gestured to Abdiel without taking his eyes off Mattie. Abdiel unlocked another door. Inside a very large supply closet were T.F. and four losos.

Mattie did not look at T.F. or any loso. She looked around the closet as if trying to discover what it was Gabriel meant her to see. She looked back at him and waited for some explanation.

He clucked in irritation. "Dissembler. Which one is it?"

"None."

"Daughter," he said, voice almost muffled, too low, "which animal is the killer?"

It was incredible that Abdiel and Gabriel did not know their own creation standing there in front of them.

"I don't understand," Mattie said.

"We will destroy these five then," Gabriel said.

"I think it is not one of them," Mattie said.

He merely laughed at her. "Arrange for their destruction, Abdiel."

"Destroy them," Mattie said, "and all your work, including the cellular information that is your singularity, will be destroyed."

"You have denied mind powers," Gabriel said. "Now you think to reassume them. Or do you pretend to have allies within our laboratories?"

"Yes. Small ones," Mattie said. "In the labs, in the surgeries, in storerooms, and in your own cells."

Gabriel and Abdiel stared at her. She saw that T.F. was listening.

"Abdiel, destroy these animals. Daughter, come to the surgery; we will proceed with your change."

"And with yours," Mattie said.

"Our changes are done. I explained to you, daughter, that our progeny will surpass us. The genetic information . . ."

"There will be no progeny. And you will change," Mattie said. "I have grown a variety of strong bacterial cultures with modified genetic information. One strain has as its target the DNA sequence that distinguishes yours from all other human cells. It can enter only human cell cultures but the 'correcting' genes will be activated only in cells containing the protein sequences of your singularity.

"Other strains are much more problematical in their effects and in their targets. They are not anaerobic. I was merely experimenting out of curiosity, much as you do. Some I recodified randomly—to modify the information in interesting ways. Some results won't show up for a long time; some perhaps not at all."

"Amusing, but I am aware of the primitive nature of your work. Michael has told me what you do. Inefficient. Uncontrollable . . ."

"And dangerous," Mattie added. "Once my microorganisms escape the containers I have hidden them in, the transmission of the genetic information they contain will be uncontrollable and unpredictable. And those I have already introduced into your stocks and tissues can only with great difficulty be traced and reversed. No wonder neither your people nor mine have used these primitive methods since the infancy of the science."

"Have I in any way led you to think me such a fool? If you had done these things, you would have said so earlier. Stopped our removal of your ovum. You would have forced us to let you communicate with your shipfathers. There would have been no need for Ramsay to flee in the dark, no need to control the mind of the female to pilot the copter."

"It was not done until now. My methods were slow and indirect, involving three or more time-consuming steps to accomplish a result your instruments can do in one. I had no submolecularomanipulator, no in vitro enhancers, no filters, no synthesizer, no wave instruments of any kind. I had to resort to parasitic means of modifying your codes."

"Daughter, I do not believe you. Come and show me these things in the laboratories."

"I will, after you let these losos go."

Gabriel said nothing. He studied the five losos.

"Yes," he said finally. "It is not that I believe you. But— Abdiel will take care of it. Let us go."

"Let them out now. Let me see them leave this place while you and Abdiel stay."

Gabriel gestured to Abdiel and Abdiel motioned to losos. He stood aside and all five came out of the closet and disappeared among the aisles and bins of the warehouse.

In the large laboratory where Mattie had worked, a number of young doctors was gathered, talking rather than working. Their voices were sharp whispers and their usually stern faces strangely animated.

They turned, thinking Gabriel had news. "What does the Earthdaughter say? Does she know what her fathers will do now?"

Gabriel brushed away their questions. "Where are these bacterial cultures, daughter?"

"Soon you will all suffer from an intestinal virus," Mattie said to the other doctors. "When the sickness if over, you will have sustained permanent cellular modification. The genome and the germ line of every individual Eastcountry-man will have been radically altered."

The young doctors looked to Abdiel. One mumbled a question. He shrugged and shook his head.

"Abdiel, doctors," Mattie said to them, "have you not watched me all along here in this lab using my microbes to study your protein sequences? It was the only harmless thing Michael let me do."

"Tell me," Gabriel said to Mattie, "if you have set these cultures free and injected others into susceptible cellular material, in vitro and parts of human organisms, why should I do as you say? It is already too late."

"I know which are the cultures I have tampered with among your supplies—and where I have hidden more in other areas of the compound. Some are in time-release containers, an envelope made of a degradable plasticol from the land vehicle. Of the others that I have already introduced directly into tissue, all I can do is transcribe the codes and so you can undo them with your far more efficient methods."

"There are thousands of samples here," a young doctor said.

"Some of my strains are among them. And some are yours but they are not what they were."

"You lie. Nothing here is touched."

"Believe what you will," Mattie said. "When the changes become evident it will be too late."

"Go and prepare the surgery," Gabriel said to the young doctors.

"But, Gabriel," Abdiel said, "she has been working with these materials. Should we not . . ."

"She controls the wills of the ignorant, Abdiel. Shall that be you?"

Abdiel bowed his head. Abdiel the abject, Mattie thought. But the other young doctors were not so easily intimidated.

"Do you think our materials are so vulnerable? Our chemicals are insulated. We . . ." one of them said directly to Mattie, in the face of Gabriel's silent disapproval.

"You have no metal," she said.

He didn't understand.

"The redesigned microbes also include genes altering the molecular adhesion of newood, changing its chemical structure. Not only will the bacteria containing the virus escape any of your containers, the container itself becomes infected.

"Besides, the chemicals in your bodies are not insulated."

"It is nonsense," Gabriel said.

But the young doctors seemed not so sure. "Why take the chance?" one asked.

"Prepare the surgery," Gabriel said, and several left the lab.

"It is too bad that I must allow so much of your work to be reduced to chaos before my colleagues get here," Mattie said. "There was so much we could have learned. I hope that not too much harm will be done from the microbes I have placed in your botany labs. I trust Doctor Ramsay had the sense to take away with him samples of the chemicals you use to adapt the field nutrients to human crops. I do not wish to see all of Dagda starve."

The remaining doctors grew more agitated. The ones who had left returned with a group of older men, only one or two of whom seemed familiar to Mattie.

"Did you destroy Ioso?" one asked, directing his question to Abdiel, not Gabriel.

Abdiel mumbled an explanation at great length and so quietly that Mattie could not hear.

"Daughter," the man said to Mattie, "fetch and destroy these viruses, now."

Gabriel laughed.

"Daughter, will you stop this disease if Gabriel will do no surgery?" another asked.

"Yes," Mattie said, "but I will kill only the most active cultures. The rest must continue until my shipfathers arrive."

"We will not admit them," a young doctor said.

"You have no conception of the power of Earth weapons," Mattie said so softly that the elders were startled. "For your own sake do not try to fight them."

"Does she dissemble now, Gabriel?" Abdiel asked.

Gabriel shook his head. "I don't know."

An hour later a man came to the lab from Halt One to say that the Eastcountrymen in the city had stopped sending and receiving messages.

The doctors had watched in silence as Mattie destroyed some of the cultures in the lab. Abdiel and some of the other microbiologists examined all of the materials on her bench and many of the samples among their own supplies, and they tested cells from their own bodies obsessively.

Mattie asked Abdiel about the losoborn baby who had been with her when she was taken captive. Had it been a subject in some particular experiment? Abdiel knew nothing about it. Michael might have known, he said. When Mattie suggested he search the records for the information, he shook his head. Too dangerous with killer loso somewhere.

In the future someone else, not Abdiel, will have to take Michael's place, Mattie thought. Abdiel will not do.

Losos continued to care for daughters, animals, and male children in the pens and dorms, but doctors would not work with them. There were no losos in the labs. Losos brought no food or supplies. At midday Mattie went into an eating room and sat by herself. The cook came out from the kitchen and approached her table.

"They say you know killer loso, daughter. No one can work with loso now, even to prepare food. Each of us when alone with loso says, 'Might that be it? Will it kill me?' Show it to us so we can work."

"I will not," Mattie said. "But you need not fear loso. It will not harm any man who does harmless work."

As he went back into the kitchen, she heard him say, "The witch promised she will not let it harm anyone but doctors."

Later two botanists came to Mattie in the labs. "Where did you put the microbes in our building?" they asked.

"I will not tell you," she said.

"Daughter, do as we say." They could not compréhend female disobedience.

"Do not worry. They are slow to reproduce themselves; they will not invade your stock germ until long after my shipmates are safely here. And even then I have slowed the plasmodesmatic movement of the virus once it is in your plant stocks. Return to your work and destroy nothing."

They did as she said.

Gabriel never appeared in the lab, but Abdiel and the other young doctors seemed never to leave it. They watched from an obedient distance as Mattie pulled materials from among their own stocks and chemically eradicated them. They dared not come close to inspect or challenge her.

While she was working, a message came from the train. The copter had fallen but its occupants had escaped to the Earth ship.

In late afternoon, Mattie sat in Gudrun's apartment. Blue shadows were already spread across the floor. It was a lonely quiet without Gudrun's rustling about among her herbs, snorting and mumbling to herself. Mattie wondered where Hans had taken her.

The room grew suddenly darker as a figure appeared in the doorway. Mattie knew the silhouette was Gabriel's.

"You have not defeated me, daughter," he said. "Dagdans

will not tolerate interference with us and our plans for them. The fathers hold us in reverence. They are in awe of our authority. They will not switch their trust to a few sinful strangers. Your people may be powerful in metal but they are few in number. Their control will be swiftly over-turned—if they take control at all."

"Your plans for mankind *are* defeated," Mattie said, "not by me or even this one mission. Your authority could not have lasted anyway, even if you had gotten the ship and all of us. Earthstates would have destroyed your oligarchy."

"Your Kyly told us they would not come after one lost ship—a ship that might well have met with an accident in space," Gabriel said.

"They will come for the crops first," Mattie said. "And then to settle. Earth will again be overpopulated. They will keep coming. Don't you see that Dagda—Anu—is no longer isolated?"

"I should have let you destroy everything. It will amount to the same thing," Gabriel said.

"No. This way you will still have yourselves. Do what you will with your own bodies—and what have you done to my body?"

"Made it somewhat taller, healthier. You will have more energy and endurance. Some other things. You will see. But it was only the first step."

Mattie shrugged and held out her arm. The last scar was gone. Gabriel saw and nodded.

"Now say, daughter, about my body, Eastcountrymen and their sons. Do you speak for your shipfathers? Will they de-stroy us?"

"If you give up your control of this population— voluntarily, before my shipfather—shipmates get here, maybe . . . If your people do not resist. You must show no force against them. Their weapons can devastate at once ev-erything you have done here."

"You will meet them with us when they come," Gabriel said.

"Do you still think you can command me?"

"No."

"I will not meet them in any case," she said.

"Nor will I," he said.

He lowered himself into Gudrun's rocker a few feet from the table where Mattie sat idly twisting some threads of dried grass through her fingers. They were silent as the room grew darker.

"Even if you persuade these shipmen this time, later your Earth geneticists will come here and devour us," he said finally. "They will steal our work and in their jealousy and contempt, destroy us—just as you have tried to do."

"The biologists on Earth will be awed," she said, "just as I was, by your achievements, whatever they may feel about your—persons."

"Now I know that you did not plant genetically infected materials! You would never destroy our science. You are as obsessed as we are. That is why you worked with me."

"True, I covet your work," she said, "but I will destroy you and it if I must. Your control over me was the hostages—the daughters and losos you had in your power to harm."

"I do not understand you, daughter," he said.

"Nor I you," she said.

The next day messages came through that many of the Earth people had left their ship and were moving north in their small machines and on a flatcar and that a large group of people from Fian had taken over the train at a halt in Plain.

Linkage

Mattie watched the OC cross the courtyard. He passed the Fians, who were raising dark, faded blue and purple tents in front of the lab and surgery building, passed the smallbrothers gathered for their lessons outside the pens and dorms, frowned as he looked down the length of the open space toward the disarray of vegetation that was Gudrun's kitchen garden, Mattie's headquarters and home. He straightened his shoulders and came on.

Mattie smiled and turned back from the window, sat in the rocker, and opened Gudrun's prescription book on her lap, its thin script and scrawls still cyphers as enigmatic as the doctors' codes had once been.

She had wondered how long it would take the Earth people to discover her. They had been in Eastcountry for five hours. Their arrival at Halt One had been reported by Abdiel. And Mattie had watched some of their progress through the window from time to time. She knew Parn had already taken Rol to botany and that Delt Marker was looking in vain for the government center.

"Mattie?" The OC peered into the darkness from the side of the doorway, allowing a narrow strip of sunlight to fall across the room and her lap. "They told me I would find you here."

She looked up at his sun-haloed head and was glad he had come alone.

"I thought . . . we believed you were dead," he said.

"So it wasn't to rescue me that you came?"

"To avenge your death," he said and laughed at the words. "At least that was *my* motive. Why didn't you meet us? Why are you hiding here?"

"Why should I greet people who wanted to lock me up? And I'm not hiding. I live here."

"But we might have attacked. When we met no resistance at all, we started to suspect sabotage—"

"I sent messages once the Fians gave you the train."

"How could I trust they were really from you?"

"But when you got here, you came in as conquerors; the gates were thrown open."

"True," he said, "wide open. We came ready to fight and found no enemy. We followed Parn through this maze, waiting for a trap, some kind of attack from the side. I thought—even until now—that there might be some trick, that you might be their hostage. They were so certain you had been destroyed, Parn and Elizabeth and the others, and here I find that Eastcountrymen seem to be your hostages! How—"

"How is Elizabeth?"

"Painting. The other one, Parn's girl, is angry. We could not, of course, bring her here. She—"

"I know. I know her. Where is Kyly?" she asked.

"I don't know." The OC began walking around the dim room, touching hanging herbs, examining the rows of jars and tiny boxes on shelves. He picked one up and sniffed.

"Better not do that," Mattie said.

He put it down and walked to stand behind her.

He touched the rough wooden rocker, moving Mattie gently—so different from Jack's exuberant energy.

"I've heard them calling you a witch," he said.

His voice was soft, almost a murmur. His hand moved from the chairback to her shoulder; his fingertips stirred the hairs on the nape of her neck.

She turned in the chair to look up at him. She watched the soft thin lips and remembered their touch.

"I hear you . . . had a . . . found a native lover, Mattie. A boy."

"Yes," she said.

He walked around to stand in front of her and she let him pull her to her feet.

"Are you taller?" He led her to the doorway and stared at her face in the sunlight. "Mattie, there is something different."

"I'm still the same."

He looked at her eyes in the light, pushed the fingers of his left hand through the loose knot of long hair tied up behind her head and held her away from him while he looked down at her body, the plain gray tunic falling over her breasts, ending above her ankles, the loso-made straw shoes, and up again at her face. He studied her lips with his fingertip, drew his hand down along her throat, found her nipple through the smooth worn cloth of the tunic.

She let him hold her. She felt the sun describe her face, felt his fingers, light and warm, trace the arc of her hip and thigh.

"You locked me up," she said. "You tried to bury me in a tomb."

"No. No, I didn't." He brought her back away from the doorway, started to kiss her, the light-winged play she had not understood.

She didn't move, didn't kiss him, let her arms rest at her sides.

"The boy?" he asked.

"He's dead."

"I know. Parn . . . They told me. But now, Mattie?" He suddenly moved harder to bend her head back, pushed his body against hers, a question, not a demand.

"The boy was very young," he said.

"And you're my shipfather, my veryoldfamilyfather," Mattie said, and reached her arms around him.

When she lay with him on the straw mattress, his mouth, his hands, his body moving on and in her charged every nerve. She met him, held him, held on, then let go. And then met him again. And again. She knew then some of the changes the Eastcountrydoctors had made.

Later they walked back to the lab building through the pens and dorms. Mattie showed the OC the flaccid women, the daughters in their eating rooms, the animals, animal people, the changed and the damaged. They passed youngdoctors who nodded solemnly to her and continued working, always in pairs and without losos, their tall, narrow bodies moving with serene dignity.

When Mattie and the OC reached the labs, they heard the voices of the other Earth people, who were gathered in the meeting room next to the main lab. The noise was odd and disturbing. Mattie stopped in the doorway. Inside she saw a group of restless strangers, misplaced in Gabriel's world.

They saw Mattie and were silent. There was Rachel, wearing a blue ribbon and a small puzzled smile. Delt Marker stood like a teacher behind Gabriel's table, arm raised, mouth open. Rol Addle, face flushed, Mr. Ricco, crisp as ever, and Parn were together on one side of the room. And there was Nat Smythy, glorious and glowing. It was Nat who smiled first and Mattie almost forgave all of them.

"My God, Mattie," Parn said. "When these people mentioned you—when I realized you were alive and unchanged ... After they shot poor Jack and dragged you off ... Wait. Mattie, is there something different?"

"Dr. Manan," Delt Marker said, "although circumstances may extenuate your behavior since we arrived on this planet, you must be aware that you have violated diplomatic and legal codes and have moreover disregarded the designated authority which—"

"Maybe it isn't Mattie," Rachel said. "Mattie would never wear a—a thing like that and look at her hair! We almost thought that Ariella was Mattie. It's some relation of her family. They are tricking us."

"It is Mattie," the OC said.

"That's not it," Parn said. "Did they do anything to you that we can't see?"

"Ridiculous," the OC said.

"Yes," Mattie said.

"Dr. Manan," Delt said, "we will suspend immediate penalties for these serious charges. Tell us now where the leaders are."

"Yes, Mattie," Nat said, "where is the 'control room' for this place? We've been searching and finding nothing."

"This is it," Mattie said. "Bioengineers are the leaders."

"But I mean where are the ones who control the whole operation, the whole country?"

"Here," Mattie said.

"Mattie is right, Marker. But why haven't we come across Sem the Doc yet?" Parn asked. He had not seen him since they were all taken from the train at different Eastcountry halts. Mattie had not seen him since his surgery.

"We searched this building," Mr. Ricco said. Mattie knew that was impossible, that they had no idea of its extent.

"I can't believe Sem the Doc could have done such things. He was always so nice," Rachel said.

"He was never nice," Parn said. "His smiles were irony; his humor detachment. If you had seen him standing with them on that train. Smiling. He didn't care what they did to us, me, Mattie, Erin."

"I asked these doctors and got no answer," Nat said. "We may never get him—or Kyly."

Mattie walked over to the lab door. "Abdiel," she said, "bring Doctor Sem the Doc to me here."

In a few minutes two youngdoctors, no loso, wheeled Sem the Doc into the room in a tall wooden chair. His change was not subtle. Even under the full togalike garment that covered him they could see the strange elongation of his lower body and its odd protrusions.

He would not look at them, but kept his hands over his face. Mattie thought that perhaps they had also altered his mind.

"You're under arrest, Sem the Doc," the OC said.

"You traitor," Parn said at the same time and moved toward the chair.

Sem the Doc jerked his head up and removed his hands. The flesh was smooth, fat, and gelatinous, no longer antique gold but the yellow of a rose that has begun to wilt before it fully opens; it was the unwrinkled face of a bloated, unhealthy baby.

The dark old canopies and rugs of the Fian camp moved faintly in the almost dead air of the barren Eastcountry courtyard. "I've been told that some of their families had resisted Eastcountry control," Mattie said to Nat and the OC as they came out through the door of the lab and surgery building. "I saw two of them once, arrested for sex crimes. What are they like?"

"Different from the Plainsmen," Nat said. "Not just the clothes and dialect. I don't know. They are softer and wilder. More romantic, but more real at the same time. And stubborn! We had a hard time. They don't listen."

Mattie thought of Ariella and understood.

The people sat together, leaning toward one another, unlike the rigid lines in which the Plainspeople formed themselves, sitting, walking, or working. And their clothes were heavier, darker, and more worn than those of the other Dagdans. They wore hoods and shawls rather than hats to protect them from the sun, long, hot-looking cloaks, and skirts.

A short dark-haired man in a very long, drab green cloak stood watching Mattie, Nat, and the OC cross the courtyard.

"That's Shamus," the OC said. "He's the only one who seems able to speak the language of Plain and Eastcountry."

There were two women, quieter than the men but not mute or blank of expression. In fact at first they looked right at Mattie with fierce, suspicious eyes. One of them looked like her mother, like Ariella. She was surely a member of the Fian Brens family that Mattie had once pretended to belong to without knowing who or what they were.

Shamus waved them to sit on the rugs and bowed slightly. The women and other men inched farther away than necessary, leaving an empty circle around Mattie, Nat, and the OC, but remained close enough to listen to words they only half-understood.

He had to know the language, Shamus said in soft lilting

tones like Ariella's, because he often came to Plain to trade goods—though the Eastcountrymen had begun to resent such exchanges that bypassed them. He also was the one who arranged the exchange of older children with distant families demanded by the Eastcountrydoctors.

Shamus sat and pulled his knees up under his chin, threw off his hood. He stared at Nat for awhile, at his dark skin and gold chain, and then looked at Mattie and shook his head.

"My people," he said, "are the children of the old Earth gods who abandoned them for their sins. We thought Earth fathers had returned at last in this time of peril to save their children here on Anu. When first Earth people came to the city from the sky, we waited but they did not come to us.

"Then we knew Earth people are not gods. They were afraid and stayed in their ship and obeyed the doctors. But when Ioso came to Fian and spoke, we knew it was a sign. It said we must act and here we are to save ourselves before it is too late."

"Save yourselves from what?" the OC asked.

Shamus looked at Mattie and did not speak.

"We are like you," Mattie said, "in our Earth families, the way we love and bear our children." She lay her open palm across the back of the OC's hand to show them. "You may speak to us without shame or fear."

Still Shamus did not speak. He looked around at his people and Mattie saw the Brenswoman nod at him. He finally drew a long breath and said, "I, Shamus, was born of my mother's flesh. This is my—my mate, Magdalena; she is Eastcountryborn. These are words we no longer say, even among ourselves.

"We are the only families left in Fian who—who love and bear our own children. There were four such families but now there are only three. We practice in secret. We accept the children the Eastcountrymen bring us but create our own too, the old way, and hide them.

"One Fian family—never mine—used to kill the children the doctors gave them. They said they were not human, but changelings, creatures of witches and fairies. We cannot bring ourselves to do this. The little ones look like us and like our own though we do not understand how this can be. And besides we must bring them every second harvest into the city hospital to be examined by the Eastcountrydoctors."

Shamus stopped and shook his head again. The woman, Magdalena, touched his arm and spoke quickly in their language.

"She says to ask you if you are a doctor?" Shamus said to Mattie. "Our own daughterborn children sometimes— need medical care. We try to take care of them ourselves. And we visit a Deechdaughter who is hidden in a forest very far to the west of Fian. Though she does not understand our speech, she understands our needs."

Not Gudrun, Mattie thought. Poor Gudrun would have been happy with daughters to care for. Some other Deech healer, left in isolation by the elves, had been luckier.

"What happened to the fourth family?" Nat asked.

"The Eastcountrymen discovered the condition of one of their familydaughters. They took her and her mate away. The others in the family were afraid. Most were old or had already given in to the Eastcountry rules. They would lose the way to make food. Some had already begun to raise their daughters in silence. We think that one of their own family told the doctors."

"And the Plainsman Lucius who came on the train with the loso? Where is he? And where is the loso now?" Mattie asked.

"We have locked him in our familyhouse. Away from our daughters. He is a bad man. Talkingloso has returned here to Eastcountry."

Mattie saw then what they had all felt, Elizabeth, Erin, even Jack. Lucius was "bad" both ways: he lusted after his familydaughters and hated them for it. He had never learned not to see them.

"Lucius is another kind of Eastcountry monster," Mattie said aloud though neither the OC or Nat knew who he was.

"And now," Shamus said, "together we will destroy

them. You are not our Earth fathers, but, like us, you are their true children, motherborn."

"This is a horrible thing they have done to your people," Nat said. "The suppression of natural functions, human affection—"

"You said you are seeking medical care. Are your daughterborn children, the ones you create yourselves the old way, both brothers and daughters, are they not healthy?" Mattie asked.

The speaker looked at her startled. He knew a witch when he saw one.

"They are sick. Help us cure them," he said. "Do not take them away. They are ours."

"Inbreeding!" Mattie said. And thought she heard Gabriel laughing.

When Mattie and the OC walked back to Gudrun's rooms, darkness had filled the courtyard almost to the top of pens and dorms. The sky above it was still white.

"The sky is never streaked or mottled," Mattie said.

"Poor bastards," the OC said. "To live in this empty, barren world, without color or—or flowers. And worst not to know love. Not to have this, what we have." He drew Mattie closer and murmured against her hair.

She put her arm around his waist and patted him just above the hip. Not fat, she thought, firm, muscled. A little fat.

"Well, at least we can change it. Give them back their bodies and their sex and their children."

"Can we?" Mattie said.

"We'll get rid of this place. Parn says we can give the farmers themselves the means to fix the soil—as soon as Parn and Rol understand it."

"No, we can't do that."

"Perhaps not yet. Even if we try to order these insane 'doctors' to do it, we can't trust them and we don't know enough yet to check that they obeyed. But once our own botanists understand everything then—"

"We will not give the knowledge or the chemicals to these Fians or any other Dagdans," Mattie said. "Not yet."

The OC withdrew his arm. "What are you saying? It's the only way to free the people. You're the one who explained to us how Eastcountry used the food supply to control every other group on the planet."

"Did you hear what he said about his 'real' children?" Mattie asked. "When you 'get rid' of this place, what do you propose to do with its inmates? What are you going to do with the Eastcountrymen themselves? Exterminate them? You'll have to. Otherwise when we leave everything will be the same again. But—without Eastcountry the Anunna will not survive."

The agronomists and plantecologists worked together in and out of the botany building, but Mattie was the only Earth scientist left in biology. She continued to learn from the Eastcountry molecular engineers as she always had, but now they worked with her all day and taught her all their techniques.

More equipment was brought from the ship's labs. Metal.

"Are you sure you need all this stuff to learn their secrets?" Nat asked, as they watched Mr. Ricco directing losos unloading the train at Halt One.

"Yes, we need it," Mattie said.

The young Eastcountrydoctors waiting for it in the lab almost showed their excitement. One of the youngest, Dom, was already rebuilding parts of the largest scope before losos had laid all the materials on the benches.

Abdiel, as Mattie had guested, was not brilliant; Dom might make a better replacement for Michael.

Mr. Ricco and Delt Marker went to other Eastcountry stations, first to the west and north and then east to cross the waterway.

"They'll never run the ferry on their own, even with losos. I doubt it has been rebuilt since we cut it loose," Mattie said.

"Can they take a boat or raft across?" Nat asked.

"You have not seen the waterway."

"Perhaps you and I can go there together," the OC said.

Mattie said nothing.

"There is a man with one arm here," Mr. Ricco said to Nat on the cube the next day. "His looks and speech are unlike those of the local people; he is living here at the ferry place, and with him is an old woman. He says he will ferry us across. Shall we trust him?"

"Say yes and tell him to bring the woman here when they return," Mattie said.

"Mr. Ricco says the old woman won't leave the place. Something about good plants and good medicine."

Mattie and Parn stood looking out from the second floor of the botany building above the crop storage area. The scene below was a flat glare of noon light. The shed and warehouse roofs, the bins, the silos and platforms, the tracks, the carts, and even the losos and men had lost their color and their shadows. Their motion alone made them visible as they piled goods for Plain, the city, and Fian at the side of the tracks by Halt Four. Beyond lay the cultivated fields merging indistinguishably into the empty, flat, motionless land, stretching without interruption to the horizon.

"It never changes," Parn said. "There is no weather. Every day is a duplicate of the one before. Long. Infinite. Sameness like the land."

"Except down in the waterway," Mattie said.

"Do you—think of Jack, Mattie?"

Mattie did not answer and thought of Jack. Jack lying beside her under the precipice, beautiful in the firelight, Jack lying dead in the courtyard.

"You seem to cross generations for your love affairs, Mattie."

"I love my shipfather," Mattie said. "You always thought I was a hard woman."

"Not hard. No one so anthropomorphic is hard. You always petted the animal's head as you injected it. But you were sometimes impatient, contemptuous of stupidity, of me."

"I never thought you stupid. Frivolous, maybe. But not anymore. You've changed. I want to tell you that—that I'm glad about Erin. I thought first that you would hurt her somehow, not see her innocence for what it was."

"Vulnerability like Jack's?"

The light was too bright and began to burn Mattie's Earth eyes, and she turned her back to it.

They walked together in silence along the dark and grainy corridor. They passed the open door of a botany lab where Rachel studied a single tall green plant hung with some kind of fruit; they heard Rol's voice booming up the front stairway, something about grass-fixing, and Seraf's stolid, softer answer.

"There is so much to do, so much to learn," Parn said, "and I am homesick. Sick to show Erin home, perhaps. Rol is right, we must not miss anything that will feed us and re-generate Earth and the other planets. But how long will it all take?"

"There is as much in biology," Mattie said. "But it cannot be taken."

"What do you mean? Mattie—"

"I'm not going back."

"But how can you stay? This place, these people. Mattie—your profession?"

"That's why. My profession. There is so much to fix."

"We can destroy Eastcountry and the people themselves will revert to normal behavior in a few generations."

"They must not revert or there will be very few genera-tions. Anunne reproduction must be controlled."

"But that's the very thing you objected to with the Eastcountrymen."

"I know."

They walked down the stairs and turned right, away from the sound of Rol's voice. As they went out into the court-yard Ioso gave Mattie water. It was T.F. Parn did not know and was startled when she said thank you.

"The botanists still speak of the modifying cultures you planted," Parn said. "I hope none of them infect any materials we need. Can you tell me where . . . Mattie?"

"Don't worry."

Parn stopped walking and looked at her.

"Mattie, did you really plant any cultures? Or attack the doctors' superman genetic codes with your correcting strains?"

"Maybe," she said.

The OC was watching them from where he sat on the bench in Gudrun's garden. Mattie waved to him.

"Come drink some wonderful tea or other witch-made beverage with us—if you dare," she said to Parn. "Gudrun's cupboard is well stocked."

As they walked on across the sunny, too-hot courtyard, Parn asked, "Does he know? Know that you plan not to go back with the ship?"

"Not yet," she said.

Harvest

"No, Rol!" Mattie shouts. "Put it back." She is running hat-less through the field just beyond the botany storage areas where Rol and Eastcountrymen with losos are piling bags onto a flat wagon. Late morning sun gives everything a short shadow.

Rol is standing on the wagon. He waves his arm at Mattie without speaking or looking at her and continues counting bags and checking a pad in his hand.

Elizabeth also has a pad in her hand, a fat earth drawing pad. She is wearing one of the dark blue shipsuits and sit-ting, legs dangling, in the open loft door of a longhouse.

Mattie stops next to the wagon and stares up at Rol. She doesn't say anything, but her anger is so loud that Elizabeth can paint it.

Rol studies the pad in his hand, keeping his back to Mattie. The Eastcountrymen look at her quickly and then away. They stop working but do not tell losos to stop.

"Rol," Mattie says.

"What?" Rol turns as if he has just noticed she is still there.

"Put it all back," Mattie says. "You may take the method, the code and plasm. You're taking Ith. You do not need to dismantle—"

"We can't afford to leave anything that might turn out later to be important."

"You're leaving us with nothing," Mattie says.

"You have Seraf and others. The food supply will be se-cure."

"But you are setting back all the progress that has been

made here. Without our equipment—it will take years—if ever—for us to recover."

"What 'us,' Mattie? You're not a native or a botanist. Just because you're crazy enough to stay—"

"That's just it. One of you botanits should stay, too. These Eastcountry plant geneticists have the ability to create more varieties, varieties designed for Earth. If only Parn stayed, he might do more for Earth than—"

Rol makes some kind of loud hooting sound. "Your business is getting biological information to Earth. You have no authority over botany. We're leaving with whatever I think is necessary."

"I'm not stopping you from taking samples of every stock, plasm, seed. Parn has the formula and the cultures for every possible microcell. You have had a harvest to harvest this material. I'm not stopping your copying any formula but—"

"You're not stopping anything. Go away." Rol again turns his back and studies his notepad.

Elizabeth thinks she sees Mattie look at the Eastcountrymen and move her hand, but it is very fast, and then Mattie is already striding back across the field.

Elizabeth hears Rol call out, "Come back!" but it is not Mattie he is calling. Losos are shuffling away in many directions, and the Eastcountrymen are walking back to the botany building. Rol and the wagon are alone.

Elizabeth stands up, so easily with shipsuit pants, shakes her legs in a little dance, and climbs down the ladder. It is time to go to work. Elizabeth's job is to teach several undamaged daughters to read, including Ariella and Erin—and Thomas when he wishes.

Elizabeth walks through the longhouse, through the narrow aisles of the large botany storage area, and then through botany itself to the courtyard, and out across the place where Jack lay dead. Three daughters are watching losos with long arms planting a half-grown tree in the place where the Fians were camped. Daughters are allowed to wander through the compound except into labs or sugeries, but most of them do not. They stay in the eating rooms or dorms. Sometimes Mattie has losos drive them out, but most of them go right back to their old seats.

The courtyard is hot under the noon sun. The shipsuit feels good to wear but it cannot insulate the body. Regular losos wipe Elizabeth's face but do not try to hold her back.

The classes are held in the rooms she shares with Ariella, rooms between Gudrun's apartment where Mattie lives and the larger apartment Mattie has made for Rebekah and Lucilla and a few other olderdaughters from pens and dorms. But it is all temporary. Mattie says when the earthship leaves they will have better places, away from Eastcountry, near the waterway, near the wild forest, but with fields, and houses, a farm of their own.

Erin is waiting for Elizabeth. Elizabeth looks to see if Erin's belly is bigger. She has a baby growing in her body. She will have two babies when she gets to earth with Parn.

"It isn't bigger since I saw you last," Elizabeth says. "It will come out of you just like the baby came out of loso."

"Mattie says it won't be so easy; it has six more months to grow."

"Mattie came out to the field," Elizabeth says.

"What field?"

"Beyond botany. Where I have been drawing losos and wagons—for three days. Look." Elizabeth drops her drawing pad on the table.

Erin turns the pages. "Oh, I like this one."

"Mattie is angry. Rol is taking too many things."

"Is the OC still angry at her?"

"He's always angry—since she told him she wasn't going back to earth—but he talks to her again and they—mate."

"Make love, not mate. I told you."

Elizabeth sighs and thinks she will never understand.

"They were fighting this morning, though," she says. "She wants the OC to give her all the ship's lab things they won't need. She says it will be no good—outdated—when they get to earth and just put in a junkheap. *Junkheap.* I looked it up; it was two words." Elizabeth pats the thick earth dictionary ready for the reading lessons.

"Who cares how many words? What else did they say? Were you listening through the window?"

"No! I was right there with them in the garden. She wants to keep all three land vehicles, not just two, and she wants more metal. That horrible metal, Erin. How will you be able to stay inside the ship for four harvests?"

"I just will. Maybe Nat will let me drive. What did the OC say?"

"He said he won't 'strip' the ship."

"What does she want him to do, break it all up?" Erin asks.

"She said they could take out some of the floors and walls. He said, 'Isn't it enough we've given you our genes, and sperm, and skin and blood, even some body parts we didn't know we had?' "

"Parn might agree about some of the lab equipment but no one else will," Erin says. "Nat won't let anyone touch the ship."

"Nat gave me his gold chain," Ariella sings as she comes in through the door followed by four daughters. Ariella displays the chain gleaming on her white neck. "He said it needs a change."

The daughters sit around the table. The two youngest ones pull their books out of their pockets. "I will read," one says. The olderdaughter looks at Elizabeth, waiting to be told what to do.

"Where is Thomas?" Mattie asks from the doorway.

Synthesis

"He is no experimental animal! Bring him back now."

"Mattie, an experimental animal is exactly what it is," Rachel said.

"And think of your own colleagues on Earth," Rol said. "What a treasure it will be for them, Mattie. And your professional reputation. They will know that the animal was your discovery, yours alone—I promise."

"Now, Dr. Manan," Delt Marker said, "there are priorities. Personal sentiment cannot compromise the interests of Earthstates. The scientists assure me that this animal is unique evidence—"

"You sent him to the ship without telling me? Like baggage?"

"It never occurred to us that it mattered," Rachel said.

"You will bring Thomas back," Mattie said. "That's all."

The light was still white as Mattie started to cross the courtyard, and the trees that Iosos had been planting looked like fine lines drawn across the bleached and blank façades of the Eastcountry buildings.

In the lab she found Abdiel bent over his bench, peering through a scope, and Parn and Rol standing behind him.

"Look, Abdiel," Parn said. "What's the matter with our men? Where's Mattie?"

"I'm here," Mattie said and moved over to her bench.

The OC pushed open the door. "What's the matter?" he asked Parn. "Why did you call me?"

"Ith is gone," Parn said. "Seraf is there but he stopped working with us. He won't talk to me."

"It started yesterday," Rol said. "They all walked away from me in the field."

"The animals won't do anything for us," Parn said.

Loso came into the lab with tea and bread for Mattie.

"Tell it to bring us some," Rol said. "Mine didn't show up this morning."

"Do you believe you own one individual loso and that it is the same one that continues to serve you?" Mattie asked.

"Mattie, for the gods' sakes, who cares? Talk to these people."

Mattie sipped her tea.

Nat burst into the lab. "Thought I'd find you here, OC. We've got trouble. Ricco called in from the train. The animals are unloading everything, dumping it all in the middle of nowhere. The native men won't move to stop them."

Rol's and the OC's fingercubes lit at the same time. It was Rachel saying that all the critical batches of certain old Earth germ strains were missing.

"It's a damned rebellion," Rol said. "They can't get away with it. We have the weapons."

Rol looked at the OC but the OC was looking at Mattie. They were all looking at Mattie.

"You win, then, Mattie, don't you?" the OC said.

"It's basically a grain alcohol," Parn said, "but it's tempered with the fruit of two wild plants from the waterway. And it's processed like a wine."

"It is strange," Rachel said, "but somehow good." She held her thick mug up in the candlelight as though it were a fine, old glass goblet from Earth.

"A toast!" Nat said, holding his own mug up, first toward Mattie and then to the OC, who sat at opposite ends of the long table that losos had carried out into the courtyard between botany and labs. "To Earth and Anu."

Nat's muscled neck gleamed in the light, always strangely naked without the gold chain. But there it was on the other side of the table on Ariella. Above its glitter her black eyes mirrored the flames. She raised her own mug high, threw back her head, and drank. She fit perfectly the drama of the night, Mattie thought.

But not Elizabeth next to her. The ship suit she had taken to wearing, which in daytime made her a sprite instead of a golden goose girl, became part of the blue-dark of night, leaving visible only her head, with the hair tied back from the too-narrow face, the lowered eyes. She gave no surface to reflect the light.

Erin's hair, however, flamed, and Parn's and the baby's faces seemed lit by it rather than the fire.

Mattie looked down the length of the table to where Delt Marker was saying something to the OC and Rachel. The OC's head was tilted as it always was when he listened to someone—or pretended to listen. His white brows hid his sharp eyes and his mustache, his fine lips. Only the broad bones of cheek and jaw glowed golden in the firelight. How had Mattie ever seen him as old or—fatherly?

He looked up then and caught her eyes before she could look away. They were both caught, locked.

Mattie rose and walked to him; he pulled her down onto the bench between him and Delt. "I'll stay," he said. "They don't need a captain."

"I think," Delt said, "that such a decision would be seen as highly—highly irregular." He raised his mug to his mouth in a highly irregular motion.

"It is Parn who should stay," Mattie said loudly so that Parn would hear. "I need someone to run botany."

"*She* needs," Rol said. He had moved his chair closest to the fire. His face shone beyond its usual exertion from the heat and from the several mugs of the alcohol he had drunk.

"The botanist who stays here until the next Earth expedition will be the real hero," Mattie continued. "All of Eastcountry experience can be turned to developing new kinds of crops, fixed for all the necessary conditions, not just salvaging old Earth strains as you have done now. They can be not only disease-resistant, protein-complete, but more adaptable to changes in temperature and depletion of the atmosphere than present Earth grasses and—"

"You'd have to do a double fix on the soil," Rol said. "And even then would be the problem of reversion. Maybe if—" He took another swallow from his mug and stared into the fire, face glistening.

"We aren't going to stay," Parn said. "I have to go home. Maybe we'll come back. If Erin wants to."

"And Erin will give birth on the ship? Without me," Mattie said.

"You know it will be all right, Mattie," Rachel said. "I think you don't want to be left here alone now that we are actually leaving."

"She's not alone," Elizabeth said. "We are here."

"What about the leader? That Gabriel," the OC said. "Where is he now? How can you be safe with him loose?"

"I've never seen him," Parn said. "In all the time I spent here I never met the man. If any of them are men anymore."

"I'd feel better if we had him," the OC said, "in chains on the ship."

"He is no threat to me. Never again," Mattie said. "And besides, I made him a promise. And—I may need him. Later."

Nat crossed in front of the fire to throw on more wood. Ariella hummed a not quite familiar tune. Losos brought food. Parn refilled the mugs.

"Elizabeth, let me try some," Thomas said, jumping to her side, reaching for her mug.

"Stop," Mattie said. "I don't know what it might do to your metab—"

Loso fingers were already removing the mug from Thomas's hand. T.F. was among the losos bringing food to the table.

"T.F.," Erin said. Elizabeth smiled at him.

The other Earth people looked at them as though they were talking to Hamlet's father.

"I want to dance," Rachel said. She moved her feet but didn't get up. "We need some vid music."

"Sometimes—when I was verysmall—my familyfathers and talldaughters in Fian used to dance," Ariella said.

Two figures emerged from the botany main door. One was Mr. Ricco, who had waited for the train at Halt Four before joining the party.

Although Mattie couldn't see the other's face, the familiar wisps of thin hair caught the light of the fire. She knew too well the small frame and curved back. It had to be Kyly.

Mattie's hands clenched around her wrists where the scars had completely disappeared. The OC's arm tightened around her.

"How did you catch him, Ricco?" he asked.

"I didn't. He came riding in on the train by himself."

Kyly sucked in a hiss. "I came as quickly as I was able. When it became clear that you have been irresponsibly altering the natural evolution of a vulnerable and unique culture, I was outraged. I am distraught. I can no longer be patient with your ignorance."

"Kyly," Parn said, "do you realize the position you're in?"

"While I can imagine, doctors, that you have the avarice and egos, I am surprised to discover that you have the learning or understanding to take an element from their own belief systems and use it to loot and destroy their civilization."

"Where have you been?" the OC asked.

"I have been among the people. I have shared their bread, but I never interfere. I say nothing that would contaminate their worldview or alter in any way the patterns and interrelatedness which compose their folkways. I observe. I listen."

"Just lock him up," Rol said without looking away from the fire. His voice was thick with disgust and alcohol.

"And you, Mattie Manan," Kyly continued, eyes almost shut, "you are the Spanish conqueror Cortez who the Aztecs thought was their god Quetzalcoatl. Their own legends were used to destroy them. Pretending that you are an archetypical figure of Anunne mythology, the evil anima from their collective unconscious—the witch."

Parn started to laugh aloud, and after a few seconds Nat

followed. The OC smiled and Mattie shifted against his chest, uncomfortable, suddenly cold and unconnected.

"You laugh in your ignorance." Kyly's voice rasped with strain but never grew louder. "Do you realize that Dagdan kinship patterns and courtship rituals are unique in human history?"

They all stared at him in silence for a second. Mattie carefully set her empty mug on the table—and then she laughed. Parn started in again, and Nat, and the OC. And then Erin, Rachel, and even Delt.

"Just lock him up," Rol said.

The OC had boarded the ship the day before. Mattie and he had met and held and let go, and today there were no more good-byes.

Mattie and Elizabeth wore gowns with full layered skirts and wide straw hats tilted against the rays of the lowering white sun. They stood with Rol and Rachel, a few working losos and Eastcountry botanists in the landing field, safely away from the ship.

Takeoff was to be fifteen seconds after sunset, Nat had said.

The sky was still white overhead, bright in the west, and dark purple in the east. Venus was alone, a wan low point, just above the southern horizon. Suddenly the sharp colors faded. The ship's shadow, a thin, sharp, black stain, seemed more real than the ship itself. It was a part of the land while the ship seemed to belong to the air—as if it were already gone.

And then it was really gone. Its rise, climb, and disappearance were almost unimportant, an afterthought.

Anu

Just when latelongafternoon becomes earlywhitenight the ship slips straight up. It is a small line growing thinner, and then it is gone. This time there is no flash, no explosion of light to signal its flight.

And they are left, a few human beings and losos in the middle of an empty field.

Mattie does not move. Her profile seems carved in the cold, gray metal of the ship. A strange, silent Rol holds Rachel's hand. The Eastcountry botanists still stare upward.

They all turn together and walk without words back toward the city. The sky grows as dark as the land, but they need no light.

Erin is gone, Elizabeth thinks. When she said she was the baby's mother, that loso who carried her was the mother, and that the Eastcountrydoctors who put together her genes were the mother, Mattie said the baby was Anu itself. And Erin named her Anu. Now Erin has gone from Dagda to earth and Elizabeth from Dagda to Anu.

"After everything is settled again," Mattie says when they reach the halt, "we'll visit Gudrun. We'll go to the waterway."

General Background

After the development of interstellar travel, Earth people colonized several habitable planets, including Anu. Within a hundred years a series of wars—the Frazan Wars— destroyed most scientific knowledge and all hard technology. The settlements were cut off from Earth.

Just before, and again three centuries after the Wars, monoculturing and irresponsible genetic manipulation almost ruined Earth's food grasses.

Four hundred years after the Wars, after reconstruction and recovery and the establishment of a centralized Earth government—Earthstates—missions were sent out to all the abandoned planets in the hope that the settlers had taken and propagated original ancestral wild plants, maybe even genetic material, plasm, which might form a new gene pool for a starving Earth.

Anu, last settled, farthest out, according to the fragmentary Earth records that remained from before the Wars, had been settled by at least four different, independent groups: a small scientific community of whom there was almost no information; farmers, "Plainsmen," from the north American continent; "The Celtic Guild," a political rather than ethnic association, in spite of its name; and another group of farmers or perhaps villagers from somewhere in the center of old Europe.

Anu, later renamed Dagda, is a massive-2e, dry planet made up of steppes, plains which are actually plateaus. Its waters are a latticework of deep gorges, fiords, narrow cuts; "sea" level is a mile below the plains which make up almost the entire surface of the planet.

There is little heavy metal so in spite of its size Anu's gravity is .9.

In two Earth years, au2, Anu circles an F5 sun which has twice the luminosity of Sol and 1.25 the mass.

Because of a 10% axial tilt, seasonal change is negligible. Anu is perfect for grass farming.

Since its sun is so young, less than 6 billion years, the planet has no highly evolved native life forms.

Anu is an Irish earth mother.

Dagda is an earth god, a wizard, associated with fruitfulness and fertility.

Acknowledgments

Thanks to Don Keller and Dave Hartwell for direction and perfect redirection; to Lynn Krauthamer for creative feedback and hundreds of hours of rereading; to Marian Parish for her patience and support from the beginning; to Chris, Kate, Peter, Kathy, and David Collins, Chris Peterson, Joan Gordon, and Alice Salews for sharing their energy with me.